The Boy Detective & The Summer of '74

AND OTHER TALES OF SUSPENSE

The Boy Detective & The Summer of '74

AND OTHER TALES OF SUSPENSE

BY Art Taylor

CRIPPEN & LANDRU PUBLISHERS
Cincinnati, Ohio
2020

For information contact:
Crippen & Landru, Publishers
P. O. Box 532057
Cincinnati, OH 45253 USA

Web: www.crippenlandru.com
E-mail: Info@crippenlandru.com

ISBN (softcover): 978-1-936363-44-5
ISBN (clothbound): 978-1-936363-39-1
First Edition: February 2020
10 9 8 7 6 5 4 3 2 1

To my parents

Gene and Jenny Taylor

a bushel and a peck

CONTENTS

Author's Note

When my story "Murder on the Orient Express" appeared in *Ellery Queen's Mystery Magazine* in December 1995, it felt like the world had opened up for me.

What more could a writer want than to debut in the world's leading mystery magazine? I'd made it to the big league my first time out! More stories were ahead, and those would surely be stepping stones toward novels too. The bestseller list awaited—fame and fortune and more. Spurred on by that first acceptance, I immediately drafted and revised another story, submitted it quickly to my new editor, certain she'd be thrilled to take it. I couldn't lose any momentum. I was on my way!

But that second story earned a rejection—deservedly so, reading the manuscript now.

The same happened with the next one.

In fact, nearly a dozen years would pass—six months shy of a dozen—before my short fiction would appear in *EQMM*'s pages again.

* * *

More than once I've told myself that that my decade-plus away from publication in *EQMM* afforded me a learning period—an opportunity to hone my craft, to explore and establish the kinds of stories I wanted to write, and to understand myself more fully as a writer.

I don't think that's entirely revisionist history.

But revisiting that debut story, I also see there the seeds not only of who I *was* as a writer, but also of who I *am* now. "Murder on the Orient Express" features so many elements of my later fiction, the themes and motifs and approaches that I keep returning to again and again: a focus on relationships, the responsibilities inherent in them, and the expectations laid on them; an understanding that imagination and anxiety are two sides of the same coin; an explicit interest in literary precursors and models (needless to say, my story title was used once before); and then a recognition that endings so often become openings toward new beginnings, for better or worse.

These two ideas aren't mutually exclusive—on the one hand, my awareness of connections between my first stories and my more recent fiction, and on the other, the conviction that I must have learned something, must have improved somehow during those intervening years.

Differences do stand out. In the stories here, you'll find more emphasis on voice ("Ithaca 37," for instance, or "Rearview Mirror"), more women protagonists ("Rearview Mirror" again and "When Duty Calls" and others), greater attention to point of view ("The Care and Feeding of Houseplants" and "Precision"), more elaborate narrative structures ("An Internal Complaint"), and occasionally a bit of experimentation, as with the first and final stories of this collection.

Time provides a key ingredient to the development of craft and even to the distillation of a single short story. "The Care and Feeding of Houseplants" was put aside for several years before I revised it. "A Voice from the Past" was written in two chunks—the first half and the second—over another span of years. And this collection's title story... well, I wrote the earliest draft of it more than a quarter of century ago, and I've been tinkering with it ever since.

* * *

Reading—I tell my students—is an important part of learning to write and of understanding ourselves as writers. One regular assignment in the workshops I lead at George Mason University involves having students choose a favorite writer or book or story, choose a sample passage, and try not only to articulate what they love about it but also to analyze what they can learn from it and apply some of those stylistic or structural strategies to their own work.

I'd hesitate to place my work alongside work by any of the writers I'd count as influences, but several writers have—directly or indirectly—provided models or inspirations for my own stories or at least set a high bar for me to aspire toward. Subscribing to *Ellery Queen's Mystery Magazine* in late elementary school into middle school, I read Ed Hoch, Hugh Pentecost, and others, and in high school, Ernest Hemingway, Flannery O'Connor, and Eudora Welty proved pivotal—that mix of literary writers and genre writers in equal measure in my education.

Stanley Ellin stands as a favorite today, alongside the short fiction of Patricia Highsmith, Daphne Du Maurier, Joyce Carol Oates, and William Trevor, among others.

When I can't figure out what to do with a story, they're still the ones I turn for ideas, guidance, motivation. Highsmith's book *Plotting and Writing Suspense Fiction* may be the least "how to" of the craft books you'll find out there, but it's been central to my own thoughts on what makes good fiction.

Many current writers have been influences too—too many to name, and I'd hate to miss someone, but I do want to express my appreciation for the late B.K. Stevens, a fine friend and a fine writer and someone whose thoughts on short fiction so often meshed with my own.

* * *

I'm grateful to the readers who've responded to my short stories with such enthusiasm, and to my fellow writers as well, especially to my friends and peers in the local chapters of Mystery Writers of America and Sisters in Crime and to everyone at Malice Domestic and at Bouchercon, groups which increasingly feel like family.

Half of the stories in this collection were originally published in *Ellery Queen's Mystery Magazine*, and as I've said before, I don't think I would have any place in the mystery world without the support of Janet Hutchings, my long-time editor there.

Always, I want to thank my wife, Tara Laskowski, one of the best writers I know—setting the bar high herself but also providing the support and encouragement to help me reach it, too.

And I owe more than I can express to my parents, Gene and Jenny Taylor, who nurtured my love of reading from childhood on and encouraged my ambition to write at every step of the way. My dad died in late June 2019, just a couple of days after I'd told him that this collection had accepted for publication. I wish that he had been here to see the book in print—a testament now to how my parents laid the foundation for so much of who I am as a reader, a writer, and a person.

* * *

The stories here have received several honors in the mystery world: an Edgar Award, an Anthony Award, three Derringers Awards, three Macavity Awards, and four Agatha Awards (if I can count "Rearview Mirror," which didn't win the award itself but was the first section of my novel in stories *On the Road with Del and Louise,* winner of the Agatha for Best First Novel). Some of these have also earned attention outside of our genre: "Mastering the Art of French Cooking" took first place in the flash fiction category of Press 53's Open Awards, and "Visions and Revisions" was a finalist for the *North American Review*'s first Kurt Vonnegut Fiction Prize.

Whenever I've mentioned feeling very fortunate for all this, friends have pointed out that it's not just luck but talent and hard work that earns success. Still, I recognize that there are many talented writers working harder than I am and not enjoying the same prosperity. Many factors play a role in writers finding their audience, and even when you get your big break, that's no guarantee that you've broken through.

Again, nearly twelve years separated my first story in *EQMM* from my second.

So will this collection here be my first or my only?

Give me a few years, and I'll get back to you on that.

Mastering the Art of French Cooking

Coq au Vin

1 onion
2 carrots
2 stalks celery
6 whole peppercorns
2 cloves garlic, pureed
1 sprig parsley
1 bay leaf
¼ tsp thyme
3 bottles Burgundy (two inexpensive, one not)
2 Tbsp white arsenic (from the hardware store)
2 Tbsp sugar
1 whole chicken
Salt and pepper
2 Tbsp olive oil
4 Tbsp butter, divided
1 Tbsp flour
1 ripe red tomato
¼ lb lardons (or thick bacon, cut into small strips)
½ pound mushrooms

With a sharp knife, dice onions and slice carrot and celery into small discs. Avoid cutting yourself. Combine onions, carrots, celery, peppercorns, and garlic into a large bowl. Tie parsley, bay leaf, and thyme into a small cheesecloth to make a *bouquet garni*; add to mixture. Douse with one bottle of wine, reserving approximately one swallow. Stir gently.

Look at the mixture. Slug the rest of the wine from the bottle.

Add the next ingredient.

Then add the next, to ease the bitterness.

Reflect on that word *bitterness*.

With a sharp knife, gut the chicken, trim away the neckbone and wing tips, and carve it into manageable pieces: breasts, legs, thighs, etc. Admire the sharpness of the knife, how easily it slides through the meat. See how it gleams. Feel your grip tighten. Listen to the sound of the television in the next room. Consider for a moment the alternatives. You've considered them before.

Submerge the chicken in the bowl of vegetables and seasonings. Hold it down tight.

The preceding stage of the recipe may be completed a day in advance. In fact, such a delay is preferred for superior taste and enriched texture. Cover the bowl tightly with plastic wrap and refrigerate.

Overnight and throughout the next day, reflect on the art of French cooking, a mix of sophistication and heartiness, style and romance. Consider how Julia Child brought these qualities into the early '60s suburban home—a sense of wonder at the wider world, a hint of possibility, as if anybody could do it.

Question why *French Women Don't Get Fat.*

Browse the internet for photos of Emmanuelle Béart, Isabelle Adjani, Marion Cottilard, Sophie Marceau, Audrey Tautou. While on the computer, scan your husband's email once or twice more, searching for the name Monique. Look at the picture she sent him, the high cheekbones, the creamy complexion, the glimpses of skin.

Reflect once more on that word *bitterness.*

Browse through several of the other words in this recipe: *ripe, bouquet, leg, thigh, breast, stalk.* Know that *coq* simply means chicken, but laugh inwardly at what it sounds like. Think about it: *coq* in wine. Understand where drunkenness can lead.

Open the second bottle of wine and have a couple of glasses, since you'll only use a cup of it later.

Ponder the word *lardons.* Regret your love of bacon. Glance down at your own thighs.

Two hours in advance of dinner, remove the chicken from the vegetable marinade and put aside. Strain the marinade, separating liquids and solids, and reserve each. Set aside the *bouquet garni.*

Heat oil and half the butter in a large Dutch oven over medium-high heat. Salt and pepper the chicken. Sear quickly and evenly until brown. Look at how the skin sizzles. Consider for a moment the alternatives. Remove from heat and set aside.

Add the reserved vegetables to the pot and cook, stirring occasionally, until browned. Sprinkle with flour, mix gently, then add reserved marinade. Return chicken to the pot. Dice and add the tomatoes. Toss in the *bouquet garni*. Remember tossing the bouquet at your own wedding. Remember an earlier wedding when you caught it yourself and gave a sly glance at the man you'd ultimately marry. Recall how happy you were. Resist sampling this mixture, no matter how appetizing it seems.

Cook over low heat for an hour and a half. Have more of that second bottle of wine, careful to reserve at least a cup for later. Watch the clock.

Lardons! You almost forgot! Conveniently, yes? As if. (Look at your thighs again.)

Cook the lardons in a small skillet over medium heat until crisp. Remove them to a plate lined with paper towels, reserving bacon fat. Add mushrooms and cook until browned. Gauge the weight of the skillet. Gauge the heat of the grease. Consider for a moment more alternatives. Add the reserved cup of wine to the bacon fat and deglaze the pan. Set the skillet aside.

When the chicken is tender and cooked through, add the bacon, mushrooms, and red wine glaze to the Dutch oven. Swirl in the remaining butter. Season with more salt and pepper—but *not* to taste, no matter how tempting a taste might be and for so many reasons. Resist dramatic exits, overt melodrama, sentimentalizing. A single tear? Well, if you insist. There's loss here, after all, for everyone. Just stir it in quickly, so no one sees.

Hear your husband say, "Something smells good" as he comes through the door. Watch him smile guilelessly. Ask how his day was. Don't believe anything he tells you.

Serve *coq au vin* warm over noodles or rice along with crusty French bread and the third bottle of Burgundy, the one your husband picked up for "some special occasion." When he sees it and asks if this is indeed a special occasion, try to muster something witty, such as, "Isn't every day a special occasion with me?" or "If one's going to enjoy a French meal, one simply *must* go all the way," or perhaps even a jaunty "Vive la France!" Try not to lace your words with sarcasm.

Consider that word *lace*. Picture the frilly underthings you assembled as a surprise for your honeymoon. Hear your mother calling it a *trousseau* and remember savoring the word. Imagine Monique in a push-up bra and a g-string. Consider the purpose of a *corset*. Consider the phrase *merry widow*.

At the last moment, beg off eating yourself. He knows how you've been lately about saturated fats. Or maybe a sudden headache and you've lost your appetite. It's more important that he enjoy it. Really any excuse will do. But yes, you'll sit with him and have some wine.

Then discover why you went to all this trouble. Hear him tell you how delicious it is. Hear him say, "What a long way from chicken and dumplings, isn't it, hon?" Hide your surprise that he remembers the first meal you made for him. Hide your surprise when he shakes his head and laughs and admits, "Good as this is, it just can't compete with those dumplings." See him recognize what he's saying.

Remember how he carried you across the threshold. Picture dancing in the living room, just the two of you, alone on a Saturday night, head on shoulder, hand on hip. Examine the crow's feet at the corners of his eyes.

In the middle of all that, change your mind.

Serve yourself a plate too.

Because marriage is about being in it together, isn't it? For better or worse?

And perhaps this isn't a melodramatic exit, but a stylish one—sophisticated even, romantic in its own way.

Toast him graciously.

Smile warmly, sincerely.

Pick up your fork and knife.

Take that first bite.

The Boy Detective & the Summer of '74

That summer, the summer of 1974, all the boys in the neighborhood wanted to be Evel Knievel—John especially, who'd gotten a brand new bike with chopper-style handles for his birthday. He and his younger brother Paul and I, like a brother myself, raced constantly around the hot asphalt of the small block where we lived. We built rough ramps out of old bricks and leftover plywood, jumped Tonka toys, a rusty wagon, a battered Big Wheel.

Other times, we tried to be like the Six Million Dollar Man, sprinting from yard to yard, mimicking with our lips that metallic reverb that meant we'd engaged our bionic powers. We liked Kwai Chang Caine from the *Kung Fu* show too, and Paul sometimes thrashed his arms in karate chops as we wandered into the woods and fields behind our neighborhood—land that my father owned and that he was waiting to develop, same as he had built each of the nine houses that made up our small corner of that North Carolina town.

Turns out that while we aspired to be Evel Knievel or Kwai Chang Caine or the Six Million Dollar Man, my father had his own ambitions for me—that was another thing about that summer.

But one dream was mine alone. Secretly, I wanted to be Encyclopedia Brown. And the summer of '74 offered the chance for that dream to come true.

* * *

We found the first bone about mid-morning one day in late June—the sun already high, the heat rising too. Meat still clung to it, chunks of muscle, scraps of reddish brown hide. The smell had drawn us to the small drainage ditch that separated John and Paul's yard from the road, and as soon as I saw it, I'd rushed home to get the Polaroid camera my father had forbidden me to use—the camera I begged my mother not to reveal I'd borrowed. ("It's a mystery," I'd told her. "I need evidence, please don't tell, please, Mom, please.")

"It's not a leg," Paul said as I photographed what I already thought of as the crime scene.

"Well, what do you think it is, stupid?" John said. "An arm?" He gripped the chopper-style handlebar of his bike, twisting his wrist back and forth like he was revving an engine.

"I'm not saying it's an arm," Paul said. "I'm saying it's not a leg, not a human leg." Then under his breath: "Idiot." He puffed up his chest. He wore a *Keep On Truckin'* t-shirt, his favorite, which seemed to give him courage.

"Animals have legs," Christine pointed out, reminding us she was there—the new girl in the neighborhood, the one we didn't yet know what to do with. Red hair and big moony eyes and this slack-jawed look, like she was being surprised every minute of her life. When she'd moved in after the end of the school year—a military transfer, her father overseas already—our mothers had warned us to play nice.

"Who asked you?" they shouted at her, and "We're not stupid" and "We *know* animals have legs."

Christine peered over my shoulder. "What do *you* think it is, Cooper?" she whispered, close enough that the front of her shirt brushed against me.

"I think it's a cow," I said. The upper leg, I thought, but I didn't want to get John and Paul started again. *Shank*, I would have said—and wrote later on the photo once I'd learned the word. "Looks like a dog or something gnawed on it."

"It stinks," Christine said.

"Girls stink," Paul said.

"It was probably Frisky," John said, and we all looked over toward the pen in Mr. Futrell's backyard. "Old Man Futrell opens his pen after everyone's gone to bed."

Protection for the neighborhood, Mr. Futrell had claimed, bristling if anyone argued about it. The dog's real name was Buster—a big Doberman who liked to jump up on people, throwing his weight at them. "He's just frisky," Mr. Futrell had explained, bristling when people complained about that too. The name had stuck.

Frisky seemed to be sleeping. I took a picture of his pen.

"But where'd he get it from?" I asked. "You think Frisky dragged the bone from one of those fields back there?" Cows wandered inside an electric fence up a dirt road off our neighborhood. Half a mile tops, an easy walk. Once, we'd dared one another to see who could keep their hands on the hot wire the longest.

"Wouldn't there be a trail of blood?" Paul asked.

"Somebody could have thrown it from a car," Christine said.

John snorted. Paul rolled his eyes. "Don't you think we'd have noticed?" John said, but she had a point.

I stared at the bone, then took pictures of the grass browning around us and the treehouse that none of us used anymore—John and Paul's decision, ever since their mother said they couldn't keep Christine out. I took pictures from various angles—gauging from each the distance someone would need to have thrown the bone.

All of it spelled danger—memories of danger suddenly everywhere: the spot where Paul lost one of his G.I. Joes in another drainage ditch; the place where a bike ramp slipped and John ended up with an oozing pavement burn; the black circle where Mark Sebastian had set his family's yard on fire with a Roman candle; the boxwoods Mark and his friends had hidden behind on Halloween, waiting to jump out at us.

Over at my house, Milton the yardman unloaded the riding lawnmower from a trailer, ready to mow our grass and then several more in the neighborhood, and that prompted the memory of my father's story about a man who lost his arm to tractor blade.

Christine jumped when Milton cranked up the mower. It woke Frisky too. He barked at Milton, stalking the length of his pen and back.

I closed my eyes then and tried to concentrate, tried to imagine the middle of the night—moonlit, the houses quiet, someone carrying a bone. But all I could see were red splotches, that high morning sun beating through my eyelids. All I could hear were Frisky's frantic barks and the roar of that mower and John urging us to give it up, come on, time to race our bikes.

Then, from the Sebastians' house, I heard laughter and the slam of a car door. I opened my eyes. A Mustang pulled from the driveway, the car packed with teenagers, Mark Sebastian in the driver's seat. Instinctively, I raised the camera and snapped a shot.

The car had sped away long before the picture developed, but I was left with that image of Mark's face glaring at us through the open window and the sudden knowledge—solid, if unsupported—that he was key to whatever we were looking for.

* * *

I still have those Polaroids now, the carpet of centipede grass a sickly green, the treehouse faded yellow to white, the figures dimmed to ghosts. The childish cursive of the captions have faded too: "Friday morning," and "sunny," and then on one of the bone itself, "about 15 inches long."

Trying to get the full crime scene, I caught photos of my mother sweeping the porch, and off behind her, Milton circling that lawnmower, and Ms. Lottie too—John and Paul's mother—in the window, her mouth open like she was singing. Christine half-in, half-out of a frame, one moony eye. Paul in his *Keep On Truckin'* shirt. John flexing a muscle for the camera—the bully of the bunch always, head butts, titty twisters, and Charlie horses—even if that muscle today looks thin and frail.

And then there's the glimpse of my father's Cadillac tooling unexpectedly into view, his own face glaring through the windshield—his expression as surprised as my own must have been.

But without the guilt. He wasn't the one caught doing anything wrong.

* * *

My father didn't park in his regular spot but stopped midway up the driveway that cut the length of our yard. He summoned me with a firm "Cooper!"—his face as stern as his voice, his jaw set, eyes unblinking. When I reached him, he held out his hand for the camera. "Not a toy," he said, and I remember wondering how he'd known about it, how he'd gotten across town so quickly, what punishment lie ahead.

But the camera wasn't why he'd come home. He had bigger lessons to teach that morning, and he marched me across the yard, toward Milton atop that John Deere mower.

When my father raised his hand—a hello? a command?—Milton cut the engine. My father put his foot on the mower's bladeguard, his wingtips shining next to Milton's tattered brogans. I stood close behind—witness more than participant, uncomfortable in more ways than one. Those pictures I'd already taken? I'd stuffed them down my pants.

"I'm hiring a helper for you," my father said. He guided me forward, hand on my shoulder.

Milton wiped his brow with a rag from his pocket. Grass clippings on the rag, smeared now on his forehead too. He was a tall, muscular black man, the barest hint of gray in his hair and sweat stains always under his arms. His yellowish eyes turned between my father and me.

"You want him to drive it?" Milton pointed toward the steering wheel.

My father laughed. "We'll let him work up to that. No, no, let him bag the clippings." He squatted down to look me in the eye. "A quarter a bag. Can't beat that kind of pay."

I don't remember speaking. I don't think it was really a question. Truth was, I barely paid attention. Over by the ditch, John stood over the bone and motioned for Christine to join him. Paul was sneaking up behind her.

My father kept talking, talking to me, past me: a learning experience, what's earned, what's valued, the choices you make, and Milton himself a good example of a strong work ethic.

"Cooper's choice to work or not to work," my father emphasized, and I did hear that—more news, and a potential out? I could get back to the bone, save the evidence. "But a lot of comic books a young man can buy with a handful of quarters, wouldn't you say, Milton?"

Milton swiped at his forehead, trying to flick away those clippings. "He should do the raking too?"

My father straightened but still stared at me—maybe measuring my size against a rake's. Paul had pushed Christine, but she'd spun free, and he and John were chasing her now.

"One thing at a time," my father said and left Milton and me to stare at one another.

* * *

Milton took turns mowing and raking, and when the piles were big enough, I swooped in with a big green garbage bag.

Between times, I continued my investigation—borrowing another bag to rescue the bone.

"You're saving it?" John straddled his bike, walking it beside me as I dragged the bone bag to the woods beyond my yard.

"It's disgusting," said Paul, tagging behind.

"It's evidence," said Christine.

I felt cheated that she said it first. The corners of the photos poked at my thigh as I walked.

After another round of grass clippings, I ducked into the house to hide those pictures in my room, then grabbed a notebook left over from the school year. I tore out all the pages I'd used—notes about "how to research" from my fourth grade class with Mrs. Bartlett. On the cover, I wrote *Casebook* in black magic marker.

I rushed through the yard chores. I rushed along that ditch and into the woods and even partway up that dirt road toward the cow pen. John and Paul taunted and teased at every step, while Christine skirted the edges. I filled up three pages with lists of evidence: cigarette butts and empty beer cans; candy wrappers and 87 cents in loose change; a pocketknife John had lost (which sparked him to join me briefly in the search); a black widow spider in an old milk carton (which got Paul on board); a frilly pink bra.

"Hubba hubba," John said, mimicking his dad. Paul picked it up and held it in front of Christine, who shrieked and ran.

Right under "bra" in my notebook is "popped balloon," but looking back, I can imagine what it really was. Paul had already made a comment about seeing Mark Sebastian and his girlfriend back here. At the time, that information had seemed proof that they were headed toward the cows—the pen I also walked to, counting the animals like I would know if one was missing.

"Something mighty interesting you kids up to," Milton said as I gathered up the last clippings.

I shook my head. I didn't want him reporting to my father. He didn't ask anything else.

* * *

Later in the afternoon, Mark came back. He was shooting hoops in his yard and that same girlfriend sat off to the side. When we asked why they'd been out in the woods, the pimples on his face flared up even angrier than usual.

"I will kill every one of you if you don't keep your mouths shut, do you hear me?" He clenched the basketball between his hands like he was going to launch it at us.

"More proof," I announced, after we'd run away. "And did you see that girl's face? She knows something."

"Maybe she just likes him," Christine said.

John and Paul snorted. *Girls*, they seemed to be saying, and Christine blushed too.

* * *

Be sure you include Christine. Do you understand me, Cooper?

Those words had become my mother's mantra each morning when I went out into the world.

But whether she said it or not, it had become clear pretty quickly that it didn't matter. Water-gun battles, hole-digging contests, even football or baseball—Christine wouldn't be shaken, despite our best efforts.

When we rode our bikes, pedaling furiously, she pedaled just as desperately, the tassels on her handlebars tearing through the air. "Tassels," said John later. "Won't catch Evil Knievel's daughters with tassels." And Paul said, "Not even Mrs. Evil Knievel."

When we'd taken turns to see who could hold their hands the longest on that cow pen's thin electric wires, Christine had looped her own fingers around them, told us it tickled. "A girl's word," Paul snorted.

When we climbed trees, daring one another to a higher spot, Christine always reached toward the next branch, even the time she wasn't dressed right for it—a yellow skirt, shiny black shoes, frilly socks—at least until John started chanting, "I see England, I see France," and Paul almost slipped laughing, and Christine shimmied down as fast as she could, her cheeks on fire. She stayed quiet the whole walk home, keeping up but also keeping me between her and the other boys—the lesser of those evils, I guess.

More questions inevitably in the evening too.

My mother always insisted on a sit-down dinner—cloth napkins, a full complement of silverware, and good posture—and my father insisted on conversation, even if that mostly meant him talking about the day's news: Vietnam, over but not over (never over), or Watergate or something that the nigras had done. (*We were South-*

ern. That's what I started to write, to try to explain. But really it was more complex than that.) If attention ever turned my way, it came out as another lecture: the value of a strong work ethic, the future laid out for me in the world of business, the same kinds of lessons he gave when he sprang those yardwork duties on me.

So whenever my mother interrupted to ask, "What did you children do today? Did you include Christine?" I mumbled something about riding bikes or being in the woods and told her that yes, I'd treated her well—because in the midst of sitting up straight and using the right fork and showing the proper attention, how could you explain that you felt good for having looked away from a girl's panties and yet bad for not facing that same girl when she fell in beside you afterward?

*   *   *

"Have you solved your mystery yet?" my mother asked as I was getting ready for dinner that day we'd found the bone.

I shrugged. "It wasn't anything serious," I told her.

"Did Christine help you?"

Later than night, it should've been satisfying to get the handful of quarters my father gave me, but I had other, more important work on my mind.

Those research skills our fourth-grade teacher had drilled into us? That set of *World Book Encyclopedias* my mother had been convinced to buy?

My casebook brimmed with information—the fact that cows had divided hoofs, *cloven* the word, and then that word *shank* I found in the chart of butcher's beef cuts.

I held those Polaroids beside the different kinds of cows: Aberdeen-Angus, Charolais, Hereford, Jersey, Guernsey, Holstein-Friesian. Wasn't Limousin the closest match to that scrap of reddish-brown skin? But were they only in France?

Among the many diseases of cows, was *blackleg*, bringing "lameness, convulsions, rapid swelling, and high fever," but how could you tell if a severed leg had been lame or feverish?

That night was the first of many perched against the bedroom window, gazing into the darkness, watching the shrubbery and the shadows under the trees, waiting for the red glow of a cigarette somewhere in the distance. Headlights might drift down the street at any minute, or better, a car without headlights, its window rolled down and an arm hanging out, flinging stray meat. I strained for a glimpse of Frisky roaming between the trees. I eased the window open to listen for growling or gnawing. The smell of pine crept through the open crack, fighting the air conditioning pushing it back out. I heard only crickets, an occasional toad.

"We need more cow," I remember saying, aloud, out into the darkness.

* * *

The appearance of a second bone, this one in a ditch behind the Sebastians' yard, confirmed my instincts about Mark. John still made noise about better things to do—his Evil Knievel vs. my Encyclopedia Brown—but he was curious. Even Paul started coming up with ideas to solve the case.

"You could put up posters," he said. "Offer a reward."

"How is he going to pay a reward, idiot?" John pushed his shoulder.

Paul swatted back. "We don't have to pay. Whoever answered, they would probably be guilty."

"Uh-uh," I said. "That would tip them off."

Them, I thought. And then *Mark*.

I swiped my father's camera again to take more pictures. I wrapped this bone in a fresh bag and laid it near the first one, even though animals had already gnawed through that plastic, stripped the meat completely. I made another list of clues, indiscriminately—uselessly, I see now.

John, Paul, and Christine huddled around me as I drew a map of the neighborhood, marking the placement of the bones and other evidence. Together, we constructed a full list of everyone who lived there, their jobs, their schedules. (I added an "es" to make *Dobbses* and *Williamses*, trying to remember what we'd learned about plurals in school. I remember being proud of spelling *bookkeeper*, having learned from Encyclopedia Brown that it was the rare word with three sets of double letters.)

I made a list of other people who came into the neighborhood: Milton, of course, and then Percy the mailman, and the old man who delivered the paper in the afternoon, whose name I didn't know, and then the trash men who roared around our block twice a week. The stink of the bone and the stench that trailed their truck linked them inevitably.

We tracked the comings and goings of our neighbors—scrupulous notes in my casebook.

Wednesday, 4:25 p.m.—Old Man Futrell takes out his trash. Two bottles of Old Crow. Party? Guests must come at night.

And:

3:23 [no day listed on this one]—*Mrs. Crawford sits on porch, wearing housecoat, reading.* And then: *Later—piano music through open window at her house, singing.*

I entertained other suspects, asking my father about our neighbors the Crouches, who'd opened a new restaurant.

"Do they serve steak?" I asked. "Flank steak? Or brisket?"

"Not fitting to eat," said my father, not looking up from his paper. "We'll get you a rib eye when we go."

I asked my mother if Mrs. Crawford's husband had died under suspicious circumstances?

"Cancer isn't suspicious," she told me.

"What does she do in there all day? She never comes out."

"She plays her piano. She reads."

"Doesn't she get bored?"

My mother thought about that. "I don't think so. Lonely maybe— lonely, of course."

"Is that why you go over there? Because you feel sorry for her."

"She's a friend, Cooper," my mother said—maybe too insistently. "You don't need to be afraid of her. She's just different—different in many ways."

Different meant *strange*, I'd thought. *Different* meant *dangerous*.

"I'm not scared of her," I said, though I was a little, how she kept to herself and the way she pulled her frizzy gray hair in a ponytail, not like other old woman. John and Paul were convinced she was a witch. We avoided her house at Halloween.

Another time, I told my mother that Mr. Karr snuck cigarettes on the back porch, smoking in the darkness.

"Don't tell Mrs. Karr," she said. "Let that be our secret, OK?"

Whenever my father invited business associates over—"drinking and dealing" as he said—I took note of the license plates, without any idea how to trace them, and I rushed out the next morning expecting another bone. But the yards were empty.

Still, no one was safe from speculation. Eavesdropping on my mother's phone calls, I wrote down *cut* and *die* and *would do it at home but don't want it to bleed.* Now, it seems clear that she was saying dye—a hair appointment—but for several days, I kept her under close scrutiny: watching her choice of knife when she cooked, studying the thin muscles of her arms and the curiously mottled texture of the back of her hand.

* * *

Most of my casebook was devoted to Mark Sebastian.

Saturday, 1:23 p.m.—Sound of door opening and closing at the Sebastians. Laughter, Mark and two girls. Small bathing suits. Mark sees us.

Tuesday, 5:18 p.m.—Mr. Sebastian comes home, drives around basketball, parks car, picks it up, picks up a cigarette butt, examines it, carries it inside.

Thursday, 7:27 p.m.—Sebastian cookout, just family. Mr. Sebastian sees us, calls to join them. Mark whispers. Mr. Sebastian says "Grow up, Mark"—angry. We run home.

Saturday morning—Items in Sebastian yard: Six pinecones not under pine trees, three cigarette butts in back yard, Zero bar wrapper, basketball in driveway again.

I gathered those cigarette butts and kept them in a bag in my room, and the Zero bar wrapper too. I'd collected other items: a stray newspaper flyer, a four-leaf clover, 13 more cents—a number that seemed significant. If it seems obsessive, it's only because I'd learned my lesson the first day, when I'd gone back to retrieve our evidence and the bra was gone.

How often did the Sebastians see us crouched down in their bushes or wandering the ditch behind their house? One afternoon after we found the second bone, Mark and his friends chased us out from behind the boxwoods, Christine giggling and John shushing her—the shushing louder than the giggling.

Another afternoon we traipsed along behind Mark and his girlfriend in the woods, crawling over branches and stumps and through vines. Soon I realized they were walking in circles, trying to lose us or maybe simply tire us out, same as John and Paul sometimes did with Christine.

"Will you go the hell home?" Mark threw a stick in our direction. John dodged it at the last minute.

"You're not supposed to say *hell*!" John shouted.

"Leave me and Felicia alone!" Mark shouted back.

"Felicia!" said Paul, and he and John began chanting "Mark and Felicia, sitting in a tree...." Even Christine joined in, her voice low and restrained but trying to take part.

I kept quiet. At that rate, we'd never figure out where they were going.

* * *

Somewhere in here, Christine had a birthday party. Between finding the second and third bone? right after finding the third bone? At the time, it hadn't seemed as important as it does now.

Christine had passed out invitations she'd decorated with glue and glitter. John and Paul and I were the only kids invited, probably the only ones she knew, moving in after the school year had ended. Three gift bags stood on the counter when I arrived—a ball inside mine, a couple of toy cars, a package of baseball cards. Same with John's and Paul's, I imagine, but they never showed up.

"We'll have cake later." Christine's mother gestured toward the oven. "I'll call when it's ready."

Christine led me around like a tour guide, those big moony eyes like they might burst into tears at any moment. Much of the house seemed unsettled: piles of boxes on the edges of the living room and in the guest room, no pictures on any of the walls. They'd barely moved in before her father had shipped overseas.

Christine's room was different—both from the other rooms and from the ones where we boys lived. A canopied bed, all pink and ruffles, teddy bears across the pillows. Raggedy Ann and Andy in oversized versions, Barbies in several outfits, a token Ken. More toys were crammed into a pink chest, her name written on top in a curlicued script.

"Do you like books?" she asked when she caught me looking at her bookcase. "We could read together." She kneeled down by the shelves.

"I wonder if John and Paul are here yet."

She stood again when I didn't plop down beside her.

"Maybe you could borrow one another time—I don't mind."

I shook my head, even though part of me envied her copy of *Where the Wild Things Are*, which my own parents had never let me read.

"Do you want to play something else? We can do whatever you want."

Her closet was half-open—the folding doors parted slightly—a crowd of dresses and skirts, plaids and pastels, frills and bows inside. I recall some soft scent of perfume, but that could hardly have been true.

"I brought a present," I told her finally. "I left it downstairs."

Christine squealed with joy when she saw what my mother had helped me pick out in the Piggly Wiggly's toy aisle: the board game *Clue*. We played immediately. "I'm Miss Scarlet," Christine said, flicking her hair back. I'm certain she let me win.

Christine's mother and I sang happy birthday. Christine blew out all 11 candles with a quick whoosh, and then turned those moony eyes my way like they had their own wishes.

The icing on the cake was so sweet that the back of my throat curled up.

"He wants more, Mama," Christine said, after I'd choked it down. I didn't feel like I could say no.

* * *

"I hear from Milton that you won't be getting paid this week." My father leveled a hard stare at me across the dinner table. "That's a lot of comic books you won't be able to buy. When I was a young man, I wouldn't have passed up that chance."

Whenever Milton had waved me over to help that day, I'd waved back, waved him off, kept moving through my investigation. I wouldn't have put it this way then—couldn't have, I'm sure—but somehow I'd realized that except through my father, Milton had no power over me. He drank water from the hose outside instead of asking for a glass and wouldn't even come in for the bathroom, even when my mother asked if he needed the facilities.

When I didn't seem regretful enough, when I reminded my father that he'd told me the work was a choice—my choice—he got huffier.

"A man chooses to earn his way. You reap what you sow, don't reap what you don't."

My late nights at the window were leaving me exhausted, drowsy over my cereal. My father was whispering to my mother words like *derelict* and *lazy*.

But I couldn't kid myself that I was accomplishing much with my own "work" either. I had my criminal—Mark Sebastian—but no motive, no real evidence.

By the time the third bone showed up, John and Paul had fully lost interest, but Christine stuck close.

"You'll solve it soon enough," she told me, her forehead nearly touching mine as I laid out the fresh garbage bag, even as I knew the bone's eventual fate: ripped plastic, bugs, maggots, rot. A strand of hair fell across Christine's eyes, and she blew it free of her face.

She reached down to smooth a wrinkled edge of the plastic, then took a corner of the bag as I lugged it toward the woods. Sally to my Encyclopedia Brown, that's what I kept telling myself, despite the way she'd looked at me at her birthday party.

As we walked, John and Paul whizzed by on their bikes. "Cooper and Christine, sitting in a tree...."

The whirring of their spokes was shrill, then duller as they sped past. The Doppler Effect, we'd learned in school, but that knowledge didn't do me much good.

* * *

Encyclopedia Brown had a calling card: "Brown Detective Agency, 13 Rover Avenue, Leroy Brown President, NO case too small, 25 cents per day, plus expenses." Brown's father, the chief of police in Idaville, relied on Encyclopedia to solve the tough cases, the ones that had stalled in his own hands, and he always found the key clue. Of course, electric clocks don't *tick*! Clearly hard-boiled eggs will spin longer than uncooked eggs! Obviously there's no Z on a telephone dial!

Night after night, reading about his adventures and solutions, I burned with envy. Nothing about our case made so much sense.

I didn't have a calling card, but it was easy enough to write a letter:

Dear Chief—
Here are pictures of the bones we found. There are three of them.
They belong to a cow. Maybe the same cow. Can we help you solve the
case? We are investigating.
                    Cooper Hobbes
                    324-3684

I pictured photos of the Chief and me in the paper. *Boy Genius Cracks Case* and *Newest Addition to Police Force.*

"I don't know why you're so sure Mark did it," John said as I led him and Christine on the long walk to the police station downtown.

"He acts guilty."

"Didn't you say we'd need *hard evidence?*" John had started taking that role, trying to beat me on my own turf, the turf I was trying to claim.

"One of the bones was near his yard."

"The first bone was in our yard, doofus. Does that mean that me or Paul did it?"

"You wouldn't have had any reason to."

"And what reason did Mark have, huh?"

I didn't answer. More investigation ahead, that was the point of the letter.

"We're gonna get in trouble if we go any further," John said, and when I didn't stop, "You better turn back or I'm gonna tell."

"You wouldn't." I whirled on him. "You won't."

He stared at me, his hands opening and shutting. *See my finger, see my thumb*, he sometimes said. *See my fist...* But I didn't blink. Christine looked nervously from one to the other of us. Paul wasn't there at all. That morning, he told his mother he'd brushed his teeth, but when she checked, the bristles were dry, so he was paying the price. Maybe the reason John tagged along now. Nothing else to do.

"You're as stupid as you look," said John, but he and Christine both fell in behind me when I kept walking.

Our town was not large, the walk was not long, but it seemed as if we crossed several worlds on our walk. The white columns at the First Citizens Bank. The smell of discarded vegetables from the back of the Piggly Wiggly next door—18-wheelers at the loading docks. Lush green lawns lined one street. Dogwoods and azaleas and boxwoods fronted sturdy brick colonials. Then those gracious houses and manicured grounds gave way to the older section of town, the colored section we'd have called it, all sagging porches and rotting wood. Those yards were dusty, chain-link fences around the border. In one yard, I remember a young child hoisted in a makeshift swing—some part of an infant's highchair hung with a couple lengths of rope.

The child's mother stared at us as we passed, and John called back, "What are you looking at?" When she didn't stop looking, John spit out an ugly word, the kind of word his own father might've said, but always behind closed doors. I tried to shush him, I called out an apology. The woman never spoke. When I glanced back, she swung the baby steady as before.

* * *

More to that day's mission, of course—more about my ambitions and fears and failures there at the edge of what I hoped would be my first success as a boy detective.

The scuff of John's shoes against the sidewalk downtown, irritatingly unhurried. The offbeat tap tap tap of Christine's as she dodged cracks, fearful of breaking her mother's back.

The smoky tint of the police department's plate-glass window and my hesitation peering at the old men loitering within.

John taunting me, "Go on in, why don't you?" Then the ringing of the bell above the door as Christine pushed through first, dragging me behind her.

A tall counter, impossibly high. A man perched against it, his neck bulging over his collar. The breath of the woman leaning over the counter, stale with cigarettes and coffee. The way her blue hair gleamed. The way she called us *children*. "Well, hello there, children."

And then the man with the bulging neck talking to me too— "You're Frank's boy, aren't you?"—and me panicking, thrusting the envelope at the blue-haired woman, shouting "It's for the chief" before I pushed my way out, the door's bell brash as an alarm.

Laughter behind me, and snatches of words: "Got a confession there" and "Bet he nabbed us a criminal" and "Got that girl leading him around" And then outside, more laughter—John telling me what an ignoramus I was.

Every one of those details stung me to the core, chased me all the way back to our neighborhood.

But in retrospect, none of it stands out today as much as what John called that black woman in the dusty yard and the memory of her steady eyes and her silence—even as she was the last thing on my mind at the time.

* * *

For days after our visit to the police station, I stayed indoors—

waiting for the chief of police to call.

"Why aren't you outside today?" my mother urged me. "Do you have a tummyache? All that ice cream you ate last night."

Another night, I heard my father tell her, "He's certainly grown fond of the phone."

"Maybe he's got a little girlfriend," my mother said.

"He doesn't see any girls other than Christine."

"Well."

Stupid, stupid, stupid, I thought—harder on myself than John ever was.

Then one afternoon, the call *was* for me.

"Head for the *treehouse,* Coop," said the voice, John or Paul, I still don't know which. "*Now.*"

* * *

John and Paul were already rocketing out of their backdoor. When I saw Paul's backpack, my mind short-circuited. Had they found a fourth bone? Would they have put it in a backpack?

Christine raced from another direction. Had they called her? To the treehouse? But she belonged there, she did.

Paul scrambled up the ladder, the backpack wobbling. John waved me past: "Go, go!" But when I got to the top, I saw why he'd stopped first. Christine hadn't been invited at all.

"Not you." His fingers stabbed the air, a hiss in his voice, his mother's warnings suddenly thrown out the window. "No girls allowed"—like something out of a comic strip or one of the *Little Rascals* cartoons they still showed on TV. Christine looked like she'd been slapped.

Pine straw matted in the corner of the treehouse. Sitting in it, Paul stretched his lips into a wide, lascivious grin as he opened the backpack. I caught a glimpse of something we didn't see on *Little Rascals*: a *Playboy* swiped from their father's drawer. Nothing to do with the case after all.

"Wait," John said when Paul started flipping through the magazine. John had climbed up, perched himself in the doorway, one foot hanging down, like he was ready to kick at Christine. "She'll leave soon."

I looked out one of the thin windows that their father had cut into the walls. Sniper holes, Mr. Bill had called them. Christine clung to the bottom of the ladder—those doe eyes, that slack jaw.

Evil Knievel, the Six Million Dollar Man, Kwai Chang Caine, even Encyclopedia Brown—those were easier roles to play. Sometimes—I think I knew this even then—there were bigger stakes about who you were going to be.

"Will you *wait?*" John shouted before I could say anything, and then he snatched the magazine from Paul's hands and thrust it toward Christine.

"See!" he said, shoving it in her face. "See why we don't want you here?"

"What are you doing?" Paul jumped up, slipping on wet pine needles.

"Go tell your mama." Spit flew from John's lips. "See if we ever talk to you then. Go on and see what happens."

Christine's eyes were as wide as ever, but her lips had shut firmly. She stared at me—not angry now, not sad, but simply empty, so blank I could hardly meet her look.

Another chance to say something. No one stopping me this time.

Finally she turned and slowly, silently made her way across the yard and out of sight.

"Do you *know* what you did?" Paul asked, "how much trouble we're going to get in?"

"She won't do anything," John said. "Not a damn thing."

The first time I'd heard him curse. Some rite of passage there. Several.

* * *

We were rapt in the presence of the *Playboy*, its wonders and mysteries—those other kinds of mysteries. A woman lying back in the surf, her body wet and shining, and another woman, a bride, slipping out of her wedding dress and beckoning to us. We sped though the pictures, then went back and lingered over them, then again and again day after day—everything except a short photo spread of a black woman.

"Who would want to see that?" Paul said.

"They ought not put it in there," John said.

Maybe black men read *Playboy* too, I thought, but I didn't say it.

We read the cartoons too, even though the jokes flew over our heads, and an illustrated ABC of sex, whose words I wrote down on a separate page in my casebook. *Cuckold* and *frigidity* I found in the dictionary, and *rhythm* and *method* as individual words, and *wife* and *swap* too, even if I couldn't add them together to anything that made sense.

The cover was a cartoon too, brightly colored—several children at the beach, three boys and a girl, coincidentally enough, and the little girl looking sad, which couldn't help but make me think of us boys and Christine. In the middle of them stood a woman, a real woman, not a cartoon. She held an inflatable raft shaped like a horse, bending forward over it and looking out at the camera. She sucked on a popsicle.

I'm not making this up.

Same as those Polaroids, I still have the magazine—the August 1974 issue—torn in places, a little waterlogged, but intact. I salvaged it when John and Paul finally got tired of it.

After all, despite my initial reaction, it did turn out to be evidence. Of a sort.

* * *

Two nights after John and Paul stole the *Playboy*, I was keeping my usual watch before bedtime, the bottom of the window cracked, the warm air seeping in, the smell of freshly cut grass from where Milton had mowed. I could still smell grass on my own hands from bagging the cuttings—guilted into doing my job, guilted in every way.

We hadn't seen Christine since the treehouse episode. She was an absence, a silence, and through the window, the whole world seemed more silent than usual.

Then I heard a bark.

I grabbed my casebook. "11:06 Friday," I wrote. "Intruder?"

Several minutes passed. The house and the yard and the world beyond—all quiet again.

"11:14," I wrote. "Investigating. I am close to solving the case."

I pulled a pair of jeans over my pajamas, shoved the casebook in my back pocket, and tiptoed down the hallway.

Inside my parents' bedroom, my mother was pulling a cotton ball across her cheek. No sign of my father. From the first floor came silence—no television, no lights.

The living room was empty. ("I came down for water," I would've said if caught.) Beyond, a dim light shone in the back room where my father usually entertained his business associates. Pressed against the kitchen wall, I heard papers being shuffled, a clink of ice.

I stepped across the floor, high, long steps, careful not to make any sound. When the kitchen window didn't offer any clearer view, I moved to the door. The deadbolt clicked free like the cocking of a gun. The creak of the door sounded like a crypt vault opening. I waited for my father's voice—"Who's there?"—but my luck held.

Easing through the crack of the door, I gazed out and, before I knew it, found myself out in the yard. I didn't close the door fully, afraid to risk that creaking and clicking again.

Investigating, I'd written, and I was determined to do just that.

Dense shadows surrounded the pine trees at the edge of our property. Beyond it, moonlight shone more clearly on the Huffmans' yard and the edge of Old Man Futrell's, but I couldn't see whether Frisky was in his pen. The Huffmans' house completely blocked the Sebastians' from view.

John and Paul's bedroom windows were dark. I was tempted to whisper-shout up at them, but the lights were still on in the living room downstairs.

I thought about sneaking over to Christine's, but after everything at the treehouse....

Tree branches shifted slightly in the breeze, scraping one against the other. Grass blades swayed, and I had the impression that some invisible animal was crossing.

I crept forward, the ground soft beneath my bare feet.

Frisky's pen was empty. *He knows me*, I told myself, *I'm not a stranger, he wouldn't attack me*, but even I didn't believe it.

Near the Huffmans' garage, I could finally see the Sebastians' house, a single light above the front door. It looked as if the door itself might be opened, same as I'd left our door ajar. Mark's car stood in the driveway, and I knew I needed to check if the hood was warm, another trick I'd learned from Encyclopedia Brown.

Then I heard a yelp near Mrs. Crawford's house. A shaft of light appeared in her backyard, only for a second. Then darkness again, followed by a low growl.

I scrambled into the Huffmans' garage, crouched between Mr. Huffman's car and a stack of two-by-fours left over from building the treehouse. My heart throbbed. Was Mark over at Mrs. Crawford's? Was *she* involved somehow? A witch, John and Paul had said. And maybe her husband's death hadn't been cancer after all.

Or maybe lonely Mrs. Crawford was indeed a victim here.

For several minutes—an eternity—I sat paralyzed in the garage. Move ahead? Run home? The growls deepened in the distance. Was it Frisky? And if it wasn't Frisky...?

What would Encyclopedia Brown have done?

Mrs. Crawford's yard stayed dark. The streetlamp shining through the trees cast more shadows than light. The low growl became a wet gnashing sound. Another bone there, I knew it, the fourth bone, and this animal—Frisky, whatever—was devouring it.

Something will happen here, I thought. *Something soon.*

Then the light above the Sebastian's door went black, and even with the moonlight and the streetlamps, a new darkness settled over the neighborhood. At nearly the same moment—at least it seems that way in memory—whatever was in Mrs. Crawford's yard began to lumber out into the light.

I never saw it clearly, only the outline of its dark shape, the bulk of the beast, and those bright eyes, otherworldly, reflecting toward me the orange light of the streetlamp.

I didn't look twice, I leaped out from the corner of the garage and ran as fast and as hard as I could back toward my house.

Our kitchen door still stood open, but the lights were all out and my parents' bedroom door closed. If they heard the door locking or my footsteps up the stairs, they never came out.

I lay in bed with darker fantasies running through my mind—and a new word echoing, not *stupid stupid stupid* now but *coward coward coward*, and I didn't know which word was worse.

* * *

Dew glistened on the ground, wetting my feet as I walked out early the next morning. The sun peeked through the trees, but shadows lingered here and there. Everything was eerily tranquil, as if waiting for something—for me, maybe.

Frisky waited in his pen too, like he'd never left it. When I came closer, he lifted an eyebrow. No blood spots stained the cement floor, no meat hung from the sides of his mouth, but it must have been him. If I hadn't seen the empty cage the night before, hadn't heard the growling in the darkness, I wouldn't have believed any of it.

I found the fourth bone in the back corner of Mrs. Crawford's yard, near the small trail that led through the woods toward town—the one that John, Christine, and I had taken to the police station. Chunks of flesh had been shredded and torn from it, same as always.

I turned to the map in my casebook. When I added the new X, I saw how this bone helped to complete a square of sorts around Mrs. Crawford's house, and I understood that whatever was happening had been completed as well—and not only because of the shape.

A cow has four legs. I'd now found the full set.

The sliding door on Mrs. Crawford's back porch was open, and I thought about the shaft of light from the night before. All those open doors—the one I'd left ajar at my house, the one I thought I'd seen at the Sebastians', all of it coming together. This wasn't simply Mark and his girlfriend playing in the woods. They were involved in something more devious, more tragic.

"Mark Sebastian," I said, aloud. "He killed her."

He'd had been watching her place, he and his girlfriend. They'd used the bones to keep Frisky occupied. The last bone had helped them break in. Mark had stolen jewels, money so he could escape his father. He and Felecia had eloped. I pictured different headlines this time: *Old Woman Killed in the Night* and *Boy Misses Chance to Save Neighbor* and *Teen Criminals Escape—Whereabouts Unknown*.

"You, boy," I heard then, and I turned to see Mrs. Crawford opening that back door wider. "What are you doing?"

"It's me, Mrs. Crawford," I said—startled, relieved, perplexed. "It's Cooper."

"I know who you are. I asked what you're doing."

I looked down at the bone, debating whether to tell her about it. "It's a bone," I said, walking closer. "We've found four of them now."

"Bones?"

"They're not people bones," I told her. "They're cow bones. I think someone was trying to throw off Frisky—Mr. Futrell's dog. I think someone broke into your house."

"Bones," she said again, but not a question this time and like she hadn't heard the rest. "From a cow." I thought she laughed, though I couldn't understand what was funny.

Her housecoat was blue, a royal blue I'd say now, fraying slightly at the edges, and her hair hung down at all angles, not yet pulled up into that ponytail. She looked off beyond my head toward the trail where the bone lay. A long moment passed.

"I think I would know if someone had broken into my home, don't you agree?"

Behind her, through the door, I caught a glimpse of bookcases. None of the books seemed to have been torn down, nothing was strewn around the room. The piano stood silent. A single mug sat on the coffee table. How long had she been watching me?

"Have you checked all the rooms?" I asked. "Maybe—"

"Nothing is amiss," she said, the word standing out so clearly that I wrote it in my casebook later. "If you'd like to come in and see for yourself... I've put on some cinnamon rolls."

Her words were welcoming, but her tone was formal, the way I'd heard other adults talk—offering something that they didn't really want to give.

"No, ma'am," I said. "I'm glad you're OK."

* * *

"Out early today?" my father asked, reading the paper, enjoying his breakfast. My mother stood at the stove. "Hard at work, or your usual lolling and moping?"

I shook my head, joined him at the table. My mother set down a plate of bacon and eggs. "Don't slouch, Cooper."

My father folded his paper, placed it with great purpose on the table. "We have company tonight. A businessman from the Outer Banks. A potential investor to help develop the woods and fields." He waved behind him. "You can learn something from this, and...."

And what else did he say? A cookout, I knew, and the Huffmans coming over, Mr. Bill and Ms. Lottie and John and Paul too—a community of support, a family community—and from my mother, a "shouldn't Christine come as well?" but I could barely hear any of it.

Would they be going in the woods? Did I need to hide the bones?

And Christine coming? We couldn't face her, didn't want to.

Somewhere in the middle of these new troubles and worries, my father hustled me away from my half-eaten breakfast and into the Cadillac—"a lesson in preparing a pitch, start to finish," he said, some steaks to pick up for the cookout. "Rib eyes. First-class, honest, American."

As we drove out of the neighborhood, I stared at the Sebastians' house with the same suspicions, at Mrs. Crawford's with fresh ones. My father's hand rested lightly on the top of the wheel, as if he didn't even need to hold it.

* * *

"Aren't we going to the store?" I asked as we passed the Piggly Wiggly.

"That's why *I'm* going to pick up the steaks."

He drove us along the same streets that John, Christine, and I had walked: past the lush lawns, toward the dusty ones, and then a left turn deeper into the colored section of town.

"Your mother doesn't like to drive here by herself," my father said. "Bet you've never been down this way at all."

A black man sat on the porch reading a newspaper. His gaze followed us. A dog crept around the corner of another house, sliding close to the wall. The makeshift swing sat empty.

My father turned again, pulled in front of a small wooden building. The front was all plate-glass windows, "Meat" frosted on it in big letters, and a few cardboard signs propped on a small ledge: "Spareribs" and "Hog Jowls." Inside, two black men bent over a refrigerated case.

Dust kicked up as I shuffled behind my father through the gravel. A bell tinkled as we entered.

"Morning, gentlemen," my father said.

"Yes, sir." One of the men stood straight. He wore an apron, some of its red stains still glistening. The other man placed small packages of chicken beneath a sign that said "Fryers" in red magic marker. The cartons were thick with juice.

"I need a half-dozen steaks, some nice rib eyes," my father said. "About an inch thick?" He held up his fingers.

"Yes, sir." The man turned through the door behind him. I caught a glimpse of a pig, headless and hoisted on a hook. The other man kept loading the refrigerated case. Ground beef now.

The bell tinkled again. A black woman began sorting through the chickens.

"Y'all got any smaller ones?" she asked the man. "This big, sometimes they's tough."

"A couple there at the bottom."

She found one. "This'll do." She pulled a small change purse from somewhere inside her purple dress.

"Take the time and get the best, right, ma'am?" my father said.

"Pay more for a big bird," the woman said, "too tough to eat."

"Some people like them bigger breasts," the man behind the counter said, winking at the woman as he handed over her change.

She bent her chin down and glared at him. "Some people get they spindly chicken neck wrung if they keep talkin' like they do."

"Come back soon," he called as the bell rang testily behind her.

"You working on hamburger patties?" asked my father, pointing to another counter. A trail of fresh red meat fell from a large metal grinder. A stack of patties stood to the side. "We'll take five or six of those too."

"Yes, sir." He turned to wrap them.

My father leaned down toward me. "Maybe it's easier to go the grocery store, or more convenient, but you don't go for what's easiest but for what's best—best quality, best deal." He patted my head.

Soon the hamburgers were laid on the counter, and the first man returned with a large package wrapped in white paper.

"This all you need?" he said.

"That'll be it." My father pulled out his wallet, handed across the money. "Where's Milton today?"

I felt my attention tighten.

"Milton?" I said, so softly that I don't think anyone heard.

"He off this weekend," the man said. "Left town this morning for his sister's up in Greensboro."

"I'll call him later," said my father. "I have some extra work for him next week."

"Our Milton?" I said again, or maybe it wasn't aloud. Still no one noticed.

The door to the back swung lightly. The pig on the hook beyond. And more meat too. Cows, surely. Cow parts. And maybe, I thought, the things that Milton had taken from the neighborhood.

The truth about the case shifted in and out of focus—about the crime and the criminal both.

Either way, not Mark after all.

My father had me carry the burgers, heavier than I'd expected. As we left the store, I turned back and looked once more at the counter and the swinging door beyond, and the two men flanking it, guarding it, watching us leave.

* * *

The freshly wrapped beef sat between us in the Cadillac. All the way home, a rich metallic smell filled the car, different from the bones we'd found—fresher, tangier—but something familiar at its core.

My father lectured me more about business, about possibilities, about attention to detail. I didn't know what to say—how to tell him we had a thief in the neighborhood, a thief my father himself had brought there.

"I didn't know that Milton worked in a meat department," I told my mother back home. I tried to be nonchalant.

"I think he does part-time work here and there," she said, distractedly, pulling her finger through a cookbook.

"You know where meat comes from?" I asked her. "Cows."

"Thank you for telling me that," she said. "I hadn't known about that. Very interesting."

* * *

I knocked on Mrs. Crawford's door with renewed conviction.

"I'm sorry, Mrs. Crawford," I said, when she answered it. "Someone has been stealing things from your house."

She smiled. "There's that imagination of yours again."

"No, really," I told her. "Milton is stealing from you. You need to do a search, a complete search of the house."

She stared at me, no longer smiling. She brushed that gray ponytail over her shoulder. "Does your mother know about this? Does she know what you're suggesting?"

"No, ma'am, but—"

"There has been *nothing* stolen from this house, nothing." Her voice had turned stern but her face didn't look angry. *Vulnerable,* that's the word I would use now picturing her expression. "You need to think about what you're saying before you say it."

"I'm sorry, but—" *But I'm right,* I was going to say. *A search is necessary.* She had already closed the door on me.

When I knocked again, she didn't answer.

When I went toward the back corner of the yard to retrieve the bone, it was gone, as if it had never been there at all.

* * *

It was the cookout that brought the whole truth together, even if I was still struggling so hard to make sense of it all that much of the evening seems a blur. My father and Mr. Bill and that business associate tending to the coals, the new man's shirt as big as a sheet and his belly protruded so much I wondered how he kept from toppling forward. The women sipped wine on the patio—the man's wife tiny with a thin face and thin brown hair, wispy fingers with large, oversized rings on them. ("She must be on top when they do it—else he'd squash her flat," Paul said later, pressing one palm hard against the other, nodding grimly. That *Playboy* had made him an authority.)

John ran back and forth through the smoke billowing out from the grill, mimicking karate moves, thrash thrash thrash with his hands: "Sniff my arm. I'm made of *fire!*" The sun rode low in the sky over the woods my father planned to develop, the woods where three of the bones rotted.

Our parents talked about the news, I know. Nixon had re-signed—the day before? weeks before? John and Paul had news too: Evil Knievel's plans to jump Snake River Canyon, live on TV, and then the commercial Paul had seen for the *Planet of the Apes* TV show. I hadn't heard about any of it.

"Evil Knievel's gonna be on an X-2 Skycycle," said John. "People all over the world will be watching it. Russia. England. Australia."

Paul shook his head. "That's a one-time jump. *Planet of the Apes* is gonna be on every week."

"Why don't you kids go play for a while?" my father said. "A game of hide and seek. We'll call you when dinner is ready."

John looked at me. "Hide and seek?" Like we were little kids again.

Paul shrugged.

And then they both looked at Christine, who'd been standing off to the side, in one of those same frilly skirts and wearing lipstick today it looked like. Her mother had shown up too, sitting back with a glass of wine herself.

I avoided looking at Christine's mother, and Christine too. (Had she told her mother about the *Playboy*?) But I couldn't dodge the glance my own mother gave me. *Play nice*, it said. *Include her.* She was the one who'd invited them.

* * *

That look from my mother? My guilt about how I'd sent Chris-tine away from the treehouse? Everything I owed her about the case?

Whatever the reason, once Paul had been tagged "it," I ran off with Christine to hide—followed her same as she'd led me into the police station that day.

"In here." She pulled me into my parents' garage, and we ducked between my father's Cadillac and the wall, under a window facing the side yard. Sunlight seeped through a gauzy curtain, leaving most of the garage in shadow.

"Ready or not, here I come," shouted Paul, his voice distant. I peeked through the window and saw him already checking behind trees in the side yard.

"He'll see us as soon as he comes past that corner," I said.

Christine was breathing heavy—from the quick run or taking the game too seriously? She pointed to the Cadillac, opened the door, climbed in the backseat. I heard Paul yell, "Got you!" and John shout "Jerk," and I dove in behind her.

"They'll find us anyway," I said—started to say. But Christine was already smearing that new lipstick against my own lips, not slack-jawed anymore but openmouthed in a more purposeful way.

"I know you're not like them," she whispered, pulling away. "You missed me. You'll miss me." Something like that—and something different in those moony eyes, lonelier, more desperate.

* * *

What happened next was probably fallout from so much of everything else that summer: her birthday party and the way I'd always been nicer to her than John or Paul, the way she'd helped with the investigation, John and Paul chanting out our names together, that *Playboy* magazine.

Playing doctor—that's what you might've called what happened in that cramped backseat, if we'd been younger.

Petting, heavy petting, if we were older—that language, those times.

I don't know what to call it at that in-between age—didn't know what to feel about Christine pulling her shirt up, about that pale stretch of belly, those flat breasts, nipples smaller than pennies.

Before I could begin to understand any of it, a face appeared in the backseat window.

Paul had found us, and then John was jabbing a finger at the glass, a vicious smile on his face.

Vulnerable. That idea again—that word, if only I'd had it.

Same as what I'd seen in Christine's face too—both when she'd kissed me and again now that we'd been caught. Same as what I saw with Mark and his girlfriend, trying desperately to hide something from us. And in Mrs. Crawford's eyes too, I realized, and now I was inside the feeling myself.

Many things I was learning, too many things becoming clear, sharply so.

The light through that gauzy curtain, the shaft of light cutting the darkness at Mrs. Crawford's house.

Frisky and that wet gnashing sound and those bones from the meat market.

Milton tall and muscular and afraid to come into the house to use the bathroom.

Mrs. Crawford and the husband she'd lost.

Lonely, my mother had said. *Lonely, of course. And different, different in so many ways.*

* * *

Our parents sat with the fat man and his rail-thin wife at one picnic table. The four of us sat at another one, half-sized—the kids' table still.

Paul dove into his burger, juices dripping on his shirt. John chewed more methodically, looking back and forth between Christine and me. He squinted his eyes at me, raised a finger and wiped at his top lip, signaling something.

I wiped my own mouth, expecting mustard or ketchup, but instead pulled away a pink smear. Christine's lipstick.

"Cooper and Christine, sitting in a tree...." John whispered, but the word he spelled out next wasn't K-I-S-S-I-N-G. The *Playboy* again, the education all of us had gotten there.

Paul giggled.

Over at the parents' table, my mother lifted her head and turned our way, even though there was no way she could've heard.

Under the table, Christine laced her fingers with mine. I slid my hand away just as quick, then slid my whole body further down the bench.

I didn't look her way again—couldn't, feeling whatever I'd felt the day we'd caught sight of her panties as she climbed the tree. But out of the corner of my eye, I saw her hands twitching when she lifted some potato salad from her plate.

Soon, she put the fork down and stopped eating at all.

* * *

The days after the cookout were crisp and cool and brilliantly sunny, but I didn't leave the house.

"Why aren't you out playing?" my mother urged me. "Is everything OK?"

I was fine, I told her. Or I didn't feel well. Or I didn't feel like playing. Day after day of it. Through the windows, I caught sight of John and Paul tromping toward the fields or racing those bikes. Out another window, I saw Christine wandering alone, aimlessly.

Thursday brought a heavy storm.

At least then I had an excuse for staying in.

As my mother sat reading, I hunkered down by the window and watched the heavy drops spatter the panes and the puddles beginning to form beyond. Over at John and Paul's house, a face appeared in the window, the disappeared as suddenly, the curtain still.

"Did something happen?" my mother asked. "Because I haven't seen the boys lately. Haven't seen Christine either, and I wondered—"

"Nothing happened."

"Well, is there anything you want to talk about?" my mother asked. "Because I'm here if you need me."

Outside the puddles widened and deepened. I thought about Frisky getting soaked in his pen. I could feel my mother watching me.

"Her family's moving, you know," she said. "Is that what's wrong? She told you that, and..."

I didn't answer.

You missed me, Christine had said. And then *you'll miss me?* Maybe she had indeed tried to tell me. Maybe that was where her urgency had come from.

The rain smacked at the glass now—loud, pelting. Beyond, everything seemed gray. Suddenly, even in the midst of it, the summer seemed a long time ago and the neighborhood far away, as if I was watching it all from a great distance, none of it part of me anymore.

"It's natural for a young boy—a young man—to have feelings for a young woman," my mother said. "You might want to see Christine and talk to her before she moves. I think—"

If it hadn't been raining, maybe I would have run from the house, jumped on my bike and torn down the driveway. I would've raced alone around the block, again and again until I was out of breath, then come home panting, gasping too hard to talk anymore.

But I didn't move, not even to turn back and look at my mother when I spoke.

"Do you know that Milton sometimes sleeps over at Mrs. Crawford's house?" I asked. I couldn't see her house through the rain, but I aimed all of my attention at it. "Do you know why he sleeps over there?"

Only then did I turn, My mother's expression looked like I'd broken something, something that couldn't be fixed.

But she wasn't asking about Christine anymore.

* * *

Maybe I'd expected a torrent of questions as strong as the rain outside, but instead my mother stood up abruptly and said she had some laundry to do. She didn't go to the washer or dryer, though, but shut the door of her bedroom. I thought I heard her voice on the phone.

That night, dinner brought the same cloth napkins, the same spread of silverware, the same quick reminder from my mother to sit up straight, but my father said nothing about the day's work or Nixon or anything. His jaws clicked lightly with each forkful.

"The man who was here the other day," I asked, to break the silence. "Is he going to come back and work on the project with you?"

My father looked as if he were surprised to see me. "That deal fell through," he said. "But good to see you taking an interest in business, son. In fact—" He gave a glance at my mother. She didn't meet it. "I'll tell you what, son. Since you've finally become interested in how we earn something in this world, I've got a proposition. Get you started on a little business of your own."

"A business of my own?" I said. I tried to catch my mother's eye, but she'd turned away from us both.

"A lawn care business, opening up right here in the neighborhood. Not only the bagging, but all of it—the mowing, the raking. A few yards, easy enough to handle. Fall's coming on, only a few more weeks of mowing anyway, and then next spring, when you're older, we'll start fresh." His enthusiasm picked up. "Not quarters but dollars now. Dollars. A growing boy needs to *earn* his way. What do you say?"

* * *

I never saw Christine again. The moving van came, the boxes were loaded, their car pulled away from the empty house.

Soon, Mrs. Crawford's house would be empty too. A real estate sign in the yard, only a few glimpses of her peeking past the drapes, and then a quick purchase, another moving van heading out. Only years later did I find out that my father had bought the house himself. "An investment," he told me without explanation, when he finally told me at all.

Milton simply disappeared from our lives. The next time my father bought steaks, he bought them from the Piggly Wiggly.

By the time Evil Knievel tried to launch that Skycycle over Snake River Canyon, John, Paul, and I were at least halfway back to normal, as if Christine had never been there. We sat together in front of the TV as the rocket built up its head of steam and flew over the canyon. John nearly wept as the parachute opened early, dragging our hero down, short of his goal.

Ford pardoned Nixon that same day, and our fathers cursed the decision, but none of that was important to us.

Soon *Planet of the Apes* would begin. Soon Paul would get his first cavity, and Ms. Lottie would buy him a *Planet of the Apes* action figure to help ease the pain. Soon Paul would get nearly all of them the same way: the astronauts and Galen and General Urko and even Zira, with her skirt and some hint of breasts. Paul would later claim that Zira wasn't worth a trip to the dentist, even as he idly rubbed those breasts, making crude comments, keeping John and me away from her.

As for Encyclopedia Brown, I...well, I gave up reading those stories, believing in them, believing in the idea of becoming Encyclopedia Brown myself. Being a boy detective was a foolish wish, the cost of it too steep.

Things were happening or failing to happen, changing or failing to change—and how were we to know which of it mattered? At that age, how could we have understood what any of it meant?

I was just a child, I kept telling myself—keep telling myself—still only a child.

Murder on the Orient Express

Caroline leaned weakly on Edward's arm as they were herded along endless cement walkways and down another flight of stairs. Edward, standing tall to offer better support, had twice glimpsed the sparkling blue and gold train, but he worried that it was taking so long to reach it. After the champagne kir and the delightful bottle of Chateau de Gaudou on the Pullman carriage and the mysterious blush which they had been given in the reception area in Folkestone, the SeaCat's turbulent crossing had been less than acceptable. Caroline had seemed to turn an even whiter shade of pale when the little English girl across the aisle had thrown up into a paper cup, and with the woman behind them, another American, quietly chanting that she was going to be sick, going to be sick, in perfect time with the rise and fall of the ship, Edward had himself felt ill—both nauseous and annoyed.

The next turn in the hallway brought them to the end of the labyrinth and the beginning of two short lines. Edward chose the one on the right because at the rear of the left one stood the Boxer. At least that was how Edward had thought of him with his crew cut and his squat bulky build and his arrogant cockney accent. They had heard him earlier at Victoria Station, talking brashly to the woman with him, a blond frizzy-haired piece. Edward had heard the word "kissy-face" and the two of them had puckered their lips at each other in such a way that he was certain that her name was Felicia or Patsy or Krissy with a K. And he was certain now, looking at the man again, that the Boxer would not be a boxer at all but just a boxer's sparring partner or perhaps merely an actor playing one, an extra who had a cartoon name like Brutus and only got to stand in the back and frown. They were at the head of the line then. The customs official gave a perfunctory glance at the passports—a courtesy which Edward attributed to the woman's sympathy for everyone's pallor—and they found themselves on the platform at last.

"Compagnie Internationale des Wagons-Lits," said Edward, stopping to read the shining gold letters in a fine French accent. "Des Grands Express Européens." The sun was beginning to set over Boulogne and in the twilight, the train appeared exceptionally regal. Its gleaming white roof seemed recently polished and its deep blue sides shone even more brightly up close than in his glimpses before. White-gloved porters stood attentive near the ends of each car, ready to assist with a small bag or a lady's boarding, and a bright red carpet stretched before them along the length of the platform. Edward pictured himself and Caroline as characters in a Fitzgerald novel—but only in the happier scenes—or perhaps a story by James. This was much better, he thought and said as much aloud.

"Beautiful," echoed Caroline, and Edward looked down to find her face still pale beneath her short blond hair, her eyes still closed. She hugged herself closer to him and scrunched up her tiny nose. "Can we find our cabin? I'd like to wash up." She seemed so pitiful that he felt a softness fall over him and a desire to comfort her. He began immediately to move along the walkway.

Though they were only going to Paris, he was pleased they had been given a cabin instead of a table in the dining car—the usual custom waived due to the availability of rooms—but as he followed the letters hung on temporary cardboard banners from the windows of each car, he wondered why they hadn't used the four-digit numbers or the names which were already there, lettered in gold along the panels; he would much rather have been searching for "Carrozza-Letti" or even "3555" than looking for the prosaic "B." His only other thought as he walked his new wife along the platform was his hope that she would open her eyes: the red carpet seemed to pass so swiftly beneath their feet.

* * *

They had been married for less than a week and he had swept her a world away from the Church of the Good Shepherd and the reception at the Cardinal Club on what he hoped would be the trip of a lifetime. This was their first excursion to Europe together and he made sure their stay in London was an elegant one. They had taken a suite at the Berkshire and shopped at Marks and Spencer down the street and strolled through Harrod's. They had eaten in the cozy intimacy of Veronica's and, at the suggestion of the concierge, had taken in "Don't Dress for Dinner" at the Duchess, though Edward would personally have preferred the revival of "An Inspector Calls." They had been pressed for time before the show and had stopped at The American Grille—their only lapse from more local cuisine—because it was quick and Caroline had felt a sudden taste for a cheeseburger. Edward regretted eating his with his hands when Caroline told him that an English couple two tables away had snickered at them and eaten theirs with a fork and knife. Except for that and the fact that they had missed the exhibition of royal wedding gowns at Kensington Palace by fifteen minutes, Edward had taken their time in London as a personal success.

But today was another matter: the centerpiece of their honeymoon, the highpoint of their trip. So far, it had gone only half and half, the channel crossing all but completely erasing the excitement of the Pullman earlier in the afternoon.

In the cabin, Edward hung up their evening clothes and settled onto the seat with its brocade of light green and black while Caroline opened the washbasin cabinet to refresh herself. He pulled out their copy of *Murder on the Orient Express*—not the first printing, which a bookseller friend had tried in vain to find, but a small 1955 Crime Club edition still well-suited to their purpose; he didn't want to forget to take it to dinner or to have the cabin steward sign it. A unique souvenir, he thought, and Caroline had been engrossed in reading it on the plane over. He placed it on the seat beside him. A packet of stationery and a trio of postcards lay on the mahogany table and he flipped through them while he waited.

"Do you wish that we were going all the way to Venice?" he asked, looking over a postcard of Canaletto's *Regatta on the Grand Canal.*

"We've never been to Paris together."

"But if we could come back to Paris?" He was thinking of midnight in the bar car, breakfast in their cabin, the brochure of the Hotel Cipriani that the two of them had admired. "We could leave the curtains open when we went to bed tonight and gaze out at the Alps."

She turned and smiled, a little of the rosiness returning to her cheeks, a little of the sprite back in her blue eyes. "We would be sleeping on bunk beds," she said and came over to hug him. "And there's no shower. I couldn't leave the cabin without a shower."

"Who says we would need to leave the cabin?" He smiled and winked. He was thinking of her trousseau and each of the evenings in London, pleasantly surprised by a side of her that he had never seen. He would have taken her again right there except for the steward just outside the door and the fact that someone else would be coming into the cabin in Paris. He worried that they would know.

* * *

The train bucked from side to side as they made their way down the hallways toward the bar car. The continental train was speeding along much faster than the British train and Edward was afraid that the movement would upset Caroline's system again. She held her hands up as she walked, bracing herself between the window and the wall, and when they reached the passways between cars, he stepped ahead to open the doors while she held on to the siderail.

He moved up again when they reached the bar car and found himself looking at Brutus, the Boxer, through the small window, the vulgar man sitting with his leg stretched out in front of the door. Edward was so unnerved by the obstruction that he found himself fumbling to turn the handle properly.

Brutus opened it for him. "Ey, mate," he laughed. "Havin' trouble with the door?" Felicia, sitting beside him, laughed as well and Edward felt himself blushing and unable to speak as he let Caroline step through before him. Boxer, he thought. Extra. The man had carried the word "door" out to what seemed like a full three syllables and didn't even pull his feet in when they walked past. As Edward stepped over the ill-mannered legs, he felt a pat on his back and heard the cockney whisper: "Don' worry, friend. Just havin' a bit o' fun."

Edward's back stiffened but he didn't comment. Instead, he continued to the bar, ordering a martini for himself and a small Coca-cola for his wife. Turning, he saw that another couple had joined Brutus and Felicia and the party seemed to take up the whole end of the car. Brutus had lit a cigar and was puffing big billows of smoke into the air, gesturing broadly, and bellowing like a hyena. Felicia leaned suggestively against his shoulder, breathing in his fumes and echoing his laugh. Edward thought for a moment how his position had been reversed; in novels, one always read about the genteel Englishman and the bellicose American. And yet, there they were.

The four of them crossed paths again an hour later. Felicia and the Boxer were seated across the aisle from Edward and Caroline at dinner—the early seating for those passengers disembarking in Paris—and Edward wished once more that they were continuing to Venice so that some part of the journey might take place without the Boxer's incivility.

Edward had expected the evening to be the pinnacle of excellence, both in terms of the food and the atmosphere, and he and Caroline had changed for the meal: Edward into the tuxedo he had worn at their wedding while Caroline wore a lavender evening dress which she had chosen just for the occasion and a string of pearls which Edward had given her at their rehearsal dinner. She also carried a small black purse to hold the novel which they hoped the chef would sign; Edward, afraid that the book alone might be improper, had preferred they be discreet.

Despite the recommendation of black tie for dinner, few of their fellow diners had gone to as much trouble as they had. The East Asian woman two tables down appeared elegant enough but her husband only dressed to the extent of a dark jacket and taupe pants, and a quartet of businessmen diagonal to them huddled in the charcoal suits they had worn in the afternoon. The Shrimptons, whom they had met on the Pullman that afternoon, were dressed in church attire further down the car; he worked with the Bank of England and it was their twenty-fifth anniversary, though they hardly seemed to Edward that much older. Felicia and Brutus were still wearing their casual clothes. The Boxer's khaki pants were wrinkled and the tie he had added was a smidgen too wide. Felicia's outfit was so tight and red that Edward thought it just short of tawdry, tolerable for the afternoon but entirely out of place as evening wear. The two of them had been seated at a table for four and were soon met by the couple who had joined them in the bar—a rough-looking pair as well. The four of them had continued to smoke and carry on.

Edward tried his best to ignore them and was pleased that Caroline as well pretended to be unfazed by it all. Her color had come back and she had told Edward that she felt well enough to share another bottle of wine. He saw the steward—a large Italian—at the next table and glanced over the menu to help with his decision.

Neither of them would touch the smoked eel appetizer but the steamed lobster and leeks with foie gras sounded delicious and the same was true of the entrée: a fillet of lamb in spiced wine and red currants, with sautéed potatoes and vegetables. The usual cheese would follow the meal and then a chestnut pancake and mignardises for dessert. The wine steward was stepping over to take their selection just as Edward turned to peruse the cartes de vins.

"And then this namby-pamby-lookin' Yank gent comes strollin' along the way they do," came the cockney voice quietly from the table across the aisle and Edward felt certain that the Boxer was talking about him. He closed his menu even as the steward was approaching. "*Buona sera, signora, signor.*"

Over the next few minutes, Edward realized that his ears had somehow managed to hear the empty part of both conversations. His wife, upholding his opinion of her as a model of discernment, took it upon herself to ask the steward for his recommendation. But though he heard her tell him that she didn't like anything too dry, he did not hear the name of the wine suggested. And though he heard the Boxer speaking of wanting to "mash" the namby-pamby "right there" and his companion's question as to why he didn't, Edward could discern no further evidence that he was the one being discussed. There had been a "laughing," he knew, and "words passed" and the "namby-pamby" hadn't stood his ground, but by the time they seemed to be moving to the crux of the story, he found himself listening to his wife as she gave her assent. "*Grazie, signora,*" said the wine steward and passed between Edward and the party across the aisle.

"And all this happened right there on the street?"

"Right there, not a stone's throw from the Bow Bells, mark my words."

So they had not been talking about him, thought Edward, relieved, and added under his breath that Brutus the Boxer looked like one who might have thrown stones.

"What?" asked his wife.

"Oh, nothing," said Edward. "Just talking to myself." And he adjusted the napkin in his lap.

The eel was brought then with a small dish of caviar, and the wine arrived almost immediately after, though the Italian broke the seal and removed the cork without Edward's being able to see the label. He felt certain that he would be given the opportunity to examine the bottle and taste it before it was served, but the man poured the wine into Caroline's glass instead. Flustered, Edward glanced quickly around at the other tables. The Asians were still examining the menu and the businessmen were engrossed in conversation, but he could almost feel the Boxer's eyes cutting his way. He pretended to be looking at the lacquered ebony wall panels where painted yellow pelicans dove for fish. Out of the corner of his eye, he saw Caroline taste the wine and nod her assent.

It was a Bordeaux he saw, peeking under the linen once the bottle had been left in its cooler: Sauternes. He had always thought of it as a dessert wine and wondered at the waiter's choice as he touched the glass to his lips. It looked gold and thick like olive oil; it tasted like honey.

"Is it all right?" Across the table, his wife wrinkled her forehead.

"Excellent," he nodded, scanning the wine list again, guilty for not having paid the proper attention. He would undoubtedly have chosen the '91 *Pouilly-Fuissé,* he thought, closing the menu, and cringed when he saw a bottle of it standing at the Boxer's elbow, which rested on the table as if it belonged.

The fish course appeared next, the red and white lobster centered in a creamy yellow sauce, with the leeks laid in a tick-tack-toe pattern across it and the pâté placed delicately to the side. He ordered a bottle of Pellegrino water from the waiter and sipped the honey again, watching the Boxer point his cigar at his dinner companion and imbibe his own wine with obvious pleasure. The waiter had served the four of them their lobster and Brutus continued to rail on as he ate. Edward could see the flesh of the lobster as the man chewed and talked, and as the meal wore on into the next course, Edward watched the lamb and the potatoes turn into a mash between his teeth. At one point, the Boxer's mouth was so full as he spoke that a chunk of lamb flew from his mouth and landed on the table. "Woops," he said, bringing his hand up in a puerile gesture of covering his mouth. Behind it, his lips were stretched into a schoolboy's grin. Felicia popped his arm lightly with her fist.

"What are you thinking about?" asked Caroline. "You've hardly said a word all dinner and you've barely touched your food."

Edward turned back to look at his wife and in a glance detected that she was as crestfallen as he was. Her eyes, fairly shining with disappointment, seemed to plead with him for something that he feared he couldn't provide. "I had just wanted this evening to be perfect," he said and knew that there was nothing to be gained by ordering another bottle of wine this late in the meal—that there were no other tables to move to and no possibility of asking Brutus to cease his ill manners.

Caroline reached across and took his hand. "Everything's fine." Her touch was warm but he could hear her lack of conviction, and he wished again that they were continuing to Venice. Those fortunate passengers were already moving through the first dining car on their way to the second seating. They were all dressed in crisp tuxedos and evening gowns, and two Scotsmen had worn dinner jackets over bright formal kilts. Edward was certain that the dinner for the people continuing to Italy would be different and that the extra time aboard the train would give the journey time to redeem itself. But it was too late now to change their plans; someone had already claimed their cabin for the balance of the journey, and Edward and Caroline had months before made their own reservations at the Ambassador in Paris.

"I had just planned," he sighed again, "on everything being so perfect."

The chestnut pancake arrived then: a crepe-thin puff folded up like a flowerbud and drizzled with a light orange syrup. As the dessert was served, the chef entered the car in his dress whites and moved from table to table greeting the guests. Edward lacked the enthusiasm to ask his wife for the book but she was already handing it across.

"*Le diner, c'est merveilleux,*" Edward told the chef with a good show of sincerity. He handed the book to him. "*Votre signature, s'il vous plaît. Pour souvenir.*"

The man glanced at the title and smiled, his tall white hat bobbing with his nod.

Pour souvenir. Le chef de cuisine, Ch. Bodiguel, Edward read after it was handed back and the chef had moved to the next table. He glanced over the other names from the afternoon: Alan, their waiter on the Pullman, who said he traveled to the States once a year for the Kentucky Derby; the Shrimptons, who had offered *Best Wishes from 25 Years Ahead* and signed their names *David and Rosemary.*

He turned to the title page then, because he had heard Brutus call out "What's 'at?" and wanted to wait for him to ask a second time.

Even without looking, he could see in his mind the Boxer pointing his fork at the book, a grotesque image of smacking lips and teeth dripping with the pancake's orange syrup. As he reread the title a fourth and then a fifth time, he entertained the thought that there *would* be a murder and Brutus the victim. When he asks me again, I'll tell him that we call it a book, he thought and he overenunciated the word in his mind. And then if he's insolent enough to ask the name, I'll pass it across to Caroline without showing it and tell him it's *The Origin of Species* and that he should be familiar with it. Edward was well into the copyright page when he thought that the sarcasm might be too subtle and then he realized that the dining car had gone quiet and slowly became aware that the Boxer had begun to choke.

Suddenly everyone was standing, either moving toward the flailing man or stepping back in horror. Felicia was screaming and jumping up and down, her face twisted in shock, her arms flailing helplessly as her body shook in fear. The Boxer's arms were spinning as well, striking the glasses from the table, thrashing at the people around him, on his right hand a single finger sticking out like it was pointing at something in the air.

"Heimlich maneuver," shouted Edward. "A doctor, a doctor." The wine steward had already managed to wrap his arms around the Boxer, and he lifted the bulky man up in the air, jarring his body, pulling and pulling against his chest until finally, a lump of pancake flung itself forth from his mouth. But Edward could see from the Boxer's color and his puffy face that help had come too late.

* * *

Soon, they were back in their cabin. Caroline sat by the window, staring out at the lights which passed so slowly in the distance. Edward had opened the cabinet again and was washing his hands in the small porcelain basin. In the mirror, he caught sight of himself and noticed that his hair was going prematurely gray.

Brutus was dead, and Edward, despite all of his attempts at rational thinking, had been unable to dismiss his sense of responsibility for the death. He could see it no other way, given the malice he had felt and the timing. The dead man had been choked in trying to wash down his pancake with the wine which Edward had envied so greatly—choked while trying to ask a question which Edward had pretended not to hear—and Edward felt sure that the Boxer's pointing finger had been aiming for him. The Boxer's real name, it turned out, was Henry Doppler and Felicia's name was Margaret and they had just been married. She had still been in hysterics when Edward and Caroline left the car, and no one had been able to learn any more than that.

Edward could not help but feel guilty, and neither could he escape the thought, obviously secondary, that he had not only killed a man but, in doing so, had ruined his and Caroline's special evening completely. His selfishness in thinking this sent him into an even deeper state of guilt and he feared, for a moment, that he would be unable to find his way out. But they would be in Paris soon, he thought, pulling into the Gare de L'Est, taking the cab to the Opera Quarter, walking under the chandeliers of the Hotel Ambassador, and he felt a little strengthened by these images and hopeful that the darkness of the evening would disappear against the glitter of the city.

"Do you think he was poisoned?" asked Caroline, and he realized the question carried the first words she had spoken since they had returned to their room.

He wiped his hands and turned to look at her. Even from that distance, he could see the strange twinkle in her eye.

"I don't know why," she went on. "I guess it was his looks, the shape of his head, and the way he acted, and my reading that book on the plane—but I had a notion from the first moment I saw him that he was a British gangster and that the woman with him was his moll. I thought that the other couple in the bar car were a part of his gang or the other man the leader of a friendly gang and that they were planning something together. And when he began to choke and point that finger like a gun, I was certain that it was a double-cross and that the other man had poisoned his food while he asked you about the book. Or maybe the chef was really with British Intelligence and had himself laced the dessert with arsenic before it ever came out. After all, didn't you think it tasted more like almonds than chestnuts?"

She stood up then and rushed quickly to hug him.

"Oh, darling, I'm sorry he's dead, but wouldn't it have been romantic if we *had* gone on to Venice and the murder had happened in the Alps and the train had been stuck in the snow and the murderer still on board. And you could have solved it! Or we could have solved it together! Or we could have just stayed in our cabin until they interrogated us, caught up helplessly in the drama of it all."

She looked up at him then, and he saw a thrill in her features that he had never seen before. She seemed transported by what had happened.

"Can you believe it?" she said, wiping the tears from her eyes. "I even made names for them. He was called Guido and she was Delores."

It was at that moment that Edward felt released from the crime and forgiven of his guilt and, what was greater, believed himself a success once more. He didn't know how he had done it, but he was suddenly glad that he had killed the young man. He felt more alive because of it, more gallant, more virile—so much so, in fact, that he felt sure he would have taken his new wife right then and there if the train hadn't been pulling into the station, if the cabin steward hadn't been just outside the door.

An Internal Complaint

And Anna Sergeyevna began coming to see Gurov in Moscow. Once in two or three months she left S——, telling her husband that she was going to consult a doctor about an internal complaint—and her husband believed her, and didn't believe her. In Moscow she stayed at the Slaviansky Bazaar hotel, and at once sent a man in a red cap to Gurov. Gurov went to see her, and no one in Moscow knew of it.

— Anton Chekhov, "The Lady with the Dog"

Philip turned worn eyes once more through his notebook: passages from Chekhov's story copied verbatim in his own handwriting, notes penned in red ink all around the margins. What had begun as an exercise (hone craft by analyzing the master, reading IS writing) had gradually sparked a passion in him, something he hadn't quite felt with the stories he'd tried to write before, had never felt in front of a classroom of dull gazes. *Only one sentence Chekhov hints at husband's point of view*, Philip had written early on, '*believed her, didn't believe her,*' and then the words that had set the whole process in motion: *A story of its own there?* Throughout, the red ink threatened to overwhelm the black, staining his skin when the pen had bled on his fingers.

An entire page of clues and conjectures about the husband: *Surname p. 574 is Von Diderits.... First name not given: perhaps Aloysha, Evgeniy (nickname Zhenya), Gavril, Piotr.... Crown Department or Provincial Government? Anna does not know. Check Britannica for background.... How large is their house? How many servants?* Elsewhere he'd jotted, *Anna's 'internal complaint' intended as double entendre?* And on another page, a chronology of the story's scenes: Yalta where Anna and Gurov meet; the city of S—— where *The Geisha* premieres; Moscow where the affair continues....

As he stared at the words and figures, Philip's mind raced to pull the pieces, the possibilities together. He could write this. This was the one, he knew it.

"So, how are things with the Russians?"

Catherine's voice, behind him. How long had she been in the room? Philip detected a floral scent and hints of fruit—pears perhaps? grapes? She couldn't have been standing there long, or he would have noticed it—unlike his wife to wear perfume. She usually smelled of finger paints and crayons, carried home from the art classes she taught at Ligon. He hooked his pen through the top of the clipboard, closed his eyes and inhaled slowly. Grapes definitely.

"It's so dark in here," she said, and he felt her hands on his shoulders. "But I'll bet you haven't even noticed."

"I hadn't really." He opened his eyes again. Except for the glow of the computer screen—Britannica.com—the only light came from the mica-shade lamp on the desk, shining down on the open copy of Chekhov. Through the window, he saw that the sun had gone down and the night was pitch black, and he was reminded of Chekhov's own counsel: *Don't tell me the moon is shining; show me the glint of light on the broken glass.* The windowsill was steeped in shadows from the streetlight. A blur of buds bloomed on the bush beyond. Still, no moon. The CD had run out as well—how long before, he didn't know. Monk he'd been listening to. "In Walked Bud," "Round Midnight," "Evidence."

"But the Russians are good." He leaned his head forward as she kneaded his shoulders. "Or at least the one I'm working with. It'll be a good story when I'm done, I just feel it. But I'm really still just making notes. Looking for the key into the whole thing."

"But you've been in here for hours."

"Oh, it couldn't have been that long," he said. "After all, what time did we have dinner?"

She laughed. "*I* ate some leftover pizza about a half-hour ago," she said. "But unless you have a stash of food in here...." And she was right. He couldn't remember having eaten.

"Oh, well." He shrugged. She stopped touching him.

"Well, try to eat something. I'm going out for awhile."

"Anyplace special?" he asked, turning in his chair to see her. She wore a bandana print skirt, sleeveless denim top. Black hair pulled back in a ponytail. Scant light came from elsewhere in the house through the open doorway behind her, falling lightly on the edge of the bookcase, a pile of mail, the guest bed that shared this room. Catherine herself was caught half-in, half-out of the mica-tinted glow, and he tried to think what word she might be: not *luminous*, not *scintillant*... *evanescent*?

"I don't know," she said. "Target, maybe? We don't really need anything, but I'm just feeling a little restless tonight. Just want to get out." The top edge of her face was shadowed (he knew this word: *chiarascuro*; she had been *captured* in *chiarascuro*), but from the turn of her chin, he imagined that her brow must have furrowed. "I may stop by Borders afterwards, flip through some magazines, get a cup of coffee. Maybe pick up a new book for the kids at school. They stay open pretty late, right?"

He nodded. "New perfume?"

"It's French," she said. "Annick Goutal. It's called '*Ce soir ou jamais.*' The woman at Belk's described it as Turkish rose gardens, wildflowers and black currants. You like?"

Black currants. He hadn't been far off with grapes.

"I feel... *enthralled*," he said, grinning. "Fragrance is a seductive thing."

She leaned over to kiss his forehead. "I left a couple of pieces of that pizza for you in the microwave," she whispered. "Don't forget them." And then she was gone.

Her scent lingered in the air as he picked up his pen, and for a moment he was unable to remember where he had been in his notes. Then, turning a new thought over in his mind, turning the key he had found, he once more began to write: *Fragrance is a significant thing.*

* * *

Evgeniy von Diderits enjoyed his breakfasts with enthusiasm. He savored the smell of frying dough almost as much as the vareniki themselves, plump with eggs and cheese or tucked tight with minced mutton—the latter his own twist on tradition. He liked dipping his curly sausages in black currant jam, and after he finished his meal, he liked to swirl a dollop of that same jam into his tea as well. As the cup cooled, he stroked his small side-whiskers or caressed the tips of his nostril hair, reading yesterday's edition of the *Kiev Telegraph* and thinking eagerly about the meetings scheduled for the day ahead. In the shadow of a good breakfast, with his wife seated just across the table and the servants bustling through their morning duties, Evgeniy believed briefly, firmly, that little could disturb the world he had created for himself and his wife—indeed, for the entire village of S—.

"I am going to Moscow today," said Anna Sergeyevna. "I think I told you. For a few days. I will be taking the morning train at eleven."

Von Diderits looked up from his paper. His wife stared dully out the window, her fair hair pinned against her head, her breakfast plate nearly untouched. He did not speak, waiting for her to turn her gray eyes back his way.

"Your food has gotten cold," he said finally, when she failed to look at him.

"I'm not hungry," she replied. "I don't feel well."

"Is it your.... Is it the 'internal complaint' again?" he asked, and the phrase became bitter in his mouth, tainting the sweet aftertaste of his meal.

Anna Sergeyevna gave a slow nod.

"You know," he continued, his voice even, unperturbed, "we have very good doctors here as well. That is part of my responsibility, the responsibility of my committee on the zemstvo, to ensure the presence of excellent doctors here. Perhaps they are not as plentiful as they are in Moscow, but they are well-trained and eager to help." They had traveled this path before—as many times now as the number of trips she had made to Moscow—and both of them knew the way. "I am happy to arrange for you an appointment."

"Zhenya," she said, his nickname a plaintive sigh, and Evgeniy at once resented her pleading, pitying tone. But before he could speak, one of the servants came in to clear more plates. The couple remained silent while the young scullion tidied the table, and after the girl left, Anna Sergeyevna once more assumed a firmer tone. "I have already made an appointment in Moscow," she said, "with the doctor I have consulted there. He already knows my situation. I trust him."

"And yet despite your trust in him, your many visits have not alleviated this internal distress, am I correct?" He smiled broadly. "Perhaps you should trust me instead this time?" Such questions were more palatable to him.

"I have already made the appointment," she explained again, not raising her voice. "I have already purchased my ticket. I have telegraphed Petersburg as well. My sister is meeting me in Moscow. We have made plans to attend the theater."

"Your sister…," began Von Diderits, thinking of the questions he could ask next—*What time will your sister's train be arriving? What play will you be seeing? Which day?*—and of the requests that he would make upon her return: *I have read about that play; remind me about the story.* And: *Where did you dine in Moscow? I have eaten there myself; did you speak with Taraykin?* She always had the correct answers, delivered without hesitation. When he checked the timetables later, he would find that the Petersburg train was in fact scheduled to arrive at the time she had said. There had indeed been a performance of *La Corsaire* at the Bolshoi or *Dyadya Vanya* at the Art Theatre. No, she had not seen Taraykin at the Prague (so there was no way for him to confirm who had accompanied her), but she had ridden the new electric tram from Strastnaya Square to Petrovsky Park—an unverifiable, and therefore useless, detail.

Evgeniy closed his paper, rose from his seat. Walking around the table, he stood over her. "Very well," he said, believing, not believing. "You may go."

He leaned down to kiss her cheek, and past the dense smell of sausage still permeating the room, he discovered, as he had dreaded, the odor of jasmine and bergamot behind her ears and around her neck. Novaya Zarya, he knew, the scent that he'd bought her at the parfumerie on Nevsky Street during one of his own trips to Moscow—and he despaired to think that she now wore it only when she was making the same contemptible journey herself....

* * *

The scene had taken Philip days to write, drafting, revising, erasing completely—more nights spent working at the computer, as furiously as ever, his "key" into the story only unlocking more questions, and so far what little had been accomplished. Now another sunset approached, Catherine out yet another evening, dinner with friends this time, a long evening ahead.

Philip penned a question mark over the work *contemptible*. Would Chekhov have really used the word in such a context? Or anything so bald as *despaired*, except in dialogue? And the problem wasn't just the individual words but the whole approach. The details smacked of too much research. Chekhov himself would have called it "the newspaper," not the *Kiev Telegraph*. He would not have bothered with the names of restaurants or the brand name of the perfume. The reference to *Dyadya Vanya* was too self-consciously clever. And Chekhov would have crafted the entire exchange with more subtlety, kept the emotions even more restrained. "When you want to touch a reader's heart, try to be colder," Chekhov had written in one of his letters. "It gives their grief, as it were, a background against which it stands out in greater relief."

Evgeniy leaned down to kiss his wife's cheek, and discovered the odor of jasmine and bergamot behind her ears and around her neck. He recognized it as the perfume that he'd bought her on one of his trips to Moscow, and he knew that she now wore it only when making the same journey herself.

The doorbell rang—just past seven p.m. One of the neighbors? A door-to-door salesman perhaps? Their friends rarely dropped by unannounced.

Philip leaned over to glance out the window. A green Land Rover sat by the front curb—not a vehicle he recognized. He turned back to his notes, waiting for the person to go away.

The doorbell rang again, the person pressing longer on the button. *Insistent*, thought Philip. Or is it *persistent? Persistently*? He laid down his pen and got up, then grabbed his copy of Chekhov and stuck his finger between the pages as he stepped into the living room. The detail would let his visitor know that he'd been interrupted. Through the window inset into the front door, he saw a man's head in profile, cocked back at the neck. The stranger's lips were pursed as he blew a stream of smoke into the air.

"Can I help you?" Philip asked, opening the door only enough to lean out.

"Hi," said the man on the porch. He shifted his cigarette to his left hand and held out the right. "You must be Philip."

The man stood slightly taller than Philip, trim and athletic. Tanned or, rather, ruddy—his red hair made him ruddy. One too many buttons loosened on the front of his Oxford, the hair thick on his chest. With the Land Rover framed above his shoulder, he looked like a commercial, but for what, Philip wasn't sure.

"Do we know each other?" Philip asked, opening the door wider and reaching his free hand out.

"No, I don't think we've met," the man said. Shake, release. "I'm a friend of Catherine's. Buddy Shelton—well, Robert really, I'm trying to get back to Robert, but back in college it was Buddy, so...." He laughed lightly. "Didn't Catherine mention I was coming by?"

"Catherine's not here. She's gone out to dinner with some friends."

Buddy smiled. "Well, I guess that would be me." Cigarette to the mouth. A deep drag. He shook his head slightly, blew the smoke out of the corner of his mouth. "I'm sorry to have bothered you. I must have misunderstood about where we were going to meet. I thought we were all getting together here first."

They were meeting several classmates from school, Buddy explained. He had just moved back to Raleigh recently, rented a house over in Vanguard Park. He was in pharmaceutical sales, and the Triangle... "well, it's about the capital of the world for that, you know. You're teaching at State, right?"

"Close," Philip said. "Wake Tech."

"Gotta start somewhere." Buddy shrugged. "And I guess it gives you plenty of time to write, huh?" It was nice to be back in the area in general, he went on. It hadn't taken him long to run into some friends from school, and the next thing you know plans were being made. "Of course, it's just like me to get the plans wrong somehow." Buddy laughed, but Philip detected no real lapse of confidence. What was the connection between *self-effacing* and *self-assured?* Philip assumed it just depended on the *self* involved.

"Well, nice meeting you," Buddy said, stepping off the porch. "Guess I'll just try to catch up with everyone." Then halfway across the yard, with a quick turn, walking backward for a moment: "Hey, wanna join us?"

"No, I've—" Philip started to hold up his book and explain that he was working, or protest that he was only wearing a t-shirt, shorts and sandals, but then realized that he wasn't expected to say yes.

Buddy had never even stopped walking. "No," Philip called after him. "You all have a good time."

"Oh, I'm sure we will," said Buddy, and he thumbed the cigarette butt into the street as he climbed in the truck. A wave from the window as he rounded the curve.

Philip started to turn back inside, but instead walked out and sat for a while on the porch swing he and Catherine had only recently found time to install. Soon the sun would go down, and even now there were few people on the street—a pair of joggers, a couple pushing a stroller, a bicyclist in Spandex shorts. The chains supporting the swing creaked, the grass in the yard had begun to wither, paint peeled on the perimeter of the porch—little chores neglected. From somewhere in the neighborhood came the dull, distant roar of a lawnmower, or perhaps a hedge trimmer. Philip's thoughts wandered back over the conversation with Buddy, and he found himself troubled by the cigarette butt in the middle of the street. The joggers, the couple with the stroller, the cyclist—none of them seemed to notice it. Finally, he walked out to pick it up, deposited it in the trashcan on the side of the house, and then came back to the porch. He opened up the Chekhov collection.

The theater scene in S—. Gurov and Anna rushing away from the crowds at intermission. They walked *senselessly along passages*, and *up and down stairs*, came to rest on a *narrow, gloomy staircase*.

"I am so unhappy," she went on, not heeding him. "I have thought of nothing but you all the time; I live only in the thought of you. And I wanted to forget, to forget you, but why, oh, why have you come?"

On the landing above them two schoolboys were smoking and looking down... Gurov drew Anna Sergeyevna to him, and began kissing her face, her cheeks, and her hands.

"What are you doing, what are you doing?... I beseech you by all that is sacred, I implore you.... There are people coming this way!"

Someone was coming up the stairs....

Philip closed the book in mid-scene, bothered as always that the "someone" never arrived. Who was that someone? And why had he or she stopped? A similar event in Yalta—Anna and Gurov sitting at breakfast: *A man walked up to them... looked at them and walked away. And this detail seemed mysterious and beautiful, too.* But what more did the detail signify? What did Chekhov intend? Simply some reminder of the outside world barging in, ever-threatening to discover the affair? And how early would Von Diderits himself have known that his marriage had gone terribly wrong?

* * *

Evgeniy shifted uncomfortably in his seat. Anna Sergeyevna glanced toward him, away from the stage, her furrowed brow asking, *Is there something wrong?* He smiled and shook his head, patted her knee. His wife smiled in response before turning her attention back to the scene before them—the Tea House of Ten Thousand Joys. A parade of kimonoed figures with thickly powdered faces danced in unison, strummed lutes, poured tea for lounging British sailors. Evgeniy's wife tapped the tip of her fan against the bridge of her lorgnette, the latter a trifle he had bought her—unnecessary since their regular stall was on the third row, but she was always pleased by such precious accessories. "Men make love the same in all countries," the Frenchwoman on stage had said. "There is only one language for love." And when the wizened Wun-Hi replied, with those troubled r's, "Yes, me know—good language before malliage, after malliage, bad language," everyone laughed.

Evgeniy had paid little mind to the plot—a stew of misguided passions, flirtations, jealousy... a song about a goldfish. It was easy enough to let one's attention wander.

> And ever as my samisen I play
> Come lovers at my pretty feet to fall,
> Who fancy—till I bid them run away—
> A geisha's heart has room enough for all!
>
> Yet love may work his will, if so he please;
> His magic can a woman's heart unlock
> As well beneath kimono Japanese
> As under any smart Parisian frock.

Evgeniy turned his eyes once more toward the Governor's box, but still saw no one but the Governor's daughter seated in front, leaning forward, her elbows on the coping. He had nodded in the direction of the box during the bustle before the start of the play, aware from the parting of the curtains behind her and the partially glimpsed hand on the sash that the Governor himself stood back there watching—that perhaps the Governor had in turn seen him. Evgeniy hoped that at the interval between acts he would have the opportunity to speak with the man. There seemed little harm in reminding a superior that you were there, that you existed at all.

At last the first act ended. The curtain fell.

"Excuse me, my darling," Evgeniy said, standing. "There are several people I must speak with." And he stooped over quickly to kiss his wife's cheek before leaving her in the stall, proud that everyone could see what a model marriage they had. She was indeed his darling, his plum, his precious baby bird. In the aisle, he encountered Pyotr Alexeitch, and the two men began speaking as they walked toward the door outside, where several other gentlemen had already gathered to smoke.

But he had barely caught the smell of tobacco drifting through the door when a brisk movement across the room seized his attention—a woman rushing hurriedly through the crowd. A mere flash of a moment, but enough for him to recognize his wife's gown, the particular way she pinned her hair back and that familiar, though now hurried, gait. Had a problem arisen? Perhaps she had suddenly taken ill. Was she searching for him?

"I beg your pardon, Pyotr," he said, with a slight bow. "I fear there is something I must attend to." It was, he considered, no breach of manners to look to your wife in her time of need.

He walked through the laughing, chattering crowd, heard a person humming one of the refrains from the play, saw another stifling a giggle as she stiffly mimicked the bow of one of the Geisha girls.

His wife had gone through this door surely, he thought, and it opened up onto a busy passageway leading around the auditorium. A glimpse of her gown to the right, and as Evgeniy moved in that direction, he saw that another man was following closely on his wife's heels.

"Excuse me," he said to each person whose elbow he jostled, "pardon me." He eased as swiftly as he could through the crowd without disrupting them too terribly, without drawing too much attention— casting a quick smile or a friendly nod to those he knew, striving at the same time to keep his eyes on the figures ahead. They seemed to move endlessly along passageways, and up and down stairs. At times Evgeniy gained on them, at others he fell behind, until at a last turn he reached the base of a narrow, gloomy staircase, hidden from the crowd. The sounds of his wife's voice echoed down the stairs— "I beseech you by all that is sacred, I implore you" —and Evgeniy mounted the first step hastily, primed to defend his wife's virtue, his own honor, until he heard an unexpected tenor in her next words: "There are people coming this way!"

He stopped in mid-step. There was an urgency in her tone that had struck him strangely, a desperation, a passion, a—

"You must go away.... I will come and see you in Moscow. I have never been happy; I am miserable now.... I swear I'll come to Moscow. But now let us part. My precious, good, dear one, we must part!"

A moment passed in silence, an emptiness in which Evgeniy's

imagination trembled. Then he heard them coming down the stairs rapidly, and he slunk back along the passageways ahead of them, once more fighting the throng as he struggled toward the security of their accustomed stall.

* * *

Near midnight, Philip sat alone in the living room, his gaze wandering from one object to another. The weave of the fabric on the couch, marred by a stain whose origin he couldn't remember. The air conditioning vent in the corner, rattling intermittently as the system switched on and off. Over the mantle hung an abstract painting that Catherine had completed in college: Two broad, bold, s-shaped swaths of color, red and purple. Divergent at each extreme, they curved closer together in the middle and touched lightly at various points. What was the name of it? *Duet* something? *Romance? Romantic Red Pairs Passionate Purple?* There was a precious cleverness to the title, Philip recalled, but his mind was too muddled to remember it clearly. Densely chaotic jazz murmured from the stereo's speakers, the volume turned low so as not to disturb Catherine's sleep.

They had kissed soon before he left their bed a half-hour before, and her lips had tingled at the time with the mint of her toothpaste, masking the faint aftertaste of her evening out. But now it was the undertones of those tastes that lingered in his memory. The briny lure of tequila, the tang of limes. Residues, cast-offs. Like the bracelet she had discarded on the end table when she walked through the door, or the pocketbook standing like a challenge on the other chair.

"Did your friend Robert find you?" he had asked her after she came home.

"Robert?" she said. "Oh, you mean Buddy. Why? Did he call here?"

"He stopped by looking for you. He assumed you were meeting here first before dinner."

"I wonder why he would have thought that," she said, and he thought she seemed genuinely puzzled. No, he hadn't mentioned stopping by, she went on to explain, had just apologized for being late when he got there and joined them at the table. How many others? Oh, five or six—let's see... Miriam and Alex, Ken, Alice, Lucy.... Buddy of course. So how many is that? Six? Seven, including Catherine. Lucky number seven. "You know, just a bunch of us who'd been together back in school."

"Sounds like fun," Philip had said, and in his mind now, he emptied out the pocketbook sitting across from him: lipstick and powder, several tissues of Kleenex, her wallet, a tampon, her cell phone, her Palm Pilot.

"Excuse me," Evgeniy said to each person whose elbow he jostled, "pardon me." He moved as swiftly as he could through the crowd without disrupting them too terribly, without drawing too much attention—struggling to cast a quick smile or a friendly nod to those he knew, to maintain some equilibrium.

"Well it's great that you got the chance to catch up with him," Philip had gone on. "Good that Buddy's turned up here in town."

"It really is nice," Catherine said. "I'd forgotten how much I missed him."

"How long has it been since you last saw him?"

Years and years ago, she replied. They had been such good friends when they were in school—had taken several classes together, gone out to the same clubs. But once graduation came, so many people headed their separate ways. Buddy had moved out to the West Coast, to Sacramento—a job he couldn't refuse. Catherine had promised to come out and visit, had really meant to. She hadn't been particularly pleased with her own job then. She'd felt aimless, unambitious… unhappy really.

I will come and see you in Sacramento. I have never been happy; I am miserable now. I have thought of nothing but you all the time; I live only in the thought of you.…

"But I never went out to see him," she said. "Eventually, each of us got so busy. I got the job at Ligon. We stopped calling each other as often as we had…. You know how easy it is to lose touch."

Soon, Catherine had prepared to go to sleep—removed her make-up, brushed her teeth, pulled on a pair of his boxers. By the time Philip joined her, she had already settled between the sheets, was nearly asleep. He turned out the light and felt his way into the bed, recognizing in the darkness the scent of the new perfume he'd first noticed several nights before. She leaned over. A kiss. Lips redolent with mint, the taste lingering as she pulled away. They lay for a while in the half-darkness together, in the glow of the streetlight through the window, under the faint outline of the ceiling fan overhead. Philip tried to catch the dim sound of its motor spinning amidst the silence.

"Did you ever?" he finally asked her. "…you know. I mean, with your friend Buddy?"

A long pause. His imagination trembled. "You men," she said after a few seconds, "the way you…" and he heard the hint of a low chuckle. A long sigh followed. "Once or twice," she said finally. "It was back in college. It was years ago."

"Excuse me," Evgeniy said to each person whose elbow he jostled,

"pardon me." He moved as swiftly as he could through the crowd without disrupting them too terribly, without drawing too much attention. Surely what he'd seen wasn't what it seemed. Surely the man following his wife wasn't… Surely the man from Yalta wouldn't dare to…. Evgeniy had been able to excuse that indiscretion, an isolated mistake, but he could not condone this, not abide such, not here in his own town. No, this was untenable, this was….

They didn't speak after that, and soon Catherine's breathing settled into a regular pattern. He listened to her for a few minutes, then realized he would be unable to sleep himself. He went downstairs, put on the Ornette Coleman CD and sat down on the sofa to stare at the air conditioning vent and the painting over the mantle and the pocketbook on the chair with her Palm Pilot within.

What was the name of that painting? he asked himself again, and this time it came to him, a conversation years ago, emerging from some tucked-away place in his memory. *Twin Passions Twined*, she'd called it, remarking to Philip that it was like them, wasn't it? like love *should* be? She wrapped her arms around him in the memory, they kissed, they… but no comfort in remembering that embrace tonight. Other thoughts intruded. She'd actually painted it in college, hadn't she? And who had the purple swath represented for her then? What had she written down in her Palm Pilot for tonight—"Dinner w/ friends"? "Dinner w/Miriam, Alex, etc."? "Dinner with Buddy"? What was listed for the evening a few nights back when she had claimed she was going to Target and Borders?

* * *

It was at the theater that Evgeniy first saw Gurov with his own eyes, but this was not his first awareness of the other man, despite his many attempts to suppress that knowledge. Looking back over all that had happened, Evgeniy realized that he had likely already lost Anna in Yalta, or even before, and he was ashamed to have arranged a witness to his own humiliation.

Yalta was his wife's first holiday in the two years since they had been married. She had grown up in Petersburg, and he knew that moving to the provinces had been an adjustment for her. He had sensed that she was sometimes restless with their surroundings, restless with the days that he spent away from her while at council and the evenings he spent building relationships to ensure a successful career. He imagined her staring all day at the gray fence opposite the house, or chasing idly after that pesky little dog she loved so, and he felt responsible for the drabness he had begun to see in her eyes.

"Why don't you take a trip, my darling?" he had asked her one evening when she complained of not feeling well. "A change of scenery will invigorate your spirits. You could travel to Moscow maybe, or to Petersburg to see your sister. Or someplace new. To Yalta perhaps. You might enjoy some time at the coast. You can stay for two weeks or a month or even more." And though she had been hesitant at first, she had eventually acquiesced. A trip was planned for late summer. She bought some clothes for her journey, a new beret, a new parasol as well. Even the preparations seemed to return some glimmer of light to her soft gray eyes, and Evgeniy felt his own spirits relieved as well. At the end of her stay at the coast, he might come down personally to fetch her. They could spend a few days together. It would be a second honeymoon.

The week before her trip, he had summoned Zhmuhin, the hotel porter, to his office. Evgeniy found Zhmuhin a despicable person in many ways. The man was gaunt and angular, with a bent nose, and Evgeniy had often sensed something smug and sneering beneath his show of truckling diffidence. Plus, Zhmuhin perennially mispronounced Evgeniy's surname as "Dridirit"—intentionally, Evgeniy believed. But Zhmuhin also possessed the keen eye and discretion necessary for his post. He was precise in his tallying of new arrivals to and departures from the town, encompassing in his recognition of small details. It had even been rumored years before that Zhmuhin was an outside agent for the Okhrana, the imperial police, and though the idea had quickly been dismissed, Evgeniy had often wondered at the possibility and as a result continued to cultivate some familiarity with the other man. As if recognizing this, Zhmuhin sometimes dropped his pretensions around Evgeniy, and too often took advantage of being treated as an equal.

After the porter had settled into one of the wingchairs opposite the mahogany desk, Evgeniy offered him a glass of cognac, asked him about who had checked in most recently at the hotel, laughed that Zhmuhin was always at the hotel, always so much work, and didn't he ever need a holiday? And when Zhmuhin replied that he arranged to go to Petersburg each May and November, the former in honor of the Emperor's birthday and the latter to commemorate the Dowager Empress, Evgeniy commented that such respect was very noble, wondering beneath his words if the man's trips to the capital might have more to do with some duties for the secret police.

"But perhaps you would also like to take another type of holiday, and sooner," continued Evgeniy. "Perhaps somewhere warmer, perhaps to a coastal climate? Perhaps to Yalta?"

A sly smile emerged at one corner of Zhmuhin's lips. "And why would I choose to go to Yalta?" he asked, tugging at the lapels of his gray porter's uniform. "Is there some specific reason for such a trip?"

"I have always said that you are a clever man," replied Evgeniy. "That you are intelligent beyond your position, and such you are." He gestured as if doffing a hat to the porter, though he wore no hat at the time. "You are correct. It is my wife. I have decided to send her to Yalta for a holiday herself, and I would like for you to go as well."

Zhmuhin's smile vanished. "That sounds little like a holiday, Mr. Dridirit," he replied, enunciating the last word. "To carry bags and open doors. I can do these things here. And you yourself have servants for such tasks. Send them along instead." He started to rise.

"You misunderstand," said Evgeniy, "please sit, please," careful to maintain his cheer, lacing his fingers together. "That is not at all what I'm asking. Even here you are too wise for such duties, I have always thought you so. No, I do not wish you to accompany my wife but to attend to her at a distance. You have a watchful nature, everyone knows this. I simply want you to keep such a watch over my wife while she is away."

Zhmuhin's eyes narrowed. He returned to his seat.

"What need is there to keep a watch over your wife?" he asked. "When I look at your wife, I see a grown woman who does not need a guardian. Don't you agree, Mr. Dridirit?" That sly smile had returned, and Evgeniy detected some hint of salacity behind the porter's comments. He chose to ignore the man's studied insolence.

"Before our marriage, my wife was surrounded by her family in Petersburg," Evgeniy replied instead, "and here she enjoys my guardianship, of course. Certainly she is a grown woman, but I have discovered that she is so young still in many ways, simple in her thoughts and her amusements, a naïf. Often I have called her my baby bird, merely a term of endearment, you see, and yet it is appropriate in so many ways that I had not intended...." He stared down at the blotter on his desk, at the inkwell and the calligraphy pen, the papers, his political responsibilities—another world in which his wife would surely be lost, and he treasured her all the more for that. "This is her first time away on her own, you see, and perhaps I fret over her well-being too much."

They had completed their deal after that. Zhmuhin was merely to watch from a distance, not to intercede unless he found Anna Sergeyevna to be in some danger. Evgeniy in turn paid for Zhmuhin's transportation, his lodging and meals, and a remuneration of 100 rubles for the six weeks' work—more than half again his salary at the hotel for the same period, but the extra would ensure his attention and discretion.

During the first fortnight that his wife was away, Evgeniy began to receive short letters from her. She wrote of her walks in Verney's pavilion and in the public gardens, of the roughness of the seas in the days and the strange light upon it in the evenings, of how everyone gathered in the harbor for the arrival of the steamer. Evgeniy smiled over her letters, envying such simple pleasures, the easy amusements that he had never been the type to enjoy. He was grateful for a wife who could appreciate them so.

Then one morning, a messenger delivered a telegram to his office. The message itself was unsigned, but in some manner the block type itself bore a familiar insolence, and despite his incomprehension of the telegram's meaning, the words at once sent the blood rushing to Evgeniy's face.

"Baby bird has found her wings."

* * *

Two nights later, Philip sat in a rented Buick half-a-block from his own home, staring at the Land Rover that had just pulled to a stop at the curb, watching his wife escorted by another man across the lawn and into their front door. As he had throughout the evening, he struggled with the word *stalker* and its connotations. But he hadn't been stalking. He had no intentions to do anything. He had merely been surveying. He was simply watching the story unfold.

He should have been in Charlottesville at this point—the lie he'd told Catherine, the one he'd had to tell her. Research for his story, a quick trip to the Center for Russian Studies at UVA, dinner with a friend from college who lived there, someone he hadn't seen in a couple of years. "So I'll have a place to stay for free," he had explained, plausibly enough. "And it'll give the two of us a chance to catch up." He'd used the last phrase deliberately—the same that he'd used when talking to Catherine about Buddy—but she hadn't seemed to notice, and he alone had been left with a sour taste in his mouth.

So far, he'd put only a dozen miles on the rental, only a few miles between each stop. Buddy's neighborhood first, a series of squat bungalows half-a-century old, freshly painted, freshly landscaped, oversized SUVs out front. A pot of begonias had already bloomed on Buddy's own stoop; his porch swing slowly swayed nearby. Then to the restaurant, following the Land Rover across town to Glenwood Avenue and to the parking lot at 518—a couple of extra miles crisscrossing the streets near the restaurant, Jones to West, Lane to Boylan, the parking lots adjacent to 42nd Street Oyster Bar, Southend and RiRa, couples leaning toward one another, groups talking and laughing, until he found Catherine's beige Camry on Harrington.

It was still back there now, he knew, abandoned for the evening, and he wondered once more what had been running through her head as she made that decision—him watching from just down the street as the two of them exited the restaurant together, the rest of the evening determined, she must have known, by whatever happened in that moment. She'd held her head low, looking down at the sidewalk; Buddy had leaned his face down to meet her eyes better, gestured for her to stay there, walked around into the parking lot. Catherine alone in front of the restaurant. Her head held low with regrets? with shame? lost in her thoughts? lost in anticipation? Philip imagined for a moment that she had been drinking, that she was drunk, that Buddy was taking advantage of her condition. Didn't it seem she was struggling to maintain her equilibrium? But no, her balance had been complete, her stance never swayed. He could almost smell the scent of her new perfume behind her ears, along her neck. She had looked up the moment he thought that. In the direction of Philip and the rented car? No, toward the tip of the Land Rover, waiting to turn out of the parking lot.

And now they had entered the house together, the story unfolding not as Philip would have chosen but, unfortunately, as he expected. He tapped his fingers against the steering wheel, its surface sticky with the sweat of someone else's hands.

A song ended on the radio and the announcer came on. Bob Rogers. WSHA. "The Blues is the Blues is the Blues," Rogers said, his tone folksy, soothing. Philip thought of evening deejays in empty studios, alone with their passions. He thought of the people who listened to those deejays and about the shape of such a shared solitude. He had always felt apart from people—shy and self-aware—but Catherine had been patient with him, indulged his eccentricities. And what had he given her in return? What had he failed to give her that had sent her away?

He picked up the cell phone and dialed their home number.

"Hello, beautiful," he said when Catherine answered, careful to keep his tone light, intent not to betray his emotions.

"Hey," she said. "Are you almost to Charlottesville?"

"Almost," he said, pulling up the car a few feet, watching which lights went on in which rooms. "I'm driving into the city limits now. What have you been up to this evening?"

"I've been out, just got back in," she said. "I got a call soon after you left and ended up meeting some people down at 518. But about halfway through the meal, I felt sick to my stomach and ended up just coming home."

An internal complaint, Philip thought. *How ironic. How fitting.*

"Well, I hate that I'm so far away," he said. He searched for the shadows of movement between the half-closed blinds. "I hate for you to be sick and all alone like that."

"Yeah, I really do feel awful," she said. "But I'll be all right. Buddy ended up driving me back here, and Miriam said she'd come over and stay the night if I wanted her to."

"Buddy's there?"

"Yeah, he said he'd stay with me for a few minutes to make sure I'm OK." A light went on in the room where Philip worked. "And he hadn't seen the house yet, so this gives him a chance to see our place." The light went off again.

"Do you want me to come back?"

"You're hours away, hon," she said, her silhouette appearing at the living room window. "Don't be ridiculous. I'll be fine."

"Well, do you want me to call you back in a little while?"

"I'll be fine," she repeated, and he watched as she shut the blinds tightly. "Don't worry. It was just something I ate. You're almost there and I know you want to catch up with Mike. I'm just going to turn down the ringer and go to bed in a few minutes, just as soon as Buddy leaves."

Turn down the ringer. Go to bed. Catch up. Half-truths easier to tell than lies.

"So." His mind scrambled in vain for a new strategy. "I guess I'll just talk to you tomorrow then."

"All right, hon. I'll give you a call on the cell when I get up, OK?"

"OK," he said. And he saw the light in their bedroom come on. "Well, good night."

"Hey!" she said then. "Aren't you forgetting something?"

"What?" he asked.

"How about 'I love you'?"

"I love you too," he replied, relieved that she had said this in front of Buddy. "I'll talk to you tomorrow. Feel better. Good night."

But his hopes gradually faded as the minutes stretched on. And it was more than an hour before the other man left the house. When the Land Rover pulled away from the street, Philip followed, dutifully.

* * *

Zhmuhin began to send letters after that, penned in his own awkward hand, bearing information about Anna Sergeyevna's indiscretions: how she had retired with the stranger to the sanctity of her hotel room; how the couple had shared a cab to Oreanda, where they had sat near a church and held hands as they stared at the sea; how they now took their meals together regularly; how they stole kisses in the square.

Zhmuhin was fastidious in his details: There was cream in the crab soup they shared at lunch on Tuesday; the wine they drank after dinner on Thursday was a Madeira, uncorked just for them. Zhmuhin had walked past them near the church in Oreanda, but had recognized no remorse in the man's eyes; the couple's kiss in the square was fleeting, the one in the garden approximately half-a-minute in duration. Gone was Zhmuhin's insolence, but his cold precision and simple matter-of-factness were perhaps more brutal, giving Evgeniy's grief little room for relief. Evgeniy wept like some sniveling child. His eyesight became bleary with tears and his face turned so red that he stayed home from the office. He caught the servants exchanging glances when he passed them in the house. What a poor excuse for a man he had become!

And what a poor choice he had made for handling this crisis. He should have traveled to Yalta at once, he would think later. He should have challenged the other man to a duel. He should have punished his wife for her indiscretion with the same firm justice with which he might forgive her for it afterwards. But instead he had written her a letter. *There is something wrong with my eyes,* he had explained. *Please come home as quickly as possible.* A weak lie to avoid a scandal. A coward's choice. He had signed it *Your husband* as if he needed to remind her of the fact—a thought whose shame he would also long bear.

Even as he dripped the wax onto the envelope and reached for his seal, he knew that any choice he made was a mistake. If he didn't confront the situation now, he would be unable to do so later. How could he admit to her in years to come that he had known all along, that he had borne her adultery in silence? And yet what ramifications would ensue if he acted rashly? His public might acquit him of any action he took now in defense of his home, but could they avoid looking upon him differently once they'd discovered him a cuckold? How would they ever trust him as a leader if they suspected that some mismanagement of domestic affairs had sent his wife into the arms of another man?

Such was simply not possible. He sealed the wax.

* * *

WSHA had gone off the air at midnight, and hours of cold, dry static had whispered from the speakers as Philip drove restlessly through the night, haunted by images, miles of worry accumulating. The Land Rover at the curb, the light in the bedroom window, the cigarette in the street... the stale aftertaste of tequila from Catherine's kiss, the feel of her lips light on his forehead several nights before... the passions in her painting, the pizza in the microwave...

her admission that Buddy was there when he called, her admission that she had slept with him before. Another man's hand rested on her hip, caressed her breast. Her fingers wandered in the hair of his chest, their lips met, their bodies twined....

Chekhov had been right, he thought, still crafting the short story in his head, trying in vain still to distract himself from the other story, from all that had happened in those recent hours. *Each of us does have two lives, one open and the other running its course in secret.* But Chekhov had missed the despair of never truly being able to know the other's secret existence, always balancing trust against doubt. Gurov had found some prurient irony in the idea of secret lives, Anna Sergeyevna had been torn asunder by her two worlds, and Evgeniy von Diderits.... But it wasn't Evgeniy's story, after all, Philip recognized, the simplest truth. Anna's and Gurov's was the grand, conflicted passion. Von Diderits's life was static, negligible. Philip had simply chosen the wrong character. And while another man had been wooing and perhaps winning Catherine, Philip had stuck himself away in 1890s Russia, missing the chance for any significance in his own story, precisely when he should have been strengthening his role.

But now he'd secured a place in both stories, had taken special pains to assure that his presence had been felt.

Dawn had broken by the time Philip drove the rented Buick back to his own house and parked it on the curb where the Land Rover had stood the night before. The neighborhood was now lit in soft tones. Sprinklers were rotating in a lawn down the street—set off by an automatic timer, as regular as clockwork, as if nothing had changed. In another yard, a cat stalked some animal unseen. As Philip walked toward his front porch, he heard the neighbor's door open and then saw her step out to pick up her paper. She stopped when she spotted him, and even from a distance he could sense her hesitancy, her apprehension. Did she not recognize him? He saw that she didn't have her glasses on. The Buick must have confused her too. Perhaps she suspected an early morning burglar?

"Good morning, Mrs. Rosen," he called out, with a nervous wave. "Just me. Philip." *Yes, just like the sprinklers,* he told himself. Act as if nothing has changed. And then he thought, *But maybe she has seen me clearly, maybe it's not that she doesn't recognize me but that she's sensed something better than she should.* He quickly turned his key in the front door, pushed it inward, not waiting for a reply.

Once inside, however, he still felt himself an intruder, as if actually breaking into some strange house. He saw even the most familiar objects as if for the first time: a piece of pottery he and Catherine had picked up in Chatham County, a photograph of them on their honeymoon in London, Catherine's purse on the chair. The painting over the mantle seemed darker than usual. The fabric of the couch didn't quite match the floor. He noticed that a Mingus CD he had left in the player had been swapped out for Moby and that an empty bottle of Pinot Noir stood on the kitchen counter. Two glasses sat in the sink.

Had Buddy touched this newspaper on the counter? Which chair had he sat in? The carpet runner in the hallway had been kicked up at the corner. The hand towel in the bathroom had a streak of grime. Was that another man's piss on the rim of the toilet? Under the fluorescent lights, he noticed that there were still traces of red on his hands—ink? No. Not ink. Not ink—not this time. He took a moment to wash them again and then waited to let them dry in the air, reluctant to share the handtowel that the other man had touched.

In their bedroom, the rising sun crept around the edges of the window, leaving the room in morning twilight, and Philip detected the thick scent of black currants again, wildflowers. Beneath the sheets wrapped around her, Catherine's breasts rose and fell in easy rhythms. Her black hair strayed out across the pillow, and a mascara stain marked the case, almost in the shape of an eyelash itself. Someone had propped a condom against the edge of the alarm clock. Durex. Unopened.

Sitting down in the chair in the corner of the room, Philip twirled the condom in his hand, examined the edges of the wrapper, the expiration date, phrases from the package: "super thin for more feeling," "nonoxynol-9," "if erection is lost before withdrawal...." It was from a box of twelve in the bathroom, he knew, and he also knew that if he hadn't come home before she awoke, if he'd really been in Virginia, then the condom would have been returned to its spot, the evidence vanished. But unopened? He started to go into the bathroom and count the ones that remained in the box, see if others were missing, but he couldn't remember with any certainty how many had been in there before he left. It had been awhile since they made love, he realized with regret, with shame.

Catherine shifted her weight, stretched an arm out to her side. Philip clasped the condom in his hand, and moved up to the bed to sit beside her.

"Catherine," he said. "Are you awake?" He laid his free hand on her arm, resisted an unexpected urge to shake it. "It's me. Philip."

"Philip?" she mumbled, still half-asleep, leaning into his touch. Her eyes parted just slightly. "It's too early, Philip, it's—" Her body tensed, her eyes opened wide, she looked up at him bewildered. "Philip?" she said again, sitting up sharply. The sheet fell away from her bare breasts, and it struck him that Buddy had seen her nakedness too, and probably not just long ago. He watched her glance toward the clock, her confusion deepen. "Where…? It's seven in the morning. I thought you were—"

"You said you were sick," he began, and despite himself, he could hear the accusation seeping into his tone. "I came home because—" But even before he said them, he knew the words weren't right, that disguising the truth would make him no better than her. Alibi or not, the very next moment would determine everything after. "I never left," he began, sternly, pridefully, recklessly, measuring his anger. "No, I've been in Raleigh the whole time. I've used up a whole tank of gas, Catherine. I've been driving, I've been thinking…. I saw him, and I don't know what to make of it all, don't know what to make of you." He caught her glancing again at the clock, at the place where the condom no longer stood, and he felt his hand clenching tighter, the foil wrapper crinkling within. "Is this what you're looking for?" he asked with a sneer, and he flicked the condom on the bedspread with his freshly washed hands. The evidence was there. She would have to admit the truth, confirm that he'd been right. Unopened or not, it was still proof. Intentions were —

But as he watched her face, her expression betrayed little. She stared down at the condom for a moment and then pushed her hair behind her ear, lifted her head to meet his gaze. As with everything else in the house, Philip had the vague sensation of seeing Catherine now for the first time, too: the cleft dividing her chin; those faint clusters of freckles across her cheeks, usually masked by powder; the uncommon color of her eyes. Her irises were a deep, impenetrable green, her pupils unfathomably opaque. He thought of the painting above the mantle, those swaths of color brushing against one another, connecting, parting. "Oh, Philip," she whispered, gently shaking her head, "Why did you go away? Why did we need to do this?" and in her wry, pained smile he glimpsed the ragged edges of her secret life, forced open, unable to be hid. *My God*, he thought, *did I make this?*—his anger fleeing him now and some other dull feeling taking its place. The next step was inevitable, he saw then, already written, and he wanted desperately now to go back and mend everything that he'd opened up, to hide his own secret life, to leave everything hid.

"Philip," she said again, reaching out to take his hand in hers, "I have something to tell you." It was too late to stop it now, and he knew that whatever she said next he would try to believe, he would never believe. And it was clear to him that no matter what happened, the most difficult and complicated part of it was likely just beginning.

Visions and Revisions

Tending the spaghetti, Sandra studied the cabinets on the wall beside her. Their whiteness, she knew, was proof that she had painted them, wasn't it? After all, they had been brown once, surely. She remembered picking them out with her ex-husband before the house was built, choosing them from the builder's ragged catalog, and later she had painted them white when the marriage was over, just to make them hers alone. One hand on the stirring spoon, she raised the other to smooth her fingers across the face of the nearest cabinet's door. It was slightly wet with steam from the boiling pot, and there was a small smudge near the handle. She'd need to clean that up. These too—the cabinets, the steam, the smudge—were real.

Her eyes swept across the kitchen: the sink, porcelain not stainless (her choice); the sponge perched on the corner, sticky with soap and destined for the trashcan; the microwave, the toaster, the can opener; the pass-through window separating kitchen and living room, its ledge decorated with a small gathering of imitation Herend rabbits, and beyond that her boyfriend Curt slapping her nine-year-old daughter Wendy; a spice rack; a series of containers for sugar, flour, coffee and tea, ceramic containers whose surfaces were shaped like basketweave; the jolt of the cabinets as his hand struck her cheek; a stray red oven mitt, just out of reach.

Sandra gripped her thumb and forefinger around the counter's edge, pressed it hard. Then she turned her attention back to stirring her spaghetti—turned her attention, in fact, more completely to its swirl and tumble in the big black pot. She half-hoped that the busy flow of bubbles or even the twist of the noodles themselves would begin to form some pattern, restore her sense of order. She half-expected, after what she'd witnessed over the last few weeks, that the spaghetti might even curl itself into a group of letters: WATCH OUT or HE DEVIL or even HELP. They didn't, of course, and as the steam formed a film on her glasses, she closed her eyes, fought the urge to thrust her hand into the pot—a burn to chase away the images that were chasing her. She knew already that later that night, after she had put Wendy to bed, after she and Curt had gone back to her bed, after they'd had sex and his snores had settled into a slow, steady rhythm, she would do as she had done too many nights recently. She would lift Curt's right hand and examine it in the moonlight straying past the dogwood just outside the window, compare his right with his left to see if it seemed any more red or any more swollen, search in vain for some proof of his violence. She would go into Wendy's room then and sit on the edge of that bed, peer down at her daughter's cheek in the light from the hallway, gently turn the girl's head from side to side to look for the bruise that was never there.

Sandra opened her eyes. The film had dissolved from her glasses. The spaghetti was almost done. She looked through the passway beneath the cabinets into the living room where Curt was simply helping Wendy with her homework, just as he'd been doing all along.

"So how much do you have then?" Curt asked her. He held his hands in front of him like a quarterback, explaining the next play to the team. "Take your time. There's no rush."

"Twelve?" Wendy said, raising an eyebrow.

"That's right," he said. He snapped his fingers, his tone excited, celebratory. "And then all you have to do is subtract the three and—"

"Nine," she said proudly.

"Great job!" Curt patted her on the shoulder. "Honey," he called into the kitchen. "You'll be so proud. Wendy's really doing just great."

Sandra watched his muscular quarterback hands, tensed at his snapping fingers, eyed that pat on the shoulder. Innocent gestures all, and yet...

"Dinner's ready," she said finally, her voice so weak that she had to repeat herself before they heard.

* * *

When had things gone so wrong? Could she now remember clearly the first time Curt asked her out—standing there in his brown UPS shorts, nervously lingering at her desk too long after she'd signed for the package? Could she remember being so impressed by the fact that he walked around to open the car door on their first date, and later being charmed that he still did it, so casually, so naturally, on their tenth? Did it matter that when she'd finally let him meet Wendy for the first time, a year and a half ago, he had taken the girl's hand and dipped all 210 pounds of himself into a curtsy and said, in an admirably poor excuse for an English accent, "My pleasure, mi'lady"? Could the memory of Wendy's face at that moment—wide-eyed and fighting back a grin—no longer ease her worries? or the fact that her daughter had herself dipped into a curtsy to match?

Hardly. In truth, few memories now seemed as vivid as that Thursday night three weeks ago. *Wheel of Fortune* had just ended, the pizza from Domino's had been eaten. Piles of crust sat on a trio of plates atop the small tray-tables they used when they ate in front of the TV. Curt and Wendy arm-wrestled on the coffee table—his biceps the size of her neck, but he was letting her win. Sandra stood up, *excuse me*, stepped past them, purposefully brushed her bare thigh against Curt's back, headed down the hallway toward the bathroom. *Don't let* Friends *start without me.*

Minutes later, coming round the corner as she returns to the living room, Sandra sees Curt holding Wendy tightly around the waist, swinging her in circles, her legs flying out into the room. Roughhousing as usual, and Wendy laughing so hard that she's not making any noise. But in that instant of Sandra's rounding that corner, Wendy's foot strikes the TV tray, sends pizza crusts flying, overturns the floor lamp. The lightbulb shatters into a thousand pieces, a million, but Curt doesn't stop spinning her. And that's when Sandra realizes that Wendy isn't laughing but crying and that her voice is silent because she's being squeezed so hard she can't breathe.

"Stop it!" Sandra screams, but in the blink of an eye, the bulb is intact, the lamp upright, the pizza still growing cold on the plate. Curt and Wendy still sit on their respective sides of the coffee table, still arm-wrestling, the young girl's tiny hand pinning Curt's against a copy of *People*. Wendy has won again. Sandra leans hard against the doorframe for support as daughter and boyfriend stare at her with wonder and worry.

In the time since, Sandra had found herself holding onto lots of things for support. Several more doorframes, the handle on the refrigerator, the arm of the couch. The seat of her chair at the dining room table, the half-empty salt shaker, a clutch of mail. Once she'd even hugged herself, just to confirm that she was there.

Still, no matter how real the refrigerator door or the toilet seat or even her own self proved to be, the hallucinations continued, seemingly random, and of varying intensities: Curt sneaking up on Wendy as if to say "Boo"; Curt grabbing her too roughly around the shoulder or the ankle while they all sat around watching television; Curt's hand pulled back as if to slap the girl or actually slapping her or even wrapped around Wendy's throat; or—the worst—Wendy motionless on the gray-green carpet with Curt hovering over her, his head moving down as if to steal a kiss.

And the reality? The two of them were just playing Old Maid or Nintendo while Sandra read the new Danielle Steel. They were all working together in the yard, Sandra pulling weeds by the house, while Curt and Wendy set up the sprinkler in the backyard. Curt helped Wendy search the Internet, tracking down pictures of Jupiter for an astronomy project. Or they weren't even in the same place at all—Wendy doing homework alone in her bedroom while Curt read *The News and Observer* or watched Peter Jennings on the evening news.

But even that paper and that TV conspired against Sandra's sanity. Was it her imagination or hadn't there been more reports of child abuse in the news over the last couple of weeks? She read about a woman in South Carolina whose boyfriend had killed her daughter, and the next day a follow-up: Violence More Likely in Non-Traditional Homes. And then the local TV news reported the story closer to home: a terrified young girl accidentally left locked in a preschool after closing, a frantic mother unable to get in and help her child. Sandra caught herself glancing at Curt's reaction, searching for parental concern. *Look up from your Sports Illustrated,* her thoughts begged in vain, *tell me how awful that story on the news is.* And meanwhile the somber reporter kept talking about the neglected child, and the paper recounted more stories of abuse, cited more statistics, and Sandra's visions became more persistent, more insistent, plaguing her wherever she turned.

* * *

Was God trying to deliver some warning? Was some guardian angel confiding a hidden truth? Neither Sandra's parents nor Sandra herself had ever been much for church-going. Still, she couldn't help but consider that some force more powerful than herself had perhaps sought her out, and was ultimately responsible for these visions. *Or perhaps,* she thought, *it's the future I'm seeing, glimpsing through some supernatural doorway.* But what did these glimpses offer? A hint of some danger Curt might pose to Wendy, perhaps to both of them? A cautionary peek at what might come to pass if she didn't take action? Or worse, a cruel preview of impending and unavoidable tragedy?

"You're just afraid that he's going to turn out to be your ex-husband all over again," said her co-worker Beverly over coffee in the Nortel breakroom. No milk, no sugar.

Dan never hurt Wendy, Sandra started to protest, *and he only hit me once,* but Randy who worked down the hall had come in and was pretending too obviously not to listen. Bev didn't seem to notice, had already trotted along with her analysis. The possibilities, it seemed, were endless. Maybe Sandra was afraid of becoming too close to another man. Maybe her subconscious was trying to sabotage the relationship. "After all, he's just started spending the night at your place over the last few months." Or maybe Sandra was jealous of Curt's friendship with her daughter. Just a little jealous because it took his attentions away from her? A little envious of how well Curt got along with the girl? Had Sandra and Wendy been getting along themselves? Does Wendy enjoy spending time with him more than with you? "You're not losing your daughter, you know,"

Bev sipped her coffee. "And anyway, I know Curt. He's a good man. You've got nothing to be afraid of. Nothing to fear but..."

Sandra had stopped listening. Hadn't she believed that Daniel was a good man all those years ago? And hadn't she discovered how wrong she was about that? The sneaking suspicions, the phone calls that just hung up, a letter that shouldn't have been left out, and then all that anger balling up and lashing out when she'd finally confronted him.

Still, Sandra had already recognized the possibilities that these visions weren't coming from somewhere "out there," but from some dark place deep within. She knew that her insides might still be reeling from the way Dan had treated her. She might be readied for the punch this time in ways she hadn't been ready with her first husband. And she realized the effect that these episodes, whatever their cause, were having on her relationship with Curt—a relationship she had taken slowly, peering into his eyes and his actions for kindness and responsibility before inviting him so fully into their lives. Yet sometimes, just as she had leaned against the wall for support, she had also found herself leaning against Curt, pressing her blond hair against his shoulder, nestling her own shoulder in the hollow of his arms, groping toward some clear, tangible connection. During the few days just after the first vision, she had actually made love to him more frequently and with near-ferocious abandon, striving for some physical understanding, some tactile reality. And afterward, she asked him questions like "Do you believe you'll ever think of Wendy as your own daughter?" and "Are you ever afraid that things seem too good to be real?" and "Do you think the truth of us is a good truth?" And as much as his touch, his words caressed her battered imagination, and she sunk off into peaceful, even blissful dreams.

* * *

But before the second week of her visions had passed, Sandra found his touch less soothing than sickening. She lost interest in sex. She went through the motions for his pleasure at the cost of her own, just so he wouldn't ask what was wrong. She found herself shrinking away from him in bed, facing the wall, even arching her body so it was difficult for him to curl his arm around her. On several occasions, she woke up in the middle of the night having maneuvered so far from his touch that she teetered on the edge of the bed.

She watched Curt more closely when Wendy was nearby, and even when her daughter was not. She watched the way he moved his hands, the way he cut his chicken, where his eyes strayed. She once loved his compliments, but didn't he now seem to be doting a little too much? She had admired the way he gathered the laundry or took out the garbage without her asking, but was he just trying to curry favor, force her guard down? She hoped that by paying close enough attention, her observations would bridge the distance between her subconscious and her conscious—or invite that higher power to contact her more directly. After all, wasn't she truly trying harder to see?

When that connection wasn't made, Sandra kept watch anyway, hoping that her vigilance would ward off any evil. Before, she had occasionally asked Curt to pick Wendy up from school, but no more. And no more trips with Wendy to the Harris-Teeter for last-minute groceries; Curt could go alone. Sandra always joined them now when they stepped out to Barnes and Noble or the mall. She and Curt didn't take turns coaching Wendy with her homework anymore, especially if she was working in her bedroom. "I just want to be more involved in your education," Sandra said. "Is that wrong?" If it meant having to leave the two of them alone, she even put off going to the bathroom until she could simply hold it no longer.

No matter how subtle she tried to be, Curt and Wendy both seemed surprised by these changes—Curt tentative with his questions about how things seemed different between them, Wendy suddenly sullen in ways she'd never been before, sulky and increasingly defiant.

"Why couldn't I ride to the store too?" Wendy finally challenged Sandra one evening, angry that Curt had been sent off for a package of butter without her.

"Because you needed to stay here and set the table."

"We've already set the table."

"You can help me finish dinner then."

"I don't *want* to cook dinner. I wanted to ride out with Curt."

"Don't you think you sometimes spend too much time with Curt?" Sandra asked. "Do you ever have times when you feel—I don't know—a little relieved when you don't have to be with him?"

Wendy stared blankly at her mother for several moments, and then Sandra felt she could see some sad insight creep into her daughter's eyes. "If things don't work out between you and Curt," Wendy finally said, her voice just above a whisper, "I won't see him again, will I? Not even a couple of times a year like when you fly me out to visit Dad."

Of course, in the midst of trying to soothe Wendy's mind again about the divorce, trying to be strong enough herself to ease her daughter's fears, Sandra couldn't confide her own fear: the thought that Curt might become the boyfriend in *The News and Observer*'s next article, the next top story for the nightly news. Sandra couldn't explain the guilt she already felt about possibly recognizing too late the warnings she should have heeded.

And so she arrived back where she had begun. *Was* it a warning? *Was* some higher power reaching down to help her? *Was* her subconscious telling her something her conscious self was either unable or unwilling to admit?

"You need to go see a psychiatrist," said her friend Bev later, her words once again strong and bitter and black.

* * *

But Sandra went to Circuit City instead, took off work early the next Thursday and went shopping for her sanity.

The camcorder she bought felt real in her hand—more real than even the doorframe, though the camera was tiny, small enough to cup in the palm of her hand. And the instructions, a thick booklet which might have intimidated her at other times, had a straightforwardness that drew her closer. If she pressed this button, the camera would record. If she pressed this button, it would stop. If she used these buttons, today's date would be set; used this one and the date would be recorded on the screen. If she hooked the red tips of this cord into the TV and the black tips into the camera, she could watch herself on the bigger screen.

She had learned quickly that the smaller the camera, the larger the price, but she couldn't skimp on this. The size was perfect, it had all the features she would need, and the salesperson—even if he lifted his left nostril at some of her more curious questions—showed her how to hook it up to a motion sensor so that she wouldn't waste her film.

Once she'd set it up the way he'd shown her in the store, she was grateful to find that it fit easily just between the plates in the top of her china display, the black body of the camera disappearing toward the rear of the cabinet just as she'd hoped. Curt and Wendy never looked there anyway; no one did, and the top shelf had the cobwebs to prove it. She tested the camera out first to make sure that it worked, stepping in front of its gaze and waving, then taking the camera back down and checking herself on instant replay. After she returned it to its place, she drove to school and picked Wendy up.

On Saturday, she woke early to the sound of rain on the roof. It was just what she wanted. She showered and dressed, made a piece of toast for breakfast, checked the Weather Channel to see how long the rain would last, then wrote a note for Curt.

In Wendy's room, she kissed her sleeping daughter's cheek then returned to the living room, switched the camera's power to "On" and grabbed both her car keys and Curt's. *If they don't have a car, they can't go anywhere. Since it's raining, they'll stay inside.* With one last look behind her, she opened the door to leave.

But just before she pulled it shut, Wendy walked into the living room, rubbing her eyes, still half-asleep.

Over the next few hours, as Sanda sat at Bev's and then as they walked through the mall, Bev chatting constantly to distract her from second-guessing herself, Sandra wouldn't be able to remember her exact conversation with her daughter, no matter how she searched her mind. What remained in her memory was, she knew, cut from the same fabric as the visions she'd seen. Where Wendy had asked, "Where are you going?" Sandra remembered, "Why are you putting me in danger?" Where she asked, "Can I come with you?" Sandra remembered, "If you took his car keys, how will he take me to the hospital if I'm hurt? How will I get away if *he* hurts *me*?" When Sandra answered, "I have to run out. I'll be back later. Curt will take care of you," what she meant was, "My world has fallen out of balance. I don't know how else to restore what I've lost. And I'm sorry."

Could she trust anything she remembered? Yes. Two things, in fact. In both her memories and the moment of her leaving, Sandra was unable to comprehend that reckless woman with the lie on her lips and the hand on the door. And when Sandra had told her daughter, "I love you, Wendy," she had meant, "I love you, Wendy."

Of course, even as she said it—perhaps *because* she said it—a part of her wanted to stop, to not go through with her plan. *What if this is the day I've been warned about?* she wondered. *Whether I catch him or not, it will still be too late. The damage will already be done.* But what she wanted was not proof that he *would* hurt her but proof that he wouldn't. The camera wouldn't lie, she knew. And when she watched them cleaning the house together or playing checkers together, she'd feel better leaving them next time. And when everything went fine that next time, she would feel even better the third time. The camera would help her to trust him again. But she couldn't entirely shake the awful thought that crept into her mind as she kissed her daughter once more and shut the door between them.

I'm making a terrible mistake.

* * *

Sandra returned home to find Curt fretting over an old clock he'd promised to fix, the pieces strewn here and there across the coffee table while he tapped a screwdriver against his knee. His brow was furrowed and he didn't look her in the eye. Was it because of some guilt? Wendy, lying on the floor with a *Goosebumps* book, gave her mother only one furtive look before she turned back to her reading.

But perhaps they had good reason to be ill at ease. Of course they did. It wasn't like her to just leave abruptly before Curt was up, to spend the day away from the two of them without any notice. As she unpacked the groceries she'd picked up on her way home, she hardly paid attention to what she said to them, could remember later little of what Curt told her. Yes, Curt said, they had cleaned the house just like her note had asked. No, they had not gone out. It was raining and they couldn't find his keys. She heard these things because she needed to, and she was certain that she'd handed him a shirt she had bought him at the mall, proof of where she had been. But she was too busy looking at Wendy's neck and arms and at Curt's hands, watching their gestures and expressions, to listen much to what they said. Was Wendy so quiet because something had happened? Or because Curt seemed so concerned about Sandra's leaving? Had that lamp been sitting so awkwardly on the table when she left? Had this floor really been vacuumed? Was the camera where she'd left it?

It was. And she kept stealing glances at it throughout the evening, which stretched on like a whole day, a week, a month. Sandra could feel herself age with each minute of anticipation. Hoping that time would go faster if she kept busy, she made a lengthy dinner—lasagna from scratch—and cleaned the dishes herself by hand as they talked about possibly going to the zoo the next day, if the weather got better. Afterward, she pulled down Trivial Pursuit and Monopoly and Life. She tried not to look at the clock and struggled to ignore the TV because she caught herself clicking off the quarter-hours by the appearance of commercials, counting off the half-hours and hours by which show was on.

Nine-o'clock finally came—time for Wendy to go to bed. They followed their evening routine, cleaning up the games and toys before Sandra and Wendy went off to the bathroom together to brush their teeth. Curt even joined them this time, brushing his own teeth right beside them, and he helped Sandra tuck her daughter into bed with a kiss on the cheek—*just like we're a real family,* Sandra thought.

But Wendy soon complained that she couldn't sleep. She got up for water, read another book, fretted and groaned, and the thought nagged Sandra that Curt had joined them in the bathroom and helped tuck Wendy in because he hadn't wanted to leave the two of them alone, hadn't wanted to give Wendy the chance to tell her mother what had happened that day. Sandra worried that Curt's kissing Wendy on the cheek bore with it some malice that troubled her rest.

Sandra stifled her thoughts as best she could, gave Curt another beer. She'd been feeding them to him throughout the night in hopes that he would turn in early. And when Wendy was finally asleep, she led Curt to their bedroom and let him have his way with her, watching the clock as they made love, knowing that he always fell asleep more quickly and slept more soundly after sex.

But after his breath had settled into that same slow, steady rhythm, she didn't check his hands and didn't look in on her daughter, didn't check first one cheek then the next. Instead she went straight for the living room, pulled the camera down from its perch, plugged red tips into the TV, black tips into the camera and set the machine to "Play." And with that first image—"Sept. 21, '99, 02:43 PM," Sandra waving at herself on the day she bought the camera, testing it to make sure that it worked—the tape began to turn.

* * *

After it was over, Sandra returned to her bedroom, edged into the chair in the corner of the room and watched Curt sleep with a peace she hadn't known in weeks. The room was quiet except for the sound of his breathing and her own, still except for the scramble of her heartbeat, the flurry of her thoughts, which raced along so quickly that she knew sleep might never overtake them.

The tape had started fine. Sandra had watched herself move away from the camera after turning it on, watched herself pick up two sets of car keys and turn for the door: "Sept. 25, '99, 07:47 AM." She saw her daughter come into the room, rubbing her eyes, still half-asleep, and heard the conversation that she had been unable to recall clearly that afternoon, as if the muddle of her memory was suddenly being cleared away. After Sandra left, Wendy walked off-camera, apparently into the kitchen, then returned with a bowl of cereal and sat down to watch cartoons. Soon after, Curt came in, tousled Wendy's hair and made a bowl for himself. He sat beside her and read the paper while they ate. Sandra couldn't hear much of their conversation: Wendy talking about where Mom had gone, telling Curt about the note, which he soon found and read before he sat down again.

They watched cartoons for most of the morning—Sandra fast-forwarded through much of this—and then they began cleaning the living room, the dull roar of the vacuum on the tape now forcing Sandra to turn down the volume on the TV. Curt was thorough to the point of exhaustion, even moving the heavy recliner aside and cleaning beneath it instead of around it. Sandra felt her eyes glazing. It was getting late and she had to admit that what she was watching was—honestly, thankfully—boring.

And then the sound of the vacuuming ceased and the image froze, Curt and Wendy suddenly stopped in time: Curt with his arm outstretched, pushing the vacuum across a broad sweep of carpet;

Wendy caught in a moment of not helping, instead jumping up and down on the couch, suspended in mid-air. Sandra thought for a moment that she had hit the "Pause" button on the camera, but no, through the tiny window, she could watch the tape still spinning itself out. And then, just as suddenly, the image shifted again, an hour later according to the time on the screen, and Curt and Wendy were playing checkers. But here too the image was still, Wendy caught in mid-move, a checker piece in her hand as she carried it across the board. And then another scene, again motionless: Curt's hands held high in the air, frozen in a moment of exasperation as Wendy peered beneath the couch—looking for those lost keys, perhaps? There was nothing disturbing about the picture, except for that unnerving stillness and...

A chill shivered down Sandra's spine as she realized that the camera's angle had changed. To get this shot, the camera couldn't have been up on the shelf behind the china, it had to be—she turned to look—over by the fireplace. But when she looked back at the TV to confirm her discovery, Curt and Wendy were no longer looking for keys. Instead they were looking at her.

The angle had changed once more, and now they sat in a different room entirely, the dining room, Curt sitting on one of the chairs with his arm around Wendy, who has settled onto his knee. This too was a still shot and they were posed as if sitting for some Olan Mills portrait, staring directly into the camera, staring directly at Sandra as she watched the screen. The image held for several minutes, no one blinking, not even Sandra, and then the scene shifted once more, a different room again, the bathroom, the sound returning and the image moving at a normal pace as Wendy brushed her teeth, while Curt stood behind her brushing his own.

Sandra felt the anger rise up inside of her, pushed on by her certainty about what had happened. They had found the camera. They were playing a joke on her. All her efforts were for *nothing*. But that anger and that certainty vanished in the wake of what she saw next: the camera panning just slightly to reveal Sandra herself standing there beside them, a toothbrush in her mouth.

The time display read "10:04 PM" that night.

And then the image jumped ahead again—Sandra and Curt pulling the cover up around Wendy's chin and kissing her good night, then Sandra staring at the clock while Curt heaved and puffed atop her—and then it jumped further: Sandra coming toward the camera to remove it from its hiding place.

And then—Sandra felt herself mesmerized—further still: "Sept. 26," the next day, at the zoo, the three of them standing in front of the bears' den, the weather perfect, not a cloud in the sky. And then "Sept. 26," at the zoo, the three of them standing under umbrellas in front of the bears' den, as the rain poured down all around them. And with that, the pictures began changing more rapidly, an MTV video gone out of control. Some of the images were still, some in motion. Some were crisp and polished, others grainy and herky-jerky like old home movies from when she was a kid. The dates and times changed so quickly that Sandra could only read a few of them. Visions like the ones she'd seen in recent weeks, images hinting toward or portraying violence, flashed and folded between others more mundane: the three of them laughing at an *Andy Griffith* rerun, having dinner at the Golden Corral down the street, playing putt-putt golf at the beach.

Sandra saw herself a year-and-a-half later at a wedding in which she was clearly the bride, and then Curt in a tuxedo gently feeding her a slice of cake. Then she saw that same year-and-a-half unfolding differently, scenes of arguments and fighting, boxes packed, a tearful departure, the same wedding scene on the same date, herself in the same off-white dress, being fed a slice of cake by another man whom she did not know. She saw herself a year later pregnant and then in the hospital delivering a son. She saw a picture of her own self as a baby and then snapshots of her own youth—Sandra's first day of kindergarten, Sandra's first kiss, Sandra's first car, her high school graduation, her wedding to Daniel, his promise to honor and cherish—as the past sped before her eyes. She saw her honeymoon with Dan, running along the beach, dinners and dancing, and then years later, his fist balling up against her, a bloodied nose, a blackened eye. She saw pictures of herself as a child in places she had never been, doing things about which she had no memory. She saw pictures of Wendy flitting past in similar scenes, and then the first day of school, first kiss, first car of her second child, the son not yet born. She saw herself without any second husband, without any second child, raising Wendy alone. She saw future jobs, lovers from her younger days and others she had never met, her first house and houses in which she was yet to live. She saw herself aged and gray and sitting alone in a metal chair on the green front porch of a house she did not recognize. She saw her past as it had been and as it might have been and her future in all of its alternate endings. She saw her self begin to divide, fragments of her straying out along each of the different paths—this fragment with eagerness, that one with dread—and the thought began to grow that she was at once all of these possibilities and none of them, that her existence had no more weight than a sitcom, no sterner gravity than a drama once its hour was up. She felt her fears shed away, her body grow lighter as the images cut so quickly they began to blur, and for a moment, a brief moment, she believed that she might simply take flight. But at that same moment the tape ended, the picture turned blue, then black. In the sudden blankness of the TV screen, Sandra caught sight of her own reflection—stark and haggard—and her mind began once more to shrivel beneath the burden of all those possibilities.

* * *

The tape had long since ended, had worn itself out and, Sandra discovered, worn her down as well. How long had it been since she'd come back into the bedroom, sat down in the corner chair? Her eyes were too muddied with tears to see the clock, but she knew it was still night and she could still hear the sound of Curt sleeping.

She dragged her body up from her chair and crawled into her bed beside him. She wriggled herself close against his warmth, pulled his arm around her, felt him shift against her and tighten his hold. She rubbed her hand along his arm, knowing that he could just as easily crush her or Wendy as he could wrap them in a hug. A year from now, which one would he be doing? A year from now, would he even be the man who shared her bed?

The weight of the unknowable pushed her more firmly into Curt's embrace and she forced herself to focus on the decisions she *could* make, the events she *could* control.

I will tell Curt about my visions, she thought, *I will tell him tomorrow and I will let him know each time they appear. I will stay with Curt for now. I will stay with him until I don't. I will leave the house for fifteen minutes while Curt watches Wendy, and there will be no camera to record what happens because I will take it down and put it back in its box. And on Monday I will take it back to the store and return it as defective. I will stop holding onto doorframes and salt shakers. If I get dizzy, I will fall down. If I fall down, I will get up. And tomorrow we will go to the zoo—rain or shine. And I will make sausage and eggs for Curt and Wendy's breakfast, but I will have corn flakes and bananas for my own. I will wear a blue blouse and white pants...*

She persuaded herself into some small comfort with such images, consoled herself with the expectation that when the sun came up it might truly bring with it a new day and a new beginning, might truly shed light where there had been darkness. And as the last hours of night crept past, she fixed her eyes on the window, waiting quietly, desperately, unblinkingly for some hint of morning to appear.

A Voice from the Past

Mere seconds after Evan told his secretary to send the call to voicemail, the extension buzzed again.

"I'm sorry, sir." His secretary's tone was plaintive. A new secretary, but she'd already learned that he didn't like to be disturbed before meeting with a client. "The man says it may be urgent."

Evan continued to thumb through the materials he'd gathered for his ten-o'clock: the American Funds 2004 edition, last quarter's statistical update, BB&T's standard application and client disclosure, a few more items—top to bottom in the order he would present them, lined crisply along the left and bottom margins. He squared the material on his desk calendar. *Organization shows respect*, his father had told him, a banker himself. *Preparation is control. Respect, power, control. First steps to success.*

"What was the name again?"

"A Mr. Dexter Hollinger. He said he knew you in school."

On the far wall hung two diplomas from the University of Virginia—undergrad and MBA, the Darden School. Just above, the clock stood at 9:54 a.m., the second hand gliding past the six.

"A friend from college?"

"High school, I believe, sir." And then, tentatively: "Boarding school is what he said, actually."

Hollinger? Dexter Hollinger? Still not a name he recalled, but something nagged at the edges of his memory. *Football?* he wondered. He hadn't kept in touch with *every*one on the team, but at least he would have remembered the name. Was it already time for annual fundraising? Passing the cup for Roll Call?

"I'll handle it." He picked up the handset just as his secretary clicked off. There was a dry emptiness as the transferred call patched through. "Good morning, Mr. Hollinger. How may I help you?"

"*Mister* Hollinger," said the man on the other end, the voice high-toned and spry, just the trace of a Southern accent. "Now *that's* a switch." He gave a small snort. A fuzziness in the connection, slightly tinny—a cell phone probably. "Twenty years ago, I'd be trembling just to have the Head Monitor pass me in the hallway—or any of the Old Boys, really. And now.... *Mister!* I mean, I'm not the Dex I was, but still...."

Head Monitor. Old Boys. New Boys. Evan hardly thought about those phrases anymore. The "Rat" System. Upperclassman initiating the incoming students. *Hold the door. Stack the plates.* Hierarchies established, humility encouraged—spoiled teenage boys coming in with smirks on their faces and swaggers in their steps and slowly molded into Southern gentlemen. So Hollinger had been three or four years beneath him? A Rat? No wonder Evan couldn't place the name.

"Been a long time," Evan said. "Dexter, of course. Dex. Sorry about the *mister*. Just habit"—though it wasn't his habit at all. First names—that was how you established a firm relationship. "Guess I was just surprised to hear from you."

"Well, wasn't like we were close, was it? Would have seemed odd for us to talk even then, much less be calling one another now...."

"You speak the truth," said Evan, unintentionally echoing a catchphrase that had been bandied about the school back in the day.

Yes, the call was "out of the blue," Dex admitted, and "a lot of water under the bridge since then, thank God," as he chatted briefly about where the last two decades had taken him, a jittery patter of information and interjections and platitudes: back to Alabama first—"Roll on, Crimson Tide"—and then out West for a while, Seattle actually, with a new wife, a new business, success better some years than others. "The road is full of...."

Some of Dexter's words were lost as the cell phone's signal drifted, and Evan only half-listened to the ones that made it through. In his files he'd found some graphs comparing five-year and ten-year performance in various growth and income investment funds, and he arranged these on small easels on the corner of his desk. The second hand continued to sweep through the minutes on the clock opposite his desk. Finally, he couldn't take it any longer.

"My secretary said that there was something urgent you—"

"Well... urgent is...," said the voice, fading in and out, "...about you and your family, of all..." and then crisper once more: "Just a dream, I know, but, I thought, why *would* I be dreaming about Evan Spruill after all this time? And so I said to myself, well, why not give him a call just to be sure, you know?"

"A dream, you say? I lost you for a moment. You had a dream of some kind?" The clock's hands now stood at 10 precisely. *Promptness a sign of respect, too.* Outside the window, a row of dogwoods lined the bank's parking lot, and over to the right a young man in shorts strutted down the sidewalk, rushing the season, the city still a little cool this late April day. Evan took a deep breath. "Well, yeah, I guess that's odd. But hey, Dex, I gotta say, it's still good to hear from you, and I wish I didn't have this meeting to —"

"...only because it was so unsettling," Dexter went on, and Evan understood that the connection was no clearer in the other direction, that Dexter hadn't heard him at all. "Like when you wake up with a start and you've had some kind of nightmare about your mom or your brother or something. First thing you want to do—three in the morning, whatever time—you want to pick up..." the sound of traffic, the roar of a truck "... in premonitions or whatever, but something about the, I don't know, the tone of it if nothing else, struck me as disturbing, and... well, just in case, that's what I did. Called the alumni office and got your number."

Somewhere down the street, a siren wailed—for a moment, Evan wasn't sure if it was coming toward him or fading away, but then it stopped abruptly, as if strangled. "Well, Dex, I appreciate your calling and letting me know, but everything's OK here, and I hope we can catch up again soon."

The static continued to course and crinkle, but through it, Evan could hear a sudden, gnawing void. For a moment, he thought Dexter might have hung up, but then the other man's words—and his disappointment—came through clear:

"Don't you want to hear the dream?"

"I'm late for an appointment. I may have a client already waiting outside."

"I'll be quick, I promise" came the reply, and Dexter sketched out the contents of his nightmare: A car breaks down, Evan's car, Evan's wife and family aboard—a daughter perhaps, at least in the dream a daughter—a dead battery the cause; Dexter is there too, at the top of a hill, and he calls down to the family stranded at the bottom, then someone tosses a book down toward them. "I don't know the title of the book," said Dexter. "And I don't know who threw it, but when I called down to you, you said that it was good to see me and that you'd changed your name to mine for some reason. Ha, ha! Imagine...." And then more people gather to try to help the family: people manning cell phones, calling from pay phones, trying to reach help; Dexter finds a gas station nearby, but instead of simply asking a mechanic for help, he tries to search on a computer for possible assistance. Suddenly, ads for pornographic websites begin popping up on the screen, and Dexter struggles to hide them, closing new windows as quickly as they open. "I know it's all fairly random," Dexter said. "But still... well, it was just unsettling, and I woke up feeling that something," and here his voice grew more somber, "that something terrible, truly terrible might happen." He laughed again, a hint of some nervousness, self-consciousness. "I wouldn't even know if you *have* a daughter—or a wife either for that matter—but still...."

"No, you were on the money," said Evan. "Wife and daughter both." He looked at the photographs on his desk. A picture of his family taken the Christmas before: his wife Karen in a red knit sweater with a green Christmas tree across its front, five-year-old Heather wearing a pair of reindeer antlers and a red plastic nose, and Evan there too, beginning to gray. He hardly recognized himself. Another photograph of his daughter in a tire swing from his own parents' house, the rope above twisted tight and the photo caught in mid-spin, Heather's hair flying out in strands as the rope uncoiled itself. *That's the kind of future you're investing in,* he sometimes told clients, pointing to the picture. *The only investment that counts.* And it was true: His family *was* his greatest asset. "But you can rest assured, Dex, we're fine. Just a dream, I guess."

"I'm glad to hear that," said Dexter, and Evan thought he heard a sigh, the sound of some genuine relief. "Well, sorry to take your time," he said, "but if the car breaks down, I guess you know who to call! But seriously, lemme give you my number in case you ever want to catch up again someday. I actually just moved back to the area— old haunts, even if not just like the old times, thank goodness. Trying to kick-start my business out here and…" Again, a fading in and out. "…I hate to say it, but given all that happened back then and all, I thought that maybe…."

"Always a possibility," Evan said, but he didn't write down the number, and he rushed with some relief through his good-bye.

Evan's client had indeed already arrived but hadn't minded waiting. The two of them discussed investment options, short- and long-term strategies. The client completed a quick survey to determine his financial type—ultimately more conservative—and then concluded the meeting by purchasing just over $12,000 in Class A shares divided over the Growth Fund of America, the Capital World Growth and Income Fund, and the American Balanced Fund. The remainder of the day continued at a similar pace—a handful more clients and two mid-day meetings—and Evan didn't give his phone call with Dexter another thought until later that afternoon when his wife Karen called to say that she and their daughter were stuck in the parking lot at Crabtree Valley Mall, the battery dead on the LandCruiser or perhaps something else wrong, she couldn't quite tell.

* * *

"It's just eerie, that's all I'm saying," Evan told his wife as they finished dinner that night—several hours after Roadside Assistance crew had started the SUV once again. As they ate, Evan had related to Karen parts of the story, editing out parts for Heather's sake, and though he agreed that it was just coincidence ("a fluke," she had said), his frustration deepened when she didn't show even the smallest evidence of some amazement—which prompted him to further overstate his case, even to raise his voice. "I mean, what are the chances? It's... it's almost supernatural or something!"

Karen edged a nod toward Heather and widened her eyes at him—the same expression she gave when someone on TV said a "grown-up word" and she wanted Evan to change the channel. He hadn't noticed how rapt his daughter's attention had become. She held her fork upright in her little fist and stared at him, her mouth just slightly parted.

"Finished, honey?" Evan asked, and when Heather nodded yes, he turned back to Karen and cocked his head into a question.

"How 'bout you go put your plate on the sink?" Karen said. "Go play in your room while Daddy and I clean up."

"Find a good book," Evan called after her, but he knew that when he went back later, she'd be watching *Finding Nemo* for the umpteenth time or taking another trip under the sea with the *Little Mermaid* CD-ROM that she'd begged them to buy her. At least the latter was educational.

They cleared the table in silence, then stood together at the sink, Karen rinsing the plates, sending a few scraps down the garbage disposal before handing them to Evan to load into the dishwasher. She turned to the pots next.

"I just don't want you scaring her," she said finally. "Eerie? OK, sure. I understand. But maybe she doesn't, you know, Evan? And after all, it was just a dead battery, and it's running fine now. Just let it go."

"But *why'd* the battery die?" he asked, the same as he'd asked earlier. He'd checked the Toyota himself once he got home: opened and closed the doors to watch the interior lights come on and go out; started the engine not once but twice, sitting in the driver's seat the first time and then stepping outside the second, just to listen to it run.

Karen set down the sponge. "I don't know either, Evan, and I'll admit that I think there's something weird about it." She glanced toward the doorway of the kitchen, as if to make sure Heather hadn't returned, and then, elbows propped on the sink's edge, turned to face him head-on. "And you know what I'm thinking?" she asked, her voice softer, more somber. She leaned in closer, and for a moment, he felt a shiver at how steady her gaze was. "I'm thinking"—her voice almost a whisper now—"that it's *gremlins.*" And with that, she finally winked and then gave him a quick kiss on the nose. She picked up the sponge again and the pan she'd been scouring. "I'll tell you what," she said, a quick nudge with her elbow, "if you can't get it off your mind, why not give the guy a call back, and talk to *him* about it. Talk it out a little bit, laugh over old times. It'll... demystify the whole thing maybe."

"I don't even remember him. He was a few years behind me." Not abnormal, Evan knew. He'd been required to memorize the names of old boys during his own Rat year, all of them looming like titans over his freshman activities: Curtis Bartlett and Dick Oglethorpe yelling at a group of first-years to "cheer harder" at a football game, and then having them run laps around the football field when the team fell 14-10. School spirit or else. Or Crispin Smith, who'd made Evan eat a half-dozen peaches when he'd grabbed one at dinner without offering the bowl to the Old Boys first. Years later, he'd run into Smith at a cocktail party and had gone over to tell him that he still couldn't stomach the taste of peaches, but the other man couldn't recall the incident—or Evan either, he eventually admitted.

"Hard to laugh over old times," Evan said now, "since the two of us didn't really *share* any times."

Karen shrugged, then handed him the pan to add to the dishwasher. "Then let's just get back to normal, OK?"

As soon as they'd finished in the kitchen, he headed back to his daughter's bedroom, stopping along the way to skim through an old yearbook from a bookcase in the living room. Dexter's picture was bland enough—he wore a tangle of blond hair and that awkwardly boyish look, thick eyebrows over dull eyes, broad lips pulled into a slim grin, a slightly jutting lower jaw—and nothing in the brief description yielded much either: straightforward information about Dexter's hometown, an address in Alabama, perhaps still his parents' address; and extracurricular listings that showed him running cross-country in the fall, going out for track and field in the spring, computing club all year. As he returned the book to its shelf, Evan regretted that none of it jogged his memory any further.

He was surprised to find Heather neither watching a video on the TV in her room nor playing *Little Mermaid* on the small Dell that her grandfather had passed along to her. Instead, she had gathered a half-dozen animals in a semi-circle around her and was reading to them from one of her *Little Bear* books—not able literally to read the words but repeating the story from memory as she turned the pages. Evan sat down Indian-style beside her and joined in the group of quiet listeners, then read another story himself to the assembled audience. Afterwards, he and Heather sat together at the computer and checked her email for the daily message from her grandfather ("just keeping in touch," he always reminded, "write back soon," the real reason for his generous gift), and then she clicked open one of the games, moving the mouse with glee as she helped Ariel dive deep into the ocean to gather precious treasure. Soon, Karen peeked in to check on them, leaned her hip against the doorway, smiled. Evan remembered an early beach vacation with Karen, the two of them swaying in a hammock and the moon over the water, and another night, years later, with Karen rocking Heather to sleep when she was just an infant, and then more recently, the three of them reading stories together. These were the moments that Evan treasured—a sense of peace and togetherness, each thing in its place, all somehow right with the world.

When he and Karen finally pulled the covers over them for bed, neither of them had mentioned the incident again. But after Karen had drifted off, Evan still found himself nagged by restless thoughts about the day's coincidence.

Irrational, he told himself finally, thinking of both his own overreaction and Dexter's overeager phone call. "Something terrible, truly terrible," he'd said—and over what? A dream? It was more than irrational. It was absurd.

Wasn't it?

* * *

Despite himself, Evan called the alumni office between prospects at work the next day. He was on the school's Board of Directors now, and he asked the board liaison for some information about Dexter Hollinger. "Haven't talked to ol' Dex in awhile," he told her, "and don't remember seeing his name in the alumni mag. Do you all have any idea what he's up to these days?"

"Looks like it's been recently updated," she said. "And you're in luck. He lives right here in town." He could hear her smile on the phone as she gave out his addresses, both physical and email, and a phone number—very likely the same number Evan had failed to write down the day before. *But of course,* Evan thought, *why wouldn't it?*

A quick Google search yielded little more, except for the name of Dexter's wife, Pam, cross-listed with an address in Seattle—proving that part of the story true as well, it seemed. He also discovered the name of Dexter's business: Spectrum Security. A sunburst image at the top of the home page touted, "For the Full Spectrum of Security, Always Go With Spectrum Security," and a list below sketched out their specialties: home, business, car. Evan paused at the word *car.* Wouldn't it be easy for a man who knew car security to bypass one himself?

That led him to call the mechanic about the LandCruiser. Was there any chance it had been tampered with? Any chance at all? He could almost hear the mechanic's confusion and distraction over the phone.

"Dead battery's a dead battery, I reckon," he said. "Was there a problem with the way I jumped it off, sir? Is it giving you more trouble? They'd probably replace it for you, but you might need to speak to my manager...."

It was a dead battery, he told himself. *A fluke. Put it out of your mind.*

He did manage that for a while, and at the end of the afternoon, he had garnered three new clients, nearly $62,000 in investments. At home, all seemed positive as well: meatloaf for dinner, and afterwards Heather went to play while Karen took a quick trip to Crabtree Valley Mall.

But then Evan returned to his study and pulled out the old yearbook again to stare at the picture. When nothing came to him, he called Neil Copley, his boarding school roommate, now living in Georgia.

"Hollinger, you say?" asked Neil. "Vaguely. Somebody from down here?"

"From school. He was a Rat the year we graduated."

"Dexter Hollinger," repeated Neil. "Wait. Blond kid? Pointy chin?" and when Evan told him yes, Neil chuckled. "Sure, how could I forget him? He was on my hall his first year. Stretch Flex Dex—don't you remember?"

"Nickname like that, you'd think I would."

"He got it running soap races," said Neil, and Evan pictured the game: new boys lined up two at a time on the dorm's coarse industrial carpet, racing to push bars of soap from one end to the other of long hallways—pushing the soap with their noses only. "Dex was like a spider, legs spread out and that skinny ass up in the air, elbows at these wild angles and his head down on its side. Never won a race; always ended up with these *huge* rug burns on his nose, down the side of his face. Then we started calling him Carpet Flecks Dex. How's he doing, anyway? You run into him up there?"

"Got a call from him yesterday." Evan stared at Dexter's picture in the yearbook and tried to imagine carpet burns along the nose, down the side of that jaw. "He'd had some kind of nightmare about me, if you can imagine." Evan told Neil parts of the dream, explained about the dead battery on the Toyota.

"Little freaky, huh?" Neil said when the story was over.

"I didn't even remember the name, remember him at all. But guess if I'd been there for the soap races on your hall, it might have stuck in my memory a little more."

"Well you oughta remember him too," Neil said, in a voice that struck Evan as somehow accusatory. "Dex got sent up a couple of times. You were there at least once."

"Send-up?" said Evan—another phrase that he hadn't heard in nearly two decades—but before he could respond any further, he felt a tugging at his sleeve. Heather in her Strawberry Shortcake pajamas.

"Daddy, how long are you gonna be on the phone?"

"Just a few more minutes, honey. Go play in your room, and I'll come in and read you a story soon, OK?"

"But I want to show you something *now*." Her eyes widened with impatience. She wiggled her hands at her side, the fingers tensed.

"I'll see it in a minute, OK? Just set it all up for Daddy and I'll be there in a minute."

Heather left the room pouting. Evan returned to his call.

"So Dexter got sent up?" Evan pictured the midnight runs, the senior monitors pulling some wayward new boy out of his bunk, standing in a circle to sling curses at him or making him run naked laps around the football field, whatever it took to straighten him out.

"More than once," said Neil. "A complete fuck-up. Fifteen years old and already on the way to being about half-alcoholic. Caught him the first time sneaking off campus, coming back drunk. 'A hundred demerits, if you get caught.' That's what I told him. 'Can you even count that high, Stretch Flex?' He didn't need it. *I* didn't need it. That was the first send-up."

"And what was the next one?" Evan asked, but as soon as Neil told him about the uproar over the pint bottle of Jim Beam they'd found in Dexter's room, Evan had already begun to remember Dexter on his own: a cold night in early December; snow in the air, some of it just barely beginning to stick. A group gathered out beyond the new soccer fields, behind the squash courts, several of the other hall monitors standing in a circle, the formal ceremony done, the cursing and shouting begun, and then the circle parting for Evan, the head monitor, to enter the ranks. The grass had crunched under his feet. A dumb rat—Evan hadn't even known his name, only his offense—down on the ground doing push-ups, his head over a puddle of bourbon one of the others boys had poured onto the dirt. The empty pint bottle lay nearby. "Put your nose in it," Neil had said as the other boys counted: 51, 52, 53. "Sniff it up now because you won't be smelling it again." A chuckle all around, and then another of the monitors had called out, "I'll give him a smell he won't forget." That monitor—Jim Moring had it been? Evan thought he could still see now that mischievous grin, remember the swagger that he walked with. Yes, it must have been Jim who'd asked that question, and then had paused just briefly as he unzipped his pants, turning toward Evan, the ranking Old Boy: "If you approve, sir," he said, half-mocking. And with a grin, Evan had assented: "It'll be a lesson he won't forget. Carry on, good man." Evan had watched it happen, the hoots and high-fives of the other Old Boys. "Bravo, good sir," Evan had said then. "Excellent aim." And he had walked off after that, leaving it to the rest of them. An exam to study for? Just tired and ready for bed? He couldn't remember those details any more than he had recalled the boy's name. And he hadn't even seen his face that night, hadn't asked the next day for any of the monitors to point out the offender. But now it came back to him: the pant and wheeze of the blond-haired Rat struggling to keep his face held just high enough, the dull spattering of urine against the already moist ground.

"Daddy," said Heather, tugging at his arm again. "I need to show you something."

"Not now, honey," said Evan as he listened to Neil tell the story. "In a few, I told you."

"But there are people on my computer," she said, pouting, and then whispering, red-faced: "People without their clothes on. And I don't know how to make them go away."

* * *

"You know," said Dexter, "when I gave you my number on the phone, I kind-of thought I got the brush-off. So I'll admit I was a little surprised when you invited me over for a drink."

"It seemed the right thing to do," said Evan, careful to keep the edge out of his voice, keep his breathing regular.

They were sitting on the back patio now. Dexter was sipping a bourbon. "Still your drink?" Evan had asked earlier, standing at the liquor cabinet, and when Dexter had replied, "Oh, no. Just ginger ale," Evan had said, "Old times' sake," and Dexter had finally agreed. Evan had studied his features carefully for some hint of the boy he'd seen in the yearbook photo, to ferret out what Dexter was thinking about that night behind the squash courts or spur some hidden memory of his own from the halls of the high school. Dexter's features betrayed nothing significant, but Evan noticed that the hand that held the bourbon twitched occasionally, and each time it did, Dexter swirled the glass, as if trying to mask the tic. He hadn't even sipped it yet.

Dexter carried the conversation with the same bumbling, nervous enthusiasm that Evan had heard on the cell phone, now admiring Evan's house and patio and taste in bourbon, commenting on the weather in North Carolina versus Seattle, asking what there was to do around town, chatting about residential real estate prices, commercial real estate prices—covering everything from the meteo-rological climate to the business one.

The tangle of blond hair the younger Dexter had worn was now closely cropped and tightly combed and darker than the picture had shown, and while that lower jaw still jutted firmly, some monument to the fact that things still stood the same, a thick mustache now bal-anced out the bottom half of his face and helped to accentuate the fact that most of the boyishness was long gone. Small furrows stood at the top of his cheeks when he smiled. Fine lines radiated from the corner of his eyes behind his sunglasses. The eyes will betray a liar, his father had once said, but Dexter hadn't taken off those glasses, hadn't dropped the smile.

Everything was hidden, Evan thought, even as he tried to hide all the images replaying in his mind from just a few night's before. Scrambling to shut down the pop-ups filling his daughter's computer screen with lewd pictures. Telling Heather again and again to *go play in the living room, honey, just go* and her just standing there, watch-ing, asking *Is everything all right, Daddy? Did I do something wrong?* And then him finally just ripping the cord from the wall, the outlet's plastic case snapping viciously as he yanked the plug free, and his daughter erupting into tears.

"My wife and I are in an apartment for the time being," Dexter said. Twitch, swirl. "Better to settle in a little and then figure out where to buy, you know. Get the lay of the land. Get the business go-ing."

"Security, right?"

"Did I mention that when we talked?" Dexter's forehead wrinkled. "I guess I must have. You really were paying attention, weren't you? Yes. Spectrum Security is the name." He leaned back, orating now: "'For the Full Spectrum of Security, Always Go With Spectrum Secu-rity.' My wife's idea, actually. She's...."

Evan nodded, not listening. He knew the slogan, had seen it when he went back to the website to get Dexter's number. And seen more then too, studying it more closely. "From your home to your car to your business, we keep you protected throughout the day." And lower down: "If someone's watching, let it be us... watching *out* for you." And then another starburst graphic with the words, "Internet Security a Specialty!" Home, car, internet—all of the details standing out in sharper, more sinister relief. Evan had felt a chill run down his spine as it all came together.

"...and she also suggested that you might know some business or-ganizations around here, networking stuff. Chamber of Commerce, sure, no brainer there, but how 'bout the Jaycees here or anything like that? And it doesn't have to be just business. I mean, my wife would love to meet some more gals around here, I'm sure. She said so herself. In fact, I was sorry your wife couldn't join us. I would've brought Pam over and introduced them."

"Karen's at her mother's," said Evan, bristling inside at Dexter's aw-shucks ramblings. "She doesn't get the chance to see her mother much, so I encouraged her to take a visit." His father's words this time: *Preparation is control. First steps to success.*

"Do tell her I'm sorry I missed her."

"I will," Evan said. But he wouldn't, of course, since Karen didn't know Dexter was there at all, and wouldn't have liked it if she'd known.

So you're saying it's revenge? Karen had asked after she'd come home and calmed Heather enough for bed. *A grown man moving across the country to engineer a dead battery in my car? And to hack into Heather's computer? All because one of your classmates made him do some push-ups twenty years ago?*

His company is all this security stuff, Evan had said, not elaborating on the coarser details of the send-up, not wanting to try to explain or defend that. *He was in the computer club in school. You know the old cliché, Karen. It takes a thief. That's all I'm saying.*

And what was the next part of the dream? Seen any books coming down the hill?

The yearbook I looked through. That could have been it, couldn't it?

You're reaching, Evan. You really are.

And who says it's a real dream and not something he made up? He talked about the two of us trading names, Karen, trading places. You've seen those movies. The babysitter that wants to take the mother's place in the family. The neighbor who admires the family next door a little too much. And what about that Robin Williams movie we rented, huh? The photo guy? This Dexter's got something planned. Who knows what'll happen next.

His concern had grown so great that night that he had double-checked the locks on the front and back door, and he'd checked the nightstand for his gun too, waiting until Karen was in the bathroom to avoid an even sterner look from her. He had the gun in his jacket pocket now.

"Well, I look forward to meeting her another time," said Dexter. "Maybe Pam and I could have the two of you over, huh? Our place isn't much yet, like I said, but—"

"You didn't mention what brought you two back."

Dexter reddened, looked away. The longest break yet in his constant banter.

"Change of pace, I guess," he said finally. A small shrug—clearly evasive. "Seattle had become a little... claustrophobic somehow. Beautiful city, don't get me wrong, but.... All that rain and—" He stopped himself, and Evan saw something breaking loose in Dexter's expression. "Well, that's not entirely true. It's my wife, you see. We've been trying to have a child, you know? Well, of course, you don't know really. I hardly mentioned it on the phone. But we have. Unsuccessfully, I should add. Doctors, treatments. Just doesn't work. And all of our friends, sympathetic, sure, but sympathy.... After awhile, all that pity from them, and then all the *reminder* of their own kids, and us just feeling... envious." His expression had darkened, his nervous energy had smoothed, and as he spoke that last word—a word brimming with raw emotion—Evan felt that he was finally seeing Dexter's true self.

Trouble having a child. Envy for other families. The dream that they'd trade places. Evan thought of his daughter laughing in that tire swing—the only investment that counts—and then crying inconsolably a few nights before—the only investment worth protecting.

Dexter brightened again, abruptly. "Like I said," he went on, with a fragile smile, "change of pace. Tough to make friends, get the business kick-started in a new place...." On and on, but Evan had had enough—he had more than enough. " My wife's actually the one who'd suggested I check and see if anyone was around from the old school and if they might—"

"Have you stopped by campus since you've been back?"

Dexter flinched. "No," he said, a wary look on his face. "Can't say I've found the time."

Evan laid down his drink. "Want to take a drive over there now?"

* * *

The year after Evan graduated, the Rat System had been abolished—an Old Boy pushing the limits too far, an ugly incident with a double-edged razor, parents involved, controversy, condemnation, the end of an era.

Evan couldn't condone the incident, but he was sorry it had shut down the whole system. Some abuse was inevitable, but excusable. Soap races, those rug burns—the Old Boys loved the sport of it, but at least you could argue that it was a bonding experience for the Rats, an initiation of some kind. Minor abuses at worst, and despite them, Evan had believed in the system and the ways it had helped many of these boys become men. So many of them had come in with a sense of entitlement, as if the world belonged to them and should stoop to their wishes, and the system taught them to respect a world that was bigger than they were—to respect community or school or family. Or other people's families. The system punished them when they stepped out of line—put some fear in them when they needed it.

Respect, power, control.

The problem wasn't in pulling out the double-edged razor, or even in pressing it against the skin. The problem had come in actually drawing blood. You just had to know how far to go.

"You passed the front gates," said Dexter from the passenger seat. Evan hadn't even slowed down. Beside them, the brick and iron fence rushed past.

"They've upped security," said Evan. "After 8 p.m., no entry on campus without authorization."

"I guess having been Head Monitor two decades back doesn't carry much weight these days, huh?" Dexter laughed hesitantly, and Evan didn't mention being on the school's board or the pride he took in still being recognized and respected on campus. He didn't mention that he could have gone through the gates with just a wave of his ID. "Oh, well," Dexter said. "Can't say it really matters much."

"Oh, we'll get there yet," said Evan, turning down a side road into a small neighborhood.

"Don't put yourself to any trouble."

"Too late. We're already here."

Houses had always surrounded the school—pictures on the walls of the school's main building showed the campus and community as far back as the Civil War—but that neighborhood had gone through a series of ups and downs over the years: farmer's houses and fields, small suburban homes, expanding city limits. Now it was experiencing a regentrification, a reinvention of itself, with developers coming in and tearing down older single-family homes to build condos. But the more things changed, the more they stayed the same. Through it all, legions of students had escaped the rigors of the school schedule by crossing those fences toward the rear of the campus, escaping into that neighborhood. And now Evan was going to use it in reverse, hoping that security back here was no tighter now that it had ever been.

"I think I snuck off campus once this way myself," said Dexter as they tromped through the woods, leaving the car parked in a dusty construction site for what looked like a series of apartments or townhouses—just the studs, the framing, a skeleton of whatever it would eventually be. "Imagine us now, both of us in our thirties, like kids sneaking back on. We must be crazy or something."

"Or something," said Evan, reaching into his coat to make sure the gun was secure enough for him to climb the chain fence. As he jumped down, it jostled but didn't dislodge. He paid more attention to the pain in his leg. *Not the boy you once were,* he thought, rue-fully. *Those shock absorbers are beginning to wear out.*

Dexter was still on the other side, staring at Evan through the links of the fence.

"You know, sneaking out this way got me in trouble more than once a few years back," he said, his expression uneasy, even behind the sunglasses. "Maybe we should go back to your house, have another drink there."

"It's summer. There's no one back here," Evan said. "Think of it as a bonding experience." He turned and walked away, and soon heard Dexter clambering over the fence.

They walked deeper into the forest, tall oaks and pine trees shadowing the setting sun, making the day appear dimmer than it really was. The air was filled with the smell of honeysuckle from a bank of vines. Hummingbirds flitted toward the flowers. Something rustled through the undergrowth—likely a squirrel, maybe a snake.

"Where does this come out again?" Dexter asked, slowing his step just slightly.

"The old squash courts up there," said Evan, just as the building came into view. Some old maintenance equipment was piled against its walls—an aging red mower, some rusted shears, a coil of wire fencing. "Remember now?"

"I never played," said Dexter, grimly.

"Well, we're not playing today either," said Evan.

As they reached the center of the small, mossy clearing, he turned and pulled out the gun. It felt heavy in his hand, but he pointed it directly into Dexter's face.

The squash courts blocked a view of the full campus, the lush grounds and stately buildings that Evan knew were just around the corner and across the soccer fields. Afternoons during the school year, those fields would be echoing with the shouts and cheers of kids chasing victory—Evan could hear those echoes in his memory now. But after dusk, it was a lonely, desolate spot—a far cry from campus. Literally.

"What the hell is this?" asked Dexter, involuntarily lifting his arms, by reflex it seemed. He struggled to support his faltering smile.

"I'm sure you recognize this place, Dex. What more do I have to say? 'For your transgressions, Dexter Hollinger, you are being sent up before a higher power....'" Though Evan spoke the words mockingly, they rolled smoothly off his tongue, and his mind recited the rest of it as if automatically: *You will submit to the school whose authority you shunned, you will bow before the code you have dishonored, you will recognize the weight of our history, of all the men who have come before you, of all the boys who will follow in your path.* He could still picture some of the new boys who'd come before him and his fellow monitors—each with the same panicked, unbelieving expression that he saw in front of him now. But Dexter should have known better. "You threatened an Old Boy's family, Dex," said Evan, "and there is a price to pay."

"What the hell are you talking about? Threatened somebody's family?"

"*My* family," said Evan. "And you're going to leave them alone."

"Is this a joke?" Dexter dared a small laugh. "I've never even met your family."

"Take off those damn glasses," Evan said, his anger bubbling forth, and when Dexter hesitated, he shouted, "Do it now!"

Dexter removed his sunglasses, and Evan looked into his eyes for the first time. He watched them, looking for the lie, and looking as well at the sides of his face. Had the soap races left any scars there? He almost hoped they had.

"Your dream," he said. "You dreamed about a dead battery, and my wife's car battery went dead just hours after you called."

"And that's my fault?" Dexter met his gaze, challenged it.

"Car security's one of your specialties, right? And Internet security? That filth you put on our computer—on my *daughter's* computer."

"Your daughter," Dexter said, and something in his expression shifted slightly—just the smallest glance to the side, but Evan knew that he'd caught him in the lie. "I never wanted—"

"But what *did* you want, Dex? Revenge for what happened all those years ago? Envy that you couldn't have a child of your own? I've been trying to figure it out myself."

"You've gone too far," he said, and the shift in expression deepened, some small collapse in the cheeks, a sagging at the corners of his lips. "Bringing me out here. You've gone too far."

"I've gone too far? What was the next step for you, Dex? You and me trading names? Wasn't that it? Where was it going to end? I'll tell you where it's going to end. Right here." He took a deep breath, jiggled the gun and then steadied it. He could see the fear in Dexter's eyes, the respect for the gun. A good decision to bring it, just the scare tactic he needed. Respect, power, control. "You have violated the rules," he said, the words coming back to him as if it were yesterday. "You have broken the code. After tonight, you will not step out of line again. After tonight, you will always remember your place." He pointed the gun toward the ground. "Now get down there."

Dexter hesitated.

"Don't make me ask twice," said Evan, leveling the gun at him. "Kneel, Rat."

At the word, Dexter's posture shifted. His eyelid narrowed and the corners of his lips tensed upward again. He straightened his back, and as he did so, his chest moved forward, stood out in pride. He seemed to be reinflating, and to grow about a foot in the process.

"No," he said.

"Get on the ground." Evan waved the gun. "I'm not afraid to use this."

"You won't use it," Dexter said, and his voice was different now, calmer, more focused, more assertive. "You can't even drive through the gates. You're not about to let that gun go off here for everyone to hear. Your car is back in the cul-de-sac, the neighbors back there could have seen us." He stepped forward. "Just admit that and put down the gun."

Evan moved back. "Don't tempt me."

Dexter stepped forward again, and Evan stumbled briefly over some tree roots that had twisted themselves out of the ground and arched across the soil. He caught his balance just in time, aiming again, at Dexter's chest this time.

"Think about it, Evan. We're not kids anymore. I'm not a Rat anymore. That's a gun, not a game."

Double-edged razors, Evan thought then, and he wondered about the boy who'd used them, about why they'd actually been used. Maybe the Rat simply hadn't been scared by the sight of them. Maybe he'd challenged the Old Boy, refused to bow down appropriately. If you didn't gain the respect in the first place, then where was the power? Where was the control? The only choice then was to prove you were willing to go all the way.

But if you're not ready to make good on the threat.... If you're not ready to draw blood, then you might as well put the gun away.

Profit and loss. Investment and return. The photo on the desk—his wife and daughter watching him. He had been doing this for them. But the next step would be too far.

Evan closed his eyes, sighed, then let his grip relax.

"Your turn," Dexter said, and Evan opened his eyes, surprised to see that Dexter had taken the gun from him. He'd been lost in thought. Dexter motioned toward the ground with his free hand.

"What do you mean?" Evan said. "This isn't a game, you said that yourself."

"*You* said it yourself," said Dexter. "Where's it going to end? If I sabotaged your car and your computer, then where would I stop?" There was a glint of evil in his eyes as he raised the gun. "You want me to leave your family alone, then you better do what I say."

* * *

The ground smelled sour, a dank, deep smell, as if the earth here had been shadowed so long by the squash courts and the tall oaks on either side that sunlight had never touched it. Evan felt his breath being almost pulled from him, as if all the oxygen had been cut off by the rank, earthy odor. The blades of grass brushed roughly against his face, and he thought about his daughter, spinning in the tire swing. *I'm doing this for her.*

"I didn't mean for you to lay down," Dexter said from behind him, out of sight. "In fact, you better not let your chest touch the dirt." Evan raised himself up on his hands. "You know what to do— same as you were gonna make me. And I want to hear you count them."

Lifting himself into position, Evan forgot about the dream that Dexter had told him and about the flat tire and the vulgar images that his daughter had been exposed to. Instead, he found himself remembering the bowl of peaches from twenty years before and the grinning face of Crispin Smith tilting it toward him. "Rats like sweet stuff, don't they?" he'd asked with a smirk, and Evan had eaten them all.

Slowly, bitterly, he began to count out the push-ups: "One… two… three…." Despite working out three times a week in the exercise room that he and his wife had set up—the room that would eventually be their second child's—Evan could feel an abnormal strain in his arms, a weakness in his joints. As he counted, he could hear himself wheezing slightly, out of breath. Listening to the pacing behind him, he tried to picture the look on Dexter's face, but all he could see was the boy from the yearbook and the grinning face of Crispin Smith, the two overlaid one across the other.

At twenty-five, he stopped counting, steadied himself at the top of the push-up's arc. "Are you satisfied now?" he asked, tilting his head. Sweat stung his eyes, but he caught Dexter's outline in his peripheral view, stilled for a moment, high up above and behind him.

"You know they killed the Rat System the year after you graduated?" Dexter said simply. "I never got the chance to pass along the fine treatment that you fellas gave me."

"So you've been after revenge all along?"

"I don't hear any counting," Dexter said simply, and he kicked the sole of Evan's shoe lightly.

Evan's muscles tightened—the stress of the push-ups, a jolt of anger pulsing through his arms. Suddenly, his body seemed to replay the sense of dread and revulsion he'd felt eating the peaches all those years ago, a sickness in the stomach.

"Twenty-six," he said through gritted teeth, lowering himself toward the ground, pushing up once more. Behind him, the pacing resumed.

At forty, Dexter spoke again.

"You know what's funny? All I wanted was to sell you a security system. That was all. We move out here and my wife says, 'Wouldn't some of your old friends be good customers?' and she nags me until I call the alumni office and get the list. And when I saw your name.... 'Why haven't you called yet?' Pam kept asking, 'foot in the door, bills to pay,' and I couldn't tell her the truth. And then I started having these... nightmares about it. Middle of the night. Cold sweat. The dream was real. I don't know where the hell it came from, but there it was. And then I thought that I shouldn't run from it again, thought maybe I could use it to my advantage, make a joke out of it, something like, 'Well, after what you guys put me through, the least you could do is send a little business my way.' Because you *did* owe me, I thought. But I was nervous even asking that. And every time I worked up the nerve to come around to it, you cut me off."

Evan had stopped his push-ups again and was propped up awkwardly in the air. He could feel the sweat coursing down his chest and the center of his back, the nausea persistent.

"I'll buy a security system," he said. "If that's it, if that's all you wanted. I'll even pay full price. And give me some business cards. I'll—"

"You think we can just go back and have a business relationship now? Work out a deal? And maybe my wife could come over next time and meet your family, too, huh?" His laugh had a hollow, bitter edge to it.

"It was a mistake, Dex," said Evan, feeling another surge of anger—at Dexter? at himself? But he struggled to keep his tone even. He thought again about his daughter, reading a story to her teddy bears, and about his wife, leaning against the doorway. Whatever it took to get him back to them, away from this. He wouldn't press charges, couldn't tell anyone the story of what had happened. "I see that now. A misunderstanding, and—"

Dexter shoved the muzzle of the gun behind Evan's ear, roughly enough that he could hear the cartilage crinkling inside his head.

"Maybe you didn't hear me earlier," he growled. "I want to hear counting. Rat."

When the metal touched his skin, the nausea surged once more, sickening shudders of it that he'd felt only once before, sitting on the cold tile of the bathroom floor of his freshman dorm, vomiting every few minutes into the toilet and then resting his cheek against the frigid tile. "I hope Crispin Smith drops dead," he'd said to his roommate, sitting beside him. He whispered the words for fear that one of the monitors on his own hall might hear them, that it would mean other consequences. His roommate was empathetic but amused too—something they'd laugh about one day. But Evan had meant it. "I hope he drops dead," concentrating with all his might in hopes that the wish might come true.

The last memory flashed across his mind and through his gut in the second that the gun rested against the back of his ear. Evan turned then, twisted himself over and lunged upward toward the gun. Dexter looked startled, stepped back, stumbled on the same roots that Evan had tripped over before. As he did, the gun went off. A scattered, wild shot, but it found its mark nonetheless, cutting through Evan's neck and clipping an artery.

He died with the taste of peaches, like some bittersweet bile, still lingering on his lips.

* * *

"And you're sticking with that story?" the policeman asked, the hint of a sneer at one corner of his lips. Detective Walters, he'd introduced himself—his third time now with some version of the same question.

"Everything I've told you is the truth," Dexter said, hoping the evidence would prove it. He still had the voicemail with Evan inviting him for drinks. The car out there was Evan's, and the gun they'd just bagged.

"And you say he pulled the gun on you because...?"

"Crazy talk. He thought I was trying to hurt his family. He thought I'd killed the battery on his car, can you believe that?"

"Did you?"

"Of course not." He made sure to meet the detective's accusatory gaze, as if the two of them were in a playground staring contest and not in the midst of a crime scene, with various officers and officials bagging evidence, taking photographs or holding the growing crowd just beyond the yards and yards of yellow tape. Finally Walters turned away.

"Don't go anywhere," he said, pointing a finger back at Dexter. An accusatory gesture there too, Dexter knew, but he'd already fought the impulse to flee when he saw Evan fall to the ground and the blood begin to seep. But he'd fled this place before, and he wasn't going to make that mistake again.

"Run!" he'd heard the Monitors yelling at him that night in the snow. "Run like the Rat that you are!" And he had, the stench of the bourbon and urine still filling his nose, the snow falling harder, mixing with the tears he'd held inside as long as he could, blurring his vision. *I won't look back,* he'd sworn, *no matter what,* trying to block out the cheers and jeers and then block the sensation of the snowballs pelting against his back and then the roar of laughter. But all of it kept echoing in his mind even after he'd made it back to the dorm, and for days later—the taunts and sniggering, the hatred he felt for them and for himself, and the little voice that woke him in the dark of the night, urging him, "Just get them back somehow. Just make them pay. You'll feel better. You will. Just be a man."

But there were consequences to choices like that, of course.

More people pushed against the police tape—people crowding up from the neighborhood where Evan had parked and others emerging from within the campus, faculty members from the school most likely. On both sides people held their hands to their mouths in shock or talked frantically on their cell phones or pointed those phones toward the scene of the crime or the body at the center of it.

Detective Walters stood with a tall, imposing man in a blue sportcoat—the headmaster, Dexter thought, seeming to recognize him from pictures in the alumni magazine. Walters pointed his way, and as the man stared toward him, Dexter felt humbled, like a student once more, waiting to be punished.

As much as he'd tried to grow past the high school, he'd never gotten far from it—that fear of stepping out of line, that desire to make a good impression, always trying to establish himself, always dreaming that this time it will be different, or else trying to make a fresh start somewhere else, hearing the desperation in his own voice as he struggled to impress some stranger and bringing that other voice back into his ears once more, nagging him for his insufficiencies, his weakness, his impotence. Recently, it had returned every more frequently, as business troubles mounted and then as he and his wife struggled with their inability to have a child—*his* inability, *his,* yes, that voice from the past melding with his wife's nagging, pleading, humbling. Not just choice and consequence, but something even crueler to torment him now.

And moving back East—fighting the voice of his insignificance by confronting his fears and the past, some burst of proving himself, twenty years past and wouldn't it be easier now? Choice, consequence, and coincidence now—and all of it cruel this time.

Still, everything he'd told Detective Walters *was* true—even back to the dream that had started it all, or parts of it. No reason, after all, to tell the whole truth.

No reason to talk about having made Evan do those push-ups—or about those other push-ups from twenty years back. He wouldn't admit that he was just using Evan to get a business deal either, and he certainly wouldn't arouse suspicions by telling how he'd broken into Evan's computer. Stopping outside the house to sketch out ideas for a security system, the proposal he was going to pitch Evan. Pulling out the laptop to make notes, seeing the wireless network "Spruill" pop-up, remembering his own dream. A quick breach to underscore the need for security. No real harm done, at least if the daughter hadn't been there. He regretted that part.

And no reason to tell about the voice and how it had come roaring into his ears again when Evan pointed the gun and called him a Rat. A deafening sound, that voice from the past, louder still as he felt the gun in his own hands and then as he forced Evan down on the ground. He would never have answered it, though, would never have pulled the trigger, never actively taken that final, fatal step. But now that revenge had arrived on its own—unbidden, unexpected....

The voice was gone at last, he knew, vanished back into the walls of that squash court and the woods back there and deep down into the soil where Evan lay, facedown in the same spot where Dexter had done his own push-ups all those years before, but Evan looking as if his elbows had simply buckled.

I did them all, Dexter thought then, shame mixed with pride this time. *Seventy-five of them. And over a puddle of liquor and piss.*

Detective Walters came back up. "We need you to make an official statement downtown," he said, a grim look on his face. "And if I find out you're lying, I swear I'm gonna throw the book at you."

Book? Throwing a book? Something about the phrase sent a sudden shiver through Dexter, but he couldn't say why.

"Everything I've told you is the truth," he said again, because what could it hurt, the things he had left out: the fear and trembling that his old Head Monitor still inspired in him; the joy he took in seeing him do those push-ups; the fact that, after all these years, Evan Spruill's death was in some ways like a dream come true.

Rearview Mirror

I hadn't been thinking about killing Delwood. Not really. But you know how people sometimes have just had *enough*. That's what I'd meant when I said it to him, "I could just *kill* you," the two of us sitting in his old Nova in front of a cheap motel on Route 66—meaning it just figurative, even if that might seem at odds with me sliding his pistol into my purse right after I said it.

And even though I was indeed thinking hard about taking my half of the money and maybe a little more—*literal* now, literally *taking* it—I would not call it a double-cross. Just kind of a divorce and a divorce settlement, I guess. Even though we weren't married. But that's not the point.

Sometimes people are just too far apart in their wants—that's what Mama told me. Sometimes things just don't work out.

That was the point.

* * *

"Why don't we take the day off," I'd asked Del earlier that morning up in Taos, a Saturday, the sun creeping up, the boil not yet on the day, and everything still mostly quiet in the mobile home park where we'd been renting on the bi-weekly. "We could go buy you a suit, and I could get a new dress. And then maybe we'd go out to dinner. To Joseph's Table maybe. Celebrate a little."

He snorted. "Louise," he said, the way he does. "What's it gonna look like, the two of us, staying out here, paycheck to paycheck, economical to say the least"—he put a little emphasis on *economical*, always liking the sound of anything above three syllables—"and then suddenly going out all spiffed up to the nicest restaurant in town?" He looked at me for a while, and then shook his head.

"We don't have to go to the nicest restaurant," I said, trying to compromise, which is the mark of a good relationship. "We could just go down to the bar at the Taos Inn and splurge on some high-dollar bourbon and a couple of nice steaks." I knew he liked steaks, and I could picture him smiling over it, chewing, both of us fat and happy. So to speak, I mean, the fat part being figurative again, of course.

"We told Hal we'd vacate the premises by this morning. We agreed."

Hal was the man who ran the mobile home park. A week or so before, Del had told him he'd finally gotten his degree and then this whole other story about how we'd be moving out to California, where Del's sister lived, and how we were gonna buy a house over there.

"Sister?" I had wanted to say when I overheard it. "House?" But then I realized he was just laying the groundwork, planning ahead so our leaving wouldn't look sudden or suspicious. Concocting a story—I imagine that's the way he would have explained it, except he didn't explain it to me but just did it.

That's the way he was sometimes: a planner, not a communicator. *Taciturn*, he called it. Somewhere in there, in his not explaining and my not asking, he had us agreeing. And now he had us leaving.

"OK," I told Del. "We'll just go then. But how 'bout we rent a fancy car? A convertible maybe. A nice blue one." And I could see it—us cruising through the Sangre de Christos on a sunny afternoon, the top slid back and me sliding across the seat too, leaning over toward him, maybe kicking my heels up and out the window. My head would be laid on his shoulder and the wind would slip through my toes and the air conditioner would be blowing full-blast since June is the Southwest is already hot as blazes. Now *that* would be nice.

"No need to blow this windfall on some extravagance," he said. "No need to call attention to ourselves unnecessarily. Our car works fine."

He headed for it then—that old Nova. Little spots of rust ran underneath the doors and up inside the wheel well. A bad spring in the seat always bit into my behind. Lately, the rearview mirror had started to hang just a little loose—not so that Delwood couldn't see in it, but enough that it rattled against the windshield whenever the road got rough.

I stood on the steps with my hip cocked and my arms crossed, so that when he turned and looked at me in that rearview mirror, he'd know I was serious. But he just climbed in the car, and sat there staring ahead. Nothing to look back at, I guess. He'd already packed the trunk while I slept. The mobile home behind us was empty of the few things we owned.

"A new day for us," he'd whispered an hour before when he woke me up, but already it seemed like same old, same old to me.

When I climbed in beside him, I slammed the passenger-side door extra hard and heard a bolt come loose somewhere inside it.

"It figures," I said, listening to it rattle down. The spring had immediately dug into my left rump.

Del didn't answer. Just put the car in gear and drove ahead.

* * *

When I first met Del, he was robbing the 7-11 over in Eagle Nest, where I worked at that time. This was a about year ago. I'd just been sitting behind the counter, reading one of the *Cosmo*s off the shelf, when in comes this fellow in jeans and a white t-shirt and a ski mask, pointing a pistol.

"I'm not gonna hurt you," he said. "I'm not a bad man. I just need a little boost in my income."

I laid the *Cosmo* facedown on the counter so that I wouldn't lose my place. "You're robbing me?" I said.

"Yes, ma'am."

I bit my lip and shook my head—no no no—just slightly.

"I'm only 26," I said.

He looked over toward the Doritos display—not looking at it, but just pointing his head in that direction the way some people stare into space whenever they're thinking. He had a mustache and a beard. I could see the stray hairs poking out around the bottom of the ski mask and near the hole where his mouth was.

"Excuse me?" he said finally, turning back to face me. His eyes were this piney green.

"I'm not a ma'am."

He held up his free hand, the one without the pistol, and made to run it through his hair—another sign of thinking—but with the ski mask, it just slid across the wool. "Either way, could you hurry it up a little. I'm on a schedule."

Many reasons for him to be frustrated, I knew. Not the least of which was having to wear wool in New Mexico in the summer.

He glanced outside. The gas pumps were empty. Nothing but darkness on the other side of the road. This time of night, we didn't get much traffic. I shrugged, opened the cash register.

"You know," I said, as I bent down for a bag to put his money in. "You have picked the one solitary hour that I'm alone in the store, between the time that Pete has to head home for his mom's curfew and the time that our night manager strolls in for his midnight to six."

"I know. I've been watching you." Then there was a little nervous catch in his voice. "Not in a bad way, I mean. Not *voyeuristically*." He enunciated that word, and then the next one too. "Just *surveillance*, you know. I'm not a pervert."

I kept loading the register into the bag. "You don't think I'm worth watching?"

Again, with the ski mask, I can't be sure, but he seemed to blush.

"No. I mean, yes," he said. "You're very pretty."

I nodded. "There's not much money here we have access to, you know? A lot of it goes straight to the safe. That's procedure."

"I'm a fairly frugal man," he said. "Sometimes I just need a little extra for… tuition."

"Tuition?"

"And other academic expenses."

"Academic expenses," I repeated, not a question this time. I thought that he had a nice voice, and then I told him so. "You have a nice voice," I said. "And pretty eyes." I gave him my phone number, not writing it down because the security camera would have picked that up, but just told him to call, repeating the number twice so he would remember it. "And my name is Louise."

"Thanks," he said, "Louise."

"Good luck with your education," I called after him, but the door had already swung closed. I watched him run out toward the pumps and beyond, admired the way his body moved, the curve of his jeans, for as long as I could make him out against the darkness. I gave him a head start before I dialed 911.

* * *

I know what you're thinking. You're thinking that I was some bored, bubble-gum-popping, *Cosmo*-reading girl, just out of her teens and disillusioned with the real world and tired already of being a grown-up and then along comes this bad boy and, more than that, *literally* a criminal and… well, sure, there's some truth there. But here again, you'd be missing the point.

It wasn't exciting that he robbed convenience stores.

It was exciting that he was brave enough to call me afterwards, *especially* in this age of Caller ID when I had his phone number and name immediately—Grayson, Delwood—and could have sent the police after him in a minute.

That *Cosmo* article? The one I was reading when he showed up in the ski mask? "Romantic Gestures Gone Good: Strange but True Stories of How He Wooed and Won Me."

Not a one of those stories held a candle to hearing Del's voice on the other end of the phone: "Hello, Louise? I, um… robbed your 7-11 the other night, and I've been percolating on our conversation ever since. Are you free to talk?"

That takes a real man, I thought. And—don't forget those academic expenses—a man who might just be *going* somewhere.

* * *

But it had been a long time since I believed we were going anywhere fast. Or anywhere at all.

We took the High Road down from Taos. That figured too: two lanes, 45 miles per hour.

"Afraid they'll get you for speeding?" I asked.

"One thing might lead to another," he said. "And anyway, the rental place stressed that it was dangerous to exceed the speed limit while pulling the trailer here."

As we drove, he kept looking up into the rearview mirror, nervously, as if any second a patrol car really was gonna come tearing around the bend, sirens wailing, guns blasting. He had put his own pistol in the glove compartment. I saw it when I went for a Kleenex.

"If we get pulled, are you gonna use it?"

He didn't answer, but just glanced up again at the mirror, which rattled against the windshield with every bump and curve.

* * *

I was doing a little rearview looking as well, I guess.

Here's the thing. Even if I had become a little *disillusioned* with Del, I don't believe I had become *disappointed* in him—not yet.

I mean, like I said, he was a planner. I'd seen my mama date men who couldn't think beyond which channel they were gonna turn to next, unless there was a big game coming up, and then their idea of planning was to ask her to pick up an extra bag of chips and dip for their friends. I myself had dated men who would pick me up and give me a kiss and then ask, "So, what do you want to do tonight," having had no idea what we *might* do except that we *might* end up in the backseat or even back at their apartment. I'm sorry to admit it with some of those men, but most times we did.

On the other hand, take Del. When he picked me up for our first date, I asked him straight out, "So where does the desperate criminal take the sole witness to his crime on their first date?" I was admiring how he looked out from under that ski mask—his beard not straggly like I'd been afraid, but groomed nice and tight, and chiseled features, I guess you'd call them, underneath that. Those green eyes looked even better set in such a handsome face. He'd dressed up a little too: a button-down shirt, a nice pair of khakis. He was older than I'd expected, older than me. Thirties maybe. Maybe even late thirties. A little grey in his beard. But I kind-of liked all that too.

"A surprise," said Del, and didn't elaborate, but just drove out of Eagle Nest and out along 64, and all of a sudden I thought, *Oh, wait, desperate criminal, sole witness.* My heart started racing and not in a good way. But then he pulled into Angel Fire and we went to Our Place for dinner. (Our Place! That's really the name.) And then my heart started racing in a better way.

And then there's the fact that he did indeed finish his degree at the community college, which shows discipline and dedication. And then coming up with that story about his sister and why we were moving, laying out a cover story in advance, always thinking ahead. And then planning for the heist itself—the "big one," he said, "the last one," though I knew better. Over the last year, whenever tuition came due, he'd hit another 7-11 or a gas station or a DVD store—"shaking up the modus operandi," he said, which seemed smart to me, but maybe he just got that from the movies he watched on our DVD player. He'd stolen that too.

* * *

That was how we spent most of our nights together, watching movies. I'd quit the 7-11 job at that point—it was too dangerous, Del said—*ironically*, he said—and got a job at one of the gift stores in town, so I was home nights. Home meaning Del's mobile home, that is, because it wasn't long before I'd moved in with him.

We'd make dinner—something out of a box because I'm not much of a cook, I'll admit—and I'd watch Court TV, which I love, while he did some of his homework for the business classes he was taking over at the college or read through the day's newspaper, scouring the world for opportunities, he said, balancing work and school and me. And then we'd watch a movie, usually something with a crime element like *Ocean's Eleven* or *Mission: Impossible* or some old movie like *The Sting* or *Butch Cassidy and the Sundance Kid* or all those *Godfather* movies like every man I've ever been with. I suggested *Bonnie & Clyde* a couple of times, for obvious reasons, but he said it would be *disadvantageous* for us to see it and so we never did.

"Is that all you do, sit around and watch movies?" Mama asked on the phone, more than once.

"We go out some too," I told her.

"*Out* out?" she asked, and I didn't know quite what she meant and I told her that.

"He surprises me sometimes," I said. "Taking me out for dinner."

(Which was true. "Let's go out for a surprise dinner," he'd say sometimes, even though the surprise was always the same, that we were just going to Our Place. But that was still good because it really was *our* place—both literally *and* figuratively—and there's romance in that.)

"He loves me," I'd tell Mama. "He holds me close at night and tells me how much he loves me, how much he can't live without me."

Mama grunted. She was in North Carolina. Two hours time difference and almost a full country away, but still you could feel her disappointment like she was standing right there in the same room.

"That's how it starts," Mama would tell me, "I can't live without you," mimicking the voice. "Then pretty soon 'I can't live without you' starts to turn stifling and sour and...."

Her voice trailed off. *And violent,* I knew she'd wanted to say.

And I knew where she was coming from, knew how her last boyfriend had treated her. I'd seen it myself, one of the reasons I finally just moved away, anywhere but there.

"I thought you were going to start a *new* life," she said, a different kind of disappointment in her voice then. "You could watch the tube and drink beer anywhere. You could date a loser here if that's all you're doing."

I twirled the phone cord in my hand, wanting just to be done with the conversation, but not daring to hang up. Not yet.

"Frugal," Mama said, making me regret again some of the things I'd told her about him. "Frugal's just a big word for cheap."

* * *

"Are things gonna be different someday?" I'd asked Del one night, the two of us laying in bed, him with his back to me. I ran my fingers across his shoulder when I asked it.

"Different?" he asked.

"Different from this."

He didn't answer at first, and so I just kept rubbing his shoulder and then let my hand sneak over and rub the top of his chest, caressing it real light, because I knew he liked that. The window was slid open and a breeze rustled the edge of those thin little curtains. Just outside stood a short streetlight, one that the mobile home park had put up, and sometimes it kept me awake, shining all night, like it was aiming right for my face, leaving me sleepless.

After a while, I realized Del wasn't gonna answer at all, and I stopped rubbing his chest and turned over.

That night when I couldn't sleep, I knew it wasn't the streetlight at all.

* * *

For that *big* one, that *last* last one, Del had roamed those art galleries in downtown Taos after work at the garage. He watched the ads for gallery openings, finding a place that stressed *cash only,* real snooty because you know a lot of people would have to buy that artwork on time and not pay straight out for it all at once, but those weren't the type of people they were after. He'd looked up the address of the gallery owner, the home address, and we'd driven past that too.

I liked watching his mind work: the way he'd suddenly nod just slightly when we were walking across the Plaza or down the walkway between the John Dunn Shops, like he'd seen something important. Or the way his eyes narrowed and darted as we rode throughout the neighborhood where the gallery owner lived, keeping a steady speed, not turning his head, not *looking* as if he was looking.

We had a nice time at the gallery opening itself, too. At least at the beginning. Del looked smart in his blue blazer, even though it was old enough that it had gotten a little shine. And you could see how happy he was each time he saw a red dot on one of the labels— just more money added to the take—even if he first had to ask what each of those red dots meant. I hated the gallery owner's tone when he answered that one, as if he didn't want Del or me there drinking those plastic cups of wine or eating the cheese. The gallery owner had a sleek suit, and his thin hair was gelled back dramatically, and he wore these square purple spectacles that he looked over when he was answering Del, and I couldn't help but feel a little resentful toward him. But then I thought, *He'll get his*, if you know what I mean. And, of course, he did.

"I like this one," I said in front of one of the pictures. It was a simple picture—this painting stuck in the back corner. A big stretch of blue sky and then the different colored blue of the ocean, and a mistiness to it, like the waves were kicking up spray. Two people sat on the beach, a man and a woman. They sort-of leaned into one another, watching the water, and I thought about me and Del and began to feel nostalgic for something that we'd never had. The painting didn't have a red dot on it, but it did have a price: $3000.

"With the money," I whispered to Del, "we could come back here and buy one of them, huh? Wouldn't that be ballsy? Wouldn't that be *ironic*?"

"Louise," he said, that tone again, telling me everything.

"I'm just saying," I said. "Can't you picture the two of us at the ocean like that? Maybe with the money, we could take a big trip, huh?"

"Can't you just enjoy your wine?" he whispered, and moved on to the next picture, not looking at it really, just at the label.

"Fine," I said after him, deciding I'd just stay there and let him finish casing out the joint, but then a couple came up behind me.

"Let's try *s* on this one," the woman whispered.

"S," said the man. "OK. S." They looked at the couple on the beach, and I looked with them, wondering what they meant by "trying *s*." The man wrinkled his brow, squinted his eye, scratched his chin—like Del when's he's thinking, but this man seemed to be only playing at thinking. "Sappy," he said finally.

"Sentimental," said the woman, quick as she could.

"Um.... Sugary."

"Saccharine."

"OK. No fair," said the man. "You're just playing off my words."

The woman smirked at him. She had a pretty face, I thought. Bright, blue eyes and high cheekbones and little freckles across them. She had on a gauzy top, some sort of linen, and even though it was just a little swath of fabric, you could tell from the texture of it and the way she wore it and from her herself that it was something fine. I knew, just knew suddenly, that it had probably cost more than the money Del had stolen from the 7-11 the night I first met him. And I knew too that I wanted a top just like it.

"Fine," she said, pretending to pout. "Here's another one. Schmaltzy."

"Better! Um…. Sad."

"No, *this* is sad," she said, holding up her own plastic wine glass.

"Agreed." He laughed.

"Swill," she whispered, dragging out the *s* sound, just touching his hand with her fingers, and they both giggled as they moved on to the next picture. And the next letter too, it turned out. T was for *tarnished*, for *trashy*, for *tragic*.

Del had made the full circuit. Even from across the room, I could see the elbows shining on his blazer. Then he turned and saw me and made a little side-nod with his head, motioning toward the door. Time to head back home.

I looked once more at the painting of the couple on the beach. I'd thought it was pretty. Still did.

I'd thought the wine had tasted pretty good, too.

But suddenly it all left a bad taste in my mouth.

* * *

A bad taste still as we drove south now.

The steep turns and drop-offs that had taken us out of Taos had given way to little villages, small homes on shaded road, people up and about, going about their lives. I saw a couple of signs pointed toward the Santuario de Chimayó, which I'd visited when I first moved out this way, picking Northern New Mexico just because it seemed different, in every way, from where I'd grown up. I'd found out about the church in Chimayo from a guidebook I'd ordered off the Internet, learned about the holy earth there and how it healed the sick. When I'd visited it myself, I gathered up some of the earth and then mailed it off to Mama —not that she was sick, but just unhappy. I don't know what I'd imagined she'd do with it, rub it on her heart or something. "Thanks for the dirt," she told me when she got it.

"Do you think they've found him yet?" I asked Del.

"They?"

"I don't know, Del. The police. Or the cleaning lady or a customer."

We were nearing another curve and Del eased the Nova around it slowly, carefully.

"Probably somebody will have found him by now. Like I told you last night, I tied him up pretty good, so I don't think he'd have gotten loose on his own. But by now...."

He sped up a little bit. I don't think he did it consciously, but I noticed.

A little while later, I asked "Are we gonna do *anything* fun with the money?"

"What kind of fun?"

"I don't know. Clothes, jewelry... a big-screen TV, a vacation. Something fun."

He scratched his beard. "That's just extravagance."

"Are you gonna make *all* the decisions?"

"All the good ones," he said. He gave a tense little chuckle. "Don't you ever consider the future?"

But again, he missed what I was saying. The future is *exactly* what I was thinking about.

* * *

We bypassed Santa Fe proper, and then Del had us two-laning it again on a long road toward Albuquerque: miles and miles of dirt hills and scrubby little bushes, some homes that looked like people still lived there and others that were just crumbling down to nothing. The Ortiz Mountains standing way out in the distance. We got stuck for a while behind a dusty old pickup going even slower than we were, but Del was still afraid to pass. So we just poked along behind the truck until it decided to turn down some even dustier old road, and every mile we spent behind it, my blood began to boil up a little more.

I know Del was picturing roadblocks out on the interstate, and helicopters swooping low, waiting for some rattling old Nova like ours to do something out of the ordinary, tip our hand—even more so after I asked about that gallery owner getting loose. But after awhile, I just wanted to scream, "Go! Go! Go!" or else reach over and grab the wheel myself, stretch my leg over and press down on the gas, hurl us ahead somehow and out of all this. And then there was all the money in the trunk and all the things I thought we could have done with it but clearly weren't going to do. Once or twice, I even thought about pulling out that pistol myself and pointing it at him. "I don't want anybody to get hurt," I might say, just like he would. "Just do like I ask, OK?" That was the first time I thought about, and that wasn't even serious.

Still, it was all I could to hide all that impatience, all that restlessness and nervous energy. None of it helped by that tap tap tap tap tap of the mirror against the windshield. I felt like my skin was turning inside out.

"I need to pee," I said, finally.

"Next place I see," said Del, a little glance at me, one more glance in the rearview. I looked in the side mirror. Nothing behind us but road. I looked ahead of us. Nothing but road. I looked around the car. Just me and him and that damn mirror tapping seconds into minutes and hours and more.

* * *

We stopped in Madrid, which isn't pronounced like the city in Spain but with the emphasis on the first syllable: MAD-rid. It used to be a mining town back in the Gold Rush days, but then dried up and became a ghost town. Now it's a big artist's community. I didn't know all that when we pulled in, but there was a brochure.

We parked lengthwise along the road by one of the rest stops at one end of the town—outhouse more like it. Del waited in the car, but after I was done, I tapped on his window. "I'm gonna stretch my legs," I said, and strolled off down the street before he could answer. I didn't care whether he followed, but pretty soon I heard the scuff scuff of his feet on the gravel behind me. I really did need a break, just a few minutes out of the car, and it did help some, even with him following. We walked on like that, him silent behind me except for his footsteps as I picked up that brochure and looked in the store windows at antiques and pottery and vintage cowboy boots. Fine arts too. "Wanna make one *last* last job?" I wanted to joke. Half-joke. "Get something for *me* this time?"

I walked in one store. Del followed. I just browsed the shelves. The sign outside had advertised "Local artisans and craftspeople," and the store had quirky little things the way those kinds of places do: big sculptures of comical looking cowboys made out of recycled bike parts, close-up photographs of rusted gas pumps and bramblebush, hand-dipped soy candles, gauzy looking scarves that reminded me about the woman at the gallery the night before. I browsed through it all, taking my time, knowing that Del was right up on me, almost feeling his breath on my back.

One shelf had a bowl full of sock-monkey keychains. A little cardboard sign in front of the bowl said, "Handcrafted. $30."

"Excuse me," I called over to the man behind the counter. He'd been polishing something and held a red rag in his hand. "Is this the price of the bowl or of the monkeys?"

"Oh," he said, surprised, as if he'd never imagined someone might misunderstand that. "The monkeys," he said, then corrected himself:

"*Each* monkey," he said. "The bowl's not for sale at all."

I turned to Del.

"Why don't you get me one of these?" I asked him, holding up a little monkey.

I tried to say it casual-like, but it was a challenge. I felt like both of us could hear it in my voice. Even the man behind the register heard it, I imagine, even though he'd made a show of going back to his polishing.

"What would you want with a thing like that?" Del said.

"Sometimes a girl likes a present. It makes her feel special." I dangled the sock monkey on my finger in front of him, and Del watched it sway, like he was mesmerized or suspicious. "Or is the romance gone here?"

"It's kind of pricey for a keychain."

I leaned in close for just a second, whispered, "Why don't you just slip it in your pocket then?"

Del cut his eyes toward the man behind the counter, and then turned back to me. His look said *hush*. "I told you last night was the last time," he said, a low growl.

I just swayed that monkey a little more.

A woman in green dress jingled through the door then and went up to the counter. "You were holding something for me," she said, and the man put down his polish rag, and they started talking.

You could tell that Del was relieved not to have a witness anymore. "C'mon, Louise," he said. "Be serious."

But me? For better or worse, I just upped the ante.

"Suppose I said to you that this monkey"—I jerked my finger so that his little monkey body bounced a little—"this monkey represents love to me."

"Love?" he said.

"The potential for love," I clarified. "The possibility of it."

'How's that?"

"Well, suppose I told you that my daddy, the last time I saw him, me only six years old, he comes into my bedroom to tuck me in and he gives me a little sock-puppet monkey, bigger than this one, but looking pretty much the same" (because the truth is they all do, handcrafted or not) "and he says to me, 'Hon, Daddy's going away for a while, but while I'm gone, this little monkey is gonna take care of you, and any time you find yourself thinking of me or wondering about me, I want you to hug this monkey close to you, and I'll be there with you. Wherever I am, I'll be here with you.' And he touched his heart."

I wasn't talking loud, but the man behind the counter and the customer had grown quiet, listening to me now even as they pretended not to. It was a small store, they couldn't help it. Del wasn't sweating, not really, but with all the attention—two witnesses to our argument now—he looked like he was or was just about to break out into one.

"And Mama was behind him, leaned against the door watching us," I went on. "Anyone probably could have seen from her face that he wasn't coming back and that it was her fault and she felt guilty, but I was too young to know that then. And I dragged that monkey around with me every day and slept with it every night and hugged it close. And finally Mama threw it away, which told me the truth. 'Men let you down,' she told me when I cried about it, because she'd just broken up with her latest boyfriend and had her own heart broken, I guess. 'Men *always* let you down,' she told me. 'Don't you ever fool yourself into forgetting that.' And I stopped crying. But still, whatever Mama told me and whether my daddy came back or not, I believed—I *knew*—that there *had* been love there, there in that moment, in that memory, you know?"

Del looked over at the wall, away from the shopkeeper and his customer, and stared at this sculpture of a cowboy on a bucking bronco—an iron silhouette. The tilt of his head and the nervous look in his eyes reminded me of the first night we'd met, at the 7-11, when he'd called me "Ma'am" and I'd told him my age. Seemed like here was another conversation where he was playing catch up, but this time he seemed fearful for different reasons.

"And maybe," I said, helping him along, "just maybe if you bought this for me for, I'd know you really loved me, for always and truly. Now," I said, "would *that* get it through your thick skull?'

Out of the corner of my eye, I saw an embarrassed look on the storekeeper's face—embarrassed for Del and maybe a little embarrassed for me too. His customer, the woman in green, cleared her throat, and the shopkeeper said to her, "Yes, ma'am, just let me find that for you."

Del shifted his lower jaw to the side—another indication, I'd learned, that his mind was working on something, weighing things. He really was sweating now, and still staring at that bucking bronco sculpture like he felt some kinship with the cowboy on top, like staring at it might give him an answer somehow.

"What was your monkey's name?" he asked me.

I gave out a long sigh, with an extra dose of irritation in it. He was missing the whole point, just like always. "I don't know," I told him. I sighed again. "Murphy," I said.

His look changed then, just a little crease of the forehead, a little raise of the eyebrow. "Murphy the monkey?" he said. He wasn't looking at the sculpture now, wasn't looking afraid anymore but something else entirely. "Well, Louise," he began. "I don't really think that this monkey represents the love we share, and the truth is that thirty dollars seems like quite a bit for—"

But I didn't hear the rest of it. I just put that monkey down, then turned and walked off, out the door, slamming it behind me the way I'd slammed the Nova's door that morning and stomping off fast back toward the car.

I can't say whether I wanted him to call for me to come back or rush out after me, something dramatic like that, but if I did, I was indeed fooling myself, just like Mama had warned. That wasn't Delwood. When I got in the car, I saw him through the window, slowly coming back—those sad little footsteps, scuff scuff scuff. No hurry at all, like he knew I'd be waiting.

* * *

We rode on in silence after that—a heavy silence, you know what I mean. More ghost towns where people used to have hopes and dreams and now there was nothing but a little bit of rubble and a long stretch of empty land. I wasn't even angry now, but just deflated, disappointed.

"Men will do that to you," my mama told me another time. "After a while you feel like it's not even worth trying." I'd known what she meant, theoretically. Now I knew in a different way.

Soon the two-lane widened, and the strip malls started up and fast food restaurants—civilization. I saw a Wendy's, and asked if it was OK to stop.

"I'll pick from the dollar menu," I said, sarcastic-like.

Del didn't say anything, just pulled through the drive-thru and ordered what I wanted. He didn't get anything for himself. I think it was just out of spite.

* * *

Late afternoon, we cruised through Winslow, Arizona, which I guess would get most people in the mind of that Eagles song. Standing on a corner and all that. But it had me thinking of the past and my old high school flame. Winslow was his name, Win everybody called him, and I couldn't help but start indulging those what-ifs about everything I'd left behind. It was a fleeting moment, Win and I had had our own troubles, of course, but it struck me hard, discontented as I was with things and people—thinking myself about running down the road and trying to loosen my own load.

Then toward evening, we stopped at a motel in Kingman, one of those cheap ones that have been there since Route 66 was an interesting road and not just a tourist novelty—the ones that now looked like they'd be rented for the hour by people who didn't much care what the accommodations were like.

Del checked us in, pulled the Nova around to the stairwell closest our room.

"Get your kicks," I said.

"Kicks?" he said, baffled.

"Route 66," I said, pointing to a sign. "Guess we couldn't afford the Holiday Inn either, huh?"

He stared straight ahead, drummed his fingers light against the steering wheel. He curled up his bottom lip a little and chewed on his beard.

"You know those court shows you watch on TV?" Del said finally. "And how you tell me some of those people are so stupid? You listen to their stories and you laugh and you tell me, 'That's where they went wrong' or 'They should've known better than that.'"

"Do you mean," I said, "something like a man who robs a convenience store and then calls up the clerk he's held at gunpoint and asks her out for a date?" I felt bad about it as soon as I said it. Part of why I fell in love with him and now I was complaining about it.

"There were extenuating circumstances in that instance," he said, and this warning sound had crept into his tone, one that I hadn't heard before. "I'm just saying that we need to be fairly circumspect now about whatever we do. Any misstep might put us in front of a real judge, and it won't be a laughing matter, I can guarantee you that." He turned to face me. "Louise," he said, again that way he does. "I love you, Louise, but sometimes.... Well, little girl, sometimes you just don't seem to be thinking ahead."

It was the *little girl* that got me, or maybe the *extenuating* or the *circumspect*, or maybe just him implying that I was being stupid, or maybe all of it, the whole day.

"Del," I said through clenched teeth, putting a little emphasis on his name, too. "I love you too, and when I say that, I mean it. But sometimes, Del, sometimes, I could just kill you."

He nodded. "Well," he said, slow and even as always, but still with that edge of warning to it, "I guess you'd go to jail for that too." He handed the room key across to where I sat. "You go on in. I want to check that things haven't shifted too badly in the back."

"Fine," I said, toughening the word up so he could hear how I felt. He stared at me for a second, then went back to get our bags. In the rearview, I watched him open the trunk, but still I just sat there.

I don't know how to describe what I was feeling. Anger? Sadness? I don't know what was running through my head, either. What to do next, I guess. Whether to go up to the room and carry on like we'd planned, like he seemed to expect I'd do, or to step out of all this, literally just step out of the car and start walking in another direction.

But then I knew if I really did leave, he'd come after me. Not dramatic, not begging, but I knew he wouldn't let me go. Can't live without you, that's what he'd said, and like Mama said, sometimes that kind of love could turn ugly fast. I'd seen it before.

"You just gonna sit there?" Del called out, the trunk blocking my view, just a voice behind me. More rearranging, I guess.

"No. I'm going up," I called back, calling to the reflection of the trunk lid, I realized. Then just before I stepped out of the car, I opened up the glove compartment and slipped the gun into my purse.

* * *

In the motel room, I locked the door to the bathroom, set down my purse, and then turned the water on real hot before climbing in. I stood there in the steam and rubbed that little bitty bar of soap over me, washing like I had layers of dust from those two lane roads and that truck we'd followed for so long.

I thought about what would happen after I got out. "Sometimes people are just too far apart in their wants," I could say. "I do love you, Del, but sometimes people just need to move on." It was just a matter or saying it. It would be easy to do, I knew. I'd done it before back with Win all those years ago, and I hadn't needed a gun to do it then. But the gun showed I was serious in a different way. More than that, it was protection. "I'm not taking all the money, Del," I might say. "That's not what's going on here. That's not the point." As if he had *ever* got the point.

I took both towels when I got out of the shower. The steam swirled around me while I stood there toweling myself off—one towel wrapped around me and one towel for my hair, leaving him none.

Would he try to talk me out of it? Would he try to take the gun away? Would I have to tie him up the way he'd left that gallery owner back in Taos? Just thinking about it made me sad.

He was sitting there when I came out of the bathroom, sitting on the one chair in the room, staring at the blank television, the screen of it covered in a light layer of dust. I hadn't taken the gun out, but just held my purse in my hand, feeling the weight of it. Thinking that I might have to use it.

I suddenly wished I'd gotten dressed first. I mean, picture it: Me wrapped in two towels and holding a gun? Hardly a smooth getaway.

Del's face was... well, *pensive* was the word that came to mind. He taught me that word, I thought. I wouldn't have known it without him. And that kept me from saying immediately what I needed to say. So I just stood there, feeling little bits of water still dripping out of my hair and onto my shoulders and then down my back.

"You never talked much about your daddy," he said, breaking the silence. "He really leave you when you were six?"

"Yes," I said, and I realized then that I felt like I was owed something for that.

Del nodded, stared at the blank television. I looked there too, at the gray curve of the screen. I could see his face there, reflected toward me, kind of distorted, distant.

"He really give you a sock monkey when he left?"

I thought about that, too, but I was thinking now about what I owed Del.

"No," I told him, and I could hear the steel in my own voice "But what Mama said, she did say that."

I stared hard at the dusty TV screen, at his reflection there. I saw then that his fists were clenched, and that he clenched them a little tighter at my answer, and I could feel myself tighten too. I knew then that he knew the pistol was gone. I didn't take my eyes off that reflection as I pulled up the strap of my pocketbook, just in case he stood up quick and rushed me. But he dropped his head down a little, and then I saw his profile in the reflection, which meant he'd turned to see me straight on.

"So you lied to me then?" He was clenching his hand hard, so much that if I'd been closer, I might have backed away. But there was a bed between us. And the pocketbook was open now.

"If that's what you want to take from it."

His eyes watched me hard. Those green eyes. First thing I'd really noticed about him up close.

"Do you believe Cora was right?"—meaning Mama. That's her name.

"I don't know. Do you?

Those eyes narrowed. Thinking again. And it struck me that I could just about list every little thing he did when he was pondering over something: how he sometimes stared hard at the wall or other times stared off into space with this faraway gaze, running his fingers through his hair or through the tip of his beard, biting at his bottom lip a little or chewing on that beard or just shifting his jaw one way or the other. Usually left, I corrected myself. Always to the left. And sure enough, just as I thought it, he shifted his jaw just that way, setting it in place.

I almost laughed despite myself. *Men always let you down*, Mama had said, but Del had come through with his little jaw jut exactly like expected. At least you could count on him for that. And all of a sudden, I felt embarrassed for having taken that purse from the glove compartment, just wanted to run out in my towel and put it back.

"Do you want a surprise?" he asked, and I almost laughed again. "It's a long drive back to Our Place."

"A new surprise."

"Sure," I said.

"The story we told back at the mobile home park, about me having a sister out in Victorville," he said then. "I really do. Haven't talked to her in a while. We were estranged." He stretched out the word. "She's in real estate. Got us a deal she worked out on a foreclosure. A little house. Said she'd let me do some work for her, at her company, now that I have a degree. It's all worked out. I just needed to get the downpayment on it, so I figured, well, one more job. One big one and that'd be it." He tapped his hand on the side of the chair, like you would tap your fingers, but his whole hand because it was still clenched. I think it was the most words he'd ever said in one breath. "That's my surprise."

Part of me wanted to go over to him, but I didn't. *Don't you ever fool yourself into forgetting*, I heard Mama saying. I stood right in the doorway, still dripping all over the floor, all over myself.

"I stole that painting you wanted too," he said, as if he was embarrassed to admit it. "We can't hang it in the house, at least not the living room, not yet, not where anyone might see, but you can take it out and look at it sometimes maybe if you want. It's out in the trunk now if you want me to get it." He gave a big sigh, the kind he might give late at night when he was done with talking to me, done with the day. But something else in his face this time, some kind of struggle, like he wanted to go quiet, but wanted to say something too. "But I was serious about that being the last one," he said finally. "This is a fresh start and I want to do it right. So I paid for this."

He opened his fist then. The sock monkey keychain was in it. Crushed a little in his grip, but there it was.

"I knew that story wasn't true, about your daddy," he said. "I knew it while you were telling it. But it being true or not, that wasn't the point, was it?"

I smiled and shook my head. No no no, that wasn't the point. And yes yes yes too, of course.

* * *

Needless to say, I didn't kill him. And I didn't take my half and hit the highway.

When we got in the car the next day, I almost didn't see the rust along the wheel well, and I closed the door so soft that I almost didn't hear that loose metal rolling around inside. While Delwood packed the trunk one more time, I slipped that pistol into the glove compartment, just like it had been in the first place. I didn't touch it again.

As Delwood drove us along 66 and out of town, I rolled down

the window and kicked up my heels a little, leaned over against him.

You might imagine that I was stuck on that $5000 painting in the trunk and that house ahead, and partly I was, but again you'd be missing the point. It was the sock monkey that meant the most to me. Light as a trinket but with a different kind of weight to it. When I hung it from the rearview mirror, the rattle there died down almost to a whisper, and it all seemed like a smoother ride ahead for a while.

The Care & Feeding of Houseplants

During one of their trysts, one of those long lunch breaks they took from the ad agency where they worked, Roger invited Felicia to bring her husband over for a Friday night cookout.

"Tell hubby it's casual," he explained to her after he'd caught his breath once more. "Tell him we'll just"—and here he grazed his fingers a little more insistently along her damp skin—"just get together and heat up some meat in the backyard."

Felicia arched a single eyebrow and then turned her head toward the far side of his bedroom—looking at what, Roger wasn't clear. Unlike the other women who'd sometimes shared his bed, often under similar circumstances, Felicia seemed a true mystery—aloof, challenging, and the more desirable for it. He followed her gaze. Her beige linen business suit was folded sensibly across a chair by his bedroom window. Beyond stood the backyard itself, the patio, the teak table and chairs. Roger could already see himself standing by the grill, making small talk with her husband. *Your wife's breasts,* he would think as he smiled and chatted with the other man. *That mole on her pelvis. That scar at the hollow of her ankle.*

"Whatever you may think," Felicia said finally, "Blanton is not a fool."

"Blanton," Roger said and then again, "Blan-ton," stretching out the syllables as if they were his to twist and toy with. "You know, I still just love his name."

* * *

Blanton's grip was unsteady as he moved the watering can from one pot to the next in the solarium behind his and Felicia's house. His fingers trembled. His attention faltered and fled. The bougainvillea got too much water, the passionflower too little. He nearly drowned a blossoming powderpuff before he jerked the can back—just in time. He looked at his hand as if it wasn't his own. The age spots there had spread like a fungus. Further up, arm hairs had begun to gray. He thought of the gray hair sprouting from his ears. Were those really *his* ears? Could he believe them?

"We've been invited for dinner." That's what Felicia had told him barely a half-hour before. "One of my co-workers."

Blanton had been making drinks at the time, their evening cocktails. Mango mojitos tonight—splitting open a mango one of his botany students had given him earlier in the afternoon, one of a quartet she'd delivered as a thank-you present. The gift had left him brimming with contentment, and he had been muddling them merrily when Felicia broke the news. An off-hand remark—or meant to be.

"Have I met her?" Blanton had asked, adding a splash of white crème de menthe to the cocktails.

"Him," she said. And the pinpricks became a knife.

"Just let me know when," he had told her, and then excused himself hastily, the plants suddenly claiming his attention, some spritzing that needed to be done. And at least he was good for that, right?

But for what else? he thought now. *Because most men in a situation like this, they'd....* But that thought struck him mercilessly too: what most men would do.

Still balancing the watering can dumbly against his side, Blanton glanced over at a lyre-flower Felicia had given him, just one of the many plants the two of them had exchanged—this one a present for his 46th birthday. "A perennial," she'd said, learning from him, remembering. "Like our love."

He was so touched by the intention that he hadn't told her the other name for the flower: old-fashioned bleeding heart. Neither had he told her how some perennials only bloomed once before dying.

"Metaphors," he laughed now, bitterly, and thought of others— the withered stalk, limp to the root—and about what he couldn't do now than "most men" still could. His fault that she'd found one of those men, his fault twice, because wasn't her infidelity his own suggestion?

He'd tried drugs first, then therapy. Then the herbal remedies he'd so thoroughly researched—not just relying on supplements but trying to grow the plants himself: panax ginseng, turnera diffusa, ginkgo biloba, ptychopetalum olacoides. Increased libido, increased bloodflow in those nether regions—empty promises, more desperation. And then....

And then, standing in the solarium, he corrected himself—the bigger, truer picture. *Most men,* he remembered from his well-worn copy of Thoreau, *lead lives of quiet desperation...* "And go to the grave with the song still in them," he muttered aloud to the plants around him, as if they might hear.

* * *

"It's biological," Felicia's mother had told her years before, when she hit her teen years. "It's evolutionary. Now that you're becoming a woman, they'll all be sniffing around you. That's what they do, that's what they'll *keep* doing, all of them wanting a piece. And it's dog eat dog for them—evolutionary again. Survival of the fittest."

Felicia hadn't wanted to believe it, but she'd found out too quickly how right her mother was. So many of them, it seemed, eyes glossing hungrily over a low-cut blouse she wore, mouths nearly salivating over a glimpse of her thigh—and not just the boys at school but men too, men passing her on the street, men at the country club where she worked weekends, teachers in high school, professors at college, her father's friends, even a distant uncle at a wedding she went to, drunk and leering. Not just dogs, but wolves more like it, sly and relentless, fangs bared, hormones howling. She'd had to learn quickly how to walk among them.

And then had come Blanton—guileless, earnest. He'd brought her an orchid for their first date. He'd typed up tips for taking care of it. He'd kissed her on the cheek at the end of the evening. And she'd said, even then, "You're not like other men, are you?" and he'd cocked his head and given her that lopsided smile. No, he wasn't. Not at all.

Felicia sipped the drink he'd made.

When life hands you mangoes, make mojitos. And when life hands you lemons....

But Felicia had tried to be supportive, she had. *It's fine, it happens. No big deal, another time. Perhaps if I...?* Or *we could try....* And then *maybe the worrying only makes it worse?* Finally, when all his efforts had fallen short and all her efforts too, he'd come home to her one afternoon flush with embarrassment, starkly vulnerable, ripe for martyrdom.

"You're still a young woman," he'd said. He held a plant in his hands, a symbol of what she wasn't sure—the offer he was making? the words he couldn't bring himself to speak? Peperomia, she found out later, its spiky flowers jutting up like tiny fingers, like phalluses. "I just ask that you keep it discreet. And, please, nothing... lengthy with anyone."

"I'm not going to do that," she'd said flatly, and she'd said it once more the next time he brought it up: "Thank you, but no."

He never mentioned it again, but it was already too late. Appreciation turned to pity, and soon pity began to fester into frustration, then flare toward anger. Where did it come from, that desire to kick a person just for being generous to you, to kick a man not just when's he's down but *because* he's down?

Ultimately, her mother had been right in more ways than one. "You'll want it too," she'd warned all those years before. "You'll *need* it. Simple biology. But just don't forget who you are in the middle of all that."

She had needed it. And then she'd taken it. But what about this next step? Dog eat dog again? Was that what this was all about?

If so, Felicia did indeed know who she was.

The bitch in the middle.

* * *

Roger had invited a fourth for dinner: Jessica, an old friend who knew about the affair—knew about all his adventures, in fact. Her curiosity always bested her disapproval, and her disapproval always gave Roger an extra little thrill. He liked witnesses to his exploits.

"This dinner," Jessica had said when she first arrived, "it's kind of a jackass thing to do, you know? And what's the point? I mean, are you *trying* to break up their marriage, is that it?"

"Things with me and Felicia are perfect just like they are," he'd told her. "The sex is *always* better with someone else's woman."

Jessica had rolled her eyes. "And so the rooster struts."

"Make up your mind, Jess? Am I a jackass or cock of the walk?"

The latter, he knew, even though she didn't answer him, just smiled and rolled her eyes and shook her head.

The first time he'd met the husband of one of his lovers—purely by chance that time, at a cocktail party—he'd felt a surge of adrenaline and pride, a sudden strut to his step. The next time he and the woman tangled in bed had been passionate, relentless, charged.

He wanted that same intensity next time with Felicia, to break through that wall of immovability that he'd tried so many times to penetrate.

"You were *bad*," he imagined Felicia saying next time, and he would tell her, "Bad's what you want. It's what you need." The victor. The conqueror.

But to do that, he needed to go to battle first—needed to one-up the competition—and so the richly marbled steaks and the fine French wine and the freshly pressed shirt, gradually mounting more proof of his superiority. So too the plant that he'd moved from the bedroom to the study, where he would lead them all at evening's end for an after-dinner glass of port—the plant that Felicia had given him just after the first time they'd slept together, now displayed prominently on a small mahogany stand.

It was all perfect, he thought, and when they arrived, he felt geared up, ready—energized even a little more when he caught his first glimpse of Felicia in the doorway, those long lashes shadowing the dark gleam of her eyes, the corners of her lips curled just on the edge of some sly, elusive grin, that knee-length sundress showcasing those tawny legs.

But when Blanton trundled across the threshold, Roger felt a surge of disappointment, and more than disappointment, revulsion. The other man was older than Roger had anticipated. His hairline was receding, his face was not just slackjawed but jowly. His polo shirt—once green, evidently—was faded beyond the point at which Roger would have cast it aside. His weighty paunch sagged across the waistband of rumpled khaki shorts, whose fabric squeezed flabby haunches.

Roger's revulsion deepened. What sense of victory could he achieve when there wasn't really a challenge in sight?

* * *

Along the curving driveway, then glimpsing the house—modern and angular—and then walking up the steps, Blanton had been struck by the feeling that he was somehow spying on his wife, spying in plain sight. Rethinking possibilities, weighing consequences, he became so lost in his thoughts that he seemed to be watching himself too—all of this, his own finger on the doorbell, the door opening in response—as if from some great distance, some other man making these small moves, unsure where it would end.

Roger Wilson, he heard the other man say, as if through a tube, tinnily echoed, and then his own voice, *Blanton Morrison*, and his own hands as if another's reaching out to shake the hand of Felicia's lover—a man who seemed to have stepped directly from the pages of some fashion catalog. Felicia handed over a bottle of wine they'd picked up on the way. Blanton offered a pair of mangos and felt himself patting the breast pocket of his coat. Somewhere the words *mint* and *drinks* and *later*—his own—and then Roger's *thanks, thanks, thanks* and *hope the directions were OK* and Felicia's reply, *No trouble getting here*. Necessary pretenses. Ruses. He knew she'd been here before.

And then another woman coming down the hallway—thick red hair, a wide smile, wiping her hands on a dishtowel—and Blanton felt relief and sudden elation. Maybe he'd been wrong?

"My, what a beautiful sight," he exclaimed, too loudly—the volume suddenly back on but turned up too high—and he felt embarrassed at his outburst. But when she giggled and opened her arms—"I adore a man who flatters first thing. That deserves a hug instead of a handshake!"—he welcomed the sense of being embraced and all that this woman seemed to mean: this evening wasn't the beginning of some horrible series of events, but a dinner to mark some end.

"Felicia didn't tell me you had such a lovely girlfriend," he said, almost on the verge of giddiness. But then he noticed the sudden hush.

"Jessica's not my girlfriend," Roger said.

"I know him too well." Jessica laughed, nervously, blushing. "I'm not his style."

There was some brief interplay of glances between the three of them, Blanton saw. Nothing was safe. None of them.

* * *

"A local artist," Roger was explaining, pointing to the headless torso of a woman on a side table: bronze, nearly all breasts and the back arched to emphasize it. "Molded from her own body."

"I've never liked that piece," said Jessica.

Felicia had never liked the sculpture either, always felt that Roger thought of all women the way the artist had presented herself: all breasts, no head. But she didn't say that now. Blanton hadn't responded either, and Felicia wondered at his quietness. A dull panic? A simple sulk?

The image prompted a memory—a college boyfriend, a sulker himself. He'd loved David Lynch movies, she remembered as Roger continued his tour of the house, Blanton commenting on the light, Jessica throwing Felicia little glances, trying to catch her attention. Felicia couldn't remember the boy's name now, only his goatee and his baggy shirts and the two of them watching *Lost Highway* in his dorm room, all the lights out and her attention wandering.

Another night, they'd gone for pizza (Paul? Peter? Philip? P certainly)—late night, a local hangout, a crush of people, frat boys at a table nearby, and the two of them in a booth of their own. The pizza arrived, and she and P. had each taken a slice, and as they ate, one of the frat boys had turned and started talking to her: "How are you doing? You're looking good tonight. That pizza smells great." And then he'd turned to P. and said, "You don't mind if I have a piece, do you?" and he'd picked up a slice of their pizza and eaten it in front of them, a smile and a wink at Felicia between bites.

"Yeah," P. had said, hesitantly, and "Um" and "We're kind of talking here."

Later, P. had fretted and moaned—all the things he should've said, the things he should've done. "I could've punched him. I could've stabbed his hand with my fork, I could've...." Revenge fantasies, underscored by hints that maybe Felicia herself should've acted differently too.

Felicia had slept with the frat boy months later, long after P. was gone from her life. She didn't remember his name now either, and wasn't sure he'd remembered her even at the time. That hadn't seemed the point, and now she couldn't quite remember what the point had been.

* * *

Standing at the grill with Blanton, Roger found himself just going through the motions of what he'd planned.

When Blanton said he liked his steaks well done, Roger said he preferred "a little more pink in the middle, the way a real man should."

When Blanton asked how things were at the office, Roger volunteered that Felicia was "a real fireball. Get her going and she just won't stop."

"I'm surprised a man like you isn't married," Blanton said at one point, as Roger checked the steaks. "Jessica seems swell, doesn't she?"

"Can't say I'm the marrying type," said Roger, not bothering to ridicule the man's *swell*. "Not really an institution I put much faith in. But there's usually someone at work who's willing to take a little lunch break, if you know what I mean. The usual ins and outs of office romance." He glanced openly toward the women on the other side of the patio—at Felicia, slender and shapely. "Truth is, I'm involved with a juicy little something myself right now." He winked.

"That kind of romancing is a younger man's game," Blanton said. "I just don't what I'd do without my Felicia."

His Felicia—and yet what had he done to keep her?

Jessica was telling a story across the patio, gesturing with her free hand, leaning toward Felicia, laughing a little. Felicia smiled, demurely, and took a sip of wine. Even from that distance, Roger could see the way her mouth left a smudge on the rim of the glass, the red outline of her lips. Despite the smoke from the grill, he could still remember—as if smelling it now—the vanilla and honeysuckle of her perfume, the scent that sometimes lingered on the pillows on the afternoons she stopped over.

Sometimes Roger had questioned why she talked so rarely about her home life. Unlike the other married women he'd had, she never went into tirades about a dull routine or demanding children, never recited *ad nauseum* bickering arguments about monies spent and monies earned or dull squabbles about whose turn it had been to take out the trash. Not once had Felicia embarked on some small drama insisting that they must stop this, they must, because she couldn't do this to her husband, couldn't do this any more. At one point, he'd admired the way she handled the affair, but now, seeing Blanton, he felt that admiration turn to pity, a sour pity, and a cruelty too. He'd enjoyed the challenge she offered—all that he saw of himself in her, that strength, that will—and the power play between them. "Three lunches a week, no more," she'd told him, wanting that control over the relationship, but then asking another time to be tied up, wanted to be dominated in ways she obviously wasn't getting at home. Now he saw that it must be weakness that held her to Blanton, and he didn't want to just dominate her but punish her for it.

* * *

While he and Roger had been alone at the grill, Blanton had tried to reason with the other man—indirectly, of course—to urge him toward Jessica, the beautiful woman available and in front of him, to throw him off the scent of his wife. On their way inside for dinner, he'd considered pulling Felicia aside, pleading with her for them to leave now, to leave forever, for her to stop this once and for all, for both their sakes, but he feared that such weakness might only drive her deeper into the other man's arms.

And then, amidst the clamor of conversation, the clatter of forks and knives, the clink of the wineglasses, he realized something: There hadn't been a plant in sight. Nothing green, nothing growing, no life. Could anyone really want to live in a place without that?

"Plants," he told Jessica toward the end of dinner when she asked what he did. "Plants are my life, really. My plants and my wife, of course." He wanted to reach out and touch Felicia's hand, but he held back. He couldn't even look at her, afraid of what he might find in her expression. "A flower is a beautiful thing. Each of them has a personality, just like we do. Each of them should be respected, tended to and cared for."

He talked on then, talking to Jessica as if she were a student of his, speaking to her but pleading with his wife. He listed the plants they had at home: begonias and caladium, bromeliads and ferns, geraniums, succulents, oleanders, ivy… plant after plant, name after name. He explained the different kinds of pots—clay, plastic, ceramic—and discussed the need to watch the humidity and to keep the house temperature in flux, stressing the importance of learning what each plant most wanted. Even when Roger tried to interrupt, Blanton kept going, stressing the difference in yellowing due to water shortage and yellowing due to iron deficiency, explaining how to watch for dormancy, lecturing about how to adjust the lighting to what each plant needed, telling how he cleaned the leaves each week, some of them with a sponge and others—"the fuzzier ones"—with a special camel-hair brush. "And yet despite all that, plants are tougher than you think," he said at one point. "They're the most adaptable things, so many of them. They'll survive even under the most adverse conditions."

After awhile, he wasn't sure what he was talking about, what he was trying to imply—was it Felicia who was the plant and he the tender? Or was he the plant, tough and adaptable, deceptively so? Metaphors popped into his mind again—more plant names: the lipstick plant; the crown-of-thorns with its red flowers and sharp spines; the screw pine, which drops its lower leaves as it gets older and sends out aerial roots instead—desperately, he thought now, considering it. But he could save the relationship still, couldn't he? Wasn't this the way?

"What was it Thoreau said?" he asked Jessica as they entered the study for more drinks, readying his favorite quote. His students joked that each time he repeated it, he pretended he was remembering it for the first time. "'The finest qualities of our nature, like the bloom on fruits, can be preserved only by the most delicate handling. Yet—'"

But his words faltered when he saw the plant sitting on one of the shelves behind the couch—a plant that he recognized too well, the peperomia he'd given to Felicia when he offered her that window of sexual opportunity, that door toward infidelity.

"Yet what?" asked Jessica. She had been, he thought then, a front-of-the-class kind of girl, and for a moment he imagined what a relationship with her might have been like, how this evening might never have happened.

"Yet," he said then, hearing the loss in his own words, the pity for himself and for them all, "Yet we do not treat ourselves nor one another thus tenderly."

* * *

The plant had never looked right anywhere—that's what Felicia thought seeing it now. The peperomia with its spiky, phallic flowers.

After Blanton gave it to her, she'd kept it at home for a few days and then taken it to the office. She'd put it on the windowsill, and then at the corner of her desk and then up on a shelf. Wherever it was, it didn't seem to belong. It caught her eye wrong, caught her mood wrong.

Or maybe it wasn't the look of the plant itself, but the reminder it provided—opportunities, possibilities, desires, needs.

When she brought it to Roger's place and placed it beside the bed, it looked even less like it belonged, but the context gave it a new life: responsibilities instead of opportunities, duties instead of desires. Sometimes even in the more blinding heat of passion, she'd look over at the plant and feel the guilt even deeper than Roger's thrusts, feel the connection to Blanton even more than to the man rising above her, falling against her.

The boy's name came to her then. Patrick it was. And she remembered how he'd stopped in the middle of their own lovemaking that night, after the incident in the pizza parlor, and looked down on her.

"You're not here," Patrick had told her, accusation in his voice, deprecation too. "This isn't…. This isn't what you…. You're thinking about *him*, aren't you?" And when she hadn't answered, he'd shook his head, rolled off her, turned himself toward the wall. He'd known, he was right. That wasn't what she wanted. *He* wasn't what she wanted—this nervous boy who'd let someone steal his pizza, this panting thing who'd retreated into a sulk. What she wanted was someone who would've taken the action, fought furiously and recklessly. She wished Patrick had hit the frat boy, wished even that he'd hit her. He could've done something, he could've done *anything*.

* * *

Damn that Jessica. No sooner had Felicia's hubby finally stopped talking than she got him started again.

"It's fascinating," she said. "I grow some herbs at home, some basil and oregano and cilantro, a little mint."

"Oh," Blanton said. "Yes, I mean…." He reddened. "That reminds me." And he looked around him, patting himself at the same time. He was like a wind-up robot, Roger thought—completely still and then suddenly in motion, and then still again until someone wound him up once more. "I forgot that I was going to provide the after-dinner drinks," he said. "The mangos and," he reached inside his pocket and smiled, "A-ha, there it is. The mint." He smiled—feebly, Roger thought—and started up on the plants again, "Could you be a dear and bring me those mangos, Jessica? Proof that plants can give pleasure, certainly."

Roger turned away from his view of the other man's bulging belly and toward Felicia's slender, sculpted form. Throughout Blanton's tirade, Roger had tried to catch Felicia's eye, but she'd steadfastly avoided his gaze, and did so again now.

"Are these like the drinks you made for me the other day?" Felicia asked Blanton.

"Yes. Mango mojitos," he exclaimed. "These were a gift from one of my students," he told them as Jessica returned. "I teach botany at the college. One of my students asked for some advice on growing a mango plant from a pit, and so I…." On and on, wound up again.

Roger pitied those students. All those plants, all that lecturing about how plants are people too. *Animals*, Roger kept thinking. *We are animals*, not *plants*, imagining the next time Felicia came over. She seemed the dutiful wife as she took one of the drinks Blanton was offering around—not just demure but tamed really—and he hated her suddenly for that too, and hated Blanton for turning the evening into a Latin American Fiesta, the drinks not just a bad match for the meal, but poorly mixed too, bitter even, though everyone pretended to enjoy them, all of them tamed.

Well, *he* would tame Felicia in his own way next time. He would treat her rougher than normal, manhandle her a little, paw at her, grasp her. "Animals," he would growl into her ear. He would pet her, caress her haunches and her loins, force some feline arch to her lithe little back. They would pant and moan and howl, driven wild with the scent of the other's sweat and desire. And then he would end it, push her aside, send her back to that pitiable man of hers. *That* would be her punishment.

Blanton had started a new lecture. "The difference is between sexual propagation, propagation by seeds, and vegetative propagation, where you just cut off a little part of the plant, and spread it somewhere else." He looked as if he was concentrating heavily, as if any of this mattered. "Take this plant here," he pointed to the plant Roger had placed in the study. Roger had forgotten about it. "*Peperomia obtusifolia*. Red margin. You could take a little cutting from this and plant it and it will grow on its own. But it also grows by seeds, and—"

"That was a gift from your wife," Roger said then. Felicia shot him an ugly look, then blushed slightly. Two emotions. Unlike her.

"I thought it might be," said Blanton, and he turned to Felicia. "A cutting, dear, or the original?"

"It's the one you gave me," said Felicia, composed again.

He nodded, and then to Roger: "She's very generous, don't you think?" And for the first time, Roger could see in the other man's eyes some spark of a challenge, some knowledge. He was finally catching on, and Roger felt his own blood begin to rise.

But before he could answer, Felicia cut him off.

"A toast," she said, "to these wonderful drinks. And to the student who gave you the mangoes. It's good to be appreciated."

"You can't use drinks to toast the drinks themselves," Roger snorted, but he raised his glass anyway.

"Then a toast to plants," said Blanton, and suddenly Roger just wanted the evening over and all of them gone.

* * *

"I'm sorry to cause any trouble," said Blanton, patting his pockets, "but I think I must have dropped my keys somewhere inside." The four of them stood in the driveway, had already said their good-byes. "No, no, ladies. You can stay out here and talk. We'll take a look inside. Roger, you don't mind helping me, do you?"

Felicia could see the reluctance in Roger's expression, but he'd turned back toward the house anyway, leading Blanton inside, leaving her with Jessica. It was the first they'd been truly alone.

"Well, the evening turned out better than I'd expected," Jessica said, and Felicia could feel the woman's eyes on her, some sense of judgment or curiosity. Maybe both.

"I'm going to end it," Felicia said, not meeting the other woman's look.

"With which one?" Jessica asked, and Felicia could tell from the tone that judgment was winning.

Felicia shook her head, leaned against her car. "What I've been doing, it's not...."

The moon was peeking over the tops of the pine trees in Roger's yard. Nearly a full moon, Felicia saw now. Other nights, there might have been something romantic about the image.

"Did you ever have boys fighting over you?" Felicia asked.

"Years ago," said Jessica. "A bar fight. Some guy sent over a drink, and my boyfriend got jealous. My *ex*-boyfriend, I should add."

"Who won?"

"Who knows? Both of them got kicked out of the bar. I decided to stay with my friends and keep drinking. Broke up with the guy by phone the next day. A real lunkhead."

"There was a boy once," Felicia said, and then she stopped, thinking about the word. *Boy* was right: needy, insecure, pitiful really. "He wanted to fight for me, wanted to *have* fought for me, and the thing was, *I* wanted him to fight for me too. I was mad at him for not being more of a man, felt like I deserved a real man." She shook her head again, she looked up at the moon. "I didn't even know what a man was."

"All of them disappoint," said Jessica. "That's the way they are."

But that wasn't what Felicia meant at all. She tried to imagine Blanton fighting for her, throwing fists, getting kicked out of a bar. But that wasn't who he was. Instead, she pictured him making those mojitos, his struggle to stay poised, some nervous attempt at grace. She thought about how complicated the adult world was, more than she'd ever imagined. Compromises and negotiations. With others, with yourself. Things weren't ever just how they looked. "I thought Blanton was weak like that boy was, but I was wrong."

Blanton and Roger came out again. Roger stood tall, framed by the doorway. Blanton took the handrail as he made his way down the front steps.

"Don't say anything about it tonight," Felicia told Jessica quickly. She felt liberated, frightened. She still didn't know what the future was going to be like, how she was going to handle her desires, her needs, how she'd explain things to either of the men. But she'd made her decision. "I'll tell Roger tomorrow that it's over. I will."

* * *

Blanton had found his keys easily enough, sitting in the study, precisely where he'd left them. Before they turned away again, he paused once more over the peperomia, Felicia's gift to her lover.

"It's a beautiful plant," he said

As he touched its leaves one last time, Blanton imagined other ways that this night could have played out. Nightshade would have been more fitting, he thought, more poetic even, and he had a particularly nice specimen of the plant at home, those purple bell-shaped flowers bowing mournfully, those shiny black berries aching to be plucked. Those he could have blended into a daiquiri.

Then, at some small moment with Roger, he might have looked over at his wife and muttered "Belladonna" under his breath, but just loud enough for the other man to hear him. "What?" Roger might have said, and Blanton would have repeated it, "Belladonna," and gestured toward Felicia. "My beautiful lady." And perhaps later, when that poison had begun to take effect, perhaps then his victim would have remembered and understood.

But the ricin was more effective, of course. More certain. And the castor bean plants had been growing on their own in the yard, even without his care. A weed really, just waiting to be used. "A toast," Blanton had said, "to plants"—seeing the little wince in Roger's expression, that bitter taste, like castor oil itself, but the mangoes had sweetened it adequately enough, just as he'd expected.

"See here, Roger," Blanton said now, before they left the study a second time. "See the way the leaves are yellowing a little? A little water, a little more attention might do this plant some good."

He turned to Roger, and saw the sneer in the other man's face, the pride, and the hints of something else, something Roger wasn't aware of himself. Soon, the symptoms would reveal themselves. The nausea would turn to vomiting, Roger's body trying to send the poison back out the way it had arrived. And then trying to expel it out the other end, bloodily so. Yes, many trips to the bathroom tonight, soiling the elegance he'd displayed so proudly, soiling himself. And then dehydration, seizures, even hallucinations perhaps, before liver and spleen and kidneys began calling it quits. No antidote. The end unavoidable now.

"Come to think of it," Blanton squinted his eyes, "a little water might do you some good too. You're looking a little peaked yourself."

* * *

When Blanton reached the car, his wife turned to face him.

"All done?" she asked.

He held up the keys. "Everything's taken care of," he replied, and they told Jessica good-bye and got in the car. Blanton wondered how long Jessica would stay, if she'd be there for the finale—nursemaid first, corpse-bearer later. He hoped she wouldn't be drawn into cleaning it all up. A nice girl, she was, and Blanton felt sorry for what she might be forced to witness.

He and Felicia hardly talked on the way back, but things were different already, he could feel it. At one point, there in the silence, she reached over and touched his hand, and he felt a tingling in his loins, a stirring that he'd nearly forgotten. He pressed down slightly on the accelerator, hurrying them homeward.

He had a dose for her too.

Family takes care of family, that's what I've learned. And us guys, we gotta protect the girls, I know that too.

Like in *The Godfather*, for instance. You might think that movie's about the mafia and mob hits and drugs, and yeah I guess it is, but it's also about family, and a lot of it's about looking after the weaker sex. Sonny and Fredo and Michael, you'll remember, none of them care much for their sister's husband, Carlo, and they're right not to. Carlo's a bad man. He cheats on Connie, he beats her up. And then Sonny, well one day Sonny, he's had enough, and he drives up on that sidewalk all in a hurry and he jumps out of the car and he chases Carlo and then he catches him. The street's busy, lots of people there, kids playing in fire hydrants, everybody watching, and then Sonny, he—

"Are you watching that movie again?" my own sister, Lilian, asks me, my baby sister still, even if she's twenty-two now. She's standing in the doorway at the edge of the kitchen. "Do you ever do anything but sit there and watch movies?"

She's dolled up. A smear of lipstick. Her shirt cut low. She's started dressing that way just recently, skimpy clothes all around, and not just because July is hot.

"Going out?" I ask her. My chair—Dad's old chair—squeaks when I turn to look her over. "Studying again?" Because that's what she used to tell me. The library, her classes, whatever.

"You need to take care of *yourself*," she tells me.

It's her favorite thing to say these days. I know where she got it.

"You look like a hooker," I tell her. Since our parents died, Mama when we were kids and then Dad about a year ago, it's just been me and her in the house. And who's gonna look after her if I don't?

"That money Dad left you, do you think it's gonna last forever? Do you think I'm going to take care of you forever? I'm telling you, I don't care what Dad said, I won't do it. "

She's got this look about her while she's talking right now. Her lips are trembling a little. She won't meet my eye. Shame. That's what it is. Again—always these days. Ashamed of the way she's dressed, the way she's been acting. She's admitted it before, how she feels. But even if she didn't, I'd know, because I know who she's been catting around with. Her own sort-of Carlo. And she knows I know. Ben is his name.

"That skirt," I tell her. "I can almost see right up it from here. A brother shouldn't see that. No one should."

She takes a deep breath. She won't look at me.

"This is going to end," she tells me. "*I'm* going to end it, Reggie. It's a fair warning, Reggie. *Fair*. If...."

There's a tear in her eye. The shame literally oozing out of her. She doesn't finish her sentence. And then she just walks out, not changing her clothes first, just closing the door behind her.

"The library," I call after her. "I get the DVDs from the library." I found them when I went looking for her there, all that studying she was supposed to be doing.

Anyway, so Sonny chases this Carlo down and then he's beating and kicking him and then biting Carlo's finger and then throwing that trashcan on him and then kicking him into the street. "You touch my sister again," Sonny says to Carlo, "I'll kill you."

Sonny, he gives Carlo a warning. He teaches him a lesson.

And I mean, yeah, I know where it all ends up for Sonny because of that, and I know that's a pretty bad place, that toll booth and dead and all, but then Michael comes in later and fixes it again with Carlo. Fixes it. That's what family does. And even if Connie didn't understand it at first, she knew it was the right thing to do. She knew in the end that she was better off.

When Dad left me the house and everything he'd saved up—left it to *me*—he left me with a mission too: "You and your sister," he told me, "you need to be there for one another." A *trust*—that's why they call it that. It's *entrusted* to you, and you gotta trust somebody before you release it. She tried to break the trust, of course, talked to the lawyer, tried to turn him against me. But Dad knew. And I think that someday Lilian will understand how I've tried to be there for her, where she's been steered wrong, and that what I'm doing tonight... well, it has to be done.

I count barely a minute after she's gone before I'm up and getting my things together, none the wiser.

* * *

Dad, he was a topographical surveyor, he was good at what he did. He looked deep into the landscape and he could see even the smallest rise, even the shallowest gulley. He could see the past of the land and the future, what lay ahead— "the contours of time," he said. He was a professional. He was the best.

Sometimes I think of myself as a surveyor too, like Dad but scouting out a different kind of landscape, watching the changes in the urban terrain, the passage of that time—all downhill if you ask me.

Sometimes I've been walking around here at night, this town we grew up in, this town we went to school in, an everybody-knows-everybody kind of place, and I've realized how hard it is to recognize it these days, even right down Main Street. The bank has changed its name twice in the last few years, and they keep changing who I work with on Dad's trust, who helps me to withdraw our money. That ladies dress shop where Lilian got her prom dress? It's a consignment store now, and Lilian's taken her prom dress back in there, I've seen it, and a pawnshop sits on the corner where the newsstand used to be, and I have to watch that so Lilian doesn't pawn anything there. That little lunch counter is gone, the one where Dad used to buy us sandwiches on Saturdays. Dwight, the guy who ran it, would make a Cherry Splash special for Lilian and then he'd tell me that I sure ate better than anyone he knew, sure enough, and Dad would ask him, "Why not make the boy another sandwich? Why not extra tuna salad this time?" And I'd eat it all. That building is boarded up now, and Dwight is gone, a heart attack. No one makes Cherry Splashes anymore.

Sometimes lately I've felt like it's not just the place I don't recognize, it's the people too, or maybe they don't recognize me. So many people have been moving out and new people have been moving in and even the people who've stayed seemed to have changed and not for the better. Even the ones I *do* still recognize, I just *don't* recognize them, if you know what I mean, or maybe they don't recognize me. Guys who used to pick on me in school passing me by like they don't see me, or sometimes glancing at me like they *might* know me but they're not sure. Girls looking the other way like they don't see me at all. People I grew up with, people I've known my whole life and some of them like strangers now.

Like in *It's a Wonderful Life*, that's what I'd think sometimes when I was out on my walk after Lilian had gone to the library—after she'd *said* she'd gone to the library—those scenes where Bedford Falls becomes Pottersville and everything is ugly and mean and no one recognizes Jimmy Stewart anymore. The one good man in the whole place, and he wasn't there to make a difference. I'd see Pottersville when I saw that pawn shop and the consignment store and the worst of it, that new bar with the shining neon and the throbbing music and the people spilling out the front door loud and vulgar and drunk. This one time there was a girl sitting on the sidewalk, mascara streaming down her face, bawling into her cell phone. And when I saw that Pottersville of our own, I'd think it was lucky that Lilian and I had been raised so good and lucky I was there for her now, right? You make a difference where you can.

And then one night, I saw her. Lilian.

I wasn't following her then, wasn't looking for her, just getting out a little, just checking the *lay of the land,* as Dad called it. And then I saw this girl standing at the front of that bar and looking in and then turning into the alley, and I followed her and I saw her duck into this back door, and I thought, "Well that sure looks like Lilian, even though it can't be." And then I thought a little more and I thought, "Maybe if something looks like something, it *is* that something." Or someone, of course. Then I went to the library and it was nearly empty and I started looking at the DVDs while I was watching the bathroom because I figured that was where Lilian must have been. And then the librarian came up and asked if she could help me and I asked her, "Where's Lilian?" and the librarian looked at me a little frightened, probably because I said it louder than I'd meant to, it being a library and all, but then she was frightened for another reason, because no, she hadn't seen Lilian that night or any other night. In fact, she didn't even know who Lilian was at all, and she wouldn't even tell me that until after I'd asked her three or four times, looking at me all the time like that librarian in *It's a Wonderful Life,* except that Jimmy Stewart had been married to that one and she'd been pretty and I wouldn't have been married to this lady if my life depended on it.

* * *

Lilian has a headstart tonight, but I'm not in a rush. And I can't rush anyway, not with my coat buttoned up tight, not with me having to *shorten my stride.* That was what Dad said when he was teaching me how to get a rough measure of length. Take your time, pace yourself. And I think of that tonight, you know, and how I need to stand up straight so that nothing sticks out, and keep my armpit clenched tight, and don't mind the sweat, and ignore that little scrape against your thigh. Because even though July is hot, this is the way it has to be, and it doesn't matter how quickly I get there. I know where Lilian's going.

I walk down the alley behind the bar first. I check that back door again tonight, and I put my ear up to it to try to hear what's going on in there, the worst of it, the high-dollar tables in the back, the strippers I've heard about, straight from the source. But it's quiet right now and so I circle around to the front of the bar and look in through the windows. I cup my free hand near the neon "i" and the "t" of the Miller Lite sign hanging there at eye level. I keep my other hand tight against my side.

Ben's Place, that's the name of the bar, like the whole place is his, like he's moved into town and laid some stake on the building and the street and the whole place and Lilian too. But it's not a bar like the one that used to be here, the one Dad took me to a couple of times once I was old enough. A bar is a line of stools, one man to a stool, one beer to a man. A bar is not women. A bar is not sofas.

But though the window, that's what I see now. Women at the bar, draping themselves across the men having their beers. A bunch of girls sitting back on a couple of sofas, laughing, and all these empty glasses spread out across what looks like a coffee table. Some of the men stand by themselves, and they're cutting their eyes at those girls, like they're looking at something they don't trust or looking for something they have to be careful about or like they're going to use one of those sofas for something else one of these days.

And then there's Lilian, sitting on a sofa herself—with Ben *himself*—just the two of them, leaning forward, hunched together, and I can tell even from here, even through the neon, that she's still upset, that she's crying, and it makes me glad that she's brought her shame with her. I imagine what she must have been thinking, about the disgrace that she had become, and then carrying that disgrace all the way over, overwhelmed by it, and then for a brief second I feel it: *relief.* She's come to her senses. She's ending it with him. It's over. "Ben," she's going to say. "Ben Ben Benny." Been around the block. Been there, done that. Not worth the trip. And I didn't need to make this trip either. I won't need to do anything now.

But then she reaches out her hand and puts it on his leg. And then he reaches out his hand and rubs her back, and then he puts his *other* hand on *her* leg, high up on her thigh. And then she leans into him.

"Comanche," I think to myself.

And then I realize I've said it aloud, "Comanche!" into the middle of that neon sign, and I wonder where did *that* word come from? And then I think *Comanche,* of course! Because sometimes what you're seeing isn't exactly everything that you're seeing. Sometimes something else knows something more than just what your *thinking* knows, you know?

John Wayne. That's what I've been thinking of. *The Searchers.*

In the movie, John Wayne plays Ethan Edwards, who sets off to find his nieces who've been kidnapped by Comanche Indians. He and his nephew, they start looking, and they find one of the girls raped and dead and that makes 'em rush to find the other one even quicker. But it doesn't go quick. They're searching and searching and it's winter and then it's like five years or more and then when they do find her she's gone Indian herself and she's almost lost and Ethan Edwards—that's John Wayne—he's ready to kill her. "Livin' with Comanches ain't being alive anyway," that's what he says, something like that, and killing the girl is just what her mama would've wanted him to do. The girl's turned wild, that's what she's done.

It's a jungle out here, that's what people say sometimes about the world, but it's a wilderness, I think. That's where the word *wild* comes from after all. And you have to have a code in the wilderness, a purpose, or else there's just an emptiness. Dad told me that one time. "A moral emptiness," he told me. "You just have to stand for something."

I look down at where I'm standing now, and I think about John Wayne and I think about the Comanche. I don't have cowboy boots, just a pair of old L.L. Bean boots that Dad got me a long time ago, a little tight but if I don't lace them all the way up, they fit OK. I've got a yellow rain slicker on too, zipped up tight, even though it's still mighty hot out here, but I had to wear it, of course, and now I see that it's like one of those cowboy coats, what are they called? A *duster*. And I feel like yes, John Wayne, yes, I can do this, I will. And I clench my armpit a little more, purposefully now, holding everything close.

When I look back through the neon, I see Ben's eyes catch mine, and then Lilian looks up quickly at me and there's surprise there, and more shame, I can see it, but shame now because she wasn't ashamed enough to break it off. She straightens herself up, smoothes her dress. She gives me the finger, a dirty thing a girl shouldn't do, and she walks toward the back and I hear myself saying *no, no* somewhere inside my head.

Ben looks at me, he shakes his head, he points at himself and then points after Lilian with his thumb—gestures I don't understand. Then he turns and disappears. Same back room.

In *The Searchers*, of course, Ethan Edwards kills a lot of Comanche but he doesn't end up killing his niece. "Let's go home, Debbie," he tells her after awhile, and she fights him at first, but then he just scoops her up and carries her back.

"Come home, Lilian," I say now, because I don't know how far she's gone, how much has been lost, if there's still time.

* * *

"If he's such a nice guy, why don't you bring him over here one night?" I'd asked Lilian a couple of times.

"You can seriously ask that?" she asked me.

"I just did," I told her. "A girl shouldn't be ashamed of her boyfriend, shouldn't be ashamed to bring him around to meet her family."

"Ashamed," she said, not to anybody, and she bit her lip, thinking about that word, thinking about herself. "You're right," she told me. "I'm ashamed." She pointed at me as she told me—the first time she'd admitted it, and she had this angry look like she was mad that I'd seen the truth.

A small battle, a war to win. Dad said that sometimes too.

If she refused to bring him by the house the way a girl should... Well, I went over to Ben's Place one afternoon my own self to meet him. The place was empty except for this big bald guy in an old t-shirt who was cleaning and stacking glasses and unpacking beers into a refrigerator. He smelled like sweat, the whole place did, and then he called out "Benny" toward this door in the back. There was some music playing behind it and then it opened just a little and Ben came out. He was about my age, tall and lean with this long face and big eyes with dark circles under them, kind of like a young Humphrey Bogart. His hair had something shiny in it. He closed the door behind him, but I could still hear the music, and I saw all of a sudden what he was up to. Like Bogart, like in *Casablanca*: the roulette tables, the card games, but these days, well, you know, worse. Bogart gone bad.

Ben reached out to shake my hand, but it would've felt like we were making a deal, so I pretended I didn't see it. And then we sat on stools the two of us, one man, one stool, but it didn't feel like old times at all.

"You own all this?" I asked him, and he told me he did, and I asked him, "You make all this money from people buying a few *beers?*" and he said it was more than beer, and I told him, "Yeah, I thought so," and I looked back at that door he'd come out of, and then while I was looking, he asked the guy in the t-shirt to show me a "cocktail menu," but I waved him off. He knew that wasn't what I was saying.

"Beer and cocktails," I told him, repeating his word. "And gambling in the back room, right?" Because I knew he'd be *shocked, shocked* that I knew, even as he was raking in the winnings.

But he didn't deny it. He just laughed. "Yep," he told me. "That's right. Thomas runs blackjack here at the bar." He pointed at the bald guy, who laughed too. "And back there," pointing at the door, "that's where the high-dollar tables are." He lowered his voice almost to a whisper—"And then there's the strippers, of course. Oh, and the drugs"—admitting to me the *worse* that I'd already anticipated. He leaned down toward me as he spoke, and he smelled like cologne, like he'd showered in it to try to cover up something ugly.

"Lilian says you watch a lot of movies," he told me. "Keeps the mind popping, huh?"

I shrugged. I didn't like that Lilian had been talking about me.

"I got a blu-ray player," Ben told me. "A vendor of mine dropped it off, a gift of sorts, but I've already got one at home. So I was wondering...."

I think it was that word *gift* that first got me thinking about *The Godfather.* Not Bogart—Brando. Like in that scene where everybody starts handing white envelopes of money to Don Corleone. But then I couldn't see Ben as Don Corleone or as Sonny or Michael. Maybe Fredo? Or maybe…. And maybe that was when I first starting thinking of him like Carlo. I don't know what Ben was wondering about while I thought all that, but he seemed to be wondering for a long time.

"How about we set you up with it?" Ben finally asked me. "That blu-ray player, huh?"

And that's when I realized what he was asking me, and I knew he was worse than Carlo.

"You're asking me to sell my sister for a blu-ray player?" I told him. "You're wanting to buy me off, buy off my OK for you to take her? You want to own her like you own this bar, is that it?"

Ben and the bald blackjack dealer—Thomas—looked at one another. I looked back and forth between them. Ben's big eyes widened a little more. Thomas shook his head. I wondered what kind of signal that was, and I felt myself going on guard, getting ready.

"You got a funny way of interpreting things," Ben finally said. "Twisting. Turning." Ben twisted in his seat himself as he said it, turned a little bit away from me.

"Is that where you're going to put her?" I asked him, because he couldn't twist out of this. "Back in your back room. Put her to work for you."

Not just Carlo but worse than Carlo, I thought. Not cheating, not beating, not yet at least or at least I didn't have any proof. But I could put together the things he was saying. And I could feel myself like Sonny wanting to hurt him.

The bald guy was staring at me now. "There's no back room," he told me.

"Your boss just told me different," I told me. "You heard."

Ben spoke then. "You don't have much of a sense of…." He looked around, looking for a word, looking for a way out. "Of irony, do you?"

"Lilian doesn't belong in that back room," I told him. I was trying to hold back from hitting him. "She doesn't belong here, she doesn't belong with you."

"I don't think Lilian belongs to anybody," Ben told me, and he laughed again. "Lilian"—he shook his head—"Lilian is her own woman, don't you think? She's a big girl, Reggie, she can take care of herself. It's… admirable for a brother to care like you do, but…. But I think she can make her own decisions. And you, you're a big boy yourself, that's what I tell her. You can take care of yourself, right?"

And that was it, the kind of thing that Lilian had been saying to me recently, and now I knew where she was getting it from, who'd been poisoning her against me.

I wished I had a trashcan to beat him with. I wished that there was a street of kids out there to watch me teach him a lesson.

"I *can* take care of myself. I can take care of *Lilian* too. And I can take care of *you* if it comes down to it."

"There's no need for that, Reggie," Ben said. "Let's try to sort this out."

But I'd already slid down off the stool by then and started backing out of the place slow, keeping the both of them in my sights.

"You touch my sister again, Carlo," I told him when I was at the door, and I pointed at him.

"Who's Carlo?" the bartender asked.

But Ben didn't ask. Ben *knew* what I meant. I figured he'd seen the movie himself, maybe on that blu-ray player he was bragging about.

* * *

Lilian was mad at me later when she found out I'd talked to Benny. She didn't understand, because girls sometimes don't.

"A brother is supposed to be there for his sister," I told her. "That's what we do."

"That's the point," she said, even as she was missing it. "You're *always* there. You're always *here*."

"You're right," I told her. "Here for *you*. And I *will* be. Always."

I keep my promises. I'm still here tonight, just as I said, standing at the window, staring through the "i" and the "t" at the empty spot on the sofa where Lilian and Benny just left, the blankness where they used to be, knowing what's next.

* * *

"Have you seen my phone, Reggie?" Lilian asked me one day, rushing from one room of the house to another, pulling up clothes and phone books and dishes, the mail that's been piling up, stuff she hadn't had time to get to with all of her catting around.

"Who do you need to call between here and work?" I asked her, but she didn't answer. It didn't matter. I knew.

When she finally gave up and left, I took the phone down to the police station. Jim, this guy I'd gone to school with, was sitting behind one of the desks in front, his uniform shining, and I walked right up to him. "I... I... I..." I tried to tell him, but I couldn't get it out, especially not with another policeman just a couple of desks away, watching us, listening, so I finally just handed the phone to Jim, and let him see for himself, the pictures she'd taken, the one she'd sent to Ben—*texted*, that's what they call it. Close-ups of her bosom, close-ups of her lips and her open mouth, close-ups of her face, winking and grinning.

Jim looked at the pictures. There was this smile growing on his face, a smile I didn't appreciate. He whistled a little.

"Lilian's sure grown up, hasn't she?" he said, and he handed me the phone back.

"Ben," I told him. "She's sending those pictures to Ben." I lowered my voice. "He wants to put her in the back room. They take off their clothes back there."

He looked at me. He narrowed his eyes. He took a deep breath and then he let it out. "What can I help you with, Reggie?" he asked me, like I'd just walked in the door.

"I want you to stop it," I told him, and I heard my voice rising, because I didn't know how he couldn't understand.

He took another of those deep breaths. "We get a lot of family issues come our way," he told me. "Stuff that those family members need to deal with themselves, you know what I mean?"

"No," I told him, because I didn't.

"Suppose your sister came in here and complained about you taking her phone, about you invading her privacy. Should we arrest you for that?" He looked over at the other cop, and I wondered for a second if he was thinking about arresting me. The other cop shook his head, and something about it reminded me of Ben, and I wondered if they knew one another.

"She came in here?" I asked Jim.

"Let's say I'm just talking hypothetically," he told me. "Nothing official. I'm just asking about what you think police business is."

I thought about it. Then I told him. "Morals," I told him. "You oughta uphold what's good and decent. That's what the police oughta do."

"Look," he told me. "You don't like who your sister's dating, that's between you and him. Maybe she doesn't like what you're doing, that's between her and you. None of it is police business. It's family business. It's between you and her."

"And Ben," I told him.

"Sure," he told me. "You and her and Ben."

And that was when I finally heard what he was telling me—the *aha* moment, the lightbulb. He was telling me what I knew all along.

You have to take care of your own. You have to take care of them *on* your own.

* * *

That back door is hanging open a little by the time I make it down the alley, and I wonder if Lilian's run out it and escaped, because I'm still having to move slowly, walking stiff, walking straight, keeping it all held tight. But then, just as I get there, somebody inside pulls the door closed again.

It's a challenge, I know that. No turning back now.

I unbutton my coat. I unclench my armpit, releasing the stock of the shotgun from where I've been holding it tight along the length of me. It nearly falls to the ground, but I catch it just in time.

* * *

"You sure this is the one you want?" the man behind the counter asked me, laying it out across the glass case. An Ithaca 37. A shotgun. *Pump action, featherlight*—those were the words he'd used. "I mean, for personal protection, it's not really the best choice," he told me. "It'll do the trick, sure, but this is more a military kind of thing. For home protection, I'd suggest you get a pistol, a nice Glock, keep it in your nightstand. Small, easier to use."

Home protection, I thought, and I thought about what that means, where home is, how it moves, how it changes.

"You're not much of a movie watcher, are you?" I asked the man.

He shrugged.

"*Get Carter*," I told him.

"With Stallone?" he asked me, and he raised an eyebrow. "Yeah, I remember that one. It's OK."

"No, no," I told him. "With Michael Caine. It was made in England."

"Can't say that I've seen it."

"It's a great movie," I said. "Michael Caine, he plays Carter. His brother's been killed and Carter, he's got to find the truth about it. So he starts looking into it, and then he finds that his niece has started doing these porn movies and that his brother found out about it and...." I thought about Carter seeing his niece in those smut films. I thought about seeing Lilian in those pictures on her phone. You have to watch awful stuff like that, because sometimes it explains everything. And that disgust that Carter felt, that's exactly what I felt. "Well, I don't want to give too much of the plot away."

"Nah, that's it," the man told me. "Same with Stallone, same sort-of thing."

"Well, I haven't seen that one," I told him. "But Michael Caine... he's the man. And this..." I stretched out my hands, and I was looking at the gun, but I was thinking something else. I was thinking: Why would somebody remake a movie when it had already been done right the first time? And then I thought, *tribute*. And I thought: You repeat it because you *want* to do it right yourself. And then I unrolled a picture of Michael Caine in *Get Carter*, a picture of the movie poster that I'd torn out of a book in the library.

"That's the gun," the man told me. "So you're a collector of sorts. A movie buff. Well, I didn't know that. That explains a lot, it sure does."

* * *

The library carries lots of movies about ordinary people like me who've had to take the law into their own hands: *Death Wish*, of course, and *Taxi Driver* and *Straw Dogs* and even some westerns like *Jeremiah Johnson*. And a lot of them, just like it was with *The Godfather*, a lot of them are about trying to take care of family or take care of women—protecting the innocent. *Taxi Driver* is probably the best of them, you know, because it's got that happy ending—Travis Bickle a hero, going back to his old life, everything OK. I think about the life I want to go back to, about getting things better between me and Lilian, getting her back home, everything back the way it was. *Trust*, I think, and I think that after this is all over and after she sees how good it is, then I'm going to ask the banker if I can give her a little more money each month from what Dad set aside. I think about that and I'm feeling good about it as I look at that backdoor I've been watching for so long, not just tonight, but lots of nights. Then I grab hold of my shotgun the way Michael Caine held it on that poster and I put my hand on the knob. I take a breath, I open the door.

And as soon as I open it, little bursts of light flash at me like camera bulbs popping. Something hits me in the side, and then something else hits my shoulder. Something skims past my head. Past it? No, no, it hits me too. The sight goes out of one eye, and I feel the pain then, sharp and sudden, and then I feel myself falling a little, and then floating somewhere, and then I hear a thud and it hurts on my other side now. Then a light comes on and everything is red, and I think of those Cherry Splashes that Dwight the counterman used to make for Lilian.

It's Lilian I see first. She's turned sideways. She's laying down, but she's got her feet on the wall and she's sticking out from it stiff. Laying down on the air? Suspended? It doesn't make sense, and I want to reach down and help her up but I can't, I want to get my shotgun but I can't find it, and then I feel my heart start pumping and then things are even more red. I look around for the roulette tables, for the dancing girls, but I can't see them from where I'm at. All I can see is a desk and then some chairs, all turned on their side too, and then a couple of TVs, little black and white ones, and in one of them I see the alley I just came from and then I can see the room I'm in, and it's like one of those old crime movies seeing it like that: the body on the floor, the woman standing over it. And then I realize the woman is Lilian and that it's not *her* who's laying down, it's *me*. Lilian's *standing*.

She looks down at me. "I tried to warn him," she tells me like it's an explanation, like it's a mistake. "*Fair* warning."

Ben's done something to me, that's what it seems like, and now she's apologizing for it, for having warned him I was coming. But then I think, how could she have tried to warn him? How could she even have known I was coming? Maybe she was watching me on TV too.

"He brought it on himself," says another voice, Ben himself it sounds like, and I move my eye but I can't see him. "Your dad too."

"Dad," she tells me, and I try to move my eye again, because is Dad here? But I just see those little TVs on the desk, and now I can see Ben standing beside Lilian in the movie there and I can see a gun, and then I see that it's Lilian who's holding it.

"What kind of man would put *him* in charge of a trust?" Ben asks her. "It's bribery, it's blackmail."

"Those damned contours of time," she tells me. "'He needs you, Lilian.' That's what he told me. 'Take care of him, Lilian.' Like I hadn't been cleaning up behind them both for years now. And then he made sure I'd be stuck with Reggie forever. No way to contest the will. No recourse. With blood, it really is til death do you part."

I wonder about that word *recourse*, what it means, and about what Lilian is saying about blood. The blood she and I share, I think, coursing, recoursing out of me. Cause I can feel it now. It hurts pretty bad.

"Well, you sure took care of him," Ben tells her.

"Yeah," Lilian tells me, but I don't know what she means here either, because I was the one who was supposed to take care of her.

There's a knock at the door, a voice.

"Remember," Ben tells her, "he would've shot *us*," and that's like a line from a movie too. "We saw someone breaking in. We saw the gun. The law's on our side here."

"The law," Lilian tells me. "Like the law has helped."

And I agree with her, thinking of Jim at the police station, and how I'll have to explain to him where he went wrong when he gets here.

"Self defense," he tells her, with this look, walking away. Lilian bends down and pushes something toward me. It's my gun. She loops my finger into the trigger. Doing it behind Ben's back. And then the voices at the door are louder, and there are faces now and then people crowding the room. It's like out there on the street, people I recognize but don't recognize, faces I think I might know through the dim and the red but they seem like strangers.

"He... he...." Lilian tells them and it sounds like she's crying. "It's my brother. He had a gun. He—"

"Self-defense." Ben's voice. He's crying with her. "Don't blame yourself. It was self-defense."

He's holding onto her. She's his now, I see, and I want to get up, I want to stop it, but nothing's working right.

"I don't know why he was here," Lilian tells them. "I left him at home and it was fine. He should've been home." And then she does something special. She lets go of Ben. She stoops down to the floor. She leans in close to me. She touches my face. When she speaks, I can hear the tears again, but I can't see them, probably because my vision is so blurry. "I should've watched after him better. I should've stayed with him."

And when she does all that and says all that, something inside *me*... well, it's my heart, I know, and it starts beating harder, happier, that blood coursing and recoursing with a new energy, just bursting out of me. Because it's my old Lilian back. And I realize now why she put the gun in my hand.

"Carlo," I try to tell her, but it comes out wrong, a sputter, as I try to lift the gun. "Comanche."

"What did you say?" she asks me. "Did you say 'come here'?" and she leans in closer to hear me, putting her hand around my neck to pull me close.

"Do it," she whispers to me, almost to herself, and I know she's urging me to pick up the gun, pick up the gun and shoot Ben, but I can't, especially with her squeezing so hard, her thumb on my neck. *Too tight, too tight,* Dad used to tell me when Lilian was a baby and I was hugging her. *Gentle now.* But it was only because I loved her so much, same as her with me now.

"Michael Caine," I tell her, "John Wayne," but I don't know what the words sound like anymore, especially now with her holding me like that. "Let's go home, Lilian," I tell her, but I don't know if she hears me.

There are sirens now, and they're coming closer, but instead of trying to pick up the gun anymore or thinking about what I have to tell Jim when he gets there, I just blot out the sound instead and blot out the faces that are crowded above us too, all but Lilian's, watching me so closely, like she's waiting for something, eager for it.

Looking up at her, I can picture us with Dad like she'd said just a few minutes before, picturing it like it's *going* to happen instead of it's *already* happened, you know, and I find myself waiting with her: Dad in his chair, and me on the sofa, and the two of us getting ready for some movie on TV, and the sound of Lilian in the kitchen, cleaning up after dinner, and Dad saying, "Hurry up, Lilian, c'mon, Lilian, it's almost going to start," and then the bang of the dishes from the kitchen, her rushing a little so she can join us, that same eagerness I see in her now, I guess. And that's what I'm thinking when I go for good—what Lilian and I are both thinking while she holds my hand there at the last—thinking of those happier times, those *family* times, the way it used to be, the way things ought to have been all along.

Parallel Play

The Teeter Toddlers class was finally drawing to a close—and none too soon, Maggie thought, keeping an eye on the windows and the dark clouds crowding the sky.

Ms. Amy, the instructor, had spread the parachute across the foam mats and gathered everyone on top of it. The children had jumped to catch and pop the soap bubbles she'd blown into the air. They'd sat cross-legged on the parachute and sung umpteen verses of "Wheels on the Bus" and two rounds of "Itsy Bitsy Spider." The routine never varied, the children's delight never waned—at least until the time came to raise that parachute with its spiral of colors into the air.

"Everybody off and let's go under," Ms. Amy said in a sing-songy voice. The children scrambled clear. The adults pulled the edges of the fabric tight. The parachute rose. All the kids raced beneath.

Or nearly all of them. Maggie's son, Daniel, grabbed her leg with his chubby fingers and held on tight.

"Don't you want to join your friends?" Maggie urged, same as she did each week. Daniel shook his head.

"No like," he mumbled into her thigh.

Despite what he said, Maggie knew he *did* like the parachute—or at least watching it, how it rose and fell, how it floated at the top for a moment and then drifted downward as the children giggled and tussled beneath. He seemed enchanted by it really—and Maggie saw some comfort there too, the parachute like a blanket slowly coming to rest, encircle, and enfold. But much as Daniel liked to watch, he refused to join the other kids underneath it, and generally he kept a distance from them, preferring to play on his own. Ms. Amy always asked one of the parents to crawl beneath as well, to keep the rowdiness under control, but the one time Maggie had volunteered, beckoning her son to join her, Daniel had stood at the edges and wept, almost frantically, until another parent—Walter, the only dad in the class—had graciously swapped places with her.

Walter was actually looking her way now too. He smiled, Maggie shrugged. What could you do?

"Maybe next time," Maggie said to Daniel, as Ms. Amy began to sing.

> Come under my umbrella, umbrella, umbrella,
> Come under my umbrella, it's starting to storm.
> There'll be thunder and lightning, and wind and rain.
> Come under my umbrella, it's starting to storm.

Maggie could hear the steady patter of rain overhead now. Through the windows, the sky was nearly black.

As she'd told Amy when they got to class late, her husband, Ben, was away on yet another business trip, and with all her hustling to get Daniel dressed and ready for class, she'd felt lucky to have gotten them out the door at all. Now she kicked herself for forgetting to check the weather earlier—and for forgetting an umbrella.

"Almost done," she whispered, more to herself than to Daniel. But as she ran her fingers through his wispy blond hair, she could feel his tension easing up a bit.

* * *

By the time they'd gotten shoes tied, hands washed, and made their way out the lobby door, the skies had indeed broken open—a hard, driving rain. Short gusts of wind pushed a cold spray under the awning, splattering it against Maggie's bare calves. First the forgotten umbrella, and now this. She kicked herself a second time for wearing such a short skirt today. She could feel that spray even when she stepped to the back of the sidewalk as other moms rushed past her to their cars, each of them hoisting a child in one arm and holding an umbrella up with the other.

All those *good* mothers, Maggie thought, the ones on top of everything.

Perched in her arm, Daniel leaned against her shoulder. She held up a hand to shield his face.

"If my wife hadn't reminded me this morning, I'd have forgotten mine, too." A man's voice, beside her. When she turned, Walter smiled and hefted a big golf umbrella, closed tight. "If you're game, mine's big enough for two. Or four, I mean." He nodded to Daniel. His own little boy—Jordan, a redhead wearing a dour look—stood beside him.

Wife, Maggie thought. At least that cleared up some things.

Another woman in the class (Kristen? Katrina?) had wondered whether Walter was a single dad or maybe a widower. Or maybe his wife worked and he stayed home? No one had asked him directly. Maggie wondered if there hadn't been some interest on Kristen/Katrina's part. Walter wore thick-rimmed glasses, was graying at the temples, but he wasn't unhandsome really, and Maggie had even caught herself admiring the way he handled his son. Unlike the occasional father who tagged along with his wife or filled in for a single class—checking his smartphone every few minutes, awkward, distracted—Walter seemed eager and attentive, always making sure Jordan didn't cut in line for any of the activities, always encouraging a "please" or a "thank you." Once, several of the mothers had gone across the street for frozen yogurt after class, and Walter had tagged along too, giving his son the bites with the most sprinkles and finally all of the cone.

"Chivalry lives?" Maggie asked.

"Common courtesy," Walter said. He shrugged. "It's up to you. But it doesn't seem like it's going to let up anytime soon."

As if on cue, a ripple of thunder rushed toward them. Heavier rain now, puddling and splashing. She turned to Daniel, who met her look with a hopeful one of his own.

"Jordan," he said, pointing down at the little boy—surprising Maggie.

Jordan stared forlornly into the parking lot, seemingly impervious to the rain, but Walter smiled again.

"If you're sure you don't mind," Maggie said. "We had to park three rows that way and then halfway up. We'd be drenched before we got there."

Walter picked up Jordan. With a flick of his hand, he opened the umbrella wide and tilted it slightly her way. Each of them tried awkwardly to match the other's pace as she led them toward her car.

"I think we're going to get soaked anyway," Walter said, raising his voice over the sound of the rain. "Here." He huddled closer to her, almost stepping on Maggie's toes—close enough she could smell his cologne, some blend of mint and leather.

"I'm fine," she started to say, or "No worries"—something like that, but then Daniel started wiggling, and it was all she could do to keep him and herself balanced.

As she opened the back door and wrestled Daniel into his seat, Walter maneuvered the umbrella over her, leaving himself almost completely in the rain. She struggled to fasten the buckles quickly, fumbled too much, then Walter walked her to the driver's side and spread the umbrella across the open door.

"Knight in shining armor," she said. "I mean it." Another gust misted the inside of the car.

Walter's face was dripping now. His glasses wore a thick sheen of water. Something twitched at one corner of his lips—maybe trying to muster a smile. "Tougher dragons to slay, I'm sure."

As she started the car, she saw in the side mirror that he'd knelt down by the rear tire. The spokes of his umbrella scraped lightly against the glass. How he kept his hold on Jordan, she wasn't sure.

He stood back up and knocked on her window.

"Your tire," he said when she rolled it down. "Looks like it may be going flat."

She nodded. "Thanks. I'll get it checked."

"Seriously," he said. "I'd be worried, if I were you."

* * *

Most of the traffic on the highway crawled through the mess, while other cars sped and weaved around the slower ones, swerving sharply to avoid the puddles rimming the road. Sometimes they missed, and water sprayed across Maggie's windshield, blinding her. A Toyota in front of her hydroplaned briefly, then righted itself. The brake lights magnified and blurred in the downpour. Her wipers could barely keep up.

By halfway home, Maggie could hear a dull rumble from the back corner, something indeed wrong with the tire, and the problem quickly got worse. Even when she turned onto the two-lane toward Clifton and was able to slow down more, she felt the whole car shimmying a little, pulling to the left. In the back, Daniel had begun to whimper.

Nowhere to stop at this point, and too many rollercoaster hills and turns still ahead. Sometimes cars barreled down right on top of you along these turns, impatient, impulsive, but the road was mostly clear today. She'd met one truck in the oncoming lane and glimpsed only a single pair of headlights far behind her, apparently as cautious as she was.

Her cell phone sat in the cup holder. She reached toward it, pressed the talk button. "Call Ben," she said and then was surprised when he picked up.

"How's my best buddy doing?" he asked, his voice tinny, distant over the speaker. Other voices in the background.

"He's fine, but I'm struggling." She explained about the tire, about the weather.

"Call Triple-A when you get home. They should be able to swap it out for the spare, at least for now." She could hear him turning away, saying something to someone else on his end.

"Wish you were here," she said.

"I know, I know. You hate to call the repairman."

But that wasn't what she'd meant.

Another bit of conversation on the other end. Then: "Sorry, hon. Between meetings, but duty's calling. Tell Danny I love him." And he was gone.

"Daddy says hello," she repeated, even though Daniel had surely heard. "He loves you."

After the call ended, the phone chirped a battery warning. Apparently she'd forgotten to charge it.

Lucky to have gotten out of the house at all that morning, just like she'd told Ms. Amy.

* * *

She breathed a little more easily when she finally turned onto the last road home, the trees overhead blocking some of the rain, the Kinseys' house and the Millers' and Frank Hadley's small field, the familiar run of mailboxes, the UPS truck parked at the top of Mrs. Beatley's drive. What an awful day for that job, she thought, rushing in and out of the weather with packages in hand—then felt a brief twinge of guilt, trying to remember if she was expecting one herself.

And then they were home, the car limping down the long, steep drive toward the house. She slowed as the water sluiced down the pavement, kept the car steady, eased them the final few feet.

More than anything, her husband had wanted a house with lots of land. No neighbors on top of you, room for Daniel to have a big yard, the kind of place Ben never had as a boy himself. Maggie understood how nice it was, especially in a dense area like northern Virginia. A refuge, a haven, Ben had said more than once, and she could see it too. But sometimes, especially with him traveling so much, and especially on a day like today, the space felt isolated, lonely even.

"Let's go, little man," she said, hoisting Daniel out of the car. They had a carport instead of a full garage, and here too the rain was sweeping underneath, but she stopped for a minute to check the tire. It was completely flat, and the edges of the wheel had been ground up a little where she'd driven on it. Ben would love that.

She went inside, took off Daniel's shoes, and was heading to call Triple-A when the doorbell rang. Daniel rushed to it immediately, darting around her, already pushing past her as she reached for the knob. He loved when the mailman came by and the UPS driver too. Poor man, she thought, readying her apology.

But it wasn't UPS at the door.

* * *

Walter's glasses were still covered by rain, the drops so thick she couldn't see his eyes, and somehow that troubled her nearly as much as having him show up on the doorstep. Jordan stood beside him, and there was something unreal about that too, as if the two of them had materialized there, same as they'd been standing back at Teeter Toddlers. Except he wasn't the same, was he? No, he wasn't holding an umbrella now and...

"The tire," he said. "I didn't think you'd make it all the way home, figured I'd have to play knight in shining armor again. But here you are."

Too stunned to answer, Maggie tried to snatch Daniel back and shut the door, but her son pulled away from her like it was a game, poked his head around one knee, then the other, and then into the doorway again.

"Hey, Daniel," Walter said, stooping down, leaning forward, releasing his own son's hand to take Daniel's instead. "It's Jordan, your friend."

"Jordan," Daniel repeated, and Maggie could hear a mix of pleasure and surprise in his voice, like when he got a new Matchbox car.

Walter stared up through those smeared glasses. "I hate to barge in for a play date unannounced, but given the circumstances..."

Maggie shook her head, tried to hold back the tears suddenly welling up behind her eyes, finally found her voice. "It's really not a good time right now. My husband—"

"Away on a business trip." Walter nodded. "I heard you talking to Amy, that's what got me thinking about this, making sure you got home in one piece." He looked at Daniel again, smiled. "Surely you could spare a few minutes for the boys to play."

She nodded—unconsciously, reflex really. "A few minutes," she said. "A few, of course."

Her words sounded unreal to her, more than his own now, and even as she said them, she knew it was the wrong decision—everything, in fact, the opposite of what she'd always thought she'd do in a case like this. But really what choice did she have, the way Walter had inserted his foot into the doorway and held so tightly to Daniel's hand?

And then there was the box cutter jittering slightly in Walter's other hand, raindrops glistening along the razor's edge, the truth behind that flat tire suddenly becoming clear.

* * *

"They call it parallel play," Walter said a few minutes later. They'd settled into the couch in the living room. The scent of his cologne seemed suddenly oppressive. Maggie was self-conscious again about having worn such a short skirt, different reasons now. The boys played on the floor a few feet away—out of Maggie's reach, but at least out of Walter's as well. Jordan still hadn't smiled, but he pushed a couple of Daniel's cars across the top of the coffee table, something Maggie didn't allow Daniel to do, since Ben worried it would scratch the wood. As Daniel pushed his own cars on the floor, he stole glances at each of them in turn—smiling broadly, as if he couldn't quite believe all this was really happening.

Maggie tried desperately to work past her own disbelief, to fight that feeling of everything crumbling and crashing, to figure out a way through this. She'd heard about the bank teller who talked the robber into releasing all his hostages, the receptionist who convinced the school shooter to lay down his guns. Such things had happened, they had.

"I don't know what you mean," she lied. "Tell me more."

"Parallel play," Walter said again. "Kids this age, they don't really play together, they just play side by side—sharing the space but not really connecting, not yet." Walter's hand rested loosely on the box cutter between them, and Maggie was vaguely grateful it was at least closer to her than to her son. "It's like us, really."

"Like us?"

"Don't you agree? Think about it, how our lives have run along these parallel paths. Both of us becoming parents about the same time, both of us having little boys, both of us struggling to teach and correct and nurture those little boys. And then us coming together at Teeter Toddlers once a week—crossing paths, chatting here and there, chasing after our kids, turning away, coming back together again." He tapped the couch with his index finger, the rest of his hand not leaving the blade. "Sometimes, between our meetings each week, I think about you."

Maggie looked around the room, at all the things she sometimes took for granted. Wedding photographs and honeymoon pictures, Ben hoisting her up in his arms on the beach in Cancun, those care-free early days. The champagne glasses from their wedding stood on a bar in the corner, the ones they took down each New Year's for a toast to renewal and recommitment. And then the photographs of Daniel as a newborn, the framed birth announcement, even the little hat he'd worn in the hospital, folded up in a small box frame—the first exciting taste of parenthood. On a higher shelf, an antique clock from her parents whirred and ticked in a glass case. She'd recently moved it out of Daniel's reach, since it was so very fragile.

Everything seemed fragile to her now, fragile and fleeting, seeing it like this.

She saw the room too with another set of fresh eyes. Those heavy candlesticks Ben's mother had given them, the marble paperweight on the desk across the room and Ben's brass letter opener beside it, the fire tools—everything she might use against Walter, all of it too far away. The phone was the closest thing to her, mere inches from the couch. But how quickly could she get to it and dial 9-1-1? And how long would it take anyone to respond—especially out here, especially today?

"I can only imagine how it's been for you," Walter went on, "but for my wife and me... Well, hardly feels like we're husband and wife anymore, some days hardly even friends. You think of being parents as being part of a team, bringing you closer, unifying you, but at best we're like a tag team, a couple of caretakers. One or the other of us takes the late shift, one or the other gets up for early morning, each of us taking note of who did what and for how long—bean-counting, pettiness. What have you done for the baby lately, huh? And with her working full time, eight to five, and my job—"

The lights flickered, browned briefly, like the whole world skipping a heartbeat. The boys perked up their heads. Daniel turned a worried eye toward his mother. The rain held a steady patter against the roof and windows. The power caught again.

"It's going to be okay," she said, to the boys, to herself. She'd been clenching the fringe of the seat cushion. Slowly she released her grip. "I think it's normal, the nature of parenting," she said to Walter then, the kind of thing she'd read in advice columns. "My husband and I are very happy."

Walter turned her way. "Are you?" He squinted a little, crow's feet at the corners. "Because the way you've looked at me sometimes in class, and then this morning, flirting a little with me—"

On the floor, Jordan grabbed at something in Daniel's hand—a little blue convertible, his favorite car.

"Stop," Daniel cried. "Mine." His face was suddenly anguished.

Jordan seemed neither angry nor concerned—simply kept his grip on the car and stared at Daniel, unremitting.

"Children, children," Walter said. "Remember to share." His voice was calm and patient, and the way he wagged his hand at them would've seemed innocent except for that box cutter. Maggie wasn't sure which of the boys he was reprimanding.

She didn't realize she was holding her breath until Walter put his hand back on the couch—the blade closer again to her instead of pointed at the boys.

* * *

Before Daniel was born and even afterward, during all those breast-feeding sessions, all that rocking him to sleep, Maggie couldn't get her fill of books and articles and blog posts about parenting a newborn: not just why to breast-feed but how, swaddling techniques and sleeping routines, advice on balancing the baby's needs with her own, tips for managing the changing relationship with her husband. Ben had joked about her addiction, but she'd found so much of it educational.

She remembered now getting caught up in a discussion board right after Daniel was born—one headlined with a single, simple question: "Would you die for your child?" There had already been pages of comments in reply, almost unanimously "yes," but Maggie had felt compelled to add her own comment.

"In a heartbeat," she'd written, with a surge of love and pride, and when she'd told Ben about it later, he'd agreed.

"What parent wouldn't do the same if it came to it?" he'd said. "What good parent?"

It had seemed so easy at the time, the world in balance somehow. Now everything seemed in disarray, verging on chaos.

Outside, the rain had intensified again. Lightning flashed. Fresh bursts of thunder sounded in the distance. Wasn't that usually before the storm—the warning signs of trouble ahead?

"Mama," Daniel said. "Juice?"

"Of course, honey," Maggie said, then caught herself. She turned to Walter. "Is it okay for me to get him something to drink?"

Walter crinkled his forehead. "Of course. Why wouldn't it be?"

When she stood, Walter rose and followed her. The living room and kitchen were an open floor plan, only a few steps away, but he'd probably considered, as she had, the knives in there, the kitchen mallet, the meat cleaver.

At least he'd be farther away from Daniel, she thought, but having him behind her, out of sight for even those few seconds walking to the kitchen, unnerved her in a different way. Step after step, she waited for him to attack. Silly, really, to have worried right then. He could've done it at any time.

He stood close to her as she poured the juice. She made a sippy cup for Jordan as well, for which Walter thanked her. As she watched the boys playing with their cars, vrooming here and there on the floor, she gauged the distance to the knives in the block. Then Walter stepped in between, gesturing at something else on the counter.

"You have a tea set," he said. "Actual silver?"

"Stainless," she said.

"Some tea would be nice, don't you think? On a day like this?"

The unreality of it all struck her again, his casual, conversational tone. Keep him happy, Maggie reminded herself, keep him satisfied. "Would you like me to make some?"

"Only if you'd like a cup yourself." He smiled. "I'd hate to impose."

* * *

"Delicious," Walter said, taking a sip with his left hand, keeping the other one between them as before. "And such a beautiful set."

She'd brought out the complete tray: a full pot, cups and saucers, a sugar and creamer, a pair of ornate spoons. A small plate of crackers too, which the boys were enjoying with their sippy cups. "Here's your favorite," she'd said to Daniel, touching his hair—some small comfort in the midst of all this uneasiness before Walter had patted the couch for her to join him again.

"You know," Walter said. "This is what I'd imagined really, when I pictured being a parent. Kids playing on the floor, my wife and I sitting on the couch—doing the crossword or reading a book or having tea like this." He held up the cup in his left hand, a little awkwardly. "But my wife these days, she'll make a cup of coffee for herself and never even think I might want one, never even think." He laughed, ugliness behind it. "Do you and your husband ever do things like this?"

She shook her head. "It's tough to find time."

"You have to *make* time." A sudden sharp edge underscored his words.

Maggie sipped her tea. She'd loaded it with sugar, but it tasted bitter.

"And isn't time what it's all about?" Walter said. "I'd thought we were lucky, my wife and me, with our situation. My schedule had always been pretty flexible—project management over at Micro-Com—and since most of us telecommuted anyway, I figured I'd stay home with Jordan, work at nap time and then nights after my wife got home. Keep him from having to go into day care immediately, you know? But it was so much harder than I'd expected, especially since Jordan has never been a good sleeper. Sometimes, you know, I wanted to shake him. Don't you know I've got emails to answer? Don't you know there's a deadline looming, and the boss is waiting? Why can't you go to sleep?"

He smiled at Jordan, who had glanced up at his name. "Isn't that right, little fella?" he said, but his son just stared back at him with another dull expression.

"And then my wife, the way she'd come home sometimes too tired to take over like we'd agreed. Too tired for him, for me, for anything, it seemed like, and all of a sudden it's falling back on Mr. Mom again, right? Me pushing back those emails and those deadlines, her pushing me away." His fingers drummed against the cushion, his palm against the box cutter, the blade catching and cutting lightly into the cushion. "Sometimes I wanted to shake her too, shake all of us up, shake everything loose. I've been so tired."

"I know." Maggie forced a small laugh. "I feel like I haven't gotten a full night's sleep since Daniel was born."

"That's not what I mean," Walter said. "It's more of an... existential tired." He shook his head. "I feel like I'm disappearing bit by bit."

The children had moved onto wooden blocks now. Daniel had built a small tower of them, and as he put a red triangle on top, Jordan calmly and deliberately pushed a pickup truck into it, toppling the pieces.

"Play nicely, boys," Maggie said, unsettled by Jordan but trying not to seem like she was reprimanding him alone. Walter didn't seem to notice, and neither of the boys responded to her, but Jordan did pick up the blocks and begin to help Daniel rebuild.

Daniel smiled. Maggie felt relieved. If it weren't for the circumstances, she'd have felt grateful her son had found a friend.

"I got laid off last week," Walter said. "And if I felt like there was nothing left of me before..." He was staring off into a corner of the room now, or maybe somewhere inside of himself, the box cutter still fraying the fabric of the cushion. "I don't know if you know how that makes a man feel. How useless, how... how impotent. And since my wife and I—" He shifted, turned toward Maggie. His grip on the cutter tightened again. "Do you know how long it's been since..."

Maggie tried to keep eye contact as he struggled to find the words. Whatever she'd been trying to do here, talking him down, whatever, she was losing faith it would work. At some point, he would force himself on her, and she could take that, she thought, she could survive it, as long as he didn't kill her. But she worried more about Daniel. Whatever Walter was going to do with her, would he do it in front of the boys? Would he take her away to the bedroom and leave the children alone out here? And what if something happened to one of them while they were—

"What is it you want?" Maggie asked finally, barely getting the words out herself. "From this, I mean."

"The way we talked this morning, I thought we might be..." He seemed to be searching for the word. "Friendly. I need a friend."

"And this is the way you try to find that?" She glanced toward the box cutter. She tried to sound firm.

"Sometimes friendliness needs a little encouragement." He smiled, satisfied. It was a terrible thing to see.

The lights flickered and browned again. Something in the distance buzzed and hummed, sizzled, burned. Then the power went out for good.

"Don't worry. It's going to be fine," Walter said, and he put his hand with the box cutter on Maggie's thigh. He seemed to intend it as a gesture of reassurance, but his hand was colder than the blade.

His talk about impotence, the comment about being existentially tired, about disappearing. His calmness. His coldness. Everything came together, and she could picture how easily, there at the end, they all might die.

* * *

In the instant after the power went out, the instant after he touched her bare leg with that cold hand, Maggie lunged forward and grabbed the teapot. She swung it toward his head. She felt the blade nick her skin, ducked from his hand as it swung upward. She pulled the top off the pot too and splashed the hot tea toward his eyes. Then she hit him again.

The room wasn't dark, only shadowed. The boys had surely seen at least dimly what she'd done. Already startled by the power outage, they hustled back on the rug, away from whatever was happening, and then jumped again when Maggie leapt past the coffee table toward them.

"It was an accident," she said. "Everything's going to be okay." She could hear Walter moaning and writhing behind her as she reached for Daniel. He squirmed and pushed against her as she started toward the door. Almost by reflex, she grabbed Jordan too.

Then she ran.

Out the door, into the rain, anywhere but in the house.

Wind and water lashed against her. The boys tucked their heads into her neck, held tight now, trying to shield themselves. At least that worked in her favor.

Daniel had grown so much heavier in recent months she'd struggled sometimes to carry him for long, and now Jordan added extra weight. Would Walter have hurt his own child if she'd left him behind? She couldn't even consider that phrase: *left behind.* Instinct, maternal instinct maybe. Either way, she would do this, she would.

But where to now?

As she ran, everything lurking at the back of her mind rushed to the forefront, and everything she saw struck her with an awful clarity. With the power out, the phone had been dead. Her own cell had been dying, useless she was sure. It didn't matter whether her tire was flat, because Walter's car was parked behind hers, angled slightly across the driveway, maybe to make sure she couldn't steer around it. As for the drive itself, the water coursing down made it impossible for her to get to the road, a steep climb even without two children.

She could've stayed in the house, she knew. Those candlesticks, the letter opener, the knives in the kitchen. But could she have used any of those things on him while the boys watched? She shuddered at the thought.

What neighbor would be home? The Millers next door wouldn't be back from work for hours. Hadn't the Kinseys gone on vacation?

Frank Hadley, who lived across the fallow field, had retired. That's all she knew about him really. Kept to himself, never much more than a wave in passing. Still her best bet, and she made for it.

Her hair matted against her, clung to her face, blocked one eye. Her arms ached. Her legs too, especially against the uneven dirt of the field. Her thigh was warm. Blood, she knew.

Daniel was crying now, soft sobs into her shoulder. Behind her, she thought she heard her name being shouted from back at her own house. Another shout, this one indistinct. A flash of lightning above.

"We're playing tag," she said. "We're playing hide and seek." She wasn't sure if either of the boys heard her, if Jordan even knew what hide and seek was, but she kept on. "It's a game, it's all a game."

She ran harder.

* * *

No car at Hadley's. The power out there as well. Maggie's ankle had turned somewhere in the field, the same leg that had been cut, and she was limping now. All of them were soaked.

"We have to hide," she said. "We've got to win the game, okay? I need you boys to help."

Daniel looked bewildered, Jordan looked dazed. She couldn't imagine what she looked like to them.

Then she heard a banging and saw a workshed behind the house, the door hanging loose where the wind had caught it. She glanced back across the field. Walter was on the far side, making his way toward them. She rushed toward the shed, hoping Jordan hadn't seen him.

The shed was the size of a small garage, the inside mostly shadowed, but light filtered through a couple of dirty windows. She could make out a small workbench with a few tools on a rack above, and more hanging on the wall. A concrete floor, covered here and there with dirt or sawdust. A small lawnmower had been pushed into one corner. A couple of sawhorses stood nearby, a faded tarp draped across them.

She put the children down, her arms nearly numb now. Water dripped from her hair, from every inch of her. "Over here, boys. Come on." She lifted the tarp. Neither of them moved. Jordan stared at her with apprehension. Daniel shook his head. They were soaked too.

"Everybody up and let's go under," she said, trying to mimic Ms. Amy's singing. Jordan seemed curious now, even if the drab tarp was a poor substitute for the colorful parachute. He moved tentatively toward her, but Daniel seemed even more fearful.

"I need you boys to do this," she said, and she felt herself beginning to crumble again—fought to keep things light. She reached out and touched her son, smoothing his wet hair behind his ear, trying to comfort. "Daniel, you've got to be my little man, okay?"

Daniel shook his head more firmly, determined. "No like," he said. Behind him the door banged, startling them all. Jordan jumped toward her, and she hugged him, easing him behind her. It wasn't

Walter yet, just the wind again, but he was coming, he'd be there soon.

She began to sing, her voice trembling and cracking. "Come under my umbrella, umbrella, umbrella. Come under my umbrella, it's starting to—" She wanted to go back to the morning, to the comfort of the class, the parachute there. She wanted to erase having accepted Walter's umbrella, to undo everything that had happened since then.

"Car," came a voice beside her. Jordan. He held up a tiny hand, one of the Matchbox cars clutched in it. She hadn't even seen. "Here," he said. He opened his hand toward Daniel.

Slowly, too slowly, Daniel moved past her, took the car, and the two of them sat down together beneath the tarp.

Maggie smiled, felt the tears finally come. She wanted to crawl under there with them, snuggle close, hide from everything. But instead she forced herself to pull down the edges of the tarp and shelter them inside. She couldn't let them see—not her tears, not any of it.

Would you die for your child?

Yes, yes. In a heartbeat.

Would you kill for him?

She lifted the pitchfork she'd seen hanging on the wall, took a quick breath, and headed toward the door.

* * *

Maggie kept Daniel and Jordan under the tarp in the shed, each of the boys sitting on one side of her, until Hadley came home. They sang "Wheels on the Bus" and "Itsy Bitsy Spider" and "Twinkle, Twinkle Little Star." Each time one of the boys tried to move away, she sang "Come Under My Umbrella" again and hugged him tighter. Daniel touched occasionally at the wound on her thigh. "Band-aid soon," she said, glad neither of the boys had noticed the blood elsewhere on her.

When she heard Hadley's car on the drive, heard the car door slam, she lifted the tarp and shouted, "We're in here." Hadley wouldn't know who *we* were. Just someone. Someone needing help, she hoped. She didn't take the boys back into the yard, didn't dare, and the minutes crept slowly before Hadley himself opened the shed door. Grizzled, stoic, he was carrying a shotgun when he came in, poised and ready. Even after he relaxed his grip on it and asked Maggie if she and the boys were all right, he kept staring at her with some mix of concern and curiosity and fear. She knew what he'd seen, could imagine why he'd been cautious about coming into the shed. "I've called the police," he told her. A comfort?

A caution? She wasn't sure, but she'd already figured he would call for help.

She heard the sirens a few minutes later, and the boys echoed the sound. When they left the shed, a police cruiser blocked their view of the body—strategically so, she thought. The rain seemed, finally, to have stopped.

Soon the whole yard buzzed with action and investigation, questions and more questions, lights circling, people moving. Social services were called for Jordan—maybe his mother too, Maggie wasn't sure.

Even as the paramedics cleaned and bandaged her thigh, she kept repeating "We're all right" and "He didn't hurt the boys" and "He didn't hurt us."

"But he would've," Ben said, when she called him from Hadley's phone. "That's what you need to remember, what you need to tell them."

Self-defense, he said more than once, and *preservation instinct* and then *maternal instinct*. She wasn't sure if he was reassuring her or building a defense—trying to be with her in the moment or already planning for the future—and when he told her how brave she was, when he called her a hero, she didn't correct him.

Maggie would tell him later about the worst images that had run through her head and about what she'd convinced herself she'd have been willing to do. And she'd tell the court too, if it came to that: what Walter had said, the way the box cutter felt on her leg, her fear for herself and her child—and for *his* son too. That was important.

But there were other things she'd never tell anyone, not even Ben. How Walter was right with so much of what he said. How lonely it had felt reading all those childcare books and articles on her own, and how lonely it still felt being nearly the sole caregiver to Daniel, with Ben's job demanding more, keeping him on the road for days, weeks at a time. How lonely it felt when Ben did come home and rushed right past her, barely a quick kiss, to give his best buddy a hug, then turn away from them both the moment his cell phone rang. And how many times had Ben simply given up on trying to rock Daniel to sleep and shrugged it off on Maggie? Even two nights ago, before this latest trip, he'd done that again, and when she'd finally fallen into their own bed, he'd nudged her into making love—exhausted, hurried, far from energetic. But after all, Ben would be leaving for several days, and it was important to connect.

It had been a pleasant surprise at Teeter Toddlers to have a handsome man offer up his umbrella, chivalry not dead and all. He had smelled nice, and she'd enjoyed for a moment that little spark of flirtation between them—innocent, of course, playful at best, but flattering. And Walter had always seemed so good with his son too, attentive in ways Ben had never been.

Those were the things she didn't want to admit, even to herself—those other thoughts that had been pushing her forward when she emerged from the shed, pitchfork in hand, and Walter rushed toward her with his arms outstretched. It wasn't bravery, and it wasn't just fear. She'd felt ashamed, she'd felt betrayed. She'd felt more alone than ever. And she'd felt sure she could drive all that away, stab after stab, as the winds whipped and the rain battered against them and the pitchfork plunged into Walter again and again and again and again.

The Odds Are Against Us

"How about a gimlet?" I asked.

"Special occasion?" Terry said, skeptical more than suspicious. "Or just a change of pace?"

"Change of pace," I said, waving it off, and Terry didn't blink an eye, just reached for a martini glass and tossed some ice in it, then turned toward the shelves of liquor behind him. There was a mirror back there, and I watched him close.

Here was the game I was playing. If he made it with gin, that meant yes, and if he made it with vodka, that meant no.

My heart sank a little when he reached for the Gordon's, and I told myself that I should've bet on the kind of gin instead: Tanqueray yes, Gordon's no, or something like that.

Terry was quick to make the drink because business was slow that night. Tuesdays always were. Just me on my side of the bar and him on his, and then some empty tables behind me and three guys playing cutthroat at the pool table near the back. I had something going there too: if one of them left before the others, that was a no, but if they left as a group, that was a yes. I'd made that bet when I caught sight of one of them reaching for his jacket. Then he'd just picked up his cue again and settled back into the game.

Terry stirred the drink, strained it into a glass he'd chilled. Age spots beginning to crop up on the back of his hands. Here I was, saw him a couple of times a week, but I'd never noticed it until tonight.

"Gimlet." He smiled broadly as he set it down in front of me, ice crystals skimming the surface. "Mixed perfect, you see if it's not."

My turn to nod. Perfect sure, but it was still gonna taste tough going down.

* * *

Outside, it was threatening rain. A cold rain coming, it had felt like, hints of a hard winter further on down the line. A Phillies game was on the TV above the bar, and it looked chilly there too, and the scroll along the bottom of the screen listed thunderstorm warnings, the wheres and the whens. A series of windows lined the top of the wall behind me, looking up at the street, and as the wind picked up, I could hear it whisper along the edges of the glass. Trouble ahead out there. But inside, the weather was always fine, which is why that pool player putting on his jacket, like it was cold in there—that didn't make sense to me.

The bar was old school—not the slick mahogany and fresh brass and fancy martinis of some of those steakhouses that were cropping up downtown, trying to look like somebody. No, this was the real deal. Black walnut bar top dinged and scratched over the years. Parts of it so sticky from spilt beer and liquor that they could hardly be cleaned, but the whole thing smelling of Murphy's oil—proof that Terry tried. Sometimes when the bar was slow, you could find him moving from one end to the other, limping a little from a bicycle accident back when we were teenagers, wiping everything clean, dusting and polishing the glasses, checking the fittings on the taps. Most of the business was pints, but Terry carried cheap spirits along the rail and high-dollar options on the higher shelves. Twelve stools along the bar, those empty tables behind me, hardwood flooring stretching the length of the room. Some of the boards were a little discolored where they'd been replaced, but not patchwork looking, no. The pool table was old but level, and fresh green felt on it, at least a year or so before. A coal-burning stove sat over to one side, the kind of thing that might just be decoration in another place, but Terry would sometimes stoop down to throw some coal in it on a winter's night, and those nights it helped give the whole place a glow.

Terry didn't own the bar, but he took pride in it, and it seemed like his.

Sometimes we liked to feel we were our own men.

* * *

"Remember Derek?" I asked. "From back in high school?" Old times drove our conversations most nights—that and sports and maybe a movie or TV show. Not politics, not ever. Tonight, this seemed like the right story to tell.

"Derek?" Terry said. "Our year? One of our group?"

"No. Couple of years older. Everybody called him Buzzhead."

"Gangly kid with the crewcut?"

"That's him. Reckless. Stole the Camaro from one of the Byerly brothers."

"Oh, yeah," said Terry. "I remember him, and the girl too, the one he stole it for. What was her name?"

"Julia," I said. I wasn't sure about that name, but I said it like I knew, confident. Sometimes that did the trick.

"Yeah, Julia." Terry was wiping down the counter, some spot I hadn't seen. "And we called her Julie, right? Or Jules maybe?"

"Something like that."

"Derek's a little vague, but man, she was a beauty, that Julie. Blonde hair down to here, and that smile. New to the school, and just like that, all the guys were in love." He pointed his dishrag my way. "You too."

"She didn't want anything to do with me," I said. "Played hard to get with all of us, seemed like."

"Smart as well as pretty." We both laughed at that.

"She wasn't smart about Buzzhead," I said, trying to keep the story on track. "All of us hanging out that night, shooting the shit, and him pulling up in a new Camaro, asking if she wanted a ride."

"Like Prince Charming coming in to claim his princess," Terry said. "I remember. And all of us blown away by where he got the money for it. Never crossed my mind he'd have stolen it."

Habit, I thought. Or reflex. The way Terry was going about his cleaning. The counter was spotless, but he touched here and there, seeing things I didn't.

"It was wrong, that," I said.

"Bad boys getting all the breaks?"

"No need to romanticize it," I said. "Almost got his arm broke, and I guess you can't blame 'em really. That was the Byerlys. Gotta look out for what's yours."

I swirled my drink, drank a little again.

We watched the game a little bit, listened to that wind outside. From that TV scroll, I saw that the weatherman had moved up the timing of the storm.

One of the guys from the pool table came over then, holding up his pitcher for a refill. While Terry pulled the tap, the pool player perched half of himself on the stool next to mine.

"How's it hanging?" he asked me.

I just looked straight ahead, didn't answer him. He seemed to take the hint.

A minute or so later, Terry handed him the pitcher, and he went back to his game.

"She moved away, didn't she?" Terry asked then. "A few months later, right? I wonder what happened to her."

"No idea," I said, and I didn't. She wasn't the reason I'd brought the whole thing all up.

* * *

There were two on base and two out when Howard stepped up to the plate. He made a couple of practice swings, pointed his bat toward the pitcher, settled his stance. I made another bet with myself. He gets a hit, that's a yes. He strikes out, that's a no. A no-brainer, seemed like it to me. Howard had been coasting on his old reputation for a while now, and I said something to that effect to Terry.

"Young, isn't he?" said Terry. "Howard's uneven maybe, but he's still got a lot of life left in him."

"A has-been. Falls apart under pressure."

"A powerhouse. They know he can jack 'em when they need it."
Terry looked straight at me when he said it.

A couple of foul balls later, and Howard was still nonchalant, just going through the motions. His heart wasn't in it.

"He's finished. Nothing left there." I said with a vehemence I didn't feel. Not his fault for being unwilling, unable, I knew, but I was holding up my end.

"You gotta have a little faith in a person," Terry said.

The funny thing was that I did, in my own way.

But instead of the strike-out I was betting on, Howard's bat connected with the next pitch, a hard crack, and that ball just soared, yes, yes, yes.

* * *

"She's probably fat now," Terry said. "Popped out a couple of kids, you know how it goes."

"Who?" I asked.

"Judy," he said. "That was her name, not Julia. I remembered it while we were sitting here. And we called her Jude."

"Yeah. That's right." And it was. I remembered now too.

"Yeah, a couple of little rugrats—or maybe bratty teens by now, you add up all the years. Spends all her time in front of the tube, eating potato chips or something. Waiting for her husband to come home. Maybe Derek. I mean, didn't he head off soon after she moved?"

Terry had made me another gimlet by this point, but I hadn't tasted it. I'd just been watching the ice crystals drift and glisten. I didn't want to bring my mouth to it yet, knowing that would melt them quicker.

"Prison," I said. "Stole another car soon after that, and the owner of that one turned it over to the cops."

"Oh, yeah." He shook his head, then laughed a little, but it was hollow. "Them were some crazy times, weren't they?"

"Simpler times," I said and caught Terry looking at me like that didn't make sense. Not skepticism now, not suspicion, just a little sadness. "Short stint in juvie," I said, covering it up. "That was it for him. Straight and narrow afterward, I heard."

On the TV, the announcer called out the next names in the line-up. At the pool table, the balls clinked, and one or two of them landed in the pockets, and the men mumbled and laughed. I felt like I could hear the coal burning in the stove too, then realized Terry hadn't put any in there.

"Do you really think she's like that?" I asked. Idle curiosity now, killing time. "Snaggletoothed? Spreading out around the middle?"

Terry gave a wry smile, just one-half of his lips curved up. "I bet she's still a beauty. A few years on her, sure, but..." He picked up a glass, a clean one, and began to wipe the rim of it with a cloth. "Truth is, I don't think people change that much, not most of us, at least."

* * *

We aren't old. Weren't. But we've been around. Been around longer than we should've, I sometimes think.

I picked up the gimlet, took a sip.

* * *

It was about that time that the three men at the back packed it in. Tossed their cues on the table instead of putting them back in the rack, leaving it all for someone else to clean up. Terry. Whoever. The other two pulled on their jackets, and they settled up their tab and headed past us into the cold night.

All three leaving together, that had meant yes, of course. Yeses everywhere I turned. Like I had much of a choice anyway.

"Another?" Terry asked me. "Or you ready to call it a night too."

I thought about it, all of it.

"One more for old times," I said. "No rush." Maybe the truest words I'd said the whole night.

But true or not, when he turned away from me to reach for the Gordon's again, I decided I couldn't put it off any longer.

A coward's way of doing things, I know, him with his back to me, but I didn't think I could bear to face him.

Didn't matter. He caught sight of me there in the mirror as I pulled the gun.

Heck, maybe he knew it was coming all along.

* * *

I called it in a few minutes later from down the street. Dutiful like that.

"It's done," I said.

"About time," came the voice on the other end. "Fella like that can't learn to keep his mouth shut, past time we shut it for him."

"You don't know Terry was the one who talked," I said, despite myself. Not dutiful now, probably should've kept my own mouth shut. I felt my teeth grinding, heard that long pause on the other end of the line.

"Sometimes," he said finally, "you just know. You know what's happening. You know what you gotta do. There's no two ways about it. No room for second-guessing." He was saying *you* but he meant *him*, of course. Or maybe just everybody. *You* as a general thing. All of us. Another long pause, heavier breathing on the other end of the line. "*I* know," he said, and I could hear the impatience in his voice, maybe something stronger. "That's all that should matter to you." I could picture him wiping his forehead the way he did. Sweat that was never there. "Either way, it'll send a message."

I nodded. Like he could see me. Then I hung up without saying anything else.

Disrespect now, that's how he probably took it, and I was sure I'd pay later, one way or another. But disrespect wasn't it.

Just nothing more to say.

* * *

I started walking then, not headed anywhere in particular, not sure where I wanted to go or even where I was part of the time. My balance was unsteady. The drinks, I told myself. And then I wandered further into the darkness.

I could've done it all night, I guess—not the walking but that second-guessing back in the bar, that betting with myself. Whether Terry was gonna shake a drink or stir it, or how many glasses he might polish to a shine in the course of ten minutes or a half-hour or an hour. Which of those guys in the back was gonna win at pool, or any number of things about that Phillies game: hits and runs, fouls and strikes and outs. Or betting on when that rain was gonna finally fall, if the weatherman was gonna get it right or miss it by a mile, if we'd get a trickle or a flood.

Sheet lightning lit up the sky in little bursts as I walked, letting me see everything clear as day, but just for a second. And then other lightning zigzagged and split, like fingers reaching down from the heavens. Watching it, listening to the rumble of thunder, feeling those clouds bunching overhead, the storm crowding all around me... well, I felt like I could pinpoint when everything was gonna break and come down hard on top of me. It wasn't just the weather now, of course, that was the least of my worries, but I turned up my collar against the wind like that made a difference, then just kept walking. No use looking for shelter, either. It wouldn't do any good.

That story I was telling, it had gotten away from me. The Camaro, that's all I was trying to talk about. Wrongs and retribution. Betrayal and loss. A sense of responsibility. The price you pay. That was where it had started, why I'd brought it up. Trying to tell him something without telling him. But along the way, it had changed into something else, and now that something else kept following me, more of it coming out than I'd remembered before, things I wished had been left forgotten.

Like me and Terry one night that same summer, that was the memory dogging me now.

Sheet lightning that night too, I could picture it, and the two of us sitting out at the high school football field, splitting a six-pack Terry had pilfered from the mini-fridge his dad kept in the garage. We'd been watching the sky, talking about girls—or I had, at least. Judy in particular. What I'd glimpsed when she bent over one time, what I felt like she was trying to show me. What I was gonna do to her when we finally got together, what she was gonna do to me. The things boys say, thinking it makes them sound like men. The things some men say too, I guess.

Terry had just shook his head. "You know, I'd just be happy to hold her hand."

I'd laughed at him for that. Hold her hand? I'd probably called him a pansy, something worse, something like that.

"Yeah," he'd said. "Take her to a movie. Hold her hand. Take her out for ice cream, and just sit there, looking into those blue eyes of hers."

"Her eyes are blue?"

"Yeah," he said. "And then there's that way her nose turns up just a little, just at the tip, and those freckles." And something about the way he said it... Well, this was right after the bike accident, and his limp was even worse back then before he'd gotten used to it. But even before the accident, he'd never seemed like the kind of guy girls went for, the kind who had any sort of a chance with them. None of us had thought that way about him.

"You should ask her out," I said, and felt bad as soon as I'd said it. An easy offer, I'd thought. Terry was no competition. He was sure to get rejected. Even more than ever, I thought he was weak, and that's what made it bad what I'd said.

But he'd shook his head again. "Nah, she's yours, gonna be. Already staked your claim, right?"—echoing one of the things I'd said, emphasizing that word *staked*. "And anyway, that's not how a fella treats his friend, stepping in like that on something that's his, something he wants. I just wouldn't feel good about that." He'd lifted his beer and taken a swig. "That's not the man I am."

It had made me happy then, what he said about Jude being mine, about him and me being friends, how funny it was him calling himself a man. All of it.

But again, those were simpler times.

Precision

The precision of the response, that's the key.

* * *

Turn your attention now to the safe. In order to discover what lies inside, you must accept this vault on its own terms. At each step of the way, you must respect your adversary.

Examine carefully the richness of its gray surface, the hint of blue woven into its texture. Let those subtler shades of black reveal themselves.

Caress the rough outer skin. Understand the thickness of the steel plates beneath, the perlite or vermiculite layered inside. Admire the airtight seal, the hidden hinges. Picture the small sanctuary at the core. Still and silent, seemingly inscrutable, a riddle, an enigma.

Resist the urge to touch the dial too quickly. Consider that silence instead. Absorb it. Discover a small peace. Renew your purpose.

Nothing exists outside of this relationship. Nothing.

And yet...

Divert your attention briefly to your client. Do not look at her, standing there behind you, those eyes boring into you (you can feel it). Instead, simply ponder why she watches you so intently. Think: Curiosity? Think: Distrust? Consider her intentions—felonious, clearly. Recognize her malice—unmistakable. Question her motives—elusive.

Remember the sound of her voice on the phone a week ago—nervous, hesitant, yet purposeful: "I need you to open a safe at my house." Remember your surprise at the spot to which her directions led you: a service road in the woods. Remember the quick glimpses of her there: the close-cropped blonde hair, the severe pantsuit as black as the night, the thinness of her frame, the dark intensity of her gaze. (Do not think of how you couldn't meet the look in her eyes. Do not trouble yourself with how you can no longer look anyone in the eye. Do not think about mirrors at all.)

Remember saying, "You have cased the property thoroughly," as you made your way along a small path through the underbrush, pines rising tall around you, a house lit up softly in the distance.

Remember her telling you, "It's my house. As I told you on the phone. I know it pretty well already."

Recall your sarcasm when you told her, "Of course, of course.

Your house. Your safe. Simply a forgotten combination, and midnight the only time you had free."

Remember her not responding, just keeping a steady pace ahead of you, leading you toward the house. Strident but silent, seemingly inscrutable, a riddle, an enigma.

Remember that nothing exists outside of—

Stop.

Arrange your tools: your battered laptop, the autodialer, the various cables. A stethoscope and a sheet of graph paper too—these latter nostalgically.

Then resist the urge to hold that stethoscope. Resist all forms of nostalgia. Forget the past completely. Recognize that you can't recall the good without revisiting the bad. Just take a deep breath and—

"How long does all this usually take?"

* * *

The technician doesn't like the interruption, Catherine can tell that much from the small shift in his shoulders, the way he doesn't turn up from his squatting position in front of the safe. The view unnerves her: plain gray coveralls, a tuft of thinning white hair, a shiny bald spot. A puff of irritation escapes the technician before he answers her: "You're watching me."

"I believe I've paid for the privilege," she says, trying to provoke some response. She imagines that the tension between them tightens yet another notch, but still the technician doesn't move.

The technician, she thinks... because that was the way he'd introduced himself a half-hour before, when the two of them met in the woods less than a mile from the house. He'd parked his car and slowly unfastened his seatbelt before emerging from it, pulling out that briefcase behind him, telling her, "I'm the technician you ordered." Formal, dignified—*just doing my job, ma'am.*

As if she didn't know his name after their conversation on the phone. As if she hadn't already known it.

He reminded her about their deal for payment up front, the first half of it at least—all of it too much. *An investment,* Catherine kept reminding herself, and as agreed, she produced the three stacks of bills, trying to catch more than a glimpse of the man's eyes as he counted the money in the thin moonlight. She believed if she saw those eyes she would understand something, but he just stared at her hands, never looked her fully in the face.

Now they stand inside the house itself, in a small office just off the master bedroom, and still she can't see his face clearly. The safe sits inside a cabinet between the desk and the bookshelves. A flat curve of black metal presses against the vault's face, hugging the dial, and the technician's hands hover just in front of the apparatus, holding a small gray cylinder with wires falling from it. His hands, his arms, his entire body seem frozen in place, suspended, waiting—waiting for Catherine to leave, apparently, no matter what price she's paid.

His response confirms it. "A privilege, yes, but perhaps also a waste of time. Shouldn't you be elsewhere? Aren't there things that you should do while I finish here?"

"I've done everything I need to do. Unlock the door, disable the alarm, lead you to the safe." All that and more. "Where do you want me to be?"

"Aren't there rounds to be made? Keeping a lookout in case the homeowners return unannounced?"

"Haven't I mentioned it? I'm the homeowner."

When he doesn't respond, she looks at the bookcase behind him, the books lining those shelves, the single photo propped beside them, two young girls in the picture just beside his head. He'd had at least that chance to see, but clearly he hadn't. Wouldn't. That was the point.

"You don't trust me," she says.

"Trust," he repeats, a scoff to the word.

His stillness is disturbing, and Catherine wonders—again—what sort of thoughts run through his head, what he's thinking about now. With his back to her, kneeling over the safe, he's already in the right place, the right position; she's seeing the same view that anyone would see—would *have* seen—coming up behind him, interrupting his work. She could finish it now, but she does want to know something more. And just as suddenly, she hates him for it—the desire, that need of her own.

"Did I break your concentration?" she says. "Is that it? The trick won't work if someone's watching? The magician doesn't want to reveal his secrets?" She can feel her temper rising, but quickly quashes it. "Your name is Cornelius, right?"

The technician does turn at that, just slightly, speaking over his shoulder, and Catherine catches a glimpse of that bunching skin behind his glasses, the plumpness of his jowls. "You use my name as if it's an accusation, as if knowing it wields some power over me." He shakes his head. "Whatever we are doing here, you are implicated as completely as I am."

Catherine nods, her emotions cooling, or at least leveling. She's willing to wait. "Yeah," she says. "Yeah, you're right there."

* * *

Close your eyes. Inhale deeply. Exhale. And again. Try to redis-cover that small peace. Try to ignore the woman in the room. Open your eyes. Focus. Focus.

Ensure that the magnetic base curves snugly against the dial. Avoid handles and hinges. Leave yourself plenty of open space to work. Not just open. Empty is best.

You may need to reposition the base several times for proper alignment. Remember to watch your hands. Respect the power of the magnets. You could lose a finger. You could lose worse.

Secure the motor to the locator stud furthest from the dial, then hang the tension belt on the nearest stud. Lock each into place.

Consider...

Consider her insistence that she owns this home. Accept that she may be telling the truth. Question her motives again.

Understand the phrase insurance fraud. *Tell yourself, "Of course." You have done this before, back in your previous life: the staged robbery, the manufactured crime scene, the client keeping both the jewelry and the insurance payout.*

Think: plausible deniability.

But recognize that you've never done such a job in the middle of the night.

Wonder at the drama of such a decision.

Gauge her plans. Calculate the consequences.

Ignore the subtle changes in the room's pressure as she shifts her weight behind you. Consider telling her that you work faster, work better, when you are alone. Reconsider. Do not look back. Do not get distracted.

Slow down.

You haven't skipped steps, but you've moved carelessly through several of them, completing them without thinking about them. Remember the importance of following these instructions as closely as possible. Remember to keep your blinders on. Nothing but the job. Nothing but the protocol. Adherence to that protocol is paramount. Precision is key. Remember what carelessness has cost you in the past. (Try not to remember too closely.)

Recheck your work: locater studs, tension belts, dial pulleys. Where were you?

Yes. Choose the appropriately sized dial pulley. Affix it to the dial. Tighten with screws.

Loop the timing belt over the dial pulley. Feel the tension.

Understand that word tension *in all of its forms. Remember to avoid carelessness but do* not *linger over that former carelessness itself. In fact, try not to remember that night at all.*

Stop.

Take a deep breath.

Still your nerves.
Steel your nerves.
Remember that memory is cruel.
Live in the now, not the then.

* * *

"You use a computer," Catherine says, surprised, surprising herself.

"The computer is more precise. Precision is key."

"I'd expected a drill. Or something explosive. Dynamite. Something more... destructive." Because that's what she's associated him with all this time. Destruction. Devastation.

The technician snorts. "You've seen too many movies. Big noise, big effects. Those are never the goal." He pauses. "Unless.... Do you need to have more damage done? For the insurance, I mean?"

It's still unnerving speaking to the back of his coveralls, offensive even, not just because of the awkwardness of it, but because of how it echoes with the past, how close it must be to what happened before. "Insurance?"

"You are the homeowner, you've said. So perhaps you would like some... evidence that whatever was in this safe has been stolen. To support your insurance claim."

Catherine shakes her head, then realizes that the technician can't see her. "No," she says, flatly. "No, you don't need to damage the safe. I just didn't know that everything was computerized."

The technician pauses. She can almost see him thinking, the wheels turning. He starts to say something, then stops, then begins to speak again.

"Everything is *scientific*," he corrects. "Everything is precise. The computer simply assists the precision." He begins tightening some sort of connection now—a cable linking the computer to the apparatus on the front of the safe, that's about all Catherine can see over his shoulder. In the briefcase beside him, she sees more cables, a pad of paper, a stethoscope. She pictures doctors, hospitals—paramedics rushing to help. Obviously not the technician's purpose.

"You use that too," she says. "The stethoscope."

"Years ago," the technician mumbles, intent on setting up the computer. "Another life for me."

Catherine thinks about that phrase. *Another life.* The passage of time, yes, but also something else: Dues paid and a fresh start. And then she thinks again: *Another life.* And for just a moment she feels her demeanor begin to shift and break once more.

"You wish to learn," the technician says. "I must focus on my work, but if you wish to learn...."

She can see those jowls again, but still not the eyes, and she wonders what she'd find there if she could. Grief? Guilt? Of course not. Pride, she imagines. Self-justification. Maybe even some hint of the self-righteous.

"Yes," Catherine says, slowly bringing herself back into control. She moves down beside him to watch more closely, despising that closer proximity to the technician, forcing herself to maintain some degree of poise. "Yes, there are definitely some things I want to learn."

* * *

Speak the steps aloud now that you have an audience. Speaking them will help you to focus.

"The unit must be off. You must plug in the power cord first, then each of the cables in order. See where this one enters the laptop? See where this one joins the stepper motor? Another cable here, very important. Understand how the order is important to the process."

Weigh the evidence that you now have at your disposal. Question your hypothesis that this is insurance fraud. Question again whether she is the homeowner. Rethink plausible deniability.

Ignore her distracting questions. Do not answer when she asks where you learned to do this. Steer clear of the question about how long you've been a safecracker. Simply correct her that you're a locksmith, a locksmith, please.

Tell her: "Turn the unit on. Turn the combination dial to O. Choose the proper configuration on the laptop."

Conjecture other possibilities for what is happening tonight. Imagine that this was her home, but there was a divorce, not an amicable one, and a dispute on property division, which you are helping to rectify. Speculate that she does not own the home but that she is being blackmailed by the homeowner over something terrible within the safe. Understand that whatever your role in whatever is happening, the events of this night are clearly illegal. Remember that you had sworn to yourself never to commit a crime again. Regret that you reneged on that decision.

Show her how to activate the program. "As simple as clicking a button."

Try not to cringe when she asks if there's ever been a safe that you couldn't crack, if there was ever a job that didn't go as planned. Try not to smell her perfume when she leans in closer to you.

Tell her: "The spindle connects the wheel pack to the drive cam." Tell her: "The number of wheels in the pack is related to the number of numbers in the combination." Tell her: "When the wheels are aligned, they form a gap." Define what it means to park the wheels.

Do not think of the scent of perfume at all, how it intrudes. Do not think of the safe you couldn't crack, the job that didn't go as planned.

Explain instead how the computer listens for the clicks to determine the number of wheels in the pack. Explain how this is just the first step. Tell her, "The wheel must be parked in stages, at intervals, and the clicking must be graphed." Tell her, "In the old days this was done by hand. By ear. The precision of the response, that was the key." Touch the stethoscope as you explain this. Feel nostalgia for the old days, despite yourself. Tell her, "The locksmith's job is to listen closely, watch closely, miss no details."

Stop.

Miss no detail yourself.

Recognize the perfume.

Recognize and consider.

Understand.

One riddle solved, other enigmas still unfolding.

Steadfastly avoid answering when she asks if there was a job that went badly.

* * *

"This conversation," the technician says. "This too seems part of the privilege you believe you've paid for."

"You don't like talking?" Catherine asks.

The technician doesn't respond to that at first, just watches the dial slowly rotate back and forth under the mechanism attached to it—Catherine still watching him watch, but up close now, closer than she ever believed she'd be, close enough to smell him. A scent like old books: musty, forgotten. No, no—more like a clogged drain. Then: He smells like an old man. And for a moment, she almost feels sympathy for him. Only for a moment.

"You've bought my services," he says finally. "My services and my time. But not this conversation. Not me."

"Of course not," says Catherine, thinking just the opposite. "It just struck me that you've done this before."

"It's my job," says the technician. "Locksmithing. You know this. You called me at my business."

"At your *legitimate* business," she says. "Of course. But you've already made it clear that you don't trust me, that you think there's something *not* legitimate about this particular job. *You're* committing no crime here—this is my house, this is my safe—but you think you're committing a crime. And that's the kind of thing I think you've done before."

The technician is watching the laptop now, watching it work through the numbers. "Those days were a lifetime ago," he says finally, as if that explains it all. Catherine swallows a sudden rise of bile.

"Were you ever in prison?" she says. "This lifetime ago, when you used to do this. I'm curious. Did a job ever go *really* wrong? Really cost you something?"

"I don't think you're curious at all," he says. "I think you know the answer to that question."

"I'll take that for a partial yes," she says. "So what was it like? Prison life?"

The technician only tinkers again with his set-up. He's only pretending he doesn't hear. "I made a mistake once," he says, but Catherine doesn't hear any remorse in it, any feeling at all. "It was a terrible mistake, a costly one. And I paid for it, paid dearly."

"Dues paid, huh? Fresh start?" Once again, she's barely able to stifle her emotions. She already knows about all that: his new reputation, his respectability. *Earned*, she guesses the technician would say. But would he say *deserved*? *Rehabilitation* he might claim, but all she can think is *recidivism*—just a matter of time before he'd be doing something like this again, wasn't it? Catherine has simply accelerated the process. She's just saving some time. She's just saving someone else the trouble, saving some beautiful someone else.

Whatever he's paid, it simply wasn't enough.

"Tell me," he says then. "This is a question I don't often ask my clients, but I'm curious myself. In this safe, what is it that you so badly want me to retrieve for you?"

He turns to her as he asks the question. Finally, she can see his eyes.

* * *

Take advantage of her sudden silence. Close your eyes. Inhale deeply. Exhale. And again. Stabilize. Turn back to your work.

Recheck the cables. Follow the calculations mounting line by line on the laptop's screen.

Clear your mind. Concentrate on the moment. Recognize how routine sustains, how the process prevails.

Do not let her words get to you. Think about penance, not prison. Know that you have indeed paid your dues. Think about the challenge in front of you—a bigger challenge than you expected—and not the ones behind.

Watch the dial as it slowly spins. Watch your back. Wonder what lies at the end of all this.

Concentrate on the moment, yes. But also focus on the immediate future. Question why you are continuing this job. Consider stopping. Consider disconnecting the cables, packing away the tension belt, the motor, and the magnetic base, simply walking away.

Recognize her motives. Consider her intentions. Evaluate more urgent exit strategies. Accept that you may need to abandon your tools.

The window is mullioned in iron. The door is the only way out.
The furniture in the room is cumbersome, blocking the path.
The books on the shelves can be grabbed and thrown.
The fireplace tongs and poker would make suitable weapons.
Regret that you didn't bring a gun.
Remember why you don't carry one.
Regret.
Stop.
Recheck the cables.
Examine window, furniture, bookshelves, fireplace once more.
Notice the photograph on the shelf beside you. Two girls.... Sisters clearly.
See them.
See.
A terrible mistake.
Stop.
Remember that you told your client this already: A terrible mistake, a costly one.

Remember that you told your wife the same thing. Circumstances spun out of control. Fate conspired against you.

Remember that you told your wife: Safecracking is not always a victimless crime, but it was never meant to be a violent one.

Remember that the past is the past, even when it seems to creep up on you in the wee hours of the morning. Even when it seems like it's being thrown in your face.

Consider telling your client this too.
Consider telling her that the past can't be undone.
Remember how you told your wife this.
Remember how you told your wife that there was nothing to be done.
Stop.
Stop.
Remember your wife.

Listen to the whir of the machinery. The computer is working, working, working. The science will complete itself—will finish all but the last stage of the job. You're needed for that, for the final precision of it all.

Understand that nothing exists outside of this relationship. Nothing.

* * *

"In this safe," he asks, "what is it that you so badly want me to retrieve for you?" and a flurry of answers and images and desires immediately crowd the front of Catherine's mind—the first of them the image of a young girl tilting her head back to drink a Pepsi, laughing at the same time, the liquid dribbling down her cheeks.

Innocence, she thinks. *Innocence restored. And guilt punished. Retribution*, she thinks. *And justice. Some balance restored.*

Your life, she thinks, and just as quickly she corrects the idea. Not just his life, but some rolling back of all the years of that life, and the reclaiming of those years for someone else.

Impossible, of course.

She had considered what to put in there for him to retrieve, another photo, a pile of photos, dead flowers, a mirror. Look at yourself! See! See!

She had even thought briefly of just leaving the safe empty—a symbol, many layers of symbolism, in fact, but too much to explain.

In the end, simplicity was best.

And it wasn't really what was in the safe at all, but the reenactment that mattered. A do-over, and the right one would die this time. *That's* what he can do for her, *that's* what he can help her to find.

But just as his question prompts this crowd of answers, he looks at Catherine—only a moment before he turns back to his work—and she finally sees those eyes head-on: the bleakness there, the vacancy.

Already dead, she thinks, and she feels cheated by the idea. Watching him continue his work, she realizes the futility of it all.

"The program has completed its run," the technician says then. "See here how it presents the numbers of the combination. There's no order yet, just the raw numbers. The next step is to try each of the sequences individually. It's a process."

Catherine looks from the technician to the picture on the shelf beside him. Two pretty girls. And she wonders which of them she was trying to bring back here. The one who died? Or the one who just died a little?

Nothing will bring either of them back.

"If you don't mind," the technician says, "I'd rather be alone for the finish. It's...."

"Yes," Catherine says. "Fine," she says. "I'll leave you alone to finish things up here." She stands. "I'll make those rounds you asked me to make."

Because that too had been the plan, even if she's not sure whether she can carry it out now.

* * *

Look at the numbers before you. The order has not been determined, but the solution is there. Only a few simple rotations stand between you and what lies inside.

Choose an order at random. Make the first turn of the dial...

...and remember that night, fifteen years before. The office safe, after hours, no security guards. An in-and-out, that's what you'd told your wife as you packed your tools: the stethoscope, the graph paper, a fresh pencil, your new pistol. Affectation, you knew, that last item. And unnecessary. An easy job.

Make another rotation of the dial now, and then a third, and consider how this is the same process you were following all those years ago, the same crouching before a safe, the same fingers turning the dial, older now, wrinkled, cramped, but...

Remember the small shift in the room's pressure that signaled someone had come up behind you. Remember the sudden scent of perfume. Smell it.

Remember attention to detail. Remember the precision of the response. Remember how you spun in place, instinct quicker than thinking, thoughtless even.

Remember thinking Why me? Why me? Why me?—*a cry that echoed through the night and the week and beyond, through the investigation and the arrest, the trial and prison, through every day, even into this day, this hour, this moment.*

This first combination of the numbers has failed to open the safe.

Do not be disappointed. The initial ordering is rarely the right one.

Rearrange the numbers. Begin again. Make the first turn of the dial.

...and remember your wife, moments before you left for that ill-fated job.

Remember how you felt packing that pistol in your toolbag. Remember joking with your wife about it, your desire to spin the gun around your finger cowboy-style, that last moment of lightness—so different from your usual self, and even more different from who you are now. Remember her not laughing with you, remember her caution that you should be careful, that someone could get hurt.

Remember kissing her goodbye.

Remember her *perfume, the way you used to get lost in that smell, holding her, loving her.*

Make another rotation of the dial, and then a third, and remember your wife telling you she loved you—the last time you heard those words from her.

This second combination has failed too. Again, do not be disappointed. Persistence is key. Patience is a virtue unto itself.

Breathe deeply now. Avoid sighing.

Rearrange the numbers again. Begin once more.

...and remember telling your wife about it when you raced home, the job unfinished, the girl's body still on the floor. Remember how your wife wouldn't look at you. Remember how you thought she was afraid for you. Remember her I told you so *attitude, and your anger that she didn't comfort, that she didn't understand. An accident really, a miscalculation. My God, couldn't anyone see?*

Remember the trial, and the evidence stacked against you. Everyone against you, everything. Prosecution, police, fate. Remember taking your wife's hand. Remember her pulling her hand away. Her too.

Remember prison and all the days she didn't visit. Remember the voicemails left unanswered, the anxious ones, then the angry ones, and the bitter letters returned, and the begging ones too, and all the words unheard, unread, unsaid. Think about the package of divorce papers and how gladly you signed them at that point, how gladly you seemed to sign them. Think about the emptiness of the apartment you moved into after you were paroled. Remember thinking, I must start again.

Then remember the mornings when you don't want to wake up, the mirror you can look into only long enough to shave, the long lonely stillness of the night.

Stop.

Regain control here—of this, of yourself.

Take out the stethoscope, listen to the safe as you make the next turns of the dial, hear the wheels move, the process working.

Remember the awkward position of the girl's body, the ill fit of her cleaning uniform, the red spot in the middle of it. Remember the nametag dangling there and the fact that you didn't look at the name.

Remember her name from the newspaper, from the trial: Rosanna.

Remember the last letter you received from your wife, and the anger you felt when she wrote that you were not the embattled hero of this story but the villain in someone else's. Remember the lines that cut you to the core: You always asked Why me? *But did you ever ask* Why her?

Forgive your wife for asking that. Forgive yourself for your answer to it.

Discover a small peace.

Renew your purpose.

Remember that the night is darkest before the dawn.

Understand the job you were hired to do.

Recognize it as the job you were meant to do.

Recognize that your story and this woman's are the same.

Take one more deep breath.

Make the final turn of this combination.

Hear the click that promises success.

Open the safe.

* * *

After she hears the safe door open, Catherine gives the technician a moment to see what's inside, to let it sink in, then she steps back into the room. The technician turns at the sound, a single sheet of paper in his hand, and that same emptiness in his features.

"Why her?" he says, very calmly, and it's the incongruity of the words, the insult of them, that pushes her over the edge.

She puts a bullet in him then. Several bullets, in fact.

Afterwards, she steps over to the corpse and takes the paper from his hand: a photocopy of Rosanna's obituary notice. Simplicity was best.

She'll need to burn that. She'll need to replace the safe with the stocks and bonds, deeds and titles she'd removed from it earlier. Her own stocks and bonds, of course, her own deeds and titles. Her house, just as she told him, and she was just protecting it from an intruder. The law would sanction that.

She picks up the photograph of her sister and herself. Rosanna was always the one with the dumb luck, always the one to make the poor choices. A custodial job—a night janitor. An innocent bystander, catching him unaware. Wrong place, wrong time—Catherine would admit that. And probably stumbling ahead stupidly—that had been Rosanna, hadn't it? But she hadn't deserved to die.

And the technician hadn't deserved a clean slate, a fresh start.

A legitimate business? Bullshit. With a single call, she'd proven that lie.

Catherine will make another call now—to the police this time. She will report the intruder, let them hear her anguish for what she's done—fright, bewilderment, some combination of the two. The police will come then, questions and answers. She'll explain that she arrived home late. She'd forgotten to set the alarm. A safe neighborhood, sometimes she just forgot. Then something about hearing a noise downstairs, stepping down to investigate, the gun she never thought she'd actually use, the blur of events that followed. A woman alone, sudden fear, wild panic. That panic would explain the number of rounds she'd put in the intruder.

She laughs lightly to herself, thinking of that word *rounds*—those *rounds* the technician had all but begged her to make.

But appropriate too, that excuse about panic, because that was what *his* excuse had been at the trial: panic, things suddenly out of control, a mistake, an accident, anything to diminish the guilt, reduce the sentence. But no matter how harsh the sentence, it never would've been enough.

And what will she say if the police discover the connection? Catherine has already considered it. A coincidence, that was the first explanation she considered, but what were the odds an ex-con would *accidentally* rob the house of a woman whose sister he'd killed years before? And then there was the explanation itself. It *was* intentional, of course. He'd been trying to set right what he'd messed up before, take something away from Catherine that he thought Catherine's family had taken from him.

All those years in prison, all those years to plot his revenge. That was a story that made sense, wasn't it?

So yes, she'll tell them that. Then tell them, with a grim laugh, that perhaps there was some perverse order to it, after all—an order the technician couldn't have planned himself.

Tell them, with a grim look: Maybe it was cosmic justice.

Tell them: Really no other way to explain it.

Tell them... well, something like that, and still time to practice it a little before they arrive, still time to get it right.

The precision of the response. Wasn't that what the technician himself said? The precision of the response—that would be the key.

A Drowning At Snow's Cut

Even though I'd driven down from Northern Virginia late the night before, my father still insisted on getting to the marina just after daybreak on Friday.

"The water is smoother early in the morning," he explained. "We'll get an early start—a full day to enjoy." Emphasis on the word *full*. After nearly 40 years, I catch the nuances.

But he was right, at least partly so. As I lugged my overnight bag and a cooler of drinks and sandwiches, I saw the serenity in the morning haze: boats moored in their slips, seagulls hopping along the dock, a sway of marsh grass, the Bogue Sound like a sheet of glass. A couple of the marina's workers were prepping for the day, but even their voices and movements seemed soft and easy—the calm before the storm when a clamor of boaters rushed in for gas and supplies and help with the lines.

Dad came up beside me. "Beautiful, isn't it?"

"Sure," I said, but the word turned into a yawn before I could catch it.

Dad stiffened, the lines around his eyes growing tighter.

"I hope you'll like the new boat at least," he said curtly and walked down the dock. A duffel and a camera bag hung from his shoulder. He squeezed hard on the new lengths of rope he carried, the veins popping up on that hand. On the other side, he carried a worn leather satchel with his thick *Waterway Guide* and a couple of John D. MacDonald novels. I'd already gotten on his bad side about those too. When he told me he'd been rereading some of the old Travis McGees, I reminded him not to get his expectations up. Our own little boat trip wouldn't have the action *or* the women.

But even as I'd said it, I'd heard Mom's voice in my head: *Don't start anything with him.* And my own conscience nagging me: *You're all he has now. Remember that.*

Then Dad turned down a small side dock, and I saw the boat for the first time. "Wow," I said, not just pretending. It was a knock-out, thirty feet or more, dark blue along the hull, the deck a bright white, and teak trim running the length of the topsides. The lines were sleek. The fiberglass gleamed. *I Dream of Doris* was written in script along the stern.

"It's a Back Cove," Dad said. "Yanmar engine. 380 horses. A couple of years old. Used, but I like it." He sounded like the salesman he'd been—manufacturing equipment in his case, big companies, big contracts, but still the same patter: the history of the company behind the boat, a legacy of quality, a friend who'd had a similar model. Then his voice faltered just slightly. "After your mother," he began, and then stopped. He seemed to be scanning that fiberglass and that teak as if he was seeing it for the first time himself. "I needed something to... to look forward to, something to be excited about," he said, and then reddened slightly, embarrassed by his own words.

"Well, this sure is something to be excited about," I said. *Stay upbeat*, Mom might've cautioned me, but I hadn't needed that nudging. For a few seconds, I simply forgot that long history of bickering and harsher arguments and forgot all those more recent phone calls—tense, brittle conversations with nothing to talk about except the weather and what each of us had eaten that night for dinner and then the weather again. Then those few seconds passed.

"A boat like this makes you wish you were making more than a reporter's salary, huh?" he said, coming to himself once more. "Get one of your own?" He laughed, the smile edged.

"Good to be back, Dad," I said with my own edge, remembering again all the times he'd encouraged me to get a *real* job. *No profit in newspapers*, he'd told me before. *Profit is important.* Or asking *Is there room for advancement at that paper of yours?* I hadn't mentioned yet about the cutbacks, of course, about me being laid off. Maybe it would've been easier just to tell him and get it over with. But it was the principle of the thing. I didn't want to give him the satisfaction.

I started to step on, then held back. "Permission to come aboard?"

"Want me to get a picture?" he asked, fumbling in his camera bag—another new toy, a little digital point-and-shoot. But I didn't wait.

"Nah," I said. I tossed my bag on deck.

"Don't forget that when you step on board, you use your right foot first," he said. "And be sure that you've got a firm grip." And so the lessons continued. "Do you remember how to tie a bowline?" he asked as I stored gear in the cabin, nowhere near a rope. "How about a square knot? A cleat hitch? We'll get the lines out later and run through them again." And then later, "Red, right, returning from sea or... when else?" He seemed to be hoping I'd get them wrong so he could set me right.

"If I flunk the test, can I go home?" I finally asked. He looked hurt, but at least he stopped.

By the time we eased the boat out of the slip, some of the morning haze had burned off, but the day was still gray and the sky overcast. Clouds seemed to be gathering and settling.

* * *

The waterway was mostly quiet. Late May, a weekday—the season had barely started. Dad had taken the helm to guide the boat through the tight, shallow channel that led away from the marina, but once we were on the waterway, he offered me the wheel: "Get it up on a plane, son. It'll do almost 24 knots if you push it, but I think it's better to keep it around 2200 rpms. Above that, it burns too much fuel too fast."

I leveled it out about 2600 RPMs, cutting the water at a fast clip. I could see him eying the tachometer, but to his credit, he didn't say a word—still sore maybe. He did take a picture this time: his son at the helm. I wondered what my expression betrayed.

Talk to him, my mother would have said. *That's all he wants. Someone to talk to.*

"Smooth," I said to him, above the roar of the wind.

He nodded, started to speak and then didn't.

Each of us left it at that.

We were heading south—Morehead City, NC, to Southport, a single night docked at a marina there, and then back the next afternoon. A short trip because I needed to get back to work, I'd told him. And that was half-true if you counted emailing out resumes to newspapers that weren't hiring or scanning the Internet for possibilities on some unseen horizon. Long empty days, little in the way of prospects. It had already been two weeks since I was laid off. A short trip with anyone else might've done me good, but I already felt the need to rush through this one, rush back.

The markers flew past, red and green alternating. The Intracoastal Waterway thinned and broadened. Along some sections, houses with grassy yards stood on the edge of water, wooden docks jutting out toward us, boats tied up and bobbing lightly in the current or else hoisted up on simple lifts. Other stretches of our trip were just sand and marsh and those windswept oaks, and an occasional sailboat or power yacht. Lone fishermen stood along the shore here and there. Elsewhere a couple of guys tossed lines out from a small skiff. We passed the quaint old fishing village at Swansboro and then the old Hatteras Yacht plant, and then cruised through the training grounds at Camp LeJeune, the signs warning boaters not to anchor, not to come ashore. Dad snapped photos of all of it, each landmark, each little patch of scenery.

Every time we'd slow for the No Wake Zones near marinas or at any of the numerous bridges that dotted the channel, Dad asked if I wanted a Coke or a pack of nabs or tried to strike up a little patch of conversation. But trouble lurked around the edge of each question.

"Working on a big story these days?" he asked.

"Same old, same old. You know how it is."

Later he tried again: "Everything I read says that the newspaper business is on the downswing. You OK?"

"Holding my own," I told him—one of his own old phrases, tossed back his way.

As soon as each No Wake Zone ended, I pushed the throttle ahead quickly, drowned out any potential for those questions to go much further, and drowned out the memories of old fights and of new failures.

* * *

We anchored for an early lunch along Snow's Cut, a thin canal that leads the ICW west toward the Cape Fear River. The canal was thin, barely 100 feet wide, with just a few slivers of beach and a couple of stretches of tall cliffs. Dad brought out some sandwiches—chicken salad. There was a small dinette just behind the cockpit but we sat down on a couple of chairs on the lower back deck, enjoying the sun. Not far from us, a pair of fishermen sat glumly on a small boat, their lines hanging slack in the water. On our other side, a cruiser had stopped for lunch—a man, a woman and a couple of small kids. "Who wants hot dogs?" said the woman. A chorus of yeses followed.

"Sandwich OK?" Dad asked.

I nodded, chewed.

"Your mother's recipe," he said. "I knew it was one of your favorites, so I dug it out. Tried my best to do it like she would've, but...."

I hardly remembered that it had once been a favorite, and would never have recognized it as hers. But he'd surprised me, and I was moved again by the way his thought trailed off and that faraway look.

I put my hand on his shoulder. "I wish she was here with us," I told him. "She would've loved to be out here."

Dad came back from wherever he was. "Well, not *here* maybe, " he laughed. "You know how she was about boats."

"Oh, she could hold her own," I said, dropping my hand off his shoulder. I remembered her at the bow as we shoved off from the dock, or taking the wheel while Dad checked the charts, or the two of us laughing as we dodged the seaspray when Dad cut across the wake of a larger boat. "She was a pro."

"She was a good sport," Dad corrected. "But she never cared for it, even from the beginning." Something sparked in his eyes. "Did I ever tell you about the first time we went out on a boat? We were just dating then—a couple of teenagers on a little Boston Whaler we'd rented. I loved it. Man, I was on seventh heaven. There was a little bit of choppiness on the water, but I just gunned the engine and cut right through it. On top of the world. And then I turned and saw your mother clutching the rails and her feet pressed hard against the hull. She was almost green—seasick right out in the middle of the channel—and she begged me to take her back to the marina. And I did, of course, and after that, I swore to her that I'd never make her go out again, not another time, not *ever*."

"There's a promise that didn't last," I said, taking another bite of the sandwich, then talking through it. "I can't remember when we didn't have a boat, and I think I could count on one hand the times she didn't go out with us."

"The boats were *her* idea, her *insistence*," he said, bristling a little. I hadn't meant it as an accusation. "I loved her enough to give up everything for her, and she loved me right back—and that meant loving what I loved, I guess. And for a while there, a big supply of Dramamine, too." He shook his head. "But if she'd ever asked—once—I'd have given it all up."

Over at the other boat, the kids were throwing little pieces of hot dog bun into the water. Seagulls had already begun to swoop in. "Stop that," called the mother, laughing. "They'll be all over us." Dad shook his head, watching the birds gather. For a few minutes neither of us spoke.

"Remember that storm we got caught in?" I said finally. "I think I was eight or so. Remember how dark it got, and the rain and the waves? I was scared to death, but Mom just kept smiling, talking about what an adventure it was, telling me how you were keeping us safe."

"She was scared to death herself, and gave me hell later," Dad said. "But she never let it show, did she?"

"She was a good sport, like you said."

"A good woman." He nodded. "We were lucky to have her."

Laughter echoed across the water, as the gulls swooped and cried. Boats passed along the channel, their wake rocking us softly. One of the fishermen stood up and began to reel in his line, then slowed and stopped, sat down again. Soon we finished our sandwiches, pulled up the anchor, and headed off again.

After that, I kept our speed a little slower—not quite coasting, still not talking much, but not rushing the way we had. Dad offered me a beer and then cracked it open for himself after I shook my head. At one point, he put his hand on my shoulder, the way I'd put mine on his. There was thought and effort behind it, but the weight felt odd.

It must have felt odd to him too. After a few seconds, he let it drop.

* * *

By 5 p.m., we'd made Southport and taken a quick walk around the town—an old fishing village turned into a couple of cross streets of shops and restaurants and sleepy cottages. Back at the marina, Dad settled down for a while on the long chaise at the stern of the boat, reading a dog-eared copy of one of those Travis McGees, *A Tan and Sandy Silence*. While he read, I slipped down to take a shower, and as I dressed, I heard his voice through the hatch, talking to someone else. "Just the night," he said, and "Down from Morehead" and "My son's a big-city reporter and a fine one." I pulled on my shirt, stepped up on deck.

"And here he is now," Dad announced as I came up.

In the slip beside us was an older boat, as big as ours but nowhere near as sleek, though Dad would praise it later as a classic. A woman stood on deck, maybe ten years or so younger than Dad, chatting amiably across the thin dock.

"Phyllis Stackley," she told me, with a little wave. She had that distinguished look that some older women get: confident, almost regal, but wearing it easily. To the manor born, to the manor settled. Her skirt was a swirl of pastels, and she wore a white top. Casual, but elegant. "And this is my husband Dennis," she said, and a man emerged at her side. I hadn't noticed him before. He'd been just inside the transom—stocky and stern where his wife seemed thin and playful. He was graying at the temples, and he gave a curt nod.

"Won't you two handsome men come join us for a cocktail?" asked Phyllis.

"Only if we can bring over our own drinks," Dad said before I could wave off the invitation.

"It's a deal," she said brightly.

"Are you sure?" I asked, directing my question at Dennis. I thought I'd glimpsed a reaction from him, something a little sullen or sour. But he greeted my question with a smile. "Certainly, certainly," he said. "It wouldn't be a party without guests."

"That's what I always say," said Phyllis. "We'll get some cheese and crackers. Come over when you're ready." She disappeared into their cabin. Her husband gave a quick look our way—that same look I'd glimpsed before—and followed behind her.

"Maybe we shouldn't intrude," I told Dad, already up at the bar of our own boat.

"Just a drink and then we'll come back and make dinner." He was pouring us a couple of bourbons. Woodford Reserve on the rocks. "Too good to mix," he explained and gave me a generous pour.

"One'll be enough, if that's the way you're making them." I laughed.

"Never skimp," he said. A lesson there too. I didn't mention that it contradicted another of his aphorisms: "Everything in moderation." We stepped across to the other boat—right foot first for balance, I remembered, just in time.

* * *

Don't skimp overruled *everything in moderation* as it turned out. One drink wasn't enough. But Dad was having a good time, and I hated to spoil it.

He and Phyllis had really hit it off, and they sat at the stern talking and laughing. She kept encouraging her husband to keep everyone's glass filled, and Dennis topped off Dad's drink with bourbon from their own bar—"No need to keep stepping over to your boat," he said—and made his wife one vodka tonic after another.

"He puts a new wedge of lime in for each round," she said. "That way we both always know how many I've had." There were four curls of lime in her glass already.

"My wife was always two drinks, never less, never more," said Dad, already on his third. "She always liked to keep her wits about her, and speaking of wit...." He told a story then about one of Mom's April Fool's jokes: something about clocks and calendars and the previous day's newspaper. He'd already been talking about Mom, and beaming all the while: how they'd met, how long they'd been together, how much she loved crosswords and books and gardening. Despite his gray hair and the creases in his face, he seemed boyish and spry. At one point, I'd stepped over to our boat for a jacket and to "check my messages at the office"—really just seeing if any bites had come back on my resumes before the end of the week—and when I came back, Dad was talking about how proud they had been of me, too. He even mentioned a local award I'd won, one that I was surprised he knew about.

Through all of it, Phyllis listened with rapt attention—laughed and sighed at all the right places, sincerely it seemed to me. It reminded me of something Dad had told me: You'll always be remembered as a fine conversationalist if you let the *other* person do all the talking. Tonight he was holding court, enjoying the attention and even opening up a little. When he talked about Mom's cancer and how it had devastated her, how it had devastated both of them, he talked about it with a frankness and emotion he'd never shared with me.

"You poor dear man," said Phyllis, putting her hand on his arm.

Dennis had stayed quiet beside me through all the talk, but as his wife touched my father's arm, he let off a little grunt and shifted in his chair.

"You say you're from Delaware?" I asked, trying to pull him into the conversation.

"The *real* Wilmington," he said with a brisk little laugh, and then Phyllis jumped in.

"Dennis is an old sourpuss," she said. "Don't mind him. He always makes that joke, every time we come through here."

"You come here often?"

"Winters in Florida," he told me, "so twice a year, once on the way down each fall, and then again on the way up in late spring."

"Since Dennis retired," said Phyllis, "we've become nautical wanderers, following wherever the current draws us." As she turned back toward my father, a little of her drink sloshed out on the deck.

"Honey," Dennis said, a quick caution.

"Oh, Dennis," she said. "It's fiberglass. It'll wash easy." She leaned toward Dad again. "I have to admit, I never enjoyed boating, and this wasn't how *I* imagined retirement at all. No, I saw travel in Europe and Asia, not salty air and seasickness. And don't get me started on what the humidity does to my hair."

"Seasickness," Dad said.

"The worst," she said. "I'm bad in a *car*, so imagine what being on the water does to me. But Dennis loves his boats, and I love him, so...." She stood up and gave a little dance, just the smallest little shimmy, holding her arms out wide and shaking them. "Now," she said. "I can take the rolling waves and the curves, and I can sleep through the whole night no matter how the boat rocks...."

Watching her, I thought of a gypsy dance—something about that word *wanderer* maybe, and that skirt she wore, muted but still colorful. If she'd had bracelets on they would've jangled, but thin plastic bands clung to each arm instead, the ones that people wear for some charity or cause. Dad and I had worn them ourselves—the breast cancer that had taken Mom. Our bracelets had been the color of Phyllis's, and I wondered if Dad had made the same connection.

Dennis himself didn't seem to soften when his wife said, "Dennis loves his boats, and I love him." He just stared at the spot of vodka tonic growing sticky on the deck. But Dad clapped lightly as she danced. Still, even though he gave a broad smile, I could tell that something hid behind it. The moment was bittersweet at best.

"Your wife's quite a charmer," I said to Dennis, trying to draw him into the conversation again.

"Yes, she is," he said. "Always some damn scene like this." He took another sip of his drink.

Phyllis had finished her dance as we talked and plopped back down beside Dad, both of them laughing. Neither of them had heard her husband.

* * *

Dad showered while I pan-grilled a couple of steaks on the cook-top. Dennis had gone down into the cabin of his own boat after our drinks, but Phyllis stayed on deck. "Smells good," she called out about the sizzling steaks.

"Come join us," I said, but I think she could tell it was just idle politeness on my part. She waved off the invitation.

"We'll just see you tomorrow," she said, and then she stood, weaving slightly, and moved unsteadily across the deck toward the hatch that led down into their cabin. En route, she paused to grab the bot-tle of vodka, and raised it toward me, as if tipping a glass my way—warm and cheerful. But a couple of moments after she'd gone below, I heard different tones, she and her husband talking. The conversa-tion wasn't loud, but I thought I detected an undercurrent of anger. Fortunately whatever was happening there stopped before Dad came up from his shower.

While we sat on the dinette and dug into our steaks and talked about the plan for the next day, Dad kept looking over at the other boat, longingly it seemed to me.

"A beauty, isn't she?" he said at one point, out of nowhere.

"How's that?"

"The Bertram," he said, and I thought he blushed, but it may have been all he'd had to drink. "That boat is a true classic. You wouldn't believe it, but it probably cost nearly as much as this one. They just don't make 'em like that anymore."

Not just longing, but that loneliness again too. Wistful, apprecia-tive. I realized for the first time, awkwardly, that he would probably date again and might someday find someone else, and I wondered what she'd be like, how similar to Mom, how different. I was glad again that the voices on the other boat had died down.

Soon, the alcohol and the big steak took their toll. While I cleaned up our plates, Dad stretched out on that long chaise at the stern again, trying to read under the lights from the dock. But every few moments he'd nod off and then jerk himself awake. "Tough to see out here," he said finally. "I'm gonna go down," and he took his book back to his berth.

There was a bar just across the small harbor and sounds of a big crowd echoing across the water, and I went over for a while to see who I might meet. No one waiting for me back in Virginia, after all, no one serious at least, so why not? I did end up talking with a couple of women, but when they asked where I was from and what I did, I realized my heart just wasn't in it. After two drinks, I headed back for the boat and sat out on the stern under the stars, listening to the lap of the waves and to the small ripples of conversation from the other boats docked throughout the marina. From down in the cabin, I heard an occasional snore from Dad.

Another memory came back to me: Dad and I arriving home after a fishing trip, returning with a cooler full of spot and croaker, and then me standing beside Mom in the kitchen while she cleaned them. "Did you have a good time?" she'd asked, and I'd shrugged. I hadn't. "What did you boys talk about?" And another shrug from me.

"Dad told me I wasn't baiting the hook right," I said finally. He had kept trying to show me what to do and how to cast the line right. We'd both ended up frustrated. "I just couldn't do it."

"Well, maybe there's a lot your father doesn't know how to do either," she said, after a moment. "Sometimes *he* tries, and he doesn't get it right either. You think he might've been *trying* to do something *he* didn't know how to do very well?"

But I just shook my head. "No," I said. "He already knew how to do it all." When he baited the hook, he'd done it just right, and he'd cast out his line with the perfect flick of the wrist. There had been a time when I'd been in awe of everything he could do, but that day I'd felt suffocated by it, and soon after I'd begun to resent it.

Mom had the bigger picture. Most days, even now, I still couldn't see it.

When I went down to bed, I saw that Dad's book was still stretched across his chest and his mouth hung slightly open. As quietly as I could, I converted the galley table into another berth the way he'd shown me, but it took awhile for sleep to come, and even then it was restless, thinking about Dad and his life and what was ahead for him, and then about me too and my own uncertain future.

About 6 a.m., barely daybreak, I thought I heard a voice again from the Bertram beside us, and then I definitely heard someone cranking it up and pulling it out of its slip, heading back toward Delaware or at least somewhere else. Our boat rose and fell slightly with the wake from their boat, and soon I drifted back to sleep.

* * *

Dad was eating cereal when I got up, almost to the end of the book he'd left open on his chest the night before. I poured my own bowl, and as we sat together, I caught him a couple of times looking at the empty slip beside us, but he didn't say anything about the boat being gone and neither did I.

When it was time to head out, he handed me a credit card to go settle up with the harbormaster. I took it—no need for an argument—and just planned to use my own, same as I always did when he offered. Dad began straightening things around the boat, prepping for the trip home.

In the office, two young men—college-aged kids working summer jobs, khaki shorts and polo shirts with the marina's logo—huddled over a VHF radio. I caught the tail end of the words on the other end, "no attempt to resuscitate," and then a squawk and dull static.

"Man," said one of the kids, shaking his head. He had a scruffy beard.

The VHF squawked again, another staticky voice: "Closest dockage is Oceana Marina. Give me your ETA and I'll—"

The other, clean-cut and well-tanned, had caught sight of me and turned down the volume, then stepped up to the counter. The first looked disappointed and leaned his head down lower toward the speaker.

"Yes, sir," he said. "How can I help you?"

"One night's dockage," I told him. "The blue boat there. *I Dream of Doris*." I pointed through the window. Dad had brought out his camera and was snapping a few photos of the docks.

"Yes, sir," said the kid behind the counter. His nametag said *Patrick*. "It's a dollar seventy-five a foot," he said. "What size is your boat again?"

I realized I didn't know. Thirtysomething, I figured. "33," I said— the age at which I'd gotten the job I'd just lost.

"$57.75," Patrick said, and I started to hand him my credit card, but the thought of being jobless made me suddenly cautious. Practicality won out over principles. I reluctantly handed him Dad's instead.

"Dude," said the bearded one, standing up. "Vodka and *Dramamine*." He shook his head. His nametag was upside down. *Billy*, it said. "I mean you don't have to be a rocket scientist to know you're not supposed to mix that stuff, do you? Not *that* much of it, I mean, and especially old people."

"You shouldn't mix it at *any* age," said Patrick, and then under his breath, "and you can't call our customers *old*."

"They *were* old," he said. "That's just a fact, Jack."

"The boat that was docked next to us," I said. "The Bertram. Is that who you're talking about?" I glanced out at Dad again. He was looking up at me now through the window. I gave a quick wave, held up a finger.

"There's been... a drowning," Patrick said, aiming for a solemn tone and respectful pause. He sounded like a TV anchorman.

"Vodka and D is just *not* a mixed drink," Billy said—to me this time. "But you know, I wonder, if you mixed vodka and Dramamine and *Red Bull* if it would all counteract itself?"

"How did you hear about this?" I asked Patrick.

"We've been listening to the Coast Guard, and I have a buddy from school who's working at the state park up at Carolina Beach. He's been following the whole thing."

"How did it happen?" I asked—going into reporter mode. Who, what, where, when, why?

"It's effed up," said Billy and then caught sight of Patrick's glare. "I mean screwed up—the story that's coming across the radio. The Coast Guard said the people had been drinking all night and then they were out on the waterway early this morning and they got into a fight and then the boat turned and the lady—" He made a movement with his hand like diving off a diving board. "They should've just stayed here until they sobered up."

See you tomorrow, Phyllis had said. She hadn't expected an early departure.

"Why did they leave so early?" I asked.

"Dude said they were getting an early start," said Billy. "He came in late yesterday just before we closed and prepaid, said he wanted to make sure they didn't miss us, said he liked to settle his debts. I told him we opened at 7, but he said he might be gone before then."

"They left about 6," I said. "I heard them." *Him,* I thought. *Dennis.* And then I saw that sour look of his and heard that snarl in his voice—"Always some damn scene like this"—as Phyllis laughed and leaned into Dad. A fight, Billy had said. About what? About last night? About Dad? My first urge was to dig deeper, find the story behind the story. But then I remembered I wasn't a reporter anymore. And anyway, I was letting my imagination run away with me. She'd been drinking heavily. She'd admitted to seasickness. Sure, her husband was a jackass, but it was a leap from there to anything else, and what would be gained by testing that leap? And then I thought about how relaxed Dad had seemed the night before, and about the look he'd given the empty boat slip this morning, and about how much he'd already lost. Practicality? Principles? Maybe a little of both this time.

"If you step down there before we go," I told the boys in the office, "don't mention any of this to my father, OK?"

They nodded, a little confused but agreeable. I signed the credit card receipt, thanked them for their time.

Dad snapped a photo of me as I came back to the boat. I tried to smile.

"What took so long?" he asked.

"Credit card machine," I said. "Everything's fine."

* * *

Not far out of Southport, I asked Dad if I could take the helm.

"Sure," he said, "And remember, we're heading North now, but we're *also* heading into port, so...." He raised an eyebrow at me.

"I got it," I said, but I caught myself smiling this time. It wasn't just pity.

I kept us at a slow pace, not a crawl but certainly slower than the way down. Snow's Cut wasn't too far ahead of us, and I wanted to give the Coast Guard time to get that Bertram into the marina before Dad and I crossed paths with the drowning.

Dad puttered with some of the instruments and relooped a couple of lines, and then turned on the VHF radio. Before I could come up with a reason for him to turn it off, the chatter had already begun: "Two Coast Guard cruisers at Snow's Cut" and another voice asking "What's the trouble?" and then the answer: "Not sure, but looks big. Suggest keeping your speed slow, no wake."

"Sounds like we should steer clear of that," I said. "Want to take the scenic route?"

"All scenic, isn't it?" Dad said. "But I don't think there's another route—at least not an easy one."

"We could cruise up the Cape Fear a little. A side trip? Let them work out whatever the trouble is?"

"Nah. Let's just take it through. You need to get back, I know, and I'm interested to see what's happening up ahead." He reached down to adjust the squelch knob.

Just as he did it, the next words came through: "Nice-looking Bertram. I heard someone went overboard."

A puzzled look. "You don't think that's...?" Dad let the question hang.

"Dad," I said, reluctantly. I pulled the throttle back and let our own boat slow, the wake from behind us catching up and bobbing us up a little as we came to a drift out on the wide, open water. "I have to tell you something."

I told him—all of it, everything I'd heard.

"Dammit, son," he said. "If you'd told me before." He pushed me aside and took the wheel. He shoved the throttle ahead. The boat nearly jumped out of the water. I grabbed the bench to keep from being thrown back, and just barely managed to right my balance.

"What are you doing?" I called out over the sudden roar of the wind.

"There may still be time." The tachometer was quickly racing toward the red line—3100 rpms, then 3200 and 3300—but he didn't pull back. "C'mon," he said. "C'mon."

"She drowned, Dad," I called out. "She's already...." I couldn't bring myself to say the word.

"I heard you the first time," he snapped. "But we have to nail that smug son of a bitch that did it."

"He was a jackass, Dad, but there's nothing to say he killed her." I didn't want to stress all the drinking again, didn't want to make it sound like her fault, but I did call out "Dramamine" again.

"What kind of reporter are you?" he asked—bitter, angry. His words didn't come through clearly over the wind and roar, but I heard him say "an eye for detail" and "pay attention!" and then "wasn't taking Dramamine. No need."

"Her seasickness," I said. "I got *that* detail. Did *you?*"

He shook his head, pushed the throttle a little further. "Doris," he said. "Doris didn't need—" The spray swept around us, cold and cutting.

"She's *not* Doris," I called out. "It's Phyllis, Dad. Phyllis. *You* try to pay attention."

He shot an angry look my way. "I *know* who she is," he shouted—the words clear this time. "I'm not *senile*, son."

Whatever distance we'd bridged between us was gone, and gone too Dad's openness the night before. He shut down and shut me out as he focused ahead. I was glad to return the favor.

The veins on his hands rose and fell as his grip pulsed against the wheel. He passed several other boats, pushing past them, leaping their wake as we left the shipping channel and swung through the twists of the ICW leading toward Snow's Cut. He cut tight by the markers, even pulled briefly out of the channel a couple of times—reckless, hurried.

"C'mon," Dad said again—to the engines, the boat. It was as if I wasn't there.

Soon, the entrance to Snow's Cut loomed—those tall cliffs rising ahead, the channel narrowing abruptly. We struck ground briefly, the depth finder letting out its shrill alarm, a brief tug at the bottom of the boat. I hoped the propeller wasn't damaged. It certainly didn't seem to be. Dad never slowed down.

Just before a bridge that spanned the waterway, we sighted the Bertram, anchored outside the channel. A Coast Guard boat was pulled up alongside, its light flashing and swirling. Another Coast Guard boat kept a slow patrol nearby, barely pushing through the water, marking a perimeter. *Like an accident on the side of the interstate*, I thought, and same as with the highway, other boats were bottlenecking the scene. Dad just swerved around them.

"Slow it down," someone shouted as we sped past, that boat rocking heavily in our wake.

From another: "Are you blind?"

"Gotta slow down," I told Dad, but he barely pulled back the throttle. The second Coast Guard boat saw us, turned on its own flashers and spun to intercept.

"Slow your vessel," a voice boomed through a loudspeaker, echoing against the walls around us. "Slow your vessel now. Do not approach."

Dad slowed and then began to wave his arms, beckoning them near. It was unnecessary. The Coast Guard boat was coming whether we wanted them to or not. Beyond them, the Bertram and the other Coast Guard cruiser bobbed as the wake from our boats reached them. An officer stood at the Bertram's stern, looking down at his feet. Was there a body lying there? I was glad we'd been stopped where we were.

"She didn't fall in," Dad called out as the Coast Guard boat pulled alongside. "He pushed her. Her husband. He had to."

The officers on the approaching boat—blue uniforms, close-cropped hair, one taller than the other—looked at him warily. The shorter one had his hand close to his sidearm, too close for my comfort. The other looked confused.

"You know something about the drowning?" that second, taller one asked.

"We just got here," I said. "We didn't see anything." I tried to look apologetic, didn't know quite how to signal them that I wasn't responsible.

"Did he say she fell in?" Dad asked. "Is that what he says? She'd been drinking? What, all night?"

"Yes, sir," the taller of them said.

"Hell, she wasn't taking Dramamine," he said. "She was—"

"You know the deceased?" the other asked.

"We met her last night," I said. "We only just met her." I turned to Dad: "Dad, she said she was seasick."

"She used bracelets," he said. "She didn't need Dramamine, because she was using motion sickness bracelets. That's what she showed us last night. Don't you remember?"

The dance, the gypsy dance, the bracelets that didn't jangle because they were plastic. *What kind of reporter are you? Where's your eye for detail?*

"We saw the Dramamine, sir," said the taller officer.

"Don't worry," said the other. "We'll do a full blood test to make sure."

"And you'll find it," said Dad. "She'll be full of it."

People were watching us now, the boats rubbernecking our scene as much as the Bertram before. Dennis had stepped out onto the stern of the boat. He watched too.

"But, Dad," I said, worried again. "You were just saying the opposite—that she *wasn't* taking Dramamine."

"Who made the drinks?" Dad said. "He did. He was making them. She wouldn't have taken Dramamine herself. She didn't need to."

The officers exchanged glances with one another. One of them opened his eyes wide, an "Oh, boy" look.

"We'll handle it, sir," one of them said.

"Just look," he said. "Look to see if she's wearing them now. If he's trying to cover his tracks, he would've taken them off of her. He would've known he'd have to. Call them. Call over there."

The taller man shrugged, went over to his radio. He turned away from us as he talked. The shorter man stood watch over us, his hand still close to his gun.

Movement over at the other boats—someone on the cruiser moving toward the Bertram, the officer there leaning over to talk. Dennis stood at stern of the Bertram and stared our way. I couldn't see his face clearly, not from this distance, but I wondered what his expression was. Grief? Worry? Did he have a reason for the latter? Had Dad been right?

The officer on the Bertram turned and knelt down. The body was indeed down there—Phyllis lying across the stern there where we'd had drinks the night before. Dennis glanced down, then back to us. The officer on the boat stood up, asked him a question. I thought I saw Dennis shake his head. Then his questioner pointed down. Dennis shook his head vigorously then, threw his arms out as if exasperated, pointed to himself. The officer held up his hand, a calming gesture. Then Dennis pointed our way, angrily, jabbing the air.

"I don't think she was wearing any bracelets," I said.

"Of course not," Dad said. His tone was still clipped, impatient. "He took them off. He was trying to cover his tracks. I just hope he threw them overboard."

"Why's that?"

"Because if they can find the bracelets on board, he can claim that she took them off. But if he threw them overboard, he has to claim that she never had them."

"Our word against his."

He shook his head. "I've got a photo. When you went back to our boat to check in at your job. Dennis took it himself."

The radio squawked on the Coast Guard boat bobbing next to us. The man answered, and then called up to us.

"He says his wife wasn't wearing any bracelets. She didn't have them on this trip."

I glanced over at Dad, looking for that "gotcha" look of his. But his features were grim and showed no sense of triumph.

"I'll get the camera," I said. I patted his arm before I headed to find it, and I thought I felt him, just for a moment, lean toward that touch.

* * *

The rest of the cruise back, we kept an easy cruising speed, enjoying the relative peacefulness of the sun and the salt air and the easy breeze. We were running later than scheduled at that point—given the statements we needed to make to the Coast Guard and then to the police—but it seemed wrong to rush.

"Want a beer, Dad?" I asked as I steered us around a turn.

He shook his head, his eyes downcast. He was sitting right beside me, but seemed worlds away.

"Wanna pull over and dock for a while?" I asked later. "Get some lunch?"

He didn't even answer that, and so we cruised along further—marsh and oaks and water and that distance between us.

Talk to him, son. That's all he wants.

"I lost my job," I said finally.

"What?" he asked, as if he was waking up.

"I was laid off," I told him. "Two weeks ago. A lot of us were. Cutbacks everywhere. The paper was just bleeding money."

He squinted his eye at me. "You were laid off," he said, but it didn't sound like a question, despite the confusion in his look. "Why didn't you tell me? Why'd you tell me you had to get back to work?"

Keep it light, Mom would've said, but I told it to him straight—no bitterness, just honesty. "Because I was afraid you'd say exactly what you said. What kind of reporter am I? And I've been wondering myself. If I was better, maybe they would've kept me on."

Dad surprised me. He didn't react, but just nodded softly. "I was wrong to say that. Sometimes I don't... think first. And—" He hesitated, as if thinking now. "I should've known better, because I— well, I wondered if something like that might have happened. I check for your articles everyday. Online. And I noticed the paper hadn't published anything lately. I've been wondering, but I just— I just didn't know how to ask."

I shook my head. He'd known all along. As usual, he was one step ahead of me and right about everything. And then more words came back to me: *You think he might've been trying to do something he didn't know how to do very well?*

He placed his hand on my shoulder then, loosely, easily. "You're a great reporter, son. Don't worry. I know you'll land on your feet."

A boat passed, and the driver waved our way. Dad hadn't noticed, but I raised a hand in return.

"And you're a good detective," I told him. "I guess those Travis McGee novels are paying off, huh? A job for your retirement maybe?"

He shook his head slowly, looked out beyond the bow of the boat, somewhere at the next marker or maybe further beyond. Ahead of us, the channel widened.

"I'm fine to read them," he said finally. "Not to live them." But he smiled a little as he said it. "Just no profit in it, son. None at all."

A Necessary Ingredient

I am not a detective—not a real one, as you'll see—and I didn't set out to write a detective story here.

But sometimes you end up in a place you didn't intend to go. Sometimes what you discover is different from what you expected to find.

* * *

For the past few years, I've rented a second-floor office in a downtown desperately committed to revitalizing itself. My office is upstairs from an ice cream parlor that's been around for decades. Next door stands an old movie theater rehabbed for party rental but rarely rented. Down the block are a pair of consignment shops trying to look like antique stores, a barber shop with an old-school rotating pole, and a tea shoppe that opened two years ago—the latter with two p's on the sign but never much business inside. Regentrification even at a loss is the case with a lot of small Eastern North Carolina towns, I imagine.

From my vantage point, the glass on my door reads:

Ambrose Thornton

Private Detective

Outside that door, a wood box holds business cards—and brochures listing the kinds of cases I won't accept. No matrimonial work, for example, and nothing involving child custody. No skip tracing or bail bonds work. No insurance fraud. No corporate espionage. Nothing involving labor relations. Nothing that requires me to spend my days at the mall searching for shoplifters.

In fact, with so many things ruled out, not much is left I *will* handle, and that's by design. Maybe if a murder investigation comes along… but the chances there are slim, and the correspondence course I took to get my license hardly equipped me to investigate crimes like that.

The bad news is that I make no money. The good news: it doesn't matter. I rent the office solely to get my father off my back.

"It's important for a man to have a job, a purpose," he told me more than once in the years after I graduated college. "A reason to get up in the morning and put in an honest day's work and then bring home a paycheck to show for it."

By that point, my father himself had transcended the business of business and simply reaped the profits, his own desk cleared of everything but the morning paper and an afternoon cocktail, and the money flowing his way while other people's desks grew cluttered and burdened.

He liked to see other people busy—and other people specifically included me.

But my father's success had become my lifestyle. Trust fund baby, thanks to his industriousness and my mother's finagling—my late mother. Gentleman's C's through high school and college—undoubtedly helped along by donations to school coffers. Too many of those bright college years still a haze of bourbon and pot and afternoons spent reading piles of pulp fiction while the business and economic textbooks slid further and further to the side—while the nagging and indignation grew and then grew exponentially the older I got.

"Son," he'd said one day, snapping his suspenders like the punctuation to a pronouncement, "you need to find something you love to do and do it."

The thing I could've asked: What if my passion might not bring home a paycheck?

Today, even with the rent on my workspace, there's still enough stipend left to keep filling the bookshelves lining two walls of that office—classic detective stories, pulp crime novels, some of them collector's editions. I spend my days reading and rereading them, watching the sunlight travel from one side of the office to the other, watching a door that stays mostly closed. But it's a door at least, an office, a business, and isn't that what my father wanted?

* * *

My first case arrived late summer a year or so after I'd opened shop. Despite the windows shut tight against the mounting heat, the sounds outside still seeped through: children playing in the greenway that runs through the center of downtown (in off-sync stereo with the squeals from the ice cream parlor downstairs), the occasional toot of a horn at the intersection, lately an occasional helicopter passing overhead. Military maneuvers, the paper had said. The sunlight had travelled halfway across the floor and then begun to fade. The radio droned softly, election updates again—the governorship teetering over business interests and concerns about the economy, the incumbent embattled, the challenger an up-and-comer with rising poll numbers. My father talked heatedly about withholding his own endorsement until he saw which way the wind blew, but I'd tuned him out and tuned out the newscast then—focused instead on my eighth or ninth reading of *Trouble Is My Business*.

That's when my own trouble walked in.

That line sounds like your traditional hard-boiled story, I know, but she wasn't tall and leggy with flowing blonde locks and an over-abundance of cleavage nicely framed for my viewing pleasure. She was short and trim with a boyish haircut. She wore an off-white oxford and scuffed jeans. And instead of some swirl of perfume, she smelled like garlic.

"I'm Esmé," she said, offering me her hand. She had a firm grip, confident instead of dainty, but her nails were bitten to the quick. In addition to garlic, there was cumin too and maybe cinnamon, and I don't know what else.

"Esmé," I repeated. "Like the new restaurant down the street?"

"We're one and the same."

Esmé's Bistro had opened up two months before, and I'd caught whiffs of those same scents in the air walking back and forth to my car.

"Have you been in?" she asked, taking her seat as I moved to my side of the desk.

"Not yet."

"And there's part of my problem."

"Business troubles?"

"Sort of." She nibbled lightly at her lower lip. It wasn't unattractive.

I was already placing bets about it. Someone on the waitstaff mishandling the tips or culling credit cards numbers. Something to do with immigration and visas, undocumented workers huddling back in the kitchen. Or maybe there was a customer who'd gotten too friendly. Stalking—another crime I steered clear of, some flipside of matrimonial work. I was already angling for an exit.

"What do you know about...tonkas?" she asked.

There in the pause before the word, she'd looked at me—green eyes intently focused my way, like she was waiting for my reaction, not just watching but watching *for* something, and she'd needed the pause to prepare for it. Her eyes didn't leave mine, even after I'd shrugged and answered.

"I played with them as a kid. A dump truck, a front-loader, something like that." I took a deep breath. "But I need to tell you upfront: I don't handle child custody cases."

Another pause, more watching, before she shook her head. Her disappointment was palpable.

"I'm not talking about toys," she said. "I'm talking about the tonka bean. It's a spice, a very powerful one." Another glance, another bit of watchfulness.

Again, I could offer nothing but bewilderment.

"I'm not a grocery store either," I said.

"It wouldn't matter if you were." Her eyes finally turned away from me. "The FDA outlawed tonkas back in the '50s. They're considered toxic. The coumarin in them, it can cause liver damage."

"So you're not looking for them," I said. "You're trying to steer clear of them. Poisoning? Someone's slipping these beans into your kitchen?"

"No, no, not that." She rolled her eyes—the stupidity of it all, that was the message, maybe my own stupidity. "The ban is ridiculous, given how much you'd need to *consume* to risk *any* effect. And you only need a little of it to…to open up a dish." She moved forward in the chair, holding her hands out as if she had a bean in her palm. "When you shave the tonka, it releases these…powerful aromas. Vanilla and cherry and a whiff of cinnamon maybe, with a complexity to it all, and the taste carries those same layers and more. Caramel and honey flavors too, and… I don't think I'm doing it justice." She moved her hands to her face. Her cheeks had flushed. "Magic, that's the better word. It's like a drug almost, that smell, that taste. Standing above it as you shave the bean can be intoxicating, overpowering. *Em*powering really."

Vanilla, cinnamon, honey…most of the flavors she mentioned seemed fairly ordinary. But the way she was saying them and the expression on her face were anything but. She seemed transported herself simply talking about it.

"I'm still not sure what you need me for," I told her.

"My restaurant is new, and I want it to be a success, and more than a success, a…."

When she leaned in, I caught a glimpse of her breasts. I couldn't help it. And thinking about that now, maybe this moment marked another turn toward this becoming a real detective story. "Someone here in the county is growing them," she went on, barely a whisper. "I've heard it—from a reliable source—and I want some for myself. I want in."

* * *

From Esmé's description and from some quick work on Google, powering up my laptop while she sat there, I gathered a few quick facts about the tonka. It's grown mostly in Central and South America—Venezuela, Colombia, and Brazil primarily. It looks less like a bean than a long raisin or a thin prune—dried, wrinkly—and the inside has the look and texture of chocolate. Even a shallow cut into the bean would release those aromas she described as intoxicating.

"French chefs have a name for it," Esmé told me. "*La fièvre tonka.* Tonka fever.*" It sounded like a disease she'd be glad to catch—the breathless way she said the words—and the way she navigated that French accent suddenly left me a little breathless too.

"You're French yourself?" I asked.

She smiled, shrugged. "Somewhere up the family tree maybe."

"And your restaurant. French too?"

Another shrug, but the smile had faded. "Eclectic, let's say. If it's not barbecue in a town like this, does the marketing matter?"

"You're not from here, then?"

"I was a sous chef in Raleigh"—she named a restaurant everyone knows—"then got lured down here to open a place of my own. Inexpensive taxes, the promise of a supportive community. Opportunities—that what I was told."

Seemed like none of that had panned out.

The FDA had indeed outlawed the bean in 1954, like she said, and there had been cases where the government had stepped in to enforce the ban—"significant fines, negative attention," Esmé explained. "The kinds of risks any beginning restaurateur would be loath to take."

Despite that ban, I found some for sale online as we sat there.

"Some of those are meant for luck, as talismans," she explained. "Dried and shellacked. You can't cook with them."

I squinted at the screen. "The description here says 'can be used in desserts and stews,'" I said. It also mentioned "used in spells" beneath it, but she didn't let me get that far.

"Most suppliers will refuse to ship to the United States anyway. And if they did ship, chances are it would be tracked."

I clicked the button to place the order anyway.

"Cancel it, please," she said, suddenly jittery.

"Why? Couldn't hurt to see what happens."

"I've talked with you. I can't risk the association here, not officially, not where it can be documented."

"You make it sound like the FDA is watching now."

"You can't know that they're not!" She leaned forward again, her hands clasped like she was begging—her fear as palpable as her desperation before. "You've read how the government tracks our emails. What if the FDA raided me? My business means everything— it's all I've got!"

"OK, OK," I said, clicking to cancel—but the screen froze. I'd need to handle it later. "You mentioned a reliable source. Someone here in town? So you already have a connection with the grower...."

"That's a dead end for me. The *supplier* in the case"—she put a stress on the word *supplier*—"showed me a few beans, but the price for more was too high. I need"—she seemed flustered—"I need someone closer to the source."

If some of her descriptions of the tonka had made it sound like a drug, this last part surely did. I conjured images of dealers on the playground, handing out samples, hooking clientele, driving hard bargains afterwards. Her desperation wasn't quite like an addict's, but it was driven by the same need. I could see it in her eyes—that deep green there, soulful and needy.

"I'll do what I can," I said with more assurance than I felt. Whatever nerves she wrangled with, I caught them too, for my own reasons—the first client I'd ever accepted. "I'll need to get you to, uh, pay a retainer. Then there might be daily expenses. And...." I pretended that it was all routine, but I had no paperwork on hand. I promised to get it to her soon. "The retainer can serve as a contract for now."

She pulled a checkbook from her purse, glanced at the register with hesitation, then wrote out the amount. I'd caught a glimpse of her balance—barely a couple of hundred more than I'd requested. I decided I wouldn't cash the check immediately, maybe not at all.

At the door, she turned again to face me—a similar pose to when she'd walked into the room. I was struck by how my image of her had changed in our short time together. The same off-white oxford, the same jeans, the same boyish haircut and sharply bitten nails. But now she seemed cosmopolitan somehow, mysterious, seductive even.

She pointed to my name on the glass. "Thornton," she said. "You're related to Ben Thornton?"

"My father," I said. "You know him? "

"My landlord," she said. "At the restaurant—or rather he's connected somehow to the company I rent from. I didn't know it myself until he became a customer too."

Other people's desks cluttered and burdened, like I said, and the money simply flowing my father's way.

* * *

I'm not sure if I can stress enough the point I've made about not actually being a private investigator.

The private detective is a myth—at least how many people picture the job. These days it's mostly background checks of one kind or another or maybe insurance fraud—usually handled in-house by the businesses themselves. On the domestic front, anyone trying to prove a partner's infidelity hardly needs a detective, what with cheap hidden cameras and recording devices or a quick search of a smartphone or a computer's browser history.

I had regularly steered potential clients in those directions, toward online resources or the webpage for Radio Shack or sometimes to local law enforcement. A friend of mine from high school, Randall Norton, was a police officer now, and I often passed along his card. Randy told me I'd have made a killing on commissions if any money had ever changed hands.

But here law enforcement couldn't help, since the tonka was illegal. Passing Esmé along wasn't an option. And I couldn't admit that I'd never taken a case before—couldn't turn her away, could I?

Maybe I simply didn't want to.

* * *

After some more research online, I visited several produce stands the next morning. More than one mystery had the solution hidden in plain sight, right?

About a block and a half from my office, a white tent was usually popped up in front of an abandoned gas station. I'd stopped by before.

Weeds broke through the concrete, and table legs leaned into holes, barely balancing baskets of apples and peaches, small containers of figs, several piles of muscadine grapes. Another table was bunched with greens—signs for *Collard* and *Mustard* and *Kale*. The nearest things to the tonka's shape were some gray butterbeans.

April, the woman who ran the stand, was cutting peaches into a paper plate labeled *Samples, Take One*. I did.

"I've got a recipe that calls for this specific bean," I told her. "I've tried the grocery store, but you know how that is...."

Play to a source's importance, that was key.

April wiped the knife on her apron.

"You got a new girlfriend?"

"How's that?"

"All you ever buy is salad and fruit." A smirk teased one corner of her mouth. "Who's the lucky girl? Or are you the lucky one?"

"We'll wait and see how the recipe turns out."

"Never heard of tonkas, but we've got plenty of beans." Before I could interrupt her, she was working through the list: those butter beans, limas, green beans, pole beans. "Maybe you could substitute. That's what I always do, but a lot's out of season already."

"No, I really need this one." I pulled out a picture I'd printed from the internet.

"Looks like a coffee bean almost," she said.

"It's more of a seed really, what I understand."

She handed me the printout. "I don't do much with seeds, but that big market out on 70 does."

By the time I'd reached that one, the sun had risen high and the heat with it. This structure was elaborate—a wood frame and big plywood signs handwritten in green, orange, and red paint. *Boiled Peanuts* and *Home Made Pies* and *Cantaloupe* and *Water Melon*. I'd stopped there before.

"Bean seeds," the farmer running it said with a curt nod, and he walked me toward a carousel of small manila packets, hand-labeled in purple ink: Blue Lake, Kentucky Wonder, State Half Runner, Yard Long Giant. I peeked into a couple on the off chance that one might hold what I needed.

"It's a specialty seed," I said. "Grown mostly in tropical climates."

A helicopter passed overhead, low enough and loud enough that I started to repeat myself, but he'd heard.

"Tropical?" he said. "You think this heat wave is gonna last long enough to grow a *tropical* plant?" He must have been sweltering in all that denim, but he didn't seem to have broken a sweat.

"Well," I said. "I wasn't really thinking about how to grow it."

"Sunlight," he said. "Heat and lots of it, months of it. And moisture probably, depending."

I stared at several piles of tomatoes on the table beside us. One pile sat under a sign that said *Heirloom*. The other said *Hothouse*.

"Would a greenhouse do it?"

He sent me to my next stop, a more professional operation with an aluminum sales area fronting a network of long greenhouses. The man who helped me there wore a thin red tie and jeans that looked like they'd been pressed with an iron.

"Tropicals?" he said. "Sure, right this way." A side door led into one of the greenhouses—hotter and muggier than outside. But when we got to our destination, the tables were all flowers: ferns and philodendrons, African violets, bromeliads, orchids, something called a bird of paradise.

"It would be more of a tree than a plant," I told him, looking at my notes. "A cumaru tree, it's called."

"Not one I've heard of," he said. "But if it's a big enough tree, you'd need more height than we have here"—pointing at the glass roof only a few feet above our heads.

All in all, a waste of time—proof maybe that I was better off not taking cases.

* * *

I could've picked up the telephone and called Esmé to update her on my progress—lack of progress—but I decided to stop by the restaurant that night instead. I hadn't been in, after all. It might help to get the lay of the land. That's what I told myself.

Business was indeed slow. I bypassed the hostess—a disinterested teen I vaguely recognized, daughter of some somebody in town— and took a stool at a small bar that dominated half the restaurant: mirrors and sleek mahogany, the counter itself curved into a loose L-shape, only one couple there, hovering over a half-bottle of wine. The dining area was crisp white tablecloths and tall candles, high-backed chairs, dark plank floors. Three tables had diners, and their voices echoed hollow in the space. A couple of them I recognized, and we exchanged brief waves. Friends of the family, friends of my father—the country club set, their days as idle as mine but dodging the judgment.

An open kitchen stretched two-thirds of the back of the restaurant, Esmé on the other side of a stainless steel counter, busy chopping something. I glanced at the cocktail menu—leather bound, labeled *Speakeasy Classics*—ordered an Old Fashioned with Booker's, and then watched Esmé for a while, hoping she would notice me and come out to speak, but she was intent on her work. *Focused*, I thought. *Driven*. It helped drive my own goals. I was going to find her those beans.

I took out my notebook and revisited what I'd learned back in the office about the growing season for the cumaru tree, why they would struggle to survive, much less thrive, in North Carolina's climate. It would indeed take a greenhouse—and given the trees' height, one several stories tall. How would you hide that? Was it worth building a greenhouse like that—and then hiding it—for a handful of seeds? None of it made any sense.

Then I started thinking of what else might need a lot of light and heat to grow. And what someone might want to keep hidden—and from bigger guns than the FDA.

Slowly, it began to make more sense.

The door opened as I finished my notes, and my father's voice preceded him into the room. "Evening, Melissa," he said to the girl at the hostess stand, and "My usual spot"—which turned out to be the bar.

He didn't greet me at first but called out hearty hellos to those same folks in the dining area who'd waved my way before, stepping over to glad-hand one of the men. As he perched himself on the bar-stool beside me, he called out "Manhattan" to the bartender, but then stopped him as he reached for the Maker's. "On second thought, let your boss lady make it when she's free"—gesturing toward that open kitchen and Esmé within. "She knows what I'd like."

His voice boomed and carried, and I thought I saw Esmé glance out at us, then quickly glance away.

I caught myself, same as some other times, wanting to ask my father what self-respecting Southerner would drink a Manhattan. But instead I gave him a curt "Dad" as he adjusted himself on the stool.

"Son," he said. An awkward moment passed. Between his teeth, he clenched an unlit cigar, which he took out and propped between two fingers. Then he returned it to his mouth. "Buy you a drink?" Before I could gesture toward my Old Fashioned, he saw it himself. "But guess I've already bought you that one. Almost forgot that your tab's still my tab these days."

"I'm working," I said.

"One of us tosses that word around without knowing what it means."

"I am working," I said. "Actually doing work. I have a case."

"Let me guess. Someone at the library misshelved a book and they need help locating it. Or maybe the neighbor lost her cat. You always liked cats, didn't you?" He leaned over toward me, whispered, "Or maybe it's another kind of pussy you're tailing? Some cheating woman, and the husband hiring you to dig the dirt?"

"I don't take matrimonial cases."

He leaned back on his stool, stared at me as if I were a stranger he was trying to recognize. "Son, do you have any idea how real people speak?" He tapped his finger against the counter. "I'd be glad to know you were getting even a *look* at the fairer sex. Always thought you needed too much encouragement in that direction."

Esmé walked up to the counter, wiping her hand on the apron she was wearing.

"Evening, little lady," my father said. "Have you met the sire of my loins here? Heir to the fortune?"

He was overloud again. Esmé blushed, maybe both us did. My father didn't seem to notice and didn't wait for either of us to answer before ordering his Manhattan again.

Despite asking for "the boss lady" in particular, he critiqued each step of her drink-making: moving her up a higher shelf in her choice of bourbon, questioning if those were the best bitters she had, cautioning her not to bruise the vermouth.

Fine liquor was his only vice, my father used to say, and then fine women too, after my mother died and he found himself on the hunt again. She'd been the buffer between us for years. Both of us missed her.

I didn't like to think of my father dating, but if his treatment of Esmé offered any indication of how he treated women, it didn't seem like an issue.

Esmé set the cocktail on the counter before him. "Compliments of the house."

"No, ma'am," he said, pulling out his money clip and sliding a twenty from it. "It's good business to pay for what you get."

For some reason, that made Esmé blush too. She seemed prone to it.

* * *

My father is not a fat man, though I realize I may have implied that somehow: the cigars, those suspenders, his booming voice. He's not a fat man, no, but he's a big man, and he fills whatever room he's in.

Sometimes there's not much space left for anyone else.

My father gave the Manhattan a curt taste then told Esmé she'd only slightly missed the mark. He asked about the business, asked about the night's specials, protested that he'd already eaten when she offered a menu, suggested she add more pork dishes—"think about what people want to eat, not what you want them to eat." He complained about a small placard on one of the bar shelves, advertising for the challenger in the governor's race—"wear your affiliations on your sleeve, you'll alienate half your clientele." He talked about me too, that phrase "heir to the fortune" again and then some blunt comments about bigger questions of inheritance, about the traits that are passed down or *should* be passed down and then something about recessive genes—"or is it re*gressive*? I can never remember."

I'm not sure exactly what I said or how I fumbled through the conversation, what Esmé may have said or done or looked like through it all, except that she appeared truly beautiful to me now in a haunted, melancholy way and I suddenly felt like I should stand up for her or for myself—and then felt equally foolish for thinking that.

"Spends his days reading," my father was saying. "Walls of bookshelves, packed tight, up in his office."

"They're reference books," I said. "Think of lawyers, their libraries."

"Want to practice law, you should've gone to law school." My father swigged the rest of his cocktail. "Want to play at law or whatever you're doing...." He waved the empty glass toward Esmé, gesturing for another.

"Reading isn't a bad thing, knowledge," said Esmé, but she was watching me like she had the first day, with suspicion beneath it now. Any authority I had with her was quickly slipping away.

That was the way the conversation went. Before long, I left—putting off my update to Esmé. After all, I didn't have much to report anyway.

* * *

I called my friend Randy the next morning and asked to meet—away from the police station.

"Another referral?" he asked.

"A consultation," I said. "I need some insider perspective."

He was free after lunch. We planned to meet downstairs early afternoon.

As I hung up, my office door opened, and Esmé stepped in. She wore a skirt this morning—her legs tan and taut, I couldn't help but notice. She had a basket under her arm.

"Croissants," she said. "Fresh out of the oven. Have you had breakfast?"

I pointed to the coffee cup on my desk—still half full. "I have more in the pot and another mug."

Another blush. "I brought a French press," she said. She pulled that out of the basket along with a couple of jars of jelly, knives, napkins—cloth ones. The cups she poured were dainty but the scent was robust.

"What's the occasion?" I asked.

"We didn't get the chance to talk last night." She cut open a croissant. "Grape or strawberry?"

"Surprise me," I said, then: "I've got a lead, just need to see where it takes me."

She'd chosen strawberry, and the knife paused briefly against the croissant—enough so I caught it. "I thought when you came by last night—"

"I'm working on it," I said. "But no, no tonkas yet." I held my hands out, palms up. She examined them, like there might actually have been a bean sitting there. Her shoulders sunk. Her whole body seemed to deflate.

"Maybe I should pay the price," she said, almost to herself.

"Is there a rush? It's been a day, hardly that. Have some faith"—trying not to think about how my father had undermined me the night before. Reminding myself to have faith too.

She nodded—unconvincingly—then handed me the croissant.

"So tell me," I asked her, "have you always wanted to be a chef?"

"Since I was a girl," she said, carefully opening a croissant for herself. Something about her words and the movement and her smile gave me a glimpse of that child she was talking about: simple and unguarded, pure excitement, a contrast to those hard-bitten nails. "I used to burrow into the cabinets of my mother's kitchen, pulling out pots and pans, banging them around, pretending I was making something. When I was old enough, five or so, my mother gave me a chance to cook for real—or that's the way I remember it. I'm sure she helped more than I knew. She was a great cook herself, taught me everything I know. Cooking school was…perfecting some of what she'd taught me. Trying to perfect it. Understanding it in a different way."

"Sounds like you were born for it," I said. I held up the croissant. "Delicious."

She took a bite of her own. A dab of jelly clung to the corner of her mouth before she licked it away. "My mother said I had a special talent—a gift for it. And I wanted to be special, to feel like I was destined for something, you know? But destiny…you have to work at it. You make your own destiny, that's what I've learned."

"You and my father would get along well," I said.

It was a casual comment really. I didn't expect Esmé to bristle at the comparison. That unrestrained smile closed up quickly, her lips tightening.

"Did I say something wrong?" I asked.

"Your father," she said. "He didn't seem very… kind…to you. Last night."

I waved my hand. "I'm used to it."

"You shouldn't get used to things like that."

"Not much choice where family is concerned."

That same watchfulness from the first day. "I hope that's not the case." And then the smile again, but forced now—a purposeful attempt to lighten the mood. "Your turn," she said. "Something about yourself. What's been your most interesting case as a detective?"

I took a bite of my croissant to cover up the pause, buy myself time, then gave her a slimmed-down version of the plot of "Red Wind"—a set of pearls connecting a woman to her one true love, a blackmailer who stole the pearls and demanded payment or else he'd tell the woman's husband about the other man, and then the detective in the middle (me, as I was telling it) trying to get those pearls back.

"But when the pearls turned up," I said. "You know, she was probably going to protect them better, get them insured, whatever. But here's the kicker—they weren't real. That one true love of hers had given her cheap fakes. So I couldn't deliver them back, couldn't deliver that news, could I? So I pretended that the blackmailer had sold the real ones, had planned to sell fakes back to her—and I got a fake pair myself, clearly fake so she wouldn't recognize them as her own, and said that I'd done my best. She didn't get the pearls back, but she got to keep the memories. You see?"

It was a favorite case, even if not my own.

I'd earned back a real smile from Esmé, some genuine warmth behind it. "Who would've imagined there was so much intrigue in a town this size?"

"Who would've imagined there was a South American tree growing here," I said, "with an outlawed bean, a *magic* bean?"

She held up the last bite of her croissant, angling it like she wanted to toast, though it took me a few seconds to catch on. I tipped the corner of my own croissant toward hers, felt some real connection as the edges touched.

* * *

It was a day of eating indulgently. I met Randy that afternoon at the ice cream parlor downstairs. He bought Rocky Road, I had vanilla. Ms. Florence, who's run the place since both of us were kids, offered Randy his cone on the house, but I insisted on paying for both.

"If buying me a cone is a good exchange," Randy said on our way out, dodging a family hurrying in, "then it must not be very valuable, this information you're looking for."

"You saying you're open to bribery?"

"If I was, it might take more than ice cream."

"Would you have rather met for a bourbon?"

"Still on duty," he said.

I don't think he would've minded, but I did. More privacy out in the open than side-by-side with whoever might have shown up at a bar, even that early in the day. Plus, given the heat, the ice cream wasn't unwelcome.

"So what're you buying here with your single scoop?"

"What you know—off-the-record—about some criminal activity that might intersect with a case I'm working."

"Criminal activity?" he said. "Intersect?"

"Intersect at best," I said. "Unrelated ultimately—directly I mean."

He waited a second, took another lick of the cone, nodded toward a park bench set off from the few small crowds on the green. Three kids took turns chasing one another with water guns. Two women sat with a stroller at another bench. Further down the green stood a table covered with political signs—these promoting the governor and a second term.

Where we sat was far enough away from all of them. No one could hear us.

"Who's growing marijuana in the county these days?" I asked once we were settled.

Randy laughed. "You looking for a buy? Missing those high school days of ours?"

"Not for me," I said. "And not small stuff, not some set-up in a closet. I meant a big plot." Big enough for a tree? The tropical plants covering for the growth underneath? I was still feeling my way.

He whistled, held up the cone. "You should've made it a double scoop." I waited. "If I knew about someone with a large-scale marijuana operation here, wouldn't I have already arrested them? Kind of my job these days."

"Could be something you know about," I said, "but you're not acting on it yet. Could be you're waiting for the right time to deal with it."

"A lot of could be's. What's leading you that way?"

"I don't think the helicopters that have been passing by are on military maneuvers."

The kids with the water guns rushed past us, squealing and shooting. Randy called after them to watch their aim, shifted his elbow.

"Caught in the crossfire?" I asked him.

He looked at me out of the corner of his eye. "By them or by you?"

"I don't know what you mean."

"The helicopters," he said. "Not ours—not that we could afford helicopters, not with our budget—and not military either, you're right there. But government somehow."

"So what are they doing?"

"Above my pay grade," he said quickly, some bitterness laced under the words, then took a bite of his cone. After a moment, he tossed the cone to the ground in front of us.

"What's the fine for littering, officer?" I asked.

"Birds will eat it," he said. "Or ants. Tastes like cardboard anyway."

Already his ice cream was puddling. I took a bite of my own cone. It tasted fine.

"The helicopters," I said again. "They're looking for marijuana, right? Hidden greenhouses? Something like that?" But he wasn't having any of it.

"Back early this summer, end of the school year, prom night," he said, "the chief stationed several cruisers on the roads leading away from the high school. He wanted to be all zero tolerance, hard as nails, catch the kids drinking and driving, pull 'em over, run 'em in." He let out a long, low breath.

"Happy senior year, yeah?" I said.

"Exactly. And I didn't want to do it, not ruin some kid's graduation. I thought about letting them ride, whoever I saw. But then that wasn't good either—some drunk kid getting into an accident, killing somebody, himself, a whole carload of kids. You know where I'm coming from?"

I did, but I didn't. I knew what it meant, couldn't see how it connected. "So you pulled them in."

"And drove them home," he said. "Got hell for it the day after from the chief. And you know what I told him?"

I shook my head.

"I told him, when's the last time you had us stake out the roads up and down from the country club on a Saturday night?"

What he was telling me, it made sense and it didn't. The helicopters were like the police staking out prom? when they should've been staking out someone else? I told him as much.

"They're not looking for *anything*," he said. "Not as far as I can tell. That's the funny thing. I asked and was told I shouldn't ask, and then I asked again anyway."

He stood up, gave me a sad smile.

"Me, my hands are tied." He squinted, like seeing something in me he hadn't seen before. "But maybe you can get further with it, given your position and all."

It wasn't lost on me here, a classic detective fiction set-up—the detective able to work outside the law, able to find what the authorities couldn't find.

"You want a lead," he said, "maybe talk to Harley."

Which proved part of my point: that Randy knowing something didn't mean he would act on it.

* * *

Detecting, no doubt about it, was a complicated business. Randy wouldn't give me any more information—didn't have any, he said—nothing specific about the helicopters, nothing about marijuana, nothing that might lead me closer to the heat at the core of the case, the literal heat, the kind that might grow not only marijuana but the tonka. That was all I cared about, even if that bean and Esmé herself were quickly getting lost under other troubles.

Harley went to high school with Randy and me, and he'd been the go-to source for weed. It had been years since I smoked pot— I'd grown up some, no matter what my father might think—and years since I'd seen Harley. But out of sight and out of mind didn't mean out of business.

Dust swirled as I pulled up the dirt road toward Harley's trailer. When I knocked on the front door, I heard shuffling inside. He looked like I'd woken him up. Maybe I had.

"Well, well," he said. "Here come old times rolling up to the door."

We shook hands, exchanged hellos. Harley sank down into a La-Z-Boy and motioned me toward a plaid couch, frayed at the arms—

a cat, I felt sure. I hadn't seen one, but I caught a whiff of litter box mixed against the pot smell that had seeped into the couch and the walls and into Harley himself.

I mentioned that Randy had sent me his way, explained what had brought me out.

Harley nodded like he knew something. "Old times rolling up, and now looking to roll something himself." Then his loose smile morphed into puzzlement. "But you don't need me to roll a joint for you, do you?"

"Looking for some information," I said. "I wanted to ask about your supply channels."

He stiffened at that, pulled himself onto the front edge of the recliner.

"You cutting in on my business?"

"I'm not interested in your business," I said. "I mean, I am, but—"

"I'm not going to be strong-armed. I've been doing this too long to be treated like that. You push me, I'll go over your head. Don't think I won't."

He was all but bouncing in his chair, spittle clotting at the corners of his mouth. A cat did appear then, skittering out from under the couch, darting through the kitchen and deeper into the trailer.

"Harley," I said, trying to bring him back to reality. "Listen to me. I'm not buying, and I don't want to sell either. That's not why I'm—"

"You? *Selling*?" he said. "Hell, no, I know you better than that. Keep up appearances, that's you in a nutshell, even back in high school. And like you'd ever need the money. But then behind the scenes, when wasn't nobody looking—different story, yeah? And now you want to slide right into the middle here and...."

Already he was pulling me up, pushing me out of the house—more threats, his anger deepening. Classic paranoia, I thought, and I tried to tell him that, but he wasn't listening. He slammed the door behind me, curses still pushing through the trailer's thin walls.

Back in the car, I felt stunned. Why had Randy sent me out this way? Had he known how Harley would react? Surely he couldn't have anticipated what happened.

Harley peeked out from around the curtains, yanked them closed.

One of the helicopters passed, not directly overhead but not far away, and Harley peered out again, then gave me the finger.

I sat for a while, thinking.

Maybe it wasn't paranoia, I decided. Maybe Harley had reason to be spooked. None of it was clear yet, where I was headed, but as I watched the chopper, I began to wonder where it went.

* * *

I was stuck to two-lane roads winding awkwardly through the farms outside of town, while the helicopter went where it wanted to. But over a couple of hours, watching the horizons, watching the skies, I got sense of its flight paths, its area of surveillance.

I rode back into town and got to the courthouse a good 45 minutes before it closed. The office for the registrar of deeds was in the basement, a large windowless room with linoleum floors. The clerk was a girl I'd known from school, as it turned out, a few years older—Sheri was her name. I'd had a crush on her years before. She was married with two kids now, had a plumpness about her.

She helped me find the names I needed—people and corporations both. Then I went back to my office, picked up the mail—a Ross Macdonald I'd ordered—and started up the laptop.

A couple of hours later, my research revealed no connections between the names I'd written down and what I thought was going on here—what I felt I knew, based on Randy's comments about the country club and Harley's accusations about me putting myself in the middle.

No connection at all.

But I did find a connection between the farmland the helicopters were monitoring and some real estate closer at hand.

All of which—I admit this with some pride—was exactly what I'd anticipated.

* * *

That night, I returned to Esmé's.

I arrived later than I had before, giving the dinner crowd, such as it was, longer to finish up—a single table still eating, a foursome in the back corner. My father was already at the bar, Manhattan in hand—likely not his first. Esmé stood back in that open kitchen.

I eased onto the barstool beside my father, ordered another Booker's Old Fashioned. The bartender rapped the counter with his knuckle, turned to make the drink.

"You're becoming a regular here," my father said, not looking my way but at the row of liquor bottles along the wall.

"Came for you, actually," I said.

"That's unexpected."

"I had a few questions about business."

He did glance my way then. "Very unexpected."

"I've always had an interest, sometimes more than others." The bartender set down my Old Fashioned. "Hear you're moving into agriculture these days."

My father sipped his Manhattan. While I waited for him to talk, I took a sip of my own. It was sweeter than I expected. Or maybe that was the moment seeping over.

"I've always kept a diverse portfolio of interests," he said. "Good business all around."

"Investments in that direction going well?"

"Better than some." He gave me a pointed glance. I wasn't an investment that was going well.

I let it slide—both the remark and the look. "So no worries about those helicopters?"

The mirror behind the bar was obscured behind the rows of liquor bottles and the placard for that gubernatorial challenger, but from what I glimpsed, my father may have actually smiled.

"Is this the case you've been working on?" He crossed his arms. "You're wasting your time. Here's the thing about business, son. By the time you reach my age, my position, you not only know how to make a deal, but you know how to be discreet about it."

"Hide it?" I asked.

"Semantics," he said. "And then there are the deals that aren't recorded at all. Those are sometimes the strongest. Power isn't always on paper."

"I wouldn't think you'd risk dirtying your hands—man of your integrity."

"Who said I was dirtying my hands?"

"Marijuana?" I whispered it. The bartender was drying some glasses at the other end of the bar—still close enough to hear. I glanced over my shoulder. The foursome in the back corner had broken up and was heading out. The waitress cleared their table. "Remember the way you used to talk about it when I was a teenager?"

My father didn't tone down his own voice. "As much money as I've been funneling to you over the years, I figured I could at least make some of it back from your kind at the other end."

"The helicopters," I said again. "Those can't be good business, can they?"

"A political dispute, that's all."

I thought of the governor's campaign heating up—the embattled incumbent, the ambitious challenger, the business vote, the power that wasn't on paper.

"The governor is extorting your endorsement."

"The words you choose, son." He tsk-tsked me like I was a toddler. "We businessmen are key to his support. We're in negotiations, that's all."

"Everything's negotiable, huh?"

"Always."

Esmé was wiping her hands on a towel, looking our way—heading our way, it seemed clear.

"OK then," I said. "Let's you and me negotiate."

This time it was definitely a smile. I couldn't see it in the mirror, but I could feel it. Or maybe it wasn't meant for me at all, but for Esmé who was indeed rounding the bar.

Fine liquor and fine women—those were the things that drove this.

"The tonkas," I said as she came up. Her eyes widened, a cautious smile there too. "That's the case I've been working on, the case I've *solved.*"

"*Solved?*" my father said. "This little lady has known where to find them all along."

"But she couldn't get them," I said. "That's why she needed me."

"A moment please," Esmé said, shifted from one foot to another. That hint of a smile had faded. "Why don't you take off the rest of the night?" she told the bartender.

"You sure?" he asked, but he was already laying down his bar rag.

"And tell Maria she can go too." The waitress I'd seen, I assumed.

While he gathered his things, Esmé looked at me in silence—from me to my father and back—with that same watchfulness she'd brought to my office the first day. That was her whole point, I think—watching us and waiting.

When the help had left, I pointed to the leather-bound cocktail menu: *Speakeasy Classics.* "This is the connection, right? And that?" Pointing to the Manhattan.

"It wasn't the drink," Esmé said. "That was only the start."

My father sighed.

"You reach a point in your life when it's all about enjoying the day," he said. He picked up his drink, stared into it. "This is the perfect cocktail—or nearest to perfection. I've got time on my hands. I wanted to see if I could indeed perfect it."

"Abbott's bitters," I said. "Made with the tonka."

Outlawed in the U.S. in the '50s along with the bean itself, I'd found. I remembered my father chiding Esmé about the bitters she used the first night I stopped in, if those were the best she had—rubbing it in, playing his hand.

"A necessary ingredient,'" he said. "The original Manhattan, way it should be, until some neb in Washington mucked it up. I found a recipe for them, figured how hard would it be to make a batch of those bitters myself? Hell, I probably could've found an antique bottle easier, paid a pretty penny for it maybe, but the money didn't matter. It's a point of pride to make something for yourself." He looked at Esmé. "Turns out I can't cook. But then someone came to town who could—or at least I thought she could."

I turned toward Esmé. "You open your business, advertising speakeasy cocktails, and he comes in with a proposal."

"He brought in a quarter pound of the tonkas." Her voice cracked. "A plastic bag, as if it was nothing. He laid it on the counter here, and the recipe beside it. He said that it should be enough, if I'd be willing to make it. And I could have, I *would* have." She was knitting her fingers together, clasping and unclasping them. "But infusion, the aging—it takes time."

"Six months," my father said. "That's what she told me, and in the meantime, she wanted more beans for herself. And I told her sure I had them, told her they were growing like wildflowers, how many did she want?"

"He never let me touch even the first batch," she said. "As soon as I asked about additional ones, he pulled the bag away from me."

"Simple supply and demand," he said.

I turned toward Esmé. "You told me in the office that the price was too high. What was the price?" I knew the answer already. Another of those blushes confirmed it.

"I wanted conversation," my father said. "Friendly companionship, that's all."

"It wasn't companionship that you wanted," Esmé said, barely a whisper.

"A fine drink goes better with a fine woman."

"He threatened to pull the lease," she told me.

"I merely reminded her that whether her restaurant succeeded or not, the rent was due on the first of the month," he said. "*Every* month. For two years."

"A lease that's not in your name," I said, "though it is in the same name as the land those helicopters have been keeping under surveillance. So what? You claim it when it's convenient, don't when it's not? And meanwhile, use it for whatever leverage you can? There's a difference between a date and a deal, Dad."

My father leaned back and smiled, reached up and gave his suspenders a satisfied pluck.

"Don't you forget, son," he said. "The little lady here used you for leverage too. Shake you up, shake me down—isn't that right, honey? And then shake some seeds out of it all for herself."

"I wasn't using him," Esmé said. "But I thought if anyone could reason with you, could *influence* you to—"

"Influence is the definition of leverage," my father said.

"Stop it, both of you," I said. "However we got here, here's where we're at." I faced my father head on. "The marijuana isn't the case I was hired for, and what's going on between you and the governor, that's between you—for now. But I'll go to the local police with it and to the press—I'll bring it all down on you, the FDA too—if you don't give Esmé access to your *other* agricultural interests—those cumaru trees you're growing."

"A coo-ma-what?" he asked. This time it was genuine perplexity—on his part and Esmé's too, but different in each case, a difference maybe neither of us had expected.

"It's the tree that grows the tonka bean," I said. "Tropical trees, in your greenhouses."

"Growing like wildflowers," Esmé added. "That's what you told me."

My father snorted—the perplexity shifting toward something else: comprehension, confidence, pleasure.

"You ever heard of a figure of speech," he said. "Grow a tree? Why the hell would I do that? Nah, I ordered the seeds online, get as many as I want. And whatever this one kept telling me"—a thumb toward Esmé—"there's nobody from the FDA been breaking down my door to get them either. And what the hell would I care if they did?"

He drank down the rest of his Manhattan, used two fingers to slide the glass to the other edge of the bar.

"Deal's off between us, missy," he said, "and that leverage you two are working on, it doesn't mean a…a hill of beans." He laughed, sharply, then stepped down off the barstool. At the door, he turned back briefly toward us. "You two are made for each other, you know that? She lives in as much of a fantasy world as you do. Waiting for magic beans to save this business, same as you sitting and reading while the world passes you by. Rent's still due same as usual, first of the month."

After he'd left, Esmé and I were alone. I thought about the things I could say to her. That I was sorry for the way my father acted. Sorry I couldn't get the beans she wanted. Sorry there weren't any beans at all—not like she'd thought.

I wanted to tell her I was there for her still. But she spoke first.

"If you do it right, it all comes together in the end," she said. "That's what my mother told me. She was talking about cooking. The ingredients, the steps—the magic there at the end. And it wasn't simply the meal itself that you created but something else for yourself. Pride maybe, or peace, or…. But you have to do it right, and this business…." She waved a hand at the empty restaurant. "I don't have enough money to pay the rent next month."

"You think getting the beans would have made the difference? would've saved you?"

"Everything could've been different," she said, talking almost to herself now. "I didn't have to know that he ordered them online. I could've denied it if the FDA *did* come in. And maybe they'd have been what I'd needed, if I'd handled all this better."

"Would you have slept with him to get them?" I asked.

I didn't need the answer there, either. She'd already mentioned in my office her temptation to pay the price. And then there was the crisp elegance of the bar where I sat and the dining room behind me, the bottom line on that check register I'd glimpsed when she hired me, the look on her face now—that same blush, deeper than ever.

You build your future, I could've said. *You build your destiny. But even then sometimes you end up somewhere you never intended to go.*

I pulled from my pocket the check she'd written, unfolded it and left it on the bar beside what was left of my Old Fashioned. She didn't stop me as I headed out the door, didn't say a word.

For better or worse, I'd closed the case.

* * *

The next morning, Randy called to ask what I'd found out. I don't think he ever knew it was my father at the end of that search—only country club types in general, class and power and something he couldn't reach and thought I could, not because of my position as a detective but because of who I was, the class I was born in.

My turn to play coy with him. No, I hadn't found what I was looking for. And that was true. The marijuana hadn't been my case at all.

That afternoon, the tonka seeds arrived—the ones I'd ordered myself. I'd forgotten to cancel them.

Esmé said they would likely be shellacked—good luck charms of some kind instead of usable ingredients—but when I cut into one of the beans, the fragrance filled my office. Vanilla and honey and caramel and cinnamon and something joyous about it, exactly like she'd described it.

I bought a can of clear varnish and sprayed the rest of the beans, packaged them up with the invoice and added a note that she'd been right after all, probably the same kinds of beans my father had dangled before her—letting her know they wouldn't have worked, wouldn't have been worth it.

I'd mail the package, since I didn't plan on stopping by again.

And then I got back to business myself—the Ross Macdonald collection that had arrived the day before. *Strangers in Town*. I'd been waiting for it, and it for me.

When Duty Calls

Keri is just setting out the silverware when the Colonel calls across from the living room with a new question. He's watching the Military Channel and finishing up the cocktail she made for him—a thimble of Virginia Gentleman, a generous portion of soda, another light splash of whiskey on top to make it smell like a stronger drink. The Colonel's house has an open floor plan from the kitchen through the dining room to where he sits, and as she's finished up dinner, she's listened to him arguing lightly with the program's depiction of Heartbreak Ridge, reminiscing about his own stint in Korea, rambling in his own way. "Last rally of the Shermans," he mused aloud, and something about "optics" and "maneuverability" and then—a different tone than Keri's heard in the four months she's known him—"Is the perimeter secure, Sergeant?"

"The perimeter?" Keri asks, cautiously. She's grown used to these sudden shifts in subject—learned quickly just to roll along with the conversation, even in the first days after she and Pete moved in. But she still stumbles sometimes to catch up and find the right response.

The Colonel turns in his chair—turning *on* her, Keri thinks, expecting his regular confusion or the occasional rebuke—but he doesn't look her way. He's listening, it seems, his jaw fixed, his chin jutting more than usual. The tendons in his frail arms tighten, his tie tugs at the skin around his neck, his whole body perches alert, if unsteadily so. Medals and photos crowd the wall behind him. Round stickers dot many of them and almost everything else in the living room: lamps, books, bookcases, the chair itself. Red, white, and blue.

"Incoming," he says.

"No one's out there, Colonel," she tries to reassure him. Not anymore, at least, since that pair of surveyors out in the woods had packed up their bags a half-hour before, one of them waving at her through the window before cranking up, heading out. They'd stayed late. She was glad to see them go.

"Vibrations," the Colonel whispers. "A good soldier can sense these things. Life and death." Just his mind wandering, she knows, just another bout of dementia, but for a moment the seriousness of his tone, the weight of his words, stop her. Despite herself, she looks toward the door. Has he actually heard something? The surveyors had forgotten something, returned unannounced. Or maybe Pete had canceled his Tuesday night classes in town to come home early. But no. There's no knock at the door, and no sound of a key turning in it. No muddy shoes being brushed against the mat. No sound of tires on the gravel drive. Just the TV program rolling on. Strategies, skirmishes, victories, defeat.

"Did Pete call?" she asks.

"Negative," the Colonel says casually, just the hint of disdain, and then he relaxes, settles back into his chair. "Radio silence has been maintained."

There's something melancholy in his answer, or maybe it's Keri's imagination this time. She wonders if he even notices how seldom the phone rings—for either of them. Calls come so rarely that she once raised the receiver to her ear just to make sure there was a dial tone there. More than once, actually.

"Lasagna's ready," she tells him, and the Colonel brightens up.

"Officer's Club," he says eagerly. Date night, she knows.

Other nights, mealtime is just "chow," but on Tuesdays Pete always stays on campus late, and the Colonel seems to love those nights best. She's not sure how she goes from being his staff sergeant to being his... wife? Girlfriend? Daughter? She's not sure about that either: which role she plays. He doesn't seem to know who she is at all, has never even spoken her name. But sometimes when Pete is out of the way, the Colonel reaches over and presses his gnarled fingers over her hand, pats, squeezes, breaking Keri's heart a little each time.

* * *

"It's a good deal," Pete said after the interview with the Colonel's daughter, after she'd offered them the job. Do a little housecleaning, make a couple of meals a day for the old man, and in exchange: free rent, a grocery stipend, a monthly bonus. A six-month stint. "The whole semester," Pete went on. "Not just a good deal, but a *great* one, especially with teaching assistant stipends these days." He didn't need to add that Keri was unemployed herself, had been for a while.

It was that last part that convinced Keri and kept her from pointing out how much of the cooking and housecleaning quickly fell to her. Pete was at least pulling his weight elsewhere, wasn't he? Teaching a freshman survey course in western drama? Pursuing his own PhD? She could hardly complain about doing the dishes when he had lessons to prep and essays to grade and all that reading to do: Shakespeare, Ibsen, O'Neill, Beckett, Miller. And then fitting in work on his doctoral dissertation around the edges. He was already the golden boy of the doctoral program, destined to be the star of some big English department. She shared those dreams, and she tried not to nag him about her own. That wasn't the woman she wanted to be—about work or marriage, about children somewhere down the line.

"We're both in school," Pete had said more than once when she talked about the future. "Student loans won't pay themselves." And that dissertation wouldn't write itself. And tenure-line jobs didn't come knocking on your door. School first, life later. She'd grown accustomed to that.

But now, with the semester living at the Colonel's, with the savings, he'd hinted more about next steps. "With the money we're saving here, we can set aside a little bit," he said, "for the future."

Maybe it was for the best for her to shoulder the work at the house while he focused on his education. And maybe there were other good reasons that Pete's duties around the house were more limited. After all, the Colonel didn't seem entirely to approve of him. He didn't like the meals that Pete tried to make ("too spicy" once, "too bland" another time), he didn't like all the time he spent reading ("needs to get off his duff"), and he generally peppered Pete with complaints on a regular basis.

"A trip to the barber in your future anytime, son?" the Colonel asked one morning. "That hardly seems regulation length."

Other mornings—more than once: "Those shoes need a good buffing, soldier."

And on the nights when Pete did join them for dinner: "Where's your tie, boy?"

The Colonel wears a tie each night for dinner, tied in an elaborate knot. "A Full Windsor," he told Keri when she asked. "Most men employ the Half-Windsor or the Four-in-Hand, but that's too casual for me."

"A little old school, don't you think?" Pete said, when Keri asked him to try it one evening, just a single meal, just to humor the old man. "And that wasn't part of the deal, now, was it?"

"Recruits these days," the Colonel sometimes says, just under his breath. "A sorry lot, all of them."

* * *

When Keri stands up to clear the table, the Colonel stands quickly as well to help. Even when she dismisses him—"No worries, I can do it" (he's dropped plates before)—he hesitates before heading back toward the TV. He's waiting for her, she knows.

"Just let me get this cleaned up," she says, "and I'll be right in, okay?"

"Roger that," he says. "Rendezvous..." He glances at his watch. "Twenty hundred hours?"

"Roger," Keri salutes, mock-serious. These days, she doesn't have to count out the real time anymore. "I'll meet you in the den."

She stores the lasagna away in squares—leftovers for the week ahead—and sets aside a large slice for Pete, though she knows he'll already have eaten dinner and probably gone out for drinks after class. Winding-down time after the intensity of the three-hour seminars, he's explained.

The window above the kitchen sink has a wide view of the yard. The gravel driveway stretches off to the right between the trees, a hundred yards to the main road, a lonely stretch leading "off base." Shadows play in the woods directly ahead, thick with oak and pine and beech, many of them now tied with red ribbons, marked for timber. Moonlight glistens on the lake off to the left, just barely in sight from this vantage, a rough shoreline that Keri and the Colonel have walked on more than one afternoon, counting Canada geese. A full moon tonight, Keri notes, as if that might explain the tension in the air.

Throughout dinner, the Colonel seemed restless, attentive. Now, as Keri scrubs at the casserole pan, she finds herself watchful too. Is there "incoming"? She thinks about the people that she's seen in and around the property sometimes. Fishermen bring small skiffs close to shore or actually trudge down the driveway in their waders, tossing a small wave toward the house as they passed. Hunters often wander through the woods, unsure whose property they've crossed into at any point. More than once, teenagers have pulled a car up the drive—couples, groups, looking for a place to hook up, get high, get into trouble. Then, beginning last week, there came the onslaught of real estate agents and the surveyors, the men from the tree service, the crew taking soil samples, the beginning of the end. Today's surveyors had lingered until almost dusk, and she'd had the feeling of being trapped somehow, or watched at least, like she and the Colonel were on display, sad curiosities. A couple of times, she caught the men just standing there, smoking cigarettes, staring toward the house. Leering, she thought, no better than construction workers, ogling passersby.

She doesn't know which is worse—the isolation she'd been feeling out here or these sudden intrusions, and the knowledge of what it means. Stuck somewhere between the two and spurred on by the Colonel's own brewing vigilance tonight, her imagination leaps ahead again, playing tricks on her. Is that the red tip of a cigarette butt? No, just one of the ribbons flapping in the moonlight. Did that shadow move? No, just a branch swaying in the breeze.

"Full moon," she says aloud, and then remembers her horoscope from earlier that day: *Surprises abound. Follow where the evening takes you. All will become clear.* Pete still makes fun of her for reading them each morning.

Behind her, the Colonel turns up the TV—hinting for her to join him. The announcer is talking about the Trojan War, the horse that made history, the importance of surprise. Keri shivers a little.

"Coming," she calls to him.

The pan still isn't clean. And she hasn't even started on the knife, crusted with cheese. She leaves both to soak until later—even till tomorrow perhaps.

* * *

"He's dotty," Margaret, the former caretaker, had said, the second time they'd met—the passing on of the keys. She was an older woman: fifties, stout, frizzy-haired. "You'll find out soon enough. And you've got your work cut out for you with him. With all of them."

The first time they'd met was when Keri and Pete had been interviewed for the job. Margaret had brooded along the edges of the conversation as Claire, the youngest of the Colonel's children, put a different spin on the situation: "The world has passed my father by," she said. "We've striven to preserve his old glories, revere his achievements." She swept an arm about the room. Medals and honors dominated one wall. Photographs with politicians and military leaders lined another, many of them long dead Keri had since learned. Several framed boxes held guns, relics of a recent past, like museum pieces but brimming with menace. "Unfortunately, everything that my father trained for, everything that he lived for—none of it has much purpose here."

Claire explained that it was just short-term. Margaret had been called to help her own father; plans were already afoot to sell the property, but might take some time; and they were finally looking into "more professional care" for the Colonel—a step they'd dreaded and delayed for too long. Claire herself had tended to him for several years after her mother died. "But I couldn't manage any longer," she explained. "Physically, yes, but emotionally... Well, watching someone you love so dearly deteriorate, become a shadow, sometimes you just feel yourself breaking down as well." Keri and Pete were a stopgap. She was sure they understood.

The Colonel was napping while they talked. Margaret had shot a couple of looks at Keri throughout the conversation: envy, disbelief, warning glares? Keri hadn't been sure. (Margaret told her later, on the sly, that Claire was a drinker. Claire, in turn, confided that Margaret was a thief—little things, but hardly negligible.)

It was after the Colonel went down for his nap another afternoon, only a week ago now, that Claire and her siblings—Beatrice and Dwight— had made their inventory. This was the first time that Keri had met the other two, since both lived just out of state, and Margaret's comment about having her work cut out for her with "all of them" echoed throughout the day.

With Pete on campus again—early office hours, eternal office hours—Keri had played host alone. Claire asked her to make a salad for lunch, "something simple, no trouble," and Keri had, laying it out on the table, not planning to join them until the Colonel insisted, asking his son to move down a seat, make room for the ladies.

Dwight had smirked at that. "Aye aye, sir," he said, taking his salad with him as he slid down.

The Colonel had seemed to recognize them only dimly, but he nodded politely when Beatrice spoke about her children's latest report cards and Dwight talked about the business finally turning a profit again last quarter—"despite what the president's doing," he insisted, which prompted Beatrice to complain bitterly about the state of political discourse in the country today. More smirks from Dwight at that, and cold looks from Claire.

The Colonel had watched all of them with interest but no reaction. Claire tried at each turn of the conversation to nudge her father to recall Beatrice's children or the nature of Dwight's business or just the name of that current president, but she had finally given up, simply watching the Colonel with a mixture of curiosity and distress. Keri had watched each of them and didn't know exactly how she felt.

After lunch was done and the Colonel had retired to his room for some light R&R, the three of them began to divvy up the belongings, prepping to make an easy sweep of it between the day they moved the old man out and the scheduled demolition of the house, quick work for the condo development ahead. Claire had brought small circular stickers to help with the division. Each of them would simply mark the items they wanted to take. "Pop will appreciate the patriotic touch," Dwight said, holding up a package of red stickers and leaving blue and white for his sisters. Unmarked items would be slated for donation to the Salvation Army. "And a military nod again," Dwight said, already beginning to stake down his claims.

When the three of them ended up squabbling about an autographed photo of Eisenhower standing with the Colonel and his late wife, Keri felt like she saw the three of them most clearly. Beatrice, the eldest, argued that the photo was hers because she was actually in the picture, cradled in their mother's arms. Dwight, now the baby of the bunch, pointed out that he'd been named after the president, "which ought to give me dibs." Meanwhile Claire—caretaker-turned-peacemaker—tried as best she could to keep the simmer from becoming a boil.

"So doesn't that give you claim to all of this, Bea?" Dwight demanded. "You saw it first, you were there first? It's all yours?" And then trying to recruit Claire to the cause: "Isn't that how it's always been?"

"That's not what I'm saying," Beatrice said. "I'm saying I'm *in* the damn picture. It's a picture of *me.*"

"Let's leave it for father, for his room at the nursing home," Claire said. "He always loved it so."

"He wouldn't even know it's there," Dwight said.

"Let's leave it unmarked then," Claire went on. "No one will take it. We can donate it somewhere. A tribute that—"

"Stick it up in some museum?" Dwight said. "Hell no. That sucker's *worth* something."

"Is that what you're planning?" Beatrice flashed with rage. "Selling it somewhere."

"Please keep your voices down," Claire said, and Keri could sense something stretched thin in her own voice. "He'll hear us."

"If he does wake up," Dwight told Keri, "just keep him in the room for a while."

"How should I do that?" Keri asked, startled by the sound of her own voice.

"Tell him," Dwight began. "Tell him the base is on lockdown." He seemed to be thinking. He grinned broadly, something cruel behind it. "There's a sniper. Delta Force is handling it. Tell him, 'Orders from the general.'"

"General." Beatrice snorted. "Is that how you picture yourself in all this?"

Bickering spun out of selfishness, anger where there should have been empathy, lies built high on the Colonel's dementia—Keri hated it all.

But later, she reflected that she wasn't much better, at least in one regard.

When the real estate agents, surveyors, and repairmen had made their rounds, Keri had dutifully pretended to the Colonel that they were visiting dignitaries, military attaches, envoys from D.C. And when the Colonel woke from his nap and asked what all the dots were for—on the lamps, on the furniture, everywhere—Keri told him "inventory" and then "supply room," trying to think of the right term, build another lie he might believe.

"Midnight requisitions," the Colonel said vaguely, with a sigh of contempt, and something about a "five-fingered discount," and then, grinning himself, just like Dwight had, "Oh, well, Sergeant, we'll just have to requisition it all back," like he knew the game.

* * *

"Lear," Pete said when Keri told him all about it. "The grasping, the selfishness. Siblings showing their true colors. Claire sounds like the best of them: 'You have brought me up and loved me, and I return you those duties back as are right and fit, obey you, love you, and most honor you.'" Pete performed the last part with a stagy British lilt.

"It didn't feel like honor," Keri said. "Or love either."

"That's what Lear thought too." Pete raised his eyebrow. "And you know how that turned out. So who got the photo?"

"Beatrice," Keri said. "She traded Dwight the dining room table for it, but he said it didn't matter, he'd get it back someday. Told her that since she was older, she'd go first. 'I'll keep these handy,' he said, and he waved his extra stickers in the air."

"Charming," Pete said. "Sorry I missed it." Keri had hoped for a little more empathy, but Pete was already moving on: "You know, I think I'll add *Lear* to the syllabus. Sub it in instead of *Othello*— that's done too much in high school anyway, don't you think? And *Lear*—"

"But what should *we* do?" Keri insisted. "What's *our* role in all this?"

She doesn't entirely remember his answer— several possibilities, comparing them to the Earl of Kent or the Fool. Did Keri have a touch of Cordelia herself? Little of substance, nothing practical, no solace. Instead, it's more of Margaret's words that have persisted: "Not a word of thanks, unless you demand it. Not a single token of appreciation, unless you take it yourself. I'm telling you: You've already been bought and paid for."

* * *

The Colonel dresses and undresses himself, handles all of his own bathroom duties, but Keri follows-up with him each morning and each night. This evening, as usual, he's had trouble with his nightclothes—his "old man jammies," Pete calls them. One side of his top hangs low, unfastened, while the skipped button bunches out on the other side, the fabric opening to reveal the aged flesh of his belly, a thin tangle of gray hairs. "He does it on purpose," Pete has joked, "just so you can fluff him up." She tries not to think about that as she straightens the buttoning, a complicated dance of discretion and helpfulness.

The Colonel always apologizes to one version or another of who he thinks she is. "Aging is an indignity, Sergeant," he's said before.

And other times: "In all our many years together, my darling, did you ever believe it would come to this?" These seem his only flashes of awareness about time and his place in it, but even those moments are dim with confusion.

"I've not been a good husband, dear," he tells her tonight. "A good father, either, to—" He stops, he catches himself. Some small reality intrudes. "Thank you for looking after me," he says. He strokes her cheek.

She puts him to bed, she tucks him in, she turns out his light. Nearly always, he's staring at the ceiling when she leaves him. Tonight, he watches the window.

"The guards," he says. "The duty roster."

"Yes, yes," she tells him, and she closes the door.

Back in her own room, she tries to go to bed, but finds herself restless, irritable, waiting once more for Pete, angry a little at him this time—and even more of each emotion tonight because of whatever's gotten into the Colonel. She lies in the darkness for a while, staring at the shadows playing outside her own window, at that full moon raging, and then she turns on the light once more to read. She wants to keep up with what Pete's doing, give them more to talk about, so she'd been following his syllabus. The class has already reached *Lear*, and she takes down the bulky *Riverside Shakespeare* from the night-stand, reminds herself again to get a more readable copy, then picks up mid-scene where she'd fallen asleep the night before:

> *This is the excellent foppery of the world,*
> *that, when we are sick in fortune—often the*
> *surfeit of our own behavior—we make guilty*
> *of our disasters the sun, the moon, and the*
> *stars: as if we were villains by necessity; fools*
> *by heavenly compulsion; knaves, thieves, and*
> *treachers, by spherical predominance; drunk-*
> *ards, liars, and adulterers, by an enforced obe-*
> *dience of planetary influence; and all that we*
> *are evil in, by a divine thrusting on: an admi-*
> *rable evasion of whoremaster man, to lay his*
> *goatish disposition to the charge of a star!*

It's near the end of the monologue that she hears the click of the front door—opening, closing. Pete at last, sooner than she expected. Sometimes he calls, usually she sees the sweep of his headlights against the window. He's surprising her this time.

She's left a note for him: "A plate of lasagna in the fridge. Micro-wave two minutes. XO. Me." But she hopes he won't see it, that he'll just come back to her, ease this troubled evening. She listens for his footsteps coming down the hallway, but instead, she hears him trip over something, and she knows then he's been drinking after class, too many drinks again, and suddenly it seems like he'll just complicate the night further instead of improving it.

She starts to go out to him, confront him, but no, she'll wait. She picks up the book again:

> Edgar—
> *[Enter Edgar.]*
> *and pat! he comes, like the catastrophe*
> *of the old comedy. My cue is villainous mel-*
> *ancholy, with a sigh like Tom o' Bedlam. O,*
> *these eclipses do portend these divisions! Fa,*
> *sol, la, mi.*

She's stopped by the sound of the front door, opening and closing once more.

He's gone out again? Keri lays the book down, steps to the window to see what he's doing. But his car's not out there at all, the yard looks empty. And then the sound of the front door opening again, and soon after, the sound of glass breaking, but muffled as if from a great distance.

Incoming, she thinks, and now her senses tingle, her whole body as alert as the Colonel's had seemed earlier.

She picks up the bedside phone. She'll call 911. She'll call Pete, already hurrying him homeward with her mind. But there's no dial tone, just a dull ominous emptiness on the receiver.

Radio silence, she thinks, and then she remembers the Colonel's other words: *Life and death.*

And then she just thinks about the Colonel himself.

* * *

His door is still closed, she sees when she leaves her own room. There's relief in that, though she recognizes the irony: the old warrior protected by the defenseless woman. But he would only add confusion on top of whatever danger is out there. And the truth is she's not entirely defenseless. She's carrying the biggest object in the bedroom—that complete Shakespeare—though she's unsure whether it might best work as a weapon or as armor. She shudders to think it might come to that.

As she eases down the hallway, she wonders who's out there. One of the leering surveyors, after all? That's why they'd stayed so late today. They were casing the house, returning now to rob it. Or one of those college kids who sometimes drove down the wrong road —a prank this time, a dare, a different kind of trouble. She remembers too how Claire called Margaret a thief, remembers Margaret's own words that you got no token of thanks unless you took it.

The living room is dark, just as she'd left it, with only the moonlight streaming in from various windows, casting shadows around the room.

Then one of the shadows near the dining room table moves, a silhouette stumbling toward the living room. The dim form lifts a pair of pictures from the wall, returns toward the table, lays the pictures flat. Its arm raises high into the air, some object in its grasp, and smashes down sharply. A crunching sound.

Dwight, she realizes, unsure where the knowledge came from. And then she looks again at the empty spaces dotting the wall, the pictures that the intruder is destroying. The Eisenhower is among the missing photos. Dwight would get it, one way or another. There truly was something evil behind that smirk of his, beneath those callous comments.

Suddenly, the book in her hand doesn't seem protection enough.

The guns on the wall, she thinks. Are any of them loaded? How easily could she break the case? Would she know how to use one? But Dwight would stop her. He stands in the way, still fidgeting with things on the table. He could get to those guns first. In fact, she understands now, he's already taken one of them from its box, hasn't he? One of the gun cases stands empty, its glass front shattered. That's the sound Keri had heard. That's what Dwight is holding over his head, what he brings down once more against the table.

The knife. The one she left soaking in the lasagna pan. She can get to that. It's a clear line into the kitchen. It's not a gun, but it's better than Shakespeare. At least she won't be entirely unarmed.

As soon as she's thought it, she's done it. A quick sprint, and she's at the sink. Hand in soapy water, fingers slipping around the handle. But Dwight has come up behind her, grabbed her arm, pushed her against the counter. Keri can't get a grip on the knife.

Hot breath brushes against her neck, carrying with it the stench of alcohol. "You should've stayed in bed," the voice huffs, a snarl there, an undertone of amusement. But it's a woman's voice. Not Dwight, not at all. "It's just a break-in," the woman slurs quietly. "Vandalism. You were asleep. You didn't hear, you didn't know." Keri tries to shuffle around, to gain an edge, but the woman holds fast, surprisingly strong. "All those years, year upon year. And they think they have any right here? They never cared about him, not once. They don't deserve any of this." She coos, she soothes: "Just let it happen. You know it's right." And then a dark whisper: "I'll compensate you."

Keri shoves her elbow back into doughy flesh, hears the sharp intake of breath. Freed for a moment, she reaches toward the sink. But there's not enough time. Before Keri can grab the knife, she feels fingers around her throat. "This isn't between you and me," the woman says, a snarl now, and maybe it wasn't their fight, but it is now. The woman's grip is relentless, squeezing, pressing. "They can't know it was me. They can't ever know."

Keri pushes off the counter then, shoving as hard as she can, and the two of them sprawl backward across the room. But the woman hangs on, and then she's on top of Keri, slamming her head against the floor. Keri's pulse throbs grimly, there's a roar in her skull, a pounding, and then an explosion as if her head has burst.

Just as quickly the grip relaxes. The other woman falls away, a thud on the floor beside her.

The lights come on soon after, blinding, and Keri hears the Colonel's voice—a single word, frail and nearly indistinct, pleading, concerned. She rises up from the floor then, and gets her first look at the body sprawled beside her—Claire's body, bleeding heavily from where a bullet has ripped through her torso—and at the damage the woman had done.

Spray paint covers the kitchen cabinets, what looks like teen graffiti, like those young joyriders had not just driven down the road but finally come in. The lampshades have been slashed methodically, and more pictures have been pulled down from the wall. Broken glass is everywhere, shards dotting the carpet. The frame on the Eisenhower is shattered, the picture itself torn. The corner of another photo peeks out from beneath a towel on the kitchen table, one of the antique pistols dropped on top of it.

At the edge of the hallway stands the Colonel, a handgun at his side, this one not an antique. He's wearing his full uniform, every button clasped perfectly, the medals gleaming in the sudden light, his posture perfect.

He speaks softly again—a second word now, perplexed and incredulous where that first word had been pleading—and then, with his own glance around the room, he finds his voice again: "Damn those guards," he booms. "The perimeter's been breached."

* * *

"Blanche DuBois," Pete says later, when it's just the two of them alone in the house, lying side by side in the darkness.

The body has been removed, and Beatrice and Dwight have been called. They'll drive in the next morning. They'll handle things now. The police took the Colonel away for questioning, for evaluation, and Keri began straightening up, picking up glass, rubbing at the paint on the cabinets, until Pete took her in his arms and held her tight and told her it was time for bed, time to let go, at least for the night.

But she couldn't do that, of course. For a while, staring at the ceiling, Keri has listened to the silence of the house, believed that she could hear the old man's absence somewhere in it. Pete has seemed far away in his own thoughts, reflecting on the loss in his own way, Keri thinks, until those sudden words of his.

"What?" she asks. She doesn't turn to look at him.

"Blanche DuBois," he says. "Tennessee Williams. *Streetcar Named Desire.* 'I've always relied on the kindness of strangers.'" Pete tries out a Southern drawl, not as good as his British voice, though it strikes her now that none of his accents is very good. "I'd thought of the Colonel like Lear, you know, but tonight, watching him with the police when they took him away, the way he stood up straight, the way he walked... Pure Blanche DuBois. Living in his own world, his delusions, the long gone past."

"He was brave," Keri says. There's light on the ceiling, from the moonlight shining down through the window and reflecting somehow off the bedspread. "Gallant."

"Gallant," Pete echoes. "But that's the tragedy of it, isn't it? The way that we take the Stella role—all of us, the reader, the audience— trying to keep the illusions aloft, maybe even believing in them a little."

In the blankness of the ceiling, Keri imagines Pete in front of the class, pacing and gesturing, holding forth, the tweed jacket, patches on the sleeve. There's pride in those patches and a strut in his step, and she's sure she heard a snicker when he repeated the word *gallant*, as if he was marking up her term paper and dissatisfied somehow with the logic of her argument.

"When you say tragedy," she asks, "are you talking about the Colonel or about Blanche?"

He shrugs beside her, a laying-down shrug, shoulders shuffling against the pillow.

"Either," he says. "Both. Killing your daughter, not knowing it. That has all the elements of something classical, doesn't it?"

Later, many years later, lying in another bed with another man, and with her children with that husband nestled safely in their own beds just down the hallway, Keri will think back once more on this night and wonder yet again if this was the exact moment when things ended between them or if it was just one in a progression of such moments that took too long to accumulate. She'll wonder again why she stayed so long with him after this night, why she didn't just get up then and walk out into the darkness, up that gravel drive—off base once and for all. Illusions, she'll think. And tragedy. And she'll think of the hundred things she might have told Pete, the hundred times she might have told him. Then she'll remind herself: *But maybe it was enough.*

"He said her name," she tells Pete. "The Colonel. After he turned on the lights and saw her there, before he wandered out into the yard, he said 'Claire' because he saw her, what she'd done, and what he'd done too. But first, just before that... He was looking for *me*, I know he was. Looking *out* for me. Before he said her name, he said mine. He called out for me. For the first time, he said Keri."

English 398: Fiction Workshop

Notes from Class & A Partial Draft By Brittany Wallace, Plus Feedback, Conference & More

Exposition should be kept to a minimum.
Alistair Pearson is a professor of English—associate professor technically, not sure why he hasn't gone further up the ranks. He's in his mid-40s, slogging through most days, feels like he's on the verge of a mid-life crisis. He's taught composition, intro lit, and creative writing at the same college for nearly 20 years; the hours are long, a professor's pay sucks, and those students… well, let's just say he's reached the point of feeling desperate for one of them to really care, to show some genuine enthusiasm, some true passion. A class should mean more than three credits closer to graduation, that's the kind of thing he says. While work has dragged him down, his home life doesn't offer any comfort because—

* * *

Remember: Show, don't tell.
Remember: Sharp prose as much as sharp plotting.
Professor Pearson types the last of the grades into the spreadsheet, a long slog through a stack of essays, now bleeding with red ink. Moving the mouse, he notices the age spots on the backs of his hands—feels some small tightness in his knuckles. Imaginary? He's too young for arthritis. (Isn't he?)

Maybe carpal tunnel syndrome? Day after day at the keyboard, week after week, semester after semester—and how many years now? A paperweight sits on the shelf. Fifteen years of service, and a couple more years since, gathering dust atop that stack of manila folders.

He closes the spreadsheet, switches to email, sees his wife's name in the inbox, an exclamation point by it. Urgent as always. Something undone, done wrong. Some new outrage, and an apology needed. No, demanded. And what does he get in return? (How long since they've slept together? That's the question. Day after day again, week after week, and—another glimpse at those age spots.)

He succumbs to temptation, switches the window on his computer one more time. RateMyProfessor.com—a weakness, he knows, this desire to see the three chili peppers there.

Hot, Hot, Hot, *he thinks with a flush of heat himself: pride, embarrassment, self-consciousness? Some combination of the three maybe.*

Better than the nagging wife.

That old Buster Poindexter song whispers through his head—and then another bit of self-consciousness. Hot Hot Hot *is a reference his students are too young to get.*

* * *

An inciting moment is necessary to get a plot in motion.

Toward the end of his office hours comes a knock at the door. Brianna from his creative writing class peers in, asks if he's busy. Lithe, colt-like, she takes her seat, carrying herself with a casual grace. When she crosses her legs, her plaid skirt sneaks up her thigh.

"I'm sorry to stop by," she says, "but…I'm having trouble with endings."

Professor Pearson nods—sagely, he thinks. "Most writers will tell you that endings are the hardest part. A blank page is one problem, getting started. But at least then all the directions are open. The story might go anywhere. But an ending…. Did you know Hemingway wrote 47 different endings to A Farewell to Arms? *You're balancing various strands of a story by that point, working against a reader's predictions and expectations, trying to make sure your resolution is—"*

"Both surprising and inevitable." Brianna's smile has widened. "I know, Professor. I do pay attention in class." She bites at her lower lip, her lipstick siren red against her alabaster skin—chewing on some hesitation. "But that wasn't what I meant."

He cocks his head, lifts an eyebrow—his regular expression (overly aware about it suddenly) to encourage a student to dive deeper into the topic at hand.

"My last semester," she says. "That ending. And the big bad world awaits."

"Ah." Professor Pearson nods again. "I'm sure you'll have no trouble finding a job. You're sharp, you're a hard worker, a great student, a—" He shuffles through a folder. "Speaking of, here's your quiz from yesterday. An A, as usual." She takes it from him without looking at it.

"It sounds like you're writing me a recommendation."

"If you ever need one…." He waves his hand into empty air.

She glances away, takes a deep breath—steeling herself somehow, it seems. "Maybe I'm asking for something else," she says. "Maybe I'm recommending something for you."

"For me?"

"For us." She blushes slightly.

She's always been eager to participate in class discussion—that's what Professor Pearson would write if she asked for a recommendation. Her contributions to class are always thoughtful and confident.

"I've enjoyed having you as my professor," she says. "I enjoy talking to you. It's not just school I'm going to miss."

She sits in the front row, he would point this out as an indication of ambition, of leadership. The kind of student who challenges a professor to stay at the top of his game.

Professor Pearson adjusts himself in his seat. "I'm flattered but—"

"Won't you miss me, professor?"

The kind of student I wish I had in all my classes. I'll certainly miss her when—

"Certainly. You're a fine—"

"More than fine, I hope." She dips one shoulder slightly, a move that has frequently drawn his attention in class and just as quickly made him embarrassed about looking her way. *He wouldn't write that on a recommendation.* "Don't you find me attractive?"

He thinks of the chili peppers on Rate My Professor. He wonders if she's given him one herself, her own anonymous recommendation of him. Inwardly, he shakes his head—then realizes he's matched the move outwardly.

"Even if I did, Brianna—find you attractive, I mean..." His wife's image springs to mind then—never eager, undermining confidence, a woman he was increasingly looking away from. "I'm married, Brianna. I wouldn't do anything to jeopardize that"—he hears his voice stumble—"that happiness."

"Wouldn't?"

"Won't." Firmly now.

She bites again at her lower lip, the lipstick holding fast, this time nothing hesitant about it. "Only a letter's difference between won't and want, you know"—and he's reminded of the cleverness of her submissions to workshop.

His mind lingers on that word submission.

* * *

How many different senses can you incorporate into a single scene?

Hints of perfume drift around her when she enters his office, swirls of honeysuckle, the scent even more seductive in close quarters than from her seat in the front row of class.

Her voice bubbles with bits of laughter, like the first pop of champagne, then turns velvety smooth.

Her scarlet nails brush the inside of his palm when he offers her the quiz—the skin of her hand taut and fresh and unblemished against the age spots on his.

He watches her nibble that lower lip. He sees the lock of auburn hair fall from behind her ear to brush her cheek. He can't help but notice the ripple of mischief each time she smiles.

We have five senses—this is another of the things he says. Can you incorporate all of them into a single scene?

"I want," he begins, then thinks better of it, then says it anyway. "I want to taste you."

Her legs uncross as she leans forward, nudging that honeysuckle smell toward him. "Taste me where?"

* * *

Plot isn't an "and then" series of events; it's driven by causality and consequence and conflict—escalation each step of the way.

A kiss here and there leads to kisses there and there and there.

Almost being caught in the office leads to embarrassment and anxiety, which lead to encounters in the backseat of a Honda Civic (a professor's salary), which lead to muscle cramps, which lead to afternoons in a motel, which lead to unreasonable expense (a professor's salary), which leads to frustration.

His wife's work conference out of town leads to a weekend tryst on the conjugal bed.

A forgotten pair of panties leads to questions, suspicions, accusations—and what's this on the credit card about the Hideaway Hotel?

* * *

Each aspect of a short story should do more than one thing. Dialogue, for example, should reveal character while also pushing the plot forward. Every word counts!

"You're going to pay for this, Alistair, and let me tell you, I mean pay. I'm going to bury you in trouble. I'm going to leave you with nothing. When my lawyer is done with you—"

* * *

Causality, consequence, conflict always.

Threats of trouble lead to thoughts of murder. Left with nothing means nothing to lose. The plot turns toward plotting, then a poisoning. Consequence leads to more conflict.

How do you bury a body?

* * *

Look at the Lester Dent model (PowerPoint on Blackboard): Pile more grief on your characters—again and again.

[Hey, workshop buddies—just some ideas here, 'k? Let me know what u think.]

The suspicious and bull-headed detective, chip on his shoulder about investigating at a university and not having a college education himself. But don't his street smarts make him sharper? "We can't find any evidence of your wife travelling to visit her sister. Her sister says she never expected her, hasn't seen her."

The college roommate, concerned, earnest, curious—her life potentially at risk because of that concern and curiosity and her chattiness. Will she spill the key clues to the cops before her own blood is spilled?

Some third character, complicating things. Maybe Brianna has a boyfriend interested in her, the jealous type, looking for revenge. Or a neighbor who caught sight of shadows moving, melding beyond the curtains the night the wife was out at that conference? Long before she disappeared for good....

Or maybe another piece of evidence: An angry letter the wife wrote to her husband, something for the police to find? Or a letter to her attorney, if she got that far?

* * *

A story's resolution should be both surprising and inevitable.
?????

[Sorry for incomplete draft. Still working on this one, guys.]

* * *

Each student in our fiction workshop is required to provide written comments on *each* draft *before* class. Feedback should be constructive and respectful. Remember that your fellow students are giving you a little piece of themselves—and it's easy to lapse into negativity.

"Conjugal bed? What century are you writing in? And 'spill the clues before her own blood is spilled'? Give me a break."

"Completely derivative. How many times have we seen this story done before? and done better? James M. Cain relocated to a college campus might have been a nice mash-up except that it comes out like a bad Lifetime Movie of the Week."

"One-dimensional, one-note characters. The professor (in our class, not the one in your story) talked about having protagonists as desire and action—wanting something, doing something. But shouldn't they be fleshed out beyond simple animal urges?"

"Somebody's hot for teacher, yeah?"

* * *

Bolded on syllabus: "A post-workshop conference with me is required; failure to participate will impact your final grade."

"Should I leave the door open or closed?" Brittany asks when she arrives for the student-teacher conference—not Brianna but Brittany, not auburn hair but blond, not porcelain-skinned or colt-like but freckled and fuller-figured. But what difference does it make, given how the students surely read her draft?

"Open," Professor Peterson says sternly—Peterson, not Pearson, a negligible distinction there too—and then reverses himself as sternly. "Closed." He shakes his head. *Open* meant someone in the hallway might overhear. *Closed* meant someone might wonder what's so private, why the secrecy, what needs hiding. *My door is always open*, this is something he's prided himself on saying, to students and colleagues alike.

From the start, the conference is a lose-lose situation.

Brittany twirls around to close the door, her short skirt spinning briefly upwards. She smooths it down when she takes her chair—scarlet nails against the plaid. These last details she hadn't changed for her submission to workshop.

Professor Peterson throws the printed pages of her story on the desk. "How are you going to explain this?"

Brittany sits up straighter—a puzzled expression playing across her face (playing? or sincere? Professor Peterson can't tell). "But professor, you told us to write what we know."

"What you—" He sputters. "What you know? What are you trying to do? Expose us? Embarrass me? And I hope you're aware, someone might even read this as a threat against my wife."

"It's fiction, professor." She nudges a pair of tortoiseshell glasses higher on her nose. "And as we've said, even if your wife doesn't make you happy anymore, the last thing we've ever wanted was for her to be hurt by all this." She shakes her head. "It's just a story."

"Well which defense are you going with? Whatever comes to mind? Because you can't have it both ways."

More puzzlement—definitely a role, he thinks. "But you yourself said that fiction is a process of transmutation—of transforming reality into something different, something more, 'the imagination unfettered,' wasn't that how you put it? And I thought you'd be proud of me for including that whole Buster Poindexter thing, which you probably think I had to look up, but"—a wink—"as you know, I'm interested in older things. Mature beyond my years and all."

"But—" He's running his fingers through his hair, scratching his head. "But no one is reading this as fiction—not with *Brianna* here and *Professor Pearson*—"

"Brianna isn't at all like me," Brittany says. "Do I look lithe and colt-like to you?"

Professor Peterson pushes on. "Even if they pretended to read it as fiction, it was only because they were more discreet about this than you were. My god, you've made me out so lecherous."

She shrugs, she smiles. "Well, in your case, not too much of an exaggeration, is it? What was it you said? Conflict is just amplifying the everyday—more drama, more conflict, more *more*?"

Her voice raises slightly, and he wonders who might be passing in the hallway outside, who might have heard her. *More more more*— the echo intentional or not? That first time in the motel room weeks before—and him the one crying out the words.

He shifts in his seat, unable to get comfortable. Already he's leaned on the right arm of the chair and then on the left and then to the right again. He leans forward now, the edge of the desk pressing against his middle—discomfort from all angles.

"Please stop quoting my lectures, Brittany. We're not talking about crafting a short story now. This was.... I don't even know what this was. What did you hope to gain from all this? In front of the class, not giving me any warning, and—"

"You were away for the weekend when I wrote it—with your wife, remember? And you've told me lately no emails and no phone calls." She crosses her arms, tilts her head slightly—a pose he's seen from students before, finding some loophole in a syllabus, challenging a grade, thick with contempt.

"So this is punishment because I was—" He taps his thumb against the desk, then drums his fingers. "She's my wife, Brittany. It's not like I don't spend time with her, like I can't—"

"The deadline was approaching, professor. The syllabus is very clear about being late. I didn't want to jeopardize my grade."

He throws up his hands, a bitter bark of a laugh. "You're bargaining for a *grade*? I'm giving you an A, Brittany. You were *always* going to get an A."

She straightens again. "I'm not *given* grades"—nothing remotely playful in her voice now. "I earn my spot on the Dean's List, thank you very much."

Brittany stares at him over the top of her glasses. He tries to meet her gaze, but breaks off first, looks around his office—a small space suddenly feeling smaller. The bookshelves stuffed thick with writing books, novels and story collections he's taught, stacks of printed lesson plans and grading books—small symbols of his dedication to his students, testaments to his reputation. The 15-year paperweight catches his eye—even if Brittany hadn't included it in her story—the memory of the university president shaking his hand, saying "We're proud of your accomplishments" with such sincerity it was like he'd meant it. And then the photograph on the shelf just below it....

Professor Peterson turns back to Brittany.

"So what *do* you want? What is it you wanted to get out of…this?" He gestures toward the paper on his desk—rudely, he realizes, dismissive if only he knew how to actually dismiss it.

"What we've always wanted," she says—stress on the *We*. "I'm graduating. I'll be free then. The department rules you've talked about, the university restrictions, none of that is going to matter anymore. We can finally be together." She smiles, a more gentle tilt of the head this time, a few strands of blond hair falling across her glasses in ways that before had seemed entrancing.

He shifts again in his seat. Through the office door, the sounds of footsteps in the hallway, a heavy tread—the department chair's footsteps, he recognizes them. He waits for the knock—half fearful and then more than half hoping. An interruption would at least put an end to the conversation.

The footsteps recede. A door further down the hallway opens, closes, then silence.

A glance at the photograph Professor Peterson had avoided—with his wife on their last real vacation, smiling, happy, for the camera at least. No, he corrects himself, truly happy then. He remembers the last night of that vacation, drinking mojitos on the beach at sunset. He remembers Sunday mornings lounging lazily in bed, and then Belgian waffles, and then their legs intertwined on the sofa reading throughout the afternoon. And not just simple times like these. She'd earned the money while he'd toiled through grad school. She'd been there when his brother had died, consoling, comforting. She'd—

He realizes that all the memories are about her in relation to him—what she'd done for him, where she'd sacrificed. And then, more recently, when she'd stopped putting him first.

"Yes, I know we talked about it…. But…things are complicated. We've been together a long time, my wife and I, we've…." He picks up a pen from the desk, twirls it in his hand. "I have to think about the best way to, to break it to her, the best timing for that kind of…. I can't just—"

Brittany is nodding, a nod that Professor Peterson recognizes as his own—the one he gives to students just before he disagrees with them on some point. That old pedagogical trick: Connect, then correct.

"Not *can't*, but *won't?*" She reaches forward, takes the pen from his hands, her fingers brushing against his. She lays the pen on the desk, sits back in her chair. "You talk in class about the importance of endings, but you seem to be the one having trouble with resolutions. Won't end things with your wife, don't want to give me up. All that talk in class about how important it is to bring a narrative arc home, how it takes vision and how it takes bravery, and meanwhile in the real world here, you—"

"Please," he says. "Please don't quote my own words back to me." His voice is soft now, less an order this time than simple begging. He starts to reach for the pen again, stops himself.

"All right." She's poised, a calm about her he finds troubling. "If not words"—she grins—"would you like pictures instead?"

The discomfort Professor Peterson has been feeling becomes a sharp pain now, jolting his whole body to attention.

"What pictures?"

"Of you." Brittany lifts her hand, looks at her nails, purposefully casual, it seems, but he's struck by the idea that she's admiring their sharpness. "Asleep in bed," she says. "Afterwards, I mean—the way men do."

"Of me?" He's still catching up.

"Of us really." She flicks the nails now. "Selfies. You know how we millennials love our selfies." She holds her hand up as if angling an imaginary camera. Smiles. "Click, click."

Finally, he's caught up, sees his images posted on the internet, sees his wife seeing the photos, sees— "So this is, this is all blackmail. What you can expose, unless I do what you want?"

"What you want," she says. "What we want. All that talk from you about how happy we'd be, how we would be together—as soon as I wasn't your student anymore, as soon as you could settle things." She taps those scarlet nails against the desk, picks up the pen she'd laid there, wags it at him. "Words have weight, that's what you told us. I wrote it down in my notebook. I believed you."

A student who listens, who pays attention, who treats a class as more than a few credits toward graduation? Wasn't this exactly what Professor Peterson had wanted? Wasn't this student in front him—all that attention and hard work and then more, more, more—*exactly* what he had wanted?

"I think you know what you need to do." Brittany points to the manuscript he'd thrown on the desk, pushes her story back toward him.

"You expect me to kill my wife?" His voice is nearly a whisper now, secretive, incredulous, seething. "For you?"

"For *us*," she emphasizes again. "Whatever you do, it will be for *us*. But no, like I said, it was only a story. It's bad enough to think about building our happiness on someone else's unhappiness, much less on someone else's...." She seems to struggle to find the right phrase, then pulls a finger across her throat. "There are other ways to end things. But if you make the wrong choice, other consequences for you, as you can imagine."

Brittany stands as she says it, the way Professor Peterson always stands as a signal that it's time to draw one of these student-teacher conferences to a close.

* * *

Reminder: Writing is revision.
Reminder: A story's resolution should be both surprising and inevitable.

Anyone Not See This Coming?
Tuesdays with Tasha
By Tasha Levine, Class of 2019

GUILTY.

A verdict brought down, justice served—so *they* say, but can one word really put a close to everything these last nine weeks have brought us? Story of the summer, *scandal* exploding all over social media.

I type that word "story," but really it's more than one—story after story, and every one thick with the tropes of this media-savage age. One more sorority sweetheart gone missing. One more party night that took a deadly turn. The story about the dangers of blacked-out binge drinking. The story about sexual assault on campus—on our campus, on all campuses, an epidemic. From keg stands to date rape, always with a blonde girl and her fam threading through the middle of it, that's the story that sells.

Then came the twist (dare I say "plot twist"?) that swung the spotlight toward Professor Peterson, sus from the start, amirite, but too well-tweeted, too Rate-My-Professor-eating-him-up, too respected-pillar-of-our-community with his *protesting* how he'd *never stoop* to doing anything *improper* with a student. And then that other cliché: the devoted wife standing by her man, "complete faith in my husband" (so she *said*), that same routine we've seen over and over with politicians and their wives—and isn't academia a kind of politics too? (Probably an upcoming column there; note to my editor: I'm calling dibs.)

More stories still as the evidence piled high. The biggest one? Victim blaming, *that* same old. Brittany infatuated, Brittany's imagination taking her into dangerous territory. Professor Peterson concerned about the content of her story, concerned about his wife's safety. Professor Peterson confronting, then defending, then covering up—him the helpless one, thinking of his family first, and then things got out of hand. So he *said*.

Our sleepy college town, and then we *all* got woke.

I have to tell you, I'm still feeling restless.

That well-tweeded professor crying his eyes out as the verdict came down—does that screenshot of "justice served" help us close up this story (these stories)? How about him led away in handcuffs? Orange jumpsuit time, but that won't bring Brittany back.

It's his wife's tears that keep coming back to me, her standing by him even at the end, humiliating herself day after day with that same "We're not a part of this, he would never have done this, this can't be happening." Had to be she saw the truth by the end, didn't she? Had to be she knew where this was going early on, no matter what she said?

Story after story after story, and many of us did know, did see—at least the loose outlines of the whole thing.

Even if we wish this worst-case scenario might have turned out different, the truth is that these things happen all the time—and women across our "fair campus," my friends, my sisters, can't we all attest to this?

A male professor's gaze hanging on a little too long, straying a little south. That moment when the Father-Knows-Best friendliness turns toward flirtation (cue those Creeper Old Man vibes). And high key, we women play our role here too, too many of us, because isn't that how we've all been *conditioned?*

My readers here have heard me before on these persistently patriarchal patterns of action and reaction—*that same story,* though I applaud the pop-up protests this summer against a campus administration determined too long to protect its own (*shame*). But instead of climbing up on that same soapbox, how about I turn this over to what other people have been saying?

From Thad Waverly, for example, who'd first informed the police that he knew Brittany was quote-unquote "hot" for Professor Peterson—all fidgety jerkers remorse at that second vigil for Brittany, the Call for Justice on Campus, but he meant well: "I could have told her he wasn't going to treat her right, *anybody* could've told her that. But instead of making a joke about it, what I wrote on her manuscript"—more fidgeting here—"I keep thinking that maybe I should've said something, something about how I felt. But I'm just, I've just never been good with sincerity." (Some lesson here for the men on campus too.)

From Mrs. Velma Radcliffe, the neighbor who caught Brittany's Miata on the Petersons' street when Mrs. Peterson was out of town—glaring at Professor Peterson from the witness stand: "Never got a good glimpse of the girl. It was past dark, like I said. But something not right about it all, parking halfway down the street like that. Why not park closer? Why weren't the porch lights on? I didn't know for sure what was going on, but nothing good was going to come of it, I did know that." ("None of my business," she'd said, but lucky for us all that she took down the license plate, evidence piled on evidence.)

From Detective William "Butch" Bannister in his courthouse press conference, thick neck straining against the collar of his button-down, eyes unblinking in the glare of the cameras: "Peterson was quickly our only significant suspect here, and it's gratifying to see him get what he deserves. While it's the kind of word the professor might use"—a sneer on the word *professor*—"there seem some *irony* in the fact that those compromising photographs and those love notes in Peterson's handwriting were all tucked into a manila folder in his own office, underneath that 15-years-of-teaching paperweight. Best we could determine, Brittany had hidden the envelope there herself—like if anything went...wrong, the evidence there would bring him down too."

See the thread here? They all saw this coming, at least where it might end up.

My argument: Brittany knew it too, where this might be headed—feared it. That's why she wrote *HERE* in big letters on that file folder, so no one would miss it.

Irony is right—that twist Brittany built in herself.

I'm glad she earned the last word.

THE BOY DETECTIVE AND THE SUMMER OF '74

The Boy Detective and the Summer of '74 is printed on 60-pound paper, and is designed by Jeffrey Marks using InDesign. The type is New Baskerville, a modern interpretation of the original Baskerville font developed by John Baskerville in 1762. The cover is by Luke Buchanan. The first edition was published in two forms: trade softcover, perfect bound; and one hundred fifty copies sewn in cloth, numbered and signed by the author. Each of the clothbound copies includes a separate pamphlet, "Burying the Bone," a short story by Art Taylor. *The Boy Detective and the Summer of '74* was printed by Southern Ohio Printers and bound by Cincinnati Bindery. The book was published in February 2020 by Crippen & Landru Publishers, Inc., Cincinnati, OH.

Publishing Acknowledgements

All of the collected stories were previously published and earned awards as follows:

"The Boy Detective & the Summer of '74," *Alfred Hitchcock's Mystery Magazine*, January/February 2020.

"The Care & Feeding of Houseplants," *Ellery Queen's Mystery Magazine*, March/April 2013; winner of the Agatha Award and the Macavity Award for Best Short Story.

"A Drowning at Snow's Cut," *Ellery Queen's Mystery Magazine*, May 2011; winner of the Derringer Award for Best Long Story.

"English 398: Fiction Workshop," *Ellery Queen's Mystery Magazine*, July/August 2018. winner of the Edgar Award and the Macavity Award for Best Short Story.

"An Internal Complaint," *Ellery Queen's Mystery Magazine*, June 2007.

"Ithaca 37," *Ellery Queen's Mystery Magazine,* September/October 2013.

"Mastering the Art of French Cooking," *PANK, Crime Issue*, September 2011; first place, flash fiction category, Press 53 Open Awards. Reprinted in 2012 Press 53 Open Awards, Press 53, 2012.

"Murder on the Orient Express," *Ellery Queen's Mystery Magazine*, December 1995. Republished in *The Mystery Megapack: 25 Modern and Classic Mystery Stories*, Wildside Press, 2011.

"A Necessary Ingredient," *Coast to Coast: Private Eyes from Sea to Shining Sea*, Down & Out Books, 2017.

"The Odds Are Against Us," *Ellery Queen's Mystery Magazine,* November 2014; winner of the Agatha Award and the Anthony Award for Best Short Story.

"Parallel Play," *Chesapeake Crimes: Storm Warning,* Wildside Press, 2016; winner of the Agatha Award and the Macavity Award for Best Short Story.

"Precision," *Gargoyle*, Summer 2014.

"Rearview Mirror," *Ellery Queen's Mystery Magazine*, March/April 2010; winner of the Derringer Award for Best Novelette. Republished in *The Crooked Road*, Volume 3: *Ellery Queen Presents Stories of Grifters, Gangsters, Hit Men, and Other Career Crooks*, Penny Publications, 2013, and in a revised version in *On the Road with Del & Louise: A Novel in Stories*, Henery Press, 2015, and *The Best American Mystery Stories 2016*, Houghton Miflin, 2016.

"Visions and Revisions," *North American Review*, Summer 2004. Republished in *Redux*, June 2013.

"A Voice From the Past," *Ellery Queen's Mystery Magazine*, August 2009.

"When Duty Calls," *Chesapeake Crimes: This Job Is Murder*, Wildside Press, 2012; winner of the Derringer Award for Best Long Story.

The story "An Internal Complaint" borrows characters from Anton Chekhov's "The Lady with the Dog" (1899) as well as several lines from the translation of the story by Constance Garnett (1917) and additional lines from *The Geisha: A Story of a Tea House* (1896), libretto by Owen Hall, lyrics by Harry Greenbank, music by Sidney Jones.

Thank you so much to Jeffrey Marks and Douglas Greene of Crippen & Landru Publishers for their support and encouragement of my work and to Ellen Geiger of Frances Goldin Literary Agency for her representation of this collection.

Finally, I would like to thank the Writers-in-Residence program at the Weymouth Center for the Arts and Humanities in Southern Pines, North Carolina, where I completed the final revisions on the title story for this collection.